THE GAME OF LOVE

Had he brought her here to seduce her? If he had, he was certainly not in a hurry to sweep her off her feet, for he stood staring down at something on the desk in the corner.

"Do you believe in fate, Caresse?" He turned toward her, his distinguished features brooding, a strange pain in his dark eyes.

"Perhaps." What was he getting at?

"Ah, *ma pauvre petite,* you wonder what you have taken on in me," he said, crossing with a few lithe strides to stand in front of her. He caressed her cheek with the tip of his finger, brushing a stray tendril of hair from where it curled near her mouth. Slowly, he traced the fullness of her lower lip, staring down at her with an unreadable expression in his depthless black eyes.

The sultry air that enveloped the room seemed to hold them in an embrace where time stopped. She shivered with delight at his touch and the awakening hunger she experienced as he traced the outline of her mouth. She wanted more of him than just the touch of his hand. She wanted to feel the burning pressure of his mouth on hers, the taste of him on her tongue.

"I want to take you, my sweet Caresse. From the first time I saw you I knew that it would come to this, my need for you is so great. *Mon Dieu,* I should not tell you this, for the knowledge will give you an advantage in our relationship."

" 'Tis not a duel we are fighting," she said, her voice a husky whisper as he bent his head to hers.

"Is that not exactly what it is, *ma belle* . . ."

DIANE GATES ROBINSON

THE ROGUE AND THE LILY

ZEBRA BOOKS
KENSINGTON PUBLISHING CORP.

For my editor, Ann La Farge, with gratitude, for opening a whole new world for me by accepting my first manuscript, also a novel about Louisiana. Her enthusiasm, knowledge, and wonderful support through all my novels will never be forgotten. *Merci,* Ann, *merci beaucoup.*

And

For James, travel companion, researcher, and photographer *extraordinaire!*

Prologue

"My only love sprung from my only hate."
                    Shakespeare, *Romeo and Juliet.*

Paris 1748
La Salpêtrière prison

"She was moved into a private cell this morning as you requested. It caused an uproar in the main chamber—our scarlet lilies are not usually allowed such privileges." The harsh rasp of the heavyset guard's voice echoed off the damp gray brick walls of the vast prison. He gestured for the tall masculine figure, cloaked in a voluminous black cape, to follow him. "My men had a hellish time restoring order after she was taken away."

"You have been paid well for your inconvenience," the cloaked figure tersely reminded the churlish guard.

"*Oui,* and 'tis a good thing," he admitted sullenly, holding a flickering torch high above their heads to light the way in the pitch black of the windowless tunnel that led to the private cells.

Damp currents of cold November air swirled down the forbidding corridor, causing the tall man to pull his black wool cape close. If anything, it

7

seemed even colder inside the vast fortress on the banks of the river Seine than outside in the street. The enclosure that had once been a saltpeter-powder magazine, converted years before into a prison for women, from the lowest prostitute to political prisoners, as well as the insane, seemed to pull the moisture from the river. The brick walls were wet with condensation.

"You will find her changed, *monsieur*," the guard warned over his shoulder as they strode down the narrow corridor. "She was proud and arrogant like all those aristocrats when she was first brought here. Two days and nights with the dregs of Paris brought her down, but when she felt the sting of the branding iron on her shoulder, felt the *fleur de lys* burned into that aristocratic skin, she wilted like the rest of them. For the rest of her life she will carry the scarlet lily on her back like a common criminal." There was satisfaction in the guard's voice.

The lips of the tall man grimaced in disgust beneath the black half-mask that concealed part of his lean visage. He found, to his surprise, he wanted this business over with quickly. The goal that had taken years of planning had been achieved, but there was no sense of triumph in realizing his revenge. He felt only a great weariness, and a desire to put it behind him.

"Here, this is the cell," the guard muttered as he stopped in front of a thick wooden door banded with iron bars. "Remember, she will look different to you," he cautioned the visitor as he turned the heavy key in the lock.

"It does not matter, for I have never set eyes upon her before this morn," he answered, in the deep cultured tones of a gentleman, as the door swung open.

The guard stared at him in surprise. It was an emotion the hardened soldier had not experienced

8

in a long time. He gave a shrug dismissing the whole matter as one more sign of the lunacy of the aristocracy. This man had been most specific about how he had wanted the prisoner treated once she had been arrested at her father's chateau on a *lettre de cachet* issued by King Louis XV in his own hand. Her father had been taken to the Bastille, but she was to be brought here to the women's prison and put in with the common prostitutes and petty thieves. She was not to be taken to the quarters reserved for aristocrats interned by royal decree. He had been most specific on that point, the guard remembered, watching the tall cloaked figure enter the damp cell. And now he said he had never seen her face. All those arrangements, all that money used to bribe officials and guards, and he had never met her. What had she done to warrant such treatment? You could never tell about the aristocracy, he had learned that in his years at La Salpêtrière. Crazy, they were all crazy, he decided with a shake of his grizzled head.

"There is no one here," the visitor said in sharp tones, turning toward the guard.

"Mademoiselle, you have a visitor," the guard called out into the gloom of the cell lit only by a thin stream of morning light from an aperture high in the brick wall.

At the guard's words, there was a stirring from a pile of straw in the corner. In the shadows a slight figure rose to her feet.

"Mademoiselle Marie-Caresse de Villier," the guard announced in a mocking tone as if they were at court. Then tiring of the game, remembering the warm fire in his quarters, he moved behind the cloaked man toward the open door. "I will be outside. Rap on the door when you are through. Remember, only a few minutes. I have other duties to attend to."

The figure came out of the shadows as the door

9

shut behind the guard. The pale gray light struck her tired, tear-streaked visage. "Who are you? What do you want?" she asked in a low, hesitant voice that still carried the intonations of her gentle birth.

A startled gasp was at first the only sound from the figure who stood a few feet away from her. She could tell nothing about him but his height, for the cloak covered him from head to foot, a hood concealed his head, a half-mask covered part of his face. His attire was not unusual, for gentlemen often concealed their identity when walking the streets of Paris, but she sensed that his costume had been donned to keep his identity a secret from all those inside the accursed walls of La Salpêtrière prison. Who was he, and what was he hiding?

"I might better ask who you are, *mademoiselle*." His voice told her nothing.

"As you heard from the guard, my Christian name is Marie-Caresse de Villier, but I am called Caresse." There was puzzlement in her reply as she took a few steps closer to the mysterious figure. After what she had gone through in the last few days, this masked stranger held no terrors for her.

The sight of her lovely heart-shaped visage tore at the man whose dark eyes burned from the eye-holes of the black velvet mask. For a brief moment he had thought he had seen a ghost. But he could see now, as he tried to hide his shock, that this beautiful stranger was not an apparition.

"Are you going to tell me who you are?" the young woman questioned, with a lift of her chin, staring at him out of huge sad gray eyes.

The eyes were not the same as those that haunted him still, for they had been blue, a deep blue, he thought, staring back at her. And this young woman's hair was ash blond, not powdered white, a silver blond that glowed like a mist in the dim

10

morning light. But the features, the delicate small-boned figure, were stunning in their resemblance.

"It matters not that you know my name," he murmured as he approached her, lifting his hand to stroke the curve of her cheek with the square tip of his long tapered finger. Dark piercing eyes seemed to search her face.

Caresse felt no fear, for something within her knew that he meant her no harm. How she could know this she had no idea, for this terrible place was filled with men who wished her nothing but harm. This man, however, was different. It was in his voice, in his dark eyes that held some inner pain, in the gentleness of his touch. Strange, she thought, there was a callus on that aristocratic hand. It was the hand of a gentleman who had labored like a peasant.

Suddenly, he knew there would have to be a slight change in his plans for retribution. Those plans which had been years in the making had been altered the moment he saw her. His will was strong, and once he had made up his mind, nothing would deter him from his goal. But this slight young woman, who resembled a delicate porcelain figurine even after all her suffering, had introduced a most remarkable new element to his scheme. Having once seen her, he could only marvel at the jest fortune was playing on him. But save her he must, for it seemed predestined. A remarkable twist of fate was forging their futures from the ashes of old hates, old passions never fulfilled.

"You will be given a choice, *mademoiselle;* either a slow wasting away till eventual death in this hellish prison, or a chance at a new life in the colony of La Louisiane," he said with a cool authority that told her she had no alternative.

"La Louisiane," she gasped in a broken whisper. What had her father done to cause such total banishment not only from the court at Versailles but

France itself? "But I thought a law had been passed that no longer allowed prisoners to be sent to La Louisiane?"

"You are well informed, *mademoiselle*," he answered with a surprised respect. "You will not be going as a prisoner but voluntarily, as one of the *filles à la cassette*."

"But they are young women sent out by the king to be brides for the French colonists," she replied in a low voice. Her huge gray eyes filled with such defeat and despair he had to steel himself to keep from looking away.

"*Oui, mademoiselle,* and if you are as intelligent as I think you are you will not inform anyone once you reach the convent in Rouen, where you will join the other young women bound for La Louisiane, that you ever spent time in La Salpêtrière." His voice was uncompromising, yet oddly gentle.

"That might be difficult, *monsieur,* since I carry the *fleur de lys* burned into my left shoulder. I am now what is known as one of the scarlet lilies of La Salpêtrière." There was a slight bitterness in the soft, cultured voice, but her chin was raised high, and her gray eyes met his with an unflinching gaze. The prison and its people had inflicted their torture upon her, but they had not broken her spirit, her pride.

"Then I would not allow anyone to see you unclothed," he replied, his voice thick and unsteady. His dark eyes seemed to pierce the distance between them, betraying for a moment an intense emotion that caused a strange heavy warmth to course through her veins even though the cell was cold and damp.

"That could prove difficult in these rags," she responded with a gesture to the once-fine silk gown that was in tatters about her person. One sleeve

12

...nd part of the shoulder of the gown had been torn away when they branded her a criminal.

He had not noticed her clothing, for he had been so struck by her lovely face and her nobility of posture. He unclasped the wool cloak from his neck and swept it from his broad shoulders to drape it about her tiny form.

Caresse gave a shuddering sigh at the luxurious warmth of the soft wool cloak as it surrounded her. Gently he fastened the clasp about her slender throat. She was so much smaller than he that it engulfed her slender form, but she relished the sense of drowning in its warmth.

"There, you are covered, *mademoiselle,*" he said, standing back and regarding her appearance with a wry smile. " 'Tis more than a bit large, but 'twill do till I arrange for other clothing to be brought to you."

"Why?" she asked. "Why are you doing this?" She stared at him in the gloom of the cell for he stood back in the shadows out of the thin stream of light, as if he realized that now she could see him more clearly. But all she saw was a form dressed in somber black velvet, a powdered wig upon his head tied back in a queue with a black ribbon at the base of his neck. He was a gentleman, but he could have been any number of the hundreds she saw when she accompanied her father to Versailles.

"I have my reasons, *mademoiselle,*" he replied cryptically. "Shall we say that fate has intervened in your case. Do as I have told you, and you will leave this place to find your destiny as so many others have in La Louisiane."

"As the correction girls did so many years ago," she said with a bitter smile. "I believe they proved to be poor colonists, so poor in fact, that only fine country girls like the *filles à la cassette* are allowed to become the brides of the men of La Louisiane.

13

I shall take care not to shock anyone with my scarlet lily, *monsieur.*" She gave a light shudder as she thought of her future. But then glancing at the moist gray brick walls of the cell, she knew that she wanted to live, and La Louisiane had to be better then this place of horrors.

"You should pray that you have their courage, *mademoiselle,* those first doomed women who sailed to La Louisiane almost thirty years ago. The women you call the correction girls came from this very prison." His voice had hardened and he turned away from her toward the closed door.

"Wait, please, answer just one more question," she pleaded, one hand outstretched in supplication. "My father, will he accompany me to La Louisiane?"

"Non, mademoiselle," he replied, turning back to face her in the gloom. "He resides in the Bastille, in those quarters reserved for special prisoners of the king. He will remain in relative comfort as long as you do as you are told." His black eyes burned into hers with a cold fire for one long moment, then he rapped on the door to be let out.

Caresse stared after her mysterious visitor, holding his cloak close about her. There was a clean masculine scent about it, a fragrance she had never smelled before, although the fops and courtiers drenched themselves in perfumes and cologne. No, this was different, smelling of rich warm wood scents that were a welcome relief from the stench of the prison.

Who was he, she wondered, rubbing her cheek against the soft material. Was he her savior or executioner? If fate were kind she would see him once again before she sailed for that Godforsaken place inhabited by savages both Indian and French.

Giving a choked, desperate laugh, she realized how foolish she was to think that anyone could, or would, deliver her from her present torment and bleak future. Overcome with hopelessness, she stumbled to the mound of straw in the corner. Wrapping the cloak about her, she sought escape from her overwhelming despair in slumber. But her last thought was of the tall dark-eyed man who had wrapped his cape about her like an embrace. She realized, with a strange aching in her heart, that by leaving France she would never see him again, and that was the greatest pain of all.

Part One

"*Je plie et ne romps pas*–I bend but do not break."
Jean de La Fontaine,
"Le Chêne et Le Roseau," from *Fables*.

"I am bewitched with the rogue's company."
Shakespeare, *Henry IV.*

One

Nouvelle Orléans, La Louisiane
June 1749

"Look! Ahead, *mademoiselle*, Nouvelle Orléans," the old sailor cried out with enthusiasm to the small, forlorn-looking young woman standing at the ship's rail, staring out at the wild tropical vegetation of the passing shoreline.

"We are almost there, it seems a miracle," Caresse de Villier murmured, brushing a wisp of blond hair from her damp forehead. Although it was only June, the sultry heat was unbelievable. It swirled around her, sapping the energy from her very bones. She stared out across the river, watching with listless gray eyes as a long-legged egret pecked for food with graceful gestures at the edge of the ochre-brown water. The white feathers of the bird stood out in bold relief against the dense jungle of the marsh, that had a sinister haunted atmosphere clinging to it like a palpable presence. *Mon Dieu,* she thought with a shudder, was this paradise, or some kind of hell on earth?

" 'Tis been a long journey, *mademoiselle*, but soon all will be over, and you will find sanctuary at the convent of the Ursuline sisters in Nouvelle Orléans.

19

They will take good care of you till you choose your husband from all those lucky men who will be fighting for the honor of your hand," he said reassuringly. This fragile-looking woman was different from the country girls, who although of good character, were simple uneducated young women, for the most part—who hoped to advance themselves by coming to Louisiana as brides for the male settlers. Mademoiselle de Villier was as different from them as fine cognac was from *vin ordinaire*, everyday table wine, the old sailor mused, rubbing his grizzled beard. She had the bearing and manner of the gentry, and he could only guess at the misfortune that had brought her so low she would agree to travel to a strange land to become the bride of a man she had never met.

Caresse's hand tightened on the wooden rail, turning her knuckles white. Once they disembarked she would be given a few days' grace at the convent of the Ursuline sisters, then she would be expected to choose a husband from those single men who would come to look over the new *filles à la cassette*. The young women had been given a *cassette*, or casket, containing a trousseau from the king so that they did not come to their new husbands without a dowry. A rueful smile crossed Caresse's trembling lips as she thought of the plain serviceable clothes in her chest. She had once worn only the most fashionable silks and satins as the daughter of one of the finest old families in France, but that had been wiped out with one stroke of the king's pen.

Taking a deep breath, she willed herself not to think of anything but the present. It was a trick she had learned to keep her sanity during the long days at sea. The past was dead, over; she had been reborn when she was taken from the prison in Paris to the Ursuline Convent of Our Lady of Victories in Rouen. For in spite of everything, she wanted to live, to make some kind of life for herself. She was not ready to give up, no matter what obstacles fate put in her path.

"It hardly looks like the Paris of the new world," commented a young woman who came to stand beside Caresse. Her thin lip curled in disgust as they stared across the swirling yellow-brown waters of the river to the forbidding cypress and live oak forest. The trees draped their melancholy festoons of gray moss, which the sailors called *barbe à l'espagnole* or Spanish beard, into the muddy water.

"I think, Yvonne, that was another exaggeration to entice colonists to La Louisiane," Caresse replied in wry tones. "The governor may be a marquis from a wealthy family, but I doubt that even the Marquis de Vaudreuil could take this wilderness and create *la petit Paris* on the mud banks of the Mississippi, even if that is what they call Nouvelle Orléans in France. It appears uninhabitable, so wild . . . so lonely," she finished with a sigh.

"Perhaps we were foolish to be relieved that we did not disembark with most of the others at the port of Mobile," said Yvonne.

"I believe we had little choice in the matter," Caresse gently corrected her. "It seemed that certain women were assigned to Mobile and some to Nouvelle Orléans. Although I do not know how they decided who was to go where."

"The captain was certainly upset when you started to disembark at Mobile," Yvonne mused aloud, shaking her coppery curls as she remembered how flustered the man had gotten, mumbling that it would be the end of him if he did not deliver Mlle de Villier to New Orleans.

"Well, there are only eight of us left. 'Twould seem that there are not as many single men here needing wives as there were in Mobile," Caresse sighed, unable, now that they were almost to Nouvelle Orléans, to put from her mind the realization

21

that somewhere out there in that sinister wilderness was the man she would be expected to marry. It was beyond her comprehension that she would spend the rest of her life here in this strange land as the wife of a man she had yet to meet.

As she stared at the eerie gray moss waving in the soft humid breeze, gilded here and there with the red-gold of the setting sun, she remembered a pair of dark, haunting eyes, the touch of a hand on her cheek. A stranger who had visited her in her dismal prison cell in Paris and taken her heart away with him. How could she be in love with a man whose name she did not know, and whose face she had never clearly seen except for the intensity of those burning eyes? But there had been something between them, some immediate spark, that still warmed her if only with its memory. She had placed his cloak at the bottom of her casket, and would from time to time take it out and press it to her cheek that she might smell the faint scent that still clung to it. A pang struck her as she wondered if she would ever be able to forget him. Would the memory of their one brief encounter continue to haunt her for the rest of her days?

"Ah, *petit Paris!*" Yvonne announced, sarcasm edging each word, as she pointed to the break in the thick forest and green lances of the canebrakes that marked the beginning of Nouvelle Orléans. A few crude structures, barely visible through the flamboyant tropical vegetation, lined a muddy road that ran below a rough levee. A church tower soared in the distance to the rose-violet sky of late afternoon, promising at least a minimum of civilization. As the ship weighed anchor out in the channel of the river, the two young women stared across the crowded wharves to the green square surrounded on three sides by government buildings and a solid-looking church of brick covered with masonry at the back. The fourth side of the square was open to the river.

" 'Tis the Place Royale, *mademoiselles*," the old sailor told them before leaving to see to his duties. "You are home."

Caresse caught Yvonne's eyes as the young woman gave a Gallic shrug that seemed to say, we are here, we might as well make the best of it. Caresse answered with a brief smile of agreement, then turned to stare once more at the busy wharves filled with all manner of sailing craft, from full-rigged frigates to crude flatboats that appeared to be only a few logs strapped together. Caresse realized with a start that the long narrow craft traversing the water had to be a canoe, and the men, paddling with swift graceful gestures, the first Indians she had ever seen. The scent she would come to associate always with Nouvelle Orléans drifted across the water to greet them. A rich overripe mixture of the Mississippi River, verdant fecund earth, the sensual perfume of tropical flowers, and the fragrance of strong hot coffee.

"Come, come, *mes enfants*," bade the gentle but insistent voice of the middle-aged nun dressed in the gray robes of the Ursuline sisters. She gestured like a mother hen to her chicks, to Caresse and Yvonne to follow her, prodding them away from the fascinating scene enfolding before them. " 'Tis time to gather your belongings. We will be disembarking as soon as the small boats arrive from the wharf."

Caresse accompanied Yvonne below deck to retrieve her *cassette*, and a small covered basket containing a gift from the old sailor. Inside, curled in an alabaster ball of fur, lay a tiny kitten. The ship's cat had given birth during the voyage and Caresse had been given one of the kittens. The old sailor had placed it in her lap on one of her bad days when she did nothing but stare out to sea for hours at a time. He had been rewarded with the first

23

smile he had ever seen on her delicate face, and from that moment Caresse and the kitten, whom she had named Blanchette, had become inseparable.

"I wonder if the men will be waiting to catch a glimpse of us?" Yvonne murmured to Caresse as they boarded one of the flimsy rowboats hovering beneath the shadow of the larger ship. "Soeur Marguerite told me it usually happens when a ship of *filles à la cassette* is expected."

The two nuns, Sister Marguerite and Sister Therese, had accompanied the young women from the convent at Rouen. It was the good sisters' duty to make sure the young women arrived at their destination.

Caresse steeled herself as the boat rowed by two burly sailors, made its way across the ochre water. Somewhere out there in that wild untamed land was the man she would marry. For a moment tears clouded her eyes as she knew that it would never be the dark-eyed stranger who had captured her heart. She had to forget him, push him out of her mind, or what was to come would be even harder, she thought, biting her lower lip to control the sob of regret that threatened to engulf her.

Then there was no more time to think of old pain, old regrets, for they were landing at the wharf, a wharf swarming with males of all descriptions, each eager to get a glimpse of the new *filles à la cassette* from France.

Waves of heat rose from the dock as Caresse was helped from the swaying boat. For a moment she felt faint as the crowd of men seemed to close around her—avid eyes devouring her face and figure. She closed her ears to the lewd remarks, clutching Blanchette's basket with both hands as her casket of clothes was lifted from the boat and placed at her feet.

The leering faces, the stench from some of the men surrounded her, suffocating her, till she felt the burning tropical sky above her pressing down, down upon her chest, sucking the breath from her lungs. When she thought she would scream from the sheer terror of being smothered alive by the crowd, she felt a hand on her arm. Mercifully, the crowd seemed to part and she could once more catch her breath.

"*Mademoiselle,* if I might be of service," a masculine voice inquired as firm, tapered fingers grasped her arm and steered her from the crowd.

When she looked up to reply, Caresse felt a shock run through her. Her breath caught in her lungs as she stared up into deep-set, dark magnetic eyes, eyes she would know anywhere even if she did not recognize the face.

" 'Tis you," she breathed, astonishment draining all color from her face.

"Forgive me, *mademoiselle,* but have we met?" The tall dark-haired man murmured coolly, a flicker of enigmatic emotion in his dark eyes. With a deft movement he managed to lead her away from the crowd of men. They seemed to defer to him, Caresse noticed, even through her shock and surprise.

"I . . . I thought for a moment that we had," she stammered, staring up at him now in confusion. Had she been so consumed with thoughts of the man she had seen only once in La Salpêtrière that she saw him in every tall man with expressive dark eyes? She reminded herself that many Frenchmen had dark eyes, and she wasn't even sure of the color of her visitor's hair, for he had worn a powdered wig.

Under his fashionable dark tricorn hat, the man standing at her side had thick luxuriant black hair that waved back from an elegant forehead to be caught at the nape of his neck in a queue. His face was lean and angular, with strongly marked black brows above the intense dark orbs veiled in thick lashes that seemed to blink far less rapidly than those of other men. Her gaze noted the cleft in the firm, unyielding chin beneath the full, unsmiling mouth. He was a man of mystery, for while his fine features were those of an aristocrat, his skin was bronzed from the sun. She was aware of the sinewy, almost predatory grace about his tall lean form, as well as the sense that this was a solitary man. His aloof manner, a certain remoteness about him hinted at depths not easily reached. She suddenly wondered what lay beneath the cool facade.

He stared down at her, the silence lengthening between them as he seemed to search her face, looking for what, she did not know. It was this intensity of gaze, she realized, that had reminded her of the stranger who had visited her in her prison cell over eight months before.

"If we had met, *mademoiselle,* I would have remembered, for once seen, a face as lovely as yours would never be forgotten," he said in a deep velvet murmur that still managed to be heard above the din of the docks.

"Please forgive me, *monsieur,* I was wrong," she replied politely, pulling away from his hand that still touched her arm. "You reminded me of someone I knew in France. How silly to think that he would be here in Nouvelle Orléans."

"Often we see what the heart wishes," he answered, a strange shadow in the depths of his opaque eyes. It flickered only for a moment, and then disappeared.

"Mlle de Villier, come away from there," Sister Marguerite called out as she hurried to Caresse's side. "Soeur Xavier will escort us to the convent. A slave will carry your *cassette* along with those of the others. There will be time to converse with gentlemen after we have become settled." She pulled Caresse firmly away from the arresting man who had come to her rescue. *"Monsieur,* you may call at the convent if you wish to speak with the *mademoiselle."*

"I shall, *Soeur,*" he replied, with a slight inclination of his dark handsome head, but his expression held a note of mockery. So did the bow he suddenly made with a lithe gesture to Caresse, sweeping his hat from his head. His ebony hair gleamed in the rays of the setting sun like a raven's wing.

Caresse allowed the nun to lead her over to where the others stood waiting next to a gentle-featured nun who, she decided, must be Sister Xavier. Yvonne's eyes lit up with curiosity as she stared at the elegant masculine figure who did not take his gaze from Caresse's petite figure as she reluctantly left his side.

"Who was that?" Yvonne asked as the two young women fell in line behind the other *filles à la cassette.* Two nuns led the line of young women away from the wharves with Sister Xavier bringing up the rear.

"I have no idea," Caresse murmured as she turned resolutely away from the last intriguing sight of the man who still watched them with an intense dark gaze.

"Perhaps, if you are lucky, he will come to the convent to ask for your hand," Yvonne said, looking over her shoulder for one last glimpse of the handsome stranger. "He seemed to go right to you as if he knew you. I watched him from the time we disembarked from the rowboat. He never took his eyes off you. I should have such luck," she sighed.

"Move quickly, *mademoiselles,* but with dignity," Sister Xavier cautioned from behind them. "We do not want to attract any more attention to ourselves then we already have with our arrival."

"Oui, Soeur," the two young women replied, trying not to laugh, for it seemed impossible that they would not attract attention. Every eye seemed to be upon them as they crossed the grassy square that the sailor had called the Place Royale.

On the right and left side of the square stood a

row of soldiers' barracks. It seemed that every window was occupied by a masculine face staring down at the those walking beneath the casements. The slaves hurrying about the town on their masters' business were the only pedestrians who did not glance in the direction of the line of young women being escorted toward the convent.

Caresse glanced at the passing scene from under the corner of her plain linen coif. The church steeple they had seen from the ship appeared to belong to the solid-looking brick church covered with masonry at the back of the square, flanking the church was a jail, the Corps de Garde, and the home of the Capuchin fathers. Tall grass and weeds seemed to grow where the tramping of feet had not beaten down a path across the square. Vines with tiny fragrant white flowers wound around the trunks of the oak trees, lending their perfume to the sultry air. Frogs serenaded the city from puddles in the muddy streets, their rasp a counterpoint to the chime of the church bells. Even with the French colonial style of the buildings there was an atmosphere about Nouvelle Orléans that was tropical and exotic to Caresse.

Reaching the corner of the square they turned down a street called the Rue de Chartres that led past well-maintained houses. Some had thatched roofs, others had rooftops with cypress shingles, but all were white-washed and set in the middle of luxuriant gardens with orange and peach trees. The tropical palm and other plants Caresse had never seen grew in profusion everywhere.

" 'Tis not far, *mes enfants*," the gentle voice of Sister Xavier encouraged them.

"Well, at least the men will not have far to come," Yvonne said with a giggle to Caresse.

"They will have no trouble, I assure you," the nun commented dryly from behind them.

"I hope you are right, especially that tall dark-haired man who was so intrigued with Mlle de Villier," Yvonne replied over her shoulder in spite of Caresse's frown.

"He, *mes enfants,* is one man in Nouvelle Orléans who will not come courting," she told them with a finality in her voice that only aroused their curiosity.

"And why is that, *Soeur?*" Yvonne persisted.

"Lucien St. Amant is not interested in a wife, I assure you," Sister Xavier answered.

"He is married then?" Yvonne continued, disappointment obvious in her voice.

"He is a widower," was the terse reply.

"Well, then, he is available," Yvonne said with satisfaction.

"Lucien St. Amant is not the kind of man a young woman would desire for a husband," said Sister Xavier with conviction. "His reputation is not what we would seek for our young women. Believe me, he will never come seeking a wife, not that one. He is a rogue, a *roué,* a dangerous man. Put him from your minds, *mes enfants.* His kind is not for you."

Caresse caught the sparkle of rebellion in Yvonne's expression and knew they were thinking the same thing. Lucien St. Amant would not be easy to forget—not any easier than the stranger who had been her savior in Paris. She could still feel the intensity of Lucien St. Amant's presence, the touch of his hand on her arm. Giving a shrug of her slender shoulders, she tried to push the memory to the back of her mind. She remembered, with a pang, that he had said he would come to the convent to see her. Would he keep his promise? She wished it didn't matter to her if he did, but a voice deep inside her knew that it mattered. It mattered a great deal.

Two

The midday sun beat down from a blue-white summer sky like a ball of fire, causing the sultry still air in the walled garden of the Ursuline convent to shimmer and distort the appearance of the precise flower and herb beds. As Caresse stared through the flickering golden waves of sun, everything appeared hazy and unreal, she thought with a sigh, wiping the moisture from her forehead with the back of her hand. She had been in Nouvelle Orléans four weeks, and the intensity of the heat still amazed her. Bending down she began once more to weed Sister Xavier's herb garden unaware she was being observed.

"Has her mood lightened?" Sister Hachard de St. Stanislas asked of Sister Xavier. She had become the closest to the melancholy Mademoiselle de Villier.

"Somewhat. I have found that having her work in the garden is the best remedy for her despairing moods," the gentle nun explained as they stared out from the long window of the small chamber she used as a pharmacy. She was in charge of making all the medicines that they used in the hospital across from the convent.

"All of the other *filles à la cassette* who came with her from France have been spoken for, but Mlle

30

de Villier refuses to even consider any of the many men who have come to ask for her hand. I fear she has gotten a reputation for being quite strange, and her delicate bone structure does not signify to most of them that she would make a hardworking wife. In spite of her beauty they have stopped making any inquiries," Sister Hachard de St. Stanislas said with a sigh.

"There has been one man, a most persistent man who wishes to be granted an interview with her, but I have tried to discourage his efforts. He does not, however, give up," Sister Xavier said quietly as the two nuns stared down at the delicate figure of Caresse de Villier working diligently in the herb bed, her tiny white kitten playing by her side.

"And who is this man?" her companion asked in amazement, for she had been unaware of this mysterious persistent suitor.

"Lucien St. Amant," she replied softly.

"I understand why you hesitated," Sister Hachard de St. Stanislas replied with a sigh. "He is looking for a wife?"

"He says, that is the reason he wishes to court Mademoiselle de Villier. It seems he thinks 'tis time for an heir. His wife has been dead for almost seven years, and as you know there were no children from that tragic marriage."

"There is an old saying that states a reformed rake makes a good husband," Sister Hachard de St. Stanislas mused, her middle-aged countenance creased in thought.

"But is he reformed?—that is the question," Sister Xavier replied. "You have known the family since his mother first came here all those years ago."

"*Oui*, I helped care for the *enfant* Lucien after his birth aboard ship. Even then he was stubborn, tough, and determined. How many babies would

31

survive such a birth? I never thought his poor mother would find a home when we arrived in Nouvelle Orléans, but then Jacques St. Amant was an unusual man. As the right hand of Governor Bienville, and having made a fortune in the fur trade in New France, he could have had his pick of women. But he chose poor Gabrielle. Jacques, of course, was Lucien's salvation, for his mother was never quite normal after all she went through. And now they are both dead, and Lucien is the sole heir to the St. Amant fortune as well as that mysterious inheritance from France."

"*Oui, le bon Dieu* works in wondrous and mysterious ways," Sister Xavier replied.

"Allow him to visit Mlle de Villier," the older nun said suddenly. "Perhaps 'tis true, and a reformed rake does make a good husband. At least the delicate Caresse will have a comfortable life as the mistress of Sans Regret and the lovely St. Amant town house. Jacques was a good father to Lucien. We can only hope that he learned something about compassion from him and from the tragic outcome of his first marriage."

"I shall do as you say, but I can only hope for the young woman's sake that you are right about Lucien's reformation," Sister Xavier said with a slight shudder, for she knew that Caresse de Villier's life could be many things as the wife of Lucien St. Amant, but comfortable would not be one of them.

Caresse finished her weeding, unaware that her future was being considered by the two nuns who had tried to help her adjust to her new life in the French colony. Picking up her basket, she checked to make sure she had several stalks of rosemary as well as sage leaves. Sister Xavier was teaching her how to make medicines from the herbs, and also which herbs were used for which ailments.

"Come, *ma chère*, I wish to speak with you," Sister Xavier said as she approached with the gliding walk that all the Ursuline sisters seemed to have perfected.

Blanchette trailing at her heels, Caresse walked over to the wooden bench under a tall magnolia in the corner of the walled garden, where Sister Xavier had sat down. "I have gathered the sage and rosemary that you requested," she said, holding out the basket.

"Très bien, ma chère," Sister Xavier said with an absent-minded smile, patting the place beside her on the bench. " 'Tis warm, you should rest a while. I wish to speak with you for a moment about an important matter."

"Oui, Soeur Xavier," Caresse answered, sitting down under the welcome shade of the magnolia, the fresh astringent scent surrounding them with a reviving fragrance.

"A man will be coming to see you this afternoon, that is, if you wish to see him." She stopped for a moment as if considering her next words. "You have met him before, if only briefly. His name is Lucien St. Amant."

Caresse felt a warm glow flow through her at the nun's announcement. He was finally coming as he had promised! Suddenly, she felt energy surge through her veins. He had not forgotten her.

"You wish to see him then?" Sister Xavier asked, already knowing the answer. When she had spoken his name it had been as if a light had been lit inside the somber Caresse. The nun felt a tug at her heart. This young woman was so vulnerable, she could only hope that they were doing the right thing by allowing Lucien St. Amant to enter her life.

"I should like to see him," Caresse replied quietly, trying to conceal her excitement.

"Bien, he will arrive at two of the clock," the nun told her. "If you wish to go to your chamber and

freshen up before his arrival I shall understand. Give me the basket and I shall take the herbs to *la pharmacie.*"

"*Merci,* my hands are dirty from the weeding," Caresse answered, rising to her feet after she handed the basket to the kindly nun.

"I shall have him await you here in the garden at two," Sister Xavier said, also rising to her feet. She could only pray that this meeting was in the young woman's best interests, but she could not help having some misgivings. Lucien St. Amant's reputation as one of the fast crowd that surrounded the governor's wife, the Marquise de Vaudreuil, was well known in the city. In the last few weeks the nun had become fond of the lovely Caresse with the sad gray eyes. She prayed that Sister Hachard de St. Stanislas was right and that this rogue had decided to reform.

Caresse had no such trepidation as she hurried across the floor of wide cypress boards of the second-story corridor to the tiny room that was her bedchamber. Her heart seemed to sing as the thought ran over and over through her mind like a prayer, *in an hour I shall see him once more.* Did she have a future after all? The other *filles à la cassette* had all chosen husbands, even Yvonne had found a stalwart Canadian, one of the *coureurs de bois* who had come down the Mississippi River from Canada and decided to settle in Louisiana. He had a small plantation outside the city on the Mississippi. They were to be married the next week at the St. Louis Parish Church on the Place Royale. And while she was happy for Yvonne, she knew she would miss the placid-natured young woman more than she cared to admit. Her life had seemed to stretch ahead of her empty and alone. She had felt no calling to join the Ursuline order, so she had become more and more despairing in the last few days about what was to become of her.

"You look so different," the familiar voice of Yvonne called out to her as Caresse hurried past her chamber. The door was open, and Yvonne could be seen working on a quilt the sisters had started for her trousseau. "What has happened?" she asked, as she stood on the threshold of Caresse's room.

"I have a gentleman caller coming in an hour," Caresse couldn't help telling her as she poured water from the pitcher into the basin that stood on the simple chest.

"Who is it?" Yvonne questioned, catching the excitement in her friend's voice.

"Lucien St. Amant," she replied, beginning to wash her hands with the lye soap.

Mon Dieu! Yvonne exclaimed. "Even the Marquise de Vaudreuil is said to fancy him. I heard all about him from Pierre. He is quite wealthy, with an indigo plantation on the Mississippi, and a fine town house here in the city. But his reputation is quite scandalous. It is rumored that two women of the town had a duel over him. Of course, Pierre said they were both drunk at the time. But, Caresse, he is so handsome, like some great dark jungle cat," Yvonne sighed, coming into the small barren chamber. "Will you accept him if he asks for your hand?"

"I . . . I do not know," Caresse stammered. "He is only coming to meet with me, after all, we have met just that one time at the wharf. She did not want to get her hopes up, the hurt would be too devastating if he never returned. Perhaps he was just toying with her, for if what Yvonne said was true he would hardly have to ask a *fille à la cassette* to be his wife. Lucien St. Amant had no way of knowing that she was from a fine old French family. He was, she thought with a sinking heart, probably only amusing himself for an afternoon.

"Are you going to change your bodice?" Yvonne

asked, for Caresse was dressed in a plain muslin bodice that had been washed many times so that the material was thin and worn. "I know you have a better one in your *cassette*." She started for the simple wooden trunk that stood at the front of the crude pine bed.

"No!" Caresse exclaimed with more force than she intended. She had always undressed when alone so that no one could see the red *fleur de lys* burned into her left shoulder. The warning of the stranger who had come to her prison cell so many months ago was burned into her mind like the scarlet lily on her shoulder. "I do not want him to think that I am trying to impress him, when he is only amusing himself on a boring afternoon. My everyday bodice will suffice," she answered, lifting her chin in a gesture which—she didn't realize—revealed her aristocratic upbringing.

Yvonne stared at her, wondering, not for the first time, who Caresse really was, where she came from, for she never spoke about her family or home back in France. When she stood like that, even though she could be dressed in rags, still anyone could see that there was nothing common about her person. Yvonne had once seen the Marquise de Vaudreuil riding by in her elegant carriage pulled by the four matched horses, and she had held her fashionably coifed head in just that manner.

"You are so lovely, Caresse, I am sure that Lucien St. Amant will not even notice what you are wearing," Yvonne told her with a smile.

"*Merci.* Oh, Yvonne, you must excuse me! I think I am having an attack of nerves," Caresse replied, giving her friend a quick hug before turning back to the polished metal rectangle that hung over the chest and served as a looking glass. She quickly straightened the simple muslin cap she wore on her hair pulled up into a chignon, one long ringlet falling over her shoulder. Tiny wisps of hair curled about her forehead from the humidity, but that was the climate in Nouvelle Orléans. She sighed, wishing she had one tiny bottle of her favorite lily scent. There was little use in wishing, for there was not a bottle of perfume in the entire convent.

"There, I shall just have to do for M. St. Amant," she said with a thin smile of bravado, as she turned to face Yvonne, smoothing down the white apron over the dark blue muslin skirt held out by a starched linen petticoat. The clothes she wore would have been scorned as too plain by the servants in her family's chateau, she thought, biting her lower lip, as memories of another time and place threatened to overwhelm her.

" 'Tis time. I hear the church bells striking two of the clock," Yvonne told her, giving her a fond little push in the direction of the stairs.

The object of their concern stood outside the wall of the convent at the cypress gate. Staring up at the massive plastered brick residence, two and one half stories high in the French Renaissance tradition, Lucien St. Amant grimaced slightly, as he lifted a slender bronzed hand to give a sharp rap on the gate with the brass ornamental knocker. He must be mad to allow such an obsession to take hold of him. But here he was at the Ursuline convent seeking admission, so that he could speak with a tiny slip of a young woman who haunted his days and turned his nights into a restless torment. Fate did, indeed, toy with him.

The peephole opened for a brief moment, then the door was flung wide by the concierge. With a gesture to follow behind, she escorted him first to the office of Sister Hachard de St. Stanislas. The nun awaited him with a calm patience that was far from Lucien's mood.

"I wished to speak with you before you visit with Mlle de Villier," the older nun explained as he crossed the threshold, the door closing behind him.

"To make sure my intentions are honorable," he replied with more than a hint of sarcasm in his deep voice.

"And are they?" She parried, standing with her back to the long casement that overlooked the herb garden.

"If that is the only way I can achieve my goal then they are honorable," he answered, his sensuous lips twisted into a cynical smile.

"Why do you wish to make her your wife?" the self-contained nun asked quietly, her eyes searching his handsome visage.

"The usual reasons a man has for asking a woman to marry him," he replied tersely, a melancholy frown flitting across his noble features, a shadow of some unreadable emotion in his dark eyes.

"I saw the resemblance too, *mon cher* Lucien," the older nun stated softly. "You cannot replace one person with another, simply because they vaguely resemble a lost opportunity."

" 'Tis not just the physical resemblance, although you are right there is one," he tried to explain, a brooding expression settling on his distinguished features like a storm cloud. "I find this difficult to explain, but there is something about her that draws me, something that is uniquely hers alone."

"But you have only seen her once, and that was a brief encounter," the sister reminded him.

" 'Tis why I am here today, Soeur," he explained with quiet emphasis. "I wish to confirm my feelings and perhaps to come to know Mlle de Villier."

"And if your feelings are confirmed?" She asked quietly.

"I shall wish to make her my wife," he answered, giving a light shrug of his broad shoulders that said, What other outcome could there be?

"She awaits you below in the garden, but before

you join her I wish to caution you," Sister Hachard de St. Stanislas told him as he joined her at the long window that looked down on the herb garden. " 'Tis not just her appearance that is frail and fragile, she is prone to melancholy moods. I do not know what tribulations she has gone through in her young life, but 'tis obvious they have left their mark on her. Nothing like your poor mother, if you will forgive me, but she needs gentle handling."

"And you do not think I am capable of gentleness, Soeur?" he asked, a muscle flicking angrily in his firm jaw.

"I think you wish to make up for old mistakes, and while this is noble of you, for that young woman's sake, I beg you to look deep into your heart before you make any commitments."

He stared down at the slender feminine figure— she was unaware that she was being observed. She had stopped to look at one of the perfect magnolia blooms that glowed alabaster against the dark leathery green leaves. Carefully, she bent down to inhale its fragrance without touching the delicate petals that would in one brief touch begin to turn brown. He felt a wild pang of yearning tear through him. She would, if what the nun had told him was true, require as gentle handling as a magnolia blossom. Amazement warred with desire within him, as he realized with stunned clarity that despite everything he had become, he was feeling tenderness toward this unusual woman. He could not remember when he had wanted to cherish, to protect a woman; not in a very long time. The women of the Marquise de Vaudreuil's set were a hard hedonistic lot who elicited many emotions in him, but tenderness was certainly not one of them.

"I had forgotten how perceptive you can be, Soeur," he told her ruefully, with a sudden mercurial smile, turning away from the window. "I promise I shall bring no harm to her."

"Ah, *mon cher* Lucien, you could be such a stubborn child one minute, and yet show that hidden streak of gentleness with your poor *maman*. 'Tis still there, I think, beneath the cold hard facade. She is one who deserves to see that hidden side of you." The nun gestured down to the solitary figure in the garden.

"Perhaps, Soeur," he said with a melancholy smile that did not reach his eyes, haunted with an old despair. "I should not keep her waiting."

"Adieu, *mon cher* Lucien, I shall pray for both of you," the nun said softly, making the sign of the cross over him.

" 'Twould not hurt to do so, Soeur. We shall probably need it," he said, giving a graceful nod of his dark head in farewell.

Caresse heard his step on the crushed-shell walk before she saw him, but there was some part of her body that sensed his presence as well. It was as if each and every nerve was stimulated to its highest threshold of awareness. She saw his tall shadow against the brick wall of the garden as he came up behind her. For a moment she stood immobilized, her breath caught in her throat, then slowly she turned around.

"*Bonjour, mademoiselle,*" he said quietly. His husky voice ran up and down her spine like the sensual touch of a lover's hand.

"*Monsieur,*" she managed to say so softly he could barely hear her.

"You are even lovelier than I remembered," he said as if thinking aloud, his dark eyes sweeping over her delicate visage, holding her shy gray gaze to him by force of will.

"You are very kind, *monsieur,*" she replied, still

in a breathy whisper, as she tried to look away from those eyes that probed too deeply into her soul.

"Lucien," he said. "I want to hear my name on your lips. Say it. Say my name," his voice commanded her softly, as he held her gaze by some invisible bonds of the heart and soul that would not allow her to look away.

"Lucien," she said, her throaty voice lingering over the word with an unknowingly sensual intonation that set his blood afire.

"Caresse, ah, Caresse," he repeated softly, savoring the sound of her name on his lips. "I have waited so long for today." His intense gaze seemed to gather her up and hold her to him.

"I thought you would never come," she murmured, making no effort to conceal the fact that she had been waiting for him as well.

"The good sisters would not allow me to see you till now. I do not have the best of reputations, *ma chère* Caresse," he replied, making no pretense that he was something that he was not.

"La, you mean you are a man with a past," she teased lightly, deep dimples appearing on either side of her delicious mouth.

"But that does not frighten you," he stated, his dark eyes gleaming with approval as one finger reached out to brush a loose tendril of hair from her cheek. He could not control himself, he had to touch her.

"I think I could never be frightened if I was with you," she said, the words coming, without any attempt at coquetry, straight from the heart.

"Ah, Caresse, why has it taken me so long to find you?" For an instant a melancholy wistfulness stole into his intense eyes—like a cloud across the sun. Then with a shrug of his broad shoulders, clad in an elegant dove gray waistcoat of the finest silk, he said in mock resignation, "But fate has allowed us to meet. One does not often receive a second chance in life."

"A second chance?" she asked, startled.

"Come, sit over here with me, and tell me something of your life here at the convent since you have come to Nouvelle Orléans," he requested, smoothly changing the subject as he knew he had revealed too much.

"There is little to tell, I am afraid my days are all rather the same. I help Soeur Xavier here in the garden and in *la pharmacie* preparing medicines. Also, I often help teach and care for the orphans in their school and infirmary," she explained carefully as she sat beside him on the bench.

"And what do you think of Nouvelle Orléans?" he queried, leaning back, but with his body turned toward her so he could give her his complete attention.

"I have seen very little of it," she said, with a wry smile. "I have gone once to the market on the quay with several of the *soeurs,* but that is hardly enough to be able to form a strong opinion."

"We shall change that this afternoon. You will accompany me on a tour of the city. I shall send for my carriage at my town house," he said, reaching out and once more brushing one of the tendrils from her cheek. The desire to keep touching her was so strong he had to fight for control.

" 'Tis a lovely thought, but the nuns will not allow us to accompany a man anywhere unchaperoned unless we are engaged," she explained with a rueful grimace.

"Mon Dieu, you might as well be in prison," he jested, only to see a strange look come over her delicate features. "Have I said something wrong, *mademoiselle?"*

"Non, only that we look at life differently, for to me the Ursuline convent is not a prison, but a ref-

uge," she replied in a low voice, looking away from him to stare at the sundial in the middle of one of the formal herb beds.

"A refuge from what, may I ask?" He questioned gently.

"From life, *monsieur*, from life," she answered, her bottom lip trembling so violently she caught it between her small white teeth.

"Then 'tis time you faced down your fears," he told her, with warmth as well as authority, placing his hands over hers where they lay clasped in her lap. "Look at me, Caresse de Villier."

Slowly, she lifted her head to stare into those compelling dark eyes. He was staring at her intently, but his gaze was as soft as a tender touch. The world ceased to exist except for this small corner of the walled garden where he held her to him by force of his magnetic will.

"Will you, Caresse de Villier, do me the honor of becoming my wife?" he asked in a low, composed voice that seemed unaware of how shocking was his proposal so soon in their relationship.

"Monsieur!" she gasped, as his hands tightened over hers, his eyes never leaving her face.

"Bien, I take that for an affirmative answer," he said dryly. "As your intended I claim a kiss to seal our pledge."

Before she could speak, she felt his hands release hers and pull her to his embrace. His lips first brushed across her mouth, and as she tried to speak she felt him claim her in a passionate kiss that caused all thought to flee in the tremors of physical pleasure that surged throughout her being. She felt her arms lift to wrap around his neck as if they had a will of their own. A small moan came from her throat, as his kiss deepened with his achingly sweet exploration of her moist responsive mouth. Tentatively, but unable to stop herself, she

43

touched his tongue with her own, and this time the moan came from deep within him.

She loved the feel of him, the wonderful sense of belonging she experienced in the sanctuary of his embrace. After all the fear of the last months, the terrible loneliness that made her despair of ever knowing happiness, she knew, held in his arms, what it was to hope. It was as if she had found the light at the end of her long tunnel of despair—in this man's embrace.

Time seemed to have stood still, for Caresse was unaware of how long they sat lost in each other's arms till the persistent ringing of a bell finally intruded on their concentration. It was as if she had been far away in another dimension where nothing mattered but Lucien St. Amant, and his heated mouth on her own. With reluctance, he lifted his lips from hers as he asked, "What is it?"

"The bell, it is a signal that we are to go to the dining hall," she replied with a sigh, her face buried in the hollow of his neck.

"I shall return on the morrow, *ma chère,* and your introduction back into life shall begin," he murmured against her temple as he lightly kissed the silk tendrils of her hair. "Now you'd best go while I still have some small amount of control."

She pulled away from him and stood up. He rose to his feet, towering above her. *"Adieu, monsieur,"* she said with a shy smile, her voice barely a whisper. Then she was gone, moving like a skittish kitten away from him down the shell walk toward the arched loggia at the end of the garden.

"Mon Dieu," he muttered, shaking his head in surprise and self-mockery. She had gotten to him in a way that no other woman had ever accomplished, and she was no more than a girl. He was not a sentimental man, but somehow she had touched his heart, and it had been his heart that had spoken, that had asked for her hand. What

44

had he done, allowing his impulse to commit him to this obsession? Caresse de Villier was, he feared, a dangerous obsession. A trick of fate to tempt him with a chance at redemption. What other tricks did fate have in store for him if he allowed this marriage to take place, he mused, a shadow of annoyance in his dark eyes as he stared down the empty path. And how would he spend the restless hours till he would be with her again?

Three

"Caresse, you have a visitor," Yvonne announced, opening the door of the pharmacy. "He awaits you with Soeur Hatchard de St. Stanislas." Her eyes danced with excitement for her friend had told her the night before of Lucien's proposal of marriage.

"You may go as soon as you fill the jar with the rest of the bay leaves," Sister Xavier told her quietly.

"Merci," Caresse replied, trying not to hurry as she filled the jar with the dried leaves and then pushed in the cork stopper. Yvonne waited impatiently for her friend to finish.

The two young women sped down the corridor. In the sultry heat of the summer morn, they were both soon panting from exertion, their faces damp with perspiration.

"Wait, before you go in, let me make you more presentable," Yvonne cautioned as they reached the office. Taking the end of her apron, she wiped the perspiration from Caresse's upper lip and brow. She pushed her plain linen cap back further on her head so that more of her ash blond hair was visible. "You have such lovely hair, it should not be covered up," she said. "There, you are ready."

Giving her friend a nervous smile of thanks, Caresse knocked softly on the heavy cypress portal. Within seconds it was opened by Lucien.

"Entrez, mademoiselle," he murmured in the deep resonant voice that she had tried to remember all through the tossing and turnings of her restless slumber. Although his manner was formal and correct, a slight smile curved his sensuous mouth and there was a sparkle in his magnetic dark eyes as he stared down at her.

"Merci, monsieur," she replied with equal formality, giving an unconscious lift of her chin as she crossed the open portal.

His tall, lithe figure seemed to diminish the nun's small spartan office, so that he appeared to dominate the entire chamber with both his physical presence and the aura of his mesmerizing personality. Caresse could feel his intense gaze upon her as she moved toward where Sister Hatchard de St. Stanislas stood behind the battered wooden desk. Every nerve in her body was aware of Lucien St. Amant.

"Soeur, you wished to speak with me," Caresse heard her voice tremble, to her chagrin, Lucien's presence was disconcerting. Clasping her hands in fists at her side, she fought for control.

"I understand, *mon enfant,* that you have agreed to marry M. St. Amant," the nun said, searching Caresse's delicate features for the answers to unspoken questions.

"Oui, Soeur, I have," Caresse replied, lifting her head to meet the nun's gaze with a cool composure that was all facade.

"Bien, then we shall have the banns posted. M. St. Amant wishes the marriage to be as soon as possible, according to the church. We have decided on three weeks from today, if you agree?"

"I agree, *Soeur,*" Caresse answered evenly. She showed none of the turmoil that was raging within her or her awareness of Lucien's intense gaze on the long elegant line of her back. She could feel those piercing ebony orbs stimulate every nerve in her spine like a physical touch.

"M. St. Amant has requested that, as your *fiancé*, he be allowed certain privileges. He wishes to escort you on a tour of the city in his carriage this afternoon. You will be stopping, I believe," she paused, looking at Lucien for confirmation, "yes, you will be taken to a dressmaker on the Rue Royale for measurements for the trousseau he wishes to provide for you."

Caresse looked at the nun with startled eyes as she realized everything her marriage to Lucien would entail. What had she gotten herself into, she thought with a surge of panic. He had seemed a solution to her problems, a chance at a life close to what she had been used to, in France. And then there had been the chord he had struck within her, the slight resemblance to the man who helped her escape the terrors of La Salpêtrière. She remembered with a pang the wonderful sense of security she had felt in his arms. But what did she know of him—and more importantly what did he know of her past? How willing would he be to marry her if he knew she carried the infamous scarlet lily on her left shoulder? And how would she keep the knowledge of that terrible brand from the dressmaker who would be fitting the gowns on her body. She knew she could not keep it a secret from her husband once they were married, but then it would be *fait accompli*, she would be Mme St. Amant. But if Lucien were to find out before their wedding day, would their marriage ever take place? Would she once more be cast out to find her own way, without family or fortune, in this exotic colony that slumbered in the languid tropic sun? What would she do? How would she ever survive?

"Mon enfant, what is wrong?" The nun's voice seemed to come from far away as Caresse sank down into the dark waiting abyss where there was

safety from the world's terrors, from questions that had no answers.

"Has this happened before, *Soeur?*" Lucien questioned sharply as he bent down beside the still white figure collapsed on the cypress floorboards.

"Oui, whenever she is faced with a new or frightening situation," the nun replied as she came to kneel beside the stricken young woman. "I warned you that she is very delicate both of body and mind. She has suffered much, *pauvre petite.* One only has to look in her sad eyes to know that life has not always been kind, that she has endured much unhappiness."

"She needs looking after," he muttered, cradling her head and shoulders against his chest, brushing the tangled tendrils of her hair fallen from under her muslin cap.

"Ah, so this draws you as well as her beauty, her terrible vulnerability," Sister Hachard de St. Stanislas murmured aloud with a melancholy smile. So like poor Gabrielle, she thought, but wisely kept this to herself. As he looked down at Caresse's pale visage with pain in his eyes, she remembered a young boy who had allowed only one tenderness to show through the hard wall he had erected about his heart, and that had been for the fragile shell of a human being who had been his mother. Lost in some private world of her own, Gabrielle had been as dependent on her husband and son as a young child. The trips into Nouvelle Orléans from their plantation had been torture for all of them, but Jacques could not leave her alone even with the trusted house slaves. He had to arrange for the shipment of his indigo crop, and Lucien had to be educated with the Capuchin fathers at their *presbytère* next to the parish church of St. Louis. How trying those visits must have been to the young Lucien, the nun mused—but he had never allowed any of the other boys to say a word about his mother, even when she had been at her most eccentric. Jacques and his son had loved that poor crazed soul till the day she found her release in death.

"You always were perceptive, *Soeur,*" Lucien said with a twisted smile, looking up from where Caresse was beginning to stir in his arms. " 'Tis all right, *ma chère,* you only fainted. You look as if you have not been eating, you are as thin as a bird," he reassured her softly as she sat up and pulled away from his embrace.

"Please forgive me, *monsieur, Soeur,* but I think you are right. I did not break my fast this morn," Caresse explained, looking away from Lucien's too-knowing gaze to the nun's gentle features.

"You stand on the threshold of a new life, *ma petite,* 'tis no wonder you feel a trifle light-headed," the sister replied, as Lucien helped her to her feet. "Do you feel that you are well enough for this afternoon's excursion outside these walls?"

"I shall see that she dines, *Soeur,*" Lucien interjected, determined she would accompany him.

"*Oui,* I am quite recovered," Caresse replied. She would make it work, this marriage, for it was her only chance at some kind of life outside these cloistered walls. And perhaps someday she could find out what had happened to her father, and to be able to help him when she was the wife of a wealthy planter. It made her cringe to think in such a calculating manner, but it was a matter of survival. She had endured things that she had not even known existed, until that night she had been taken from the sanctuary of her family home to the constant fight for survival and sanity that had been La Salpêtrière. She would use her wits, and somehow make a life here in Louisiane with this mercurial, intriguing man as her husband.

"*Très bien,* then as you have no family here in Nouvelle Orléans I shall serve as such," the nun said with a gentle smile. "The betrothal ring," she looked toward Lucien.

He turned toward Caresse, with some indefinable emotion in his opaque black eyes, reaching for her left hand. From an inner pocket in his waistcoat he took a small circlet that flashed gold in the sunlight coming through the long casement window.

A strange tingling warmth seemed to travel through her veins at the touch of his hand, the slightly callused caress of his fingertips, as he slid the ring on her finger. When her eyes glanced down at the betrothal ring that fit her finger as if it had been fashioned only for her, her body stiffened. The ring was a thin circlet of gold forming a graceful *fleur de lys* in the middle with a scarlet ruby on either side. Lifting her stunned gray eyes to meet his dark and unfathomable gaze, she was speechless. She seemed to feel the *fleur de lys* burning on her left shoulder as if it had just been put there.

"It belonged to my mother. My father had it fashioned for her. Someday I will tell you the special significance it had for them," he promised, lifting her hand to his lips in a gesture that was more the sealing of a vow.

Turning as if in a daze, Caresse bent her head as the nun said a prayer, giving a blessing to their betrothal. The design of the ring was only a coincidence, she tried to rationalize. The gold Bourbon *fleur de lys* flew on the white silk flag that fluttered from its high pole over the Place Royale. As the symbol of *la belle* France it could be seen everywhere in Nouvelle Orléans. She had, however, the uneasy feeling that Lucien had awaited a reaction from her as she stared down at the ring. But why? No one here in Louisiane knew that she carried the mark of the convicted felon on her shoulder. Or did they? It had been arranged that she be whisked from the prison in Paris to the convent at Rouen by someone, perhaps the mysterious visitor whom she had never forgotten. Had the mother superior at the convent in Rouen known her secret? Caresse struggled with the uncertainty that the ring had aroused. A sixth sense told her that Lucien had known that the design would have a disquieting effect on her. Once they were married it would be impossible to keep from him the fact that she was a scarlet lily from La Salpêtrière prison. But, she thought, biting her lower lip, they would already be married in the church, she would be safe. He might despise her, but she would have the security of his name.

"Now go, *mes enfants,* for your afternoon," Sister Hatchard de St. Stanislas said with a brief smile.

Caresse realized she had not listened to anything the nun had been saying, so lost was she in her own uneasy thoughts. From the expression of dismissal on the nun's gentle face she understood that they were being allowed to leave.

"Come, *ma chère* Caresse," Lucien ordered quietly, holding out his arm. "My carriage awaits outside the gate."

Her composure a fragile shell around her, she allowed him to lead her from the office. The hall was empty, and she realized that Yvonne had disappeared. What was she doing, leaving this safe sanctuary for a life with a man she knew nothing about? A man—Yvonne had confided—who was considered a rogue among men in a town notorious for them. He had confessed that his life had been less than exemplary, but what had that meant?

The white-hot July sun was streaming down through the green leathery leaves of the magnolia trees in the walled garden, as they strode down the crushed shell path between the manicured herb beds contained by their borders of boxwood. There was a silence and tranquillity about the hidden garden that was a contrast to the street outside the gate. Never had Caresse been so aware of leaving a place of safety as when they walked out onto the Rue de Chartres to Lucien's waiting carriage. She gave a light shudder as the heavy portal of the gate shut tight against all intruders.

"Life awaits you out here in the streets of Nouvelle Orléans, *ma petite,*" Lucien said, taking her arm and helping her up into the open carriage, which gleamed in the afternoon sun. The gray cushioned seats were a luxury Caresse had not experienced for a very long time.

An African man dressed in blue and gold livery flicked a whip high in the air over the heads of the matched ebony horses and they were off, rolling down the muddy street still damp from a shower. Nouvelle Orléans had a subtropical climate and showers that did nothing to cool the air occurred almost daily during the sultry summer.

Caresse's fear of leaving the sanctuary of the convent was soon stilled by her awakening interest in the colorful city that she had not really seen since her arrival. They were headed for the center of activity in Nouvelle Orléans, the Place Royale. She noticed along the Rue de Chartres both one and two-storied wooden structures, most plastered over in white or pastel tints, constructed in the style described to her by the nuns as French West Indian, with high-sloping shingled roofs slanting down to deep galleries that ringed the first and second story. Everywhere was the lush foliage of Louisiane, glimpsed through tantalizing cracks in the fences. The sultry air was filled with the fragrance of fruit and vegetables ripening in the hot sun, as well as with the perfume of jasmine, rose, and other exotic flowers. But there was always that earthy under-note of mud, river, and decay.

"The city is laid out in a grid pattern of twelve squares along the river as it was designed by the royal engineer Pierre Le Blond de La Tour in

1722," Lucien explained as the carriage rolled toward the Place Royale. "The streets are arranged in blocks called islets because of the ditches dug around them for drainage. Nouvelle Orléans is surrounded by river, lake, and swamp marsh. It also, as you have come to find out, rains like the devil. Thus the need for the ditches, or every structure's first floor would flood during a heavy rain. There is a moat or canal at the edge of town to collect the run-off from the many ditches. Not quite Paris, is it, *ma chère,* or perhaps you are from another part of *la belle* France?" His question seemed to hang in the air.

Caresse looked away from him at several passing slaves balancing produce on their heads in baskets woven by friendly Indians that lived in the cypress swamps. "My family is from Lyons, *monsieur,*" Caresse answered softly, keeping her gaze turned toward the passing scene. What she said was technically correct, for the de Villiers were one of the oldest families in Lyons, and their factories produced the finest silk woven in all France. Their fortune from silk—and their large land holdings—had supported her father's and mother's lavish life at the royal court of Versailles.

"They were workers in the silk trade?" he asked.

"You might say that, *monsieur,*" she replied wryly.

"Please, *ma chère,* we are betrothed. I told you once I enjoyed hearing my name on your lovely lips. I meant it. From now on 'tis not *monsieur* but Lucien," he corrected with a small sigh of exasperation.

"*Oui* . . . Lucien," she murmured, her voice a breathy whisper that sent a languid warmth through his veins.

What was wrong with him, he thought in disgust. This tiny slip of a girl could set his pulse pounding with the simple recitation of his name. How some of the ladies of Nouvelle Orléans—who had been at one time or another his sophisticated partners in the games of *amour*—would laugh at the idea of jaded Lucien St. Amant being stirred by something so trivial.

"What else do you wish to know . . . Lucien?" Caresse asked as a cold knot formed in her stomach. Better to get it over with, to smooth the way with some half-truths, she thought, clenching her hands together in her lap.

"What is your favorite color—and scent?" he answered, giving her a pleasant surprise.

"But . . . I do not understand," she stammered, turning toward him.

"How may I buy you scent, or those gifts dear to a feminine heart that a bridegroom should give his bride, if I do not know your taste?" he chided tenderly, his dark eyes looking kind.

"I prefer the scent of *le muguet* and my favorite color is *la rose de Pompadour,*" said Caresse naming the pink made popular by King Louis's mistress. It had been so long since anyone had cared for her preferences in the more delicate things of life. To talk about perfume, and colors in fashion, reminded her for a heart-breaking moment of a time that seemed an eternity away from Nouvelle Orléans and yet it had not really been all that long ago.

"Ah, 'twould suit you, the scent of lily of the valley. But how does a simple young woman from Lyons know about the most fashionable color at the Versailles court?" Lucien asked, with a slight edge to his deep voice.

Caresse looked away, searching for a plausible explanation, realizing that she had almost given herself away. What, indeed, would a simple country girl know of such things? She could feel him waiting for her answer like a predatory cat toying with its prey, enjoying the game. It was clear he guessed she was not what she seemed. "My family, as I said, worked in the silk trade, so they were aware of the most popular color with the nobility. It was in great demand," she replied, turning toward him with a smile that could only be described as triumphant.

"*Touché, ma chère,*" he said, amusement and respect flickering in the compelling eyes that met hers. "We shall see if Mme Cecil has any silk of that color for a gown."

"Mme Cecil?"

"She will be creating your trousseau. Her shop on Rue Royale is the finest in Nouvelle Orléans. She is also a *femme de couleur libre,* one of our free women of color. You will find that many of our finest artisans and craftsmen are *gens de couleur libre.* They are given a certain status in the community and some even own slaves of their own," he explained as the carriage rolled past the parish church of St. Louis.

"I have heard of these people," Caresse replied, staring across the sunburnt grass of the square. "They are the discarded mistresses of French gentlemen, I believe, as well as the grown children of those liaisons."

"You are well informed for someone kept in seclusion behind convent walls," he said wryly.

"My friend Yvonne has been out and about with her fiancé, Pierre. She tells me all manner of things, especially the latest gossip," she said with a teasing sidelong glance.

"I see," he murmured, "and has she told you anything about me?"

"Perhaps."

"Do not believe everything you hear, *ma chère.* Although I am the first to admit I have been no saint, remember, appearances can be deceiving. I find that often the mask that people wear has little relation to what is in their heart." He looked away from her for a moment, but not before she saw the shadow of melancholy in his eyes.

"And what is in your heart?" Her question was a whisper on the soft air.

" 'Tis a dark place, I fear, Caresse," he replied, then changed his tone. "Enough of such melancholy talk. Look at what I have to show you," he said, indicating the two-story house plastered in light blue in front of which their carriage was just coming to a stop. There were dark blue long shutters at each window that gleamed real glass. Many of the houses in Nouvelle Orléans still had linen cloths at the windows instead of glass.

She felt foolish for wishing to hear that his heart was filled with love for her. It was ridiculous to expect to hear such words, for they barely knew one another. Marriages in France were often arranged with little consideration for the feelings of the man and woman concerned. Property and wealth, as well as social standing, were what was important in such matters. But, she thought with dismay, she brought none of these things to Lucien. Why did he desire her as his bride?

"Well, what do you think?" he asked her, his words cutting through the cloud of her thoughts.

" 'Tis lovely, but why are we stopping?" She answered, forcing a slight smile to her lips.

"I thought you would like to see what will be your town house when we are married. Of course during the heat of summer I spend most of my time at Sans Regret, my plantation outside the city on the river," he explained, alighting gracefully from the carriage, then turning to help her down.

"Without regret—what an unusual name," she murmured, feeling her pulse race at the warm touch of his fingers on her own.

" 'Twas the motto of my father's life, to live each day fully, without trepidation, without care what others might think, so that when he drew his last breath there would be no regrets for what might have been," Lucien told her, a brooding quality in his liquid gaze as if old memories had taken him away from her.

"He must have been a very brave man," she replied as he led her across the gallery to the tall double doors.

"He was," Lucien answered tersely, opening the heavy portal.

They entered a long hall that ran the width of the house. The luxuriant foliage of the back garden could be seen through the French doors at the far end. Wide cypress boards gleamed under their feet from frequent polishing. Open doors led into four chambers, two on either side of the foyer. It was a cool, quiet sanctuary from the burning sun of the street.

"M'sieur, forgive me but I was out in the kitchen house," a voice speaking the patois of the African slave called out as they heard the light sound of her step on the floor. Out of the shadows came a slender, graceful middle-aged woman dressed in light blue muslin, her white apron as starched and immaculate as the turban, called a *tignon,* tied in two erect points above her high-cheekboned face, the color of coffee with cream.

Caresse turned to greet her, and as she did so the woman stopped, her hand rising to her mouth, her velvety brown eyes registering shock and disbelief.

"Mon Dieu, m'sieur, have you raised the dead?" The woman's horrified question hung in the still humid air like the dust motes in the stream of sunlight through the far French doors.

Four

"This is my fiancée, Caresse de Villier, Dominique," Lucien said with a silken thread of warning in his cold exact voice. "She is the guest I told you about. We wish to dine in the garden."

"Oui M'sieur," the woman managed in a strained voice, never taking her eyes from Caresse.

"Ma chère, this is Dominique, the housekeeper both here in Nouvelle Orléans and at Sans Regret, although at the plantation we also have Zoé as cook. She oversees the house servants when we are away."

"Bonjour Dominique," Caresse said with a slight smile. "I am sure there is much you can teach me about being the mistress of a plantation. We must have a talk about the two households after my marriage to M. St. Amant."

"Oui mam'zelle," Dominique replied softly. "Forgive me my outburst, but you resemble someone I knew long ago. In the shadows it seemed for a moment that you were a ghost."

"And does this woman live in Nouvelle Orléans?" Caresse asked, curious even though she sensed the subject was making Lucien uneasy.

"She is dead, *mam'zelle,"* Dominique replied, then turned and walked with a gliding step toward the French doors at the end of the hall.

"Pay her no mind. She has been with my family

since she and her mother came here from Saint-Domingue many years ago. Now that her mother is dead I fear her daughter has taken over her protective attitude toward the family," Lucien explained. "Come out to the garden so we may have our *déjeuner*. I promised the good sister that I would see that you had some food. Then I shall take you on a tour of the house."

"Does Soeur Hatchard de St. Stanislas know that you meant we would be dining tête-à-tête at your town house?" Caresse inquired with a mischievous smile, as she allowed him to escort her past chambers filled with elegant furniture such as could be found in a salon in Paris.

"What the good sister does not know will not upset her," he said, his mouth curving into the mercurial smile she had come to love for it softened the stern expression of his handsome but melancholy face.

The formal garden separated the main house from the kitchen, with *garçonnière* apartments, lodging for young bachelor visitors, above, the stables and servants' wing at the rear. Tall oaks and magnolias shaded the flagstones, orange and peach trees added their fragrance to that of the sweet olive bushes and the twining vines of the jasmine. Banana plants cast the long shadows of their emerald leaves across the bronze sundial held up by three marble cherubs that was the centerpiece of the garden. It was an intimate, secluded retreat in the middle of the city. A wrought-iron table and chairs stood under the spreading branches of a smooth-trunked crape myrtle heavily laden with deep pink blooms.

"How lovely," Caresse sighed as Lucien seated her at the table set with gleaming silver and fine china. For the first time since she had been taken from her family's chateau to La Salpêtrière prison she was sitting down at a table set with luxury, as in her former life.

"Do you think you could be happy here?" he asked quietly, sitting down across from her, his dark eyes watching her intently from the shadows.

"I believe I could," she said with a shy smile.

"Wait until you visit Sans Regret. I prefer the country, although I find it necessary to come into Nouvelle Orléans frequently. Does the idea of living miles from town on a plantation frighten you?" He seemed to be waiting for her answer with a certain tenseness in his lithe form.

"I am sure I shall enjoy living on a plantation . . . Lucien," she told him, trying not to shudder as she remembered the sinister look of the swamp marsh she had seen from the ship.

"Some women find the atmosphere too lonely, too oppressive," he said, with a shrug of his elegant shoulders, the melancholy shadow once more in his expressive gaze.

"I do not frighten easily," Caresse said with a wry twist to her lips, remembering the horrors of La Salpêtrière. "Besides, Blanchette will love it."

"And who pray tell is Blanchette?" he asked, raising one heavy black brow.

"My cat, more precisely kitten," she replied, lifting a delicate crystal goblet to her nose and inhaling the fragrance of the first fine wine she had seen since dining at her father's table.

"Bruno may raise some objection, but I am sure they will work it out in their own fashion," he said dryly, noting how she held the wine glass. It was the attitude of one used to the best, hardly the gesture of a country girl who worked at the silk weaver's trade.

"Bruno?"

"My dog of rather undetermined lineage, rather like his master," he spoke softly, mockingly.

"I . . . beg your pardon," she stammered, moving the glass away from her lips without tasting it.

"To us, to our life together. May it give us both what we are seeking," he said suddenly, as he held his glass to hers. "And to Blanchette and Bruno: may they find a peaceful coexistence at Sans Regret."

Caresse touched the rim of her glass to his, wondering what private turmoil caused his sudden changes of mood, the sardonic self-mocking expression that often crossed those handsome features. Then her dark thoughts were lightened by the sensation of the delicate dry wine slipping down her throat like silk.

The meal passed quickly as, with another quicksilver change of mood, Lucien became the most entertaining of dining companions. He regaled her with stories of Nouvelle Orléans and the often strange and amusing citizens who walked her muddy streets. The food served by the reserved Dominique was delicious, seasoned with piquant herbs and spices that were new to Caresse. Lucien explained that the seasoning was a blend of the herbs brought by slaves from the West Indies and native Indian plants, such as the powdered leaves of the sassafras plant, known as the filé and used in the dish called gumbo.

"Would you care to see the rest of the house?" he asked as they finished the last of the strong hot coffee and rich dessert.

"I would, although I think I could sit here forever," Caresse sighed in contentment. The warm sun, the soft humid air, the wine and delicious food, had filled her with a languor that she had never experienced.

"A quick tour, then we must leave for Mme Cecil's," he reminded her.

"Of course," she replied as he pulled out her chair.

The chambers on the first floor were furnished with marble-topped tables and polished furniture of walnut, cypress, and cedar, in the style of the provinces of France. Large gilt-framed mirrors decorated with what Caresse surmised was the St. Amant crest, mantel sconces with enameled flowers, and several tapestries, all of a quality that could grace the finest chateau, hung against the plastered walls. Settees upholstered in blue and gold damask stood on either side of the gray marble fireplace in the main salon.

It was quite lovely and so unexpected in such a wilderness. But there was a loneliness about the house, as if it were a stage set rather than a home, Caresse mused as she followed Lucien throughout the first floor. He said little, seeming to watch her reaction to the contents of every room, and it soon began to wear on her nerves. Climbing the narrow curving stair to the second floor, she felt a definite sense of oppression close over her. He was so silent, so withdrawn, she could only wonder if she had done something to offend him. She found herself wishing it was time to leave for the dressmaker. She had not looked forward to the appointment, with the necessity to conceal her scar, but she almost welcomed the opportunity to escape from this brooding atmosphere that seemed to grow between them as they toured the house.

"This will be our chamber," he announced abruptly, gesturing toward the room on the right.

High-ceilinged, with long French doors that opened onto the rear gallery, the room had a definite masculine aura that told Caresse this was where he slept. " 'Tis all very fine," she said, at a loss for words. Had he brought her here to seduce her before the wedding, she wondered idly, but without concern. If he had, he was certainly not in a hurry to sweep her off her feet, for he stood staring down at something on the desk over in the corner.

"Do you believe in fate, Caresse?" He turned toward her, his distinguished features brooding, a strange pain in the depths of his dark eyes.

"Perhaps, I am really not sure," she admitted with a slight shrug. What was he getting at?

"Ah, *ma pauvre petite*, you wonder what you have taken on in agreeing to marry me," he said, with a wry twist of his sensual lips, crossing with a few lithe strides to stand in front of her. He caressed her cheek with the tip of his finger, brushing a stray tendril of hair from where it curled near her mouth. Slowly, he traced the fullness of her lower lip, staring down at her with an unreadable expression in his depthless black eyes that seemed to pull her in, mesmerizing her with the force of his will.

It felt like warm honey was slipping through her veins, filling her with a languid warmth that soothed away any objection. The sultry air that enveloped the room seemed to hold them in an embrace where time stopped, where nothing existed but the space in which they stood. As she stared up into those eyes, she shivered with delight at his touch and the awakening hunger she experienced as he traced the outline of her mouth. She wanted more of him than just the touch of his hand. She wanted to feel the burning pressure of his mouth on hers, the taste of him on her tongue.

"I want to take you, my sweet Caresse, to taste the honey of your mouth, feel the silk of your skin. From the first time I saw you I knew that it would come to this, my need for you is so great. I should not tell you this, for the knowledge will give you a decided advantage in our relationship." The words had clearly cost him something to say.

" 'Tis not a duel we are fighting," she said, her voice a husky whisper as he bent his head to hers.

"Is that not exactly what it is, *ma belle?*" he murmured, as his tongue traced the line his finger had made.

In one motion she was in his arms, his mouth covering hers, devouring its softness, demanding a response. Like the petals of a blossom opening at the touch of the morning sun, her lips parted, beckoning him, allowing him entry.

Feeling her respond to him, the hesitant seeking of her tongue for his, as he swept inside the moist cavern of her mouth, he felt his own passion rise till he had to fight for control. The expertise in lovemaking that he had used to overcome any reluctance in other conquests suddenly struck him with its tawdry manipulation, for he realized this slight trembling woman he held in his embrace was different from the others. It was not only that Caresse was an innocent, but that his feelings toward her were different. For the first time in his life Lucien experienced a new emotion, shame. He knew he could not continue with his ignoble seduction of this gentle woman who trusted him. He had meant to sample the lovely Caresse before their marriage by seducing her this afternoon. There had been entirely too many sleepless nights because of his desire for her. He had not intended to wait three weeks until their wedding for release; Lucien St. Amant waited for nothing. But something had happened when he looked into those wide trusting gray eyes as she reached up to wrap her arms around his neck. It was as if he had been looking into a mirror, a mirror that reflected an image he did not want to see, an image of a selfish, self-serving *roué*. Suddenly, he wanted to be everything that Caresse saw when she looked at him. He wanted to be the knight in shining armor that she thought he was, the savior come to rescue her from the horror her life had become.

"We must leave, *ma chère,* while I still have the strength to resist," he whispered huskily against the silken hollow of her neck, moving his lips away from the burning temptation of her mouth. Taking her arms from about his neck, he held her wrists in his firm fingers, lifting both tiny hands to his lips before he stepped back and away from what he desired above all else, the perfection of her slender form, the beauty of her heart-shaped face.

"You are wiser and stronger than I," she said with a catch in her voice, making no attempt to pretend that she did not want him with an overwhelming passion. For a brief moment, held close to his heart, she had felt affection, and the spark of hope that perhaps there was some happiness in the world for her, after all the misery.

"The courage and honesty I see in your lovely eyes make me humble, *ma petite*," he said, with a faint tremor in his voice. The pain and melancholy in his dark gaze seemed to deepen for a moment as he stared down at her as if he were memorizing every delicate feature.

"*Mon coeur*," she breathed, a slight smile curving the mouth that still burned from his kisses. "I thank *le bon Dieu* for allowing us to meet, for truly I was lost without purpose or hope when I stepped upon the wharf my first day in Nouvelle Orléans."

"They say fate works in mysterious ways," he muttered, looking away from her, an edge of mockery in his husky voice.

"I . . . do not understand," Caresse stammered, realizing that there was an underlying meaning to his words that she could not comprehend.

"No matter what you ever hear about me, know this, *ma chère* Caresse: that I want to be what you think I am, that I shall care for and cherish you for all the days of our life together. This I vow." There was an intensity in his voice that she had never heard before. Looking up into those magnetic eyes she saw a hurt that pierced her, leaving her shaken.

"I care little what others say or think," Caresse assured him, meeting his gaze with her gentle gray eyes. "What we were before we met is in the past. Our lives began again today, so nothing matters that went before."

"Ah, *ma chère*, if only it were that easy," he said wearily, shaking his dark head. He looked away and seemed to lose himself in memories that she knew nothing about.

How long he would have stood there she did not know. She knew only that she felt in the marrow of her bones that those memories were somehow a danger to their relationship. It was the sound of the church bells from the Place Royale striking the hour that seemed to pull him from his reflections. Giving a slight shrug, as if he could thrust the melancholy away from him, he turned toward her and, holding out his arm, led her from the bedchamber and down the stairs to the first floor.

"You are leaving, *m'sieur?*" the soft voice of Dominique questioned from the shadows near the open French door.

"Mlle de Villier has a fitting at Mme Cecil's," Lucien replied. "Tell Pascal to bring the carriage around."

"Oui, m'sieur," she replied, but her sable-brown eyes never left Caresse's face. It was as if she was transfixed by the sight of the young woman.

"Now, Dominique," he reminded her tersely.

The housekeeper disappeared out the French door as Lucien gestured for Caresse to precede him into the front salon to await the carriage. She took the opportunity to look around the chamber which she had seen only briefly before going up to the second floor. It was darkened and full of shadows, for the wooden louvers at the windows had been tilted almost shut against the fierce afternoon sun. Even in the gloom she was drawn to a portrait over the marble mantel. It was of a young woman dressed in the style of twenty years before, but the eyes were what had captured her attention. They were large and dark, filled with a strange sadness. She knew that this must be a relative of Lucien for there was a striking resemblance in the melancholy ebony eyes and the full sensuous mouth.

"Who is the beautiful woman in the portrait?" Caresse inquired, more to break the long silence between them than out of curiosity.

"Gabrielle St. Amant, nêe de Clouet. Does this name mean anything to you?"

"No, but she is a member of your family?" Caresse asked, startled by the fierce look on his handsome features. She felt once more that he was playing some strange game with her where only he knew the rules.

"She was my mother," he replied in a flat, controlled voice. "My father had the portrait painted by an artist visiting from Paris when I was eight years old."

"Her eyes are so sad," Caresse could not help muse aloud.

"She had reason to be sad," he answered, with a husky rasp to his voice. "You see, she was haunted by the past, and what could never be."

"You mean there was some tragedy in her life that she could not forget?" Caresse asked, staring up at the portrait.

"The carriage is here," Lucien announced abruptly. "Come, Mme Cecil will be waiting."

Allowing him to escort her out to the open carriage, Caresse realized he had not answered her question about his mother, but she was so anxious to leave the oppressive atmosphere of the house, that she said nothing to delay their departure. Somehow, she thought, when she was Mme St. Amant she would have to find a way to lighten the ambiance within the town house.

Fierce white-hot rays of the summer sun greeted

them, blinding after the darkened salon. Caresse had to shade her eyes with her hand. Heavy heat and humidity seemed to grip the streets, for they were almost deserted as the couple drove down St. Peter Street toward Royal. The usually muddy streets had dried into dusty ruts under the relentless sun, causing the carriage to sway. After they traversed one deep hole Caresse was tossed against Lucien.

"We should be at Sans Regret during this weather," he said, placing his arm around her to try to cushion her from the rough jolting of the carriage. "The good sisters, however, have put nothing but obstacles in the path of our marriage from the first, and now we must wait another three weeks till we can leave this heat for the cool of the country."

"What do you mean obstacles?" Caresse asked in surprise, trying not to show how exhilarating it was to feel his lean body hard against hers. The wonderful sense of having someone care for her after so many long months alone.

"I have tried to convince the good sisters to allow me to call on you from the first week you arrived in Nouvelle Orléans," he explained.

"But they never told me! Why would they not allow you to call on me?"

"I believe my reputation in the city was known to them, even behind their cloistered walls." His mouth twisted in a smile that could only be described as sardonic as they hit yet another rut in the road as they turned onto the Rue Royale.

"Are you really so wicked?" she teased, deep dimples appearing beside her smiling mouth, her gray eyes sparkling.

"Many in Nouvelle Orléans think so," he said wryly.

"And how did you gain this infamous reputation?" she continued.

"I think that would be better left for another time, although there are many who will be glad to enlighten you. But enough talk about me, this was to be a tour of the city, and I can think of no better street than Royal for the continuation of our tour," he said smoothly, changing the subject. "As you can see it is wider than the other streets, seven feet to be exact, and that is because it cuts directly through the middle of the town and is the main business street of Nouvelle Orléans."

"There seem to be many fine shops," Caresse said in surprise, for they had passed numerous small establishments advertising everything from wigmaking to candles. Even in the heat of the day there could be seen a few customers slowly going about their shopping as well as slaves doing their masters' errands. Through the haze of dust that hung in the still sultry air like a mist, she saw dealers in fine fabrics, furniture, jewelry, as well as hairdressers for both men and women, even an undertaker's establishment. For a few moments she could forget that a wild reptile-infested cypress swamp came up to the edge of the city, that there was still fear of Indian attack outside the boundaries of Nouvelle Orléans only a few streets away. If she did not look too closely she could almost believe that she was in a town in France.

"Here we are," Lucien said as they stopped in front of a building of pale peach tint. Two long narrow windows, with dark green shutters and lace curtains pulled against the summer sun gave the shop a quiet secluded air.

"'Tis more like a private residence than a shop," Caresse commented as he helped her down from the carriage to the rough wooden planks that were called *banquettes*.

As he reached for the polished brass handle on the green lacquered door, it suddenly swung open to reveal a rather plump middle-aged woman dressed in an elaborate gown of sky blue brocade silk taffeta trimmed with delicate lace at the elbow-length sleeves and about the low-cut décolletage of the bodice. Her powdered hair was swept back from her heavily made-up face into a chignon and her head was covered by a small lace coif *à la parisienne* made fashionable in Paris by Madame de Pompadour. Diamonds sparkled in her ears and about her rather short thick neck. Large lustrous blue eyes, her only attractive features, swept with disdain over Caresse's plain gown, but lit up as they fastened on Lucien.

"Mon cher, but how lovely to see you," she trilled, tapping his chest with her folded fan in a flirtatious gesture. "What are you doing at Madame Cecil's, you rogue? Buying some lucky woman a frock I wager."

"One can not fool such an observant woman as you, Solange," Lucien replied, bending over her plump outstretched hand covered in rings that flashed in the sunlight.

"Really, you should be ashamed for robbing the cradle with this . . . child." She made the word sound like an insult.

"Allow me, to present my fiancée, Caresse de Villier," Lucien drawled, his dark eyes glinting with a hint of malice. "Caresse, may I present the Marquise de Vaudreuil."

"Enchantée, Marquise," Caresse said coolly with a graceful curtsy, but her head was held high and her eyes met the older woman's disdainful gaze.

"You must tell me sometime how you managed it, *mademoiselle.* How you convinced this *diable* to allow you to take him to the altar," Solange de Vaudreuil said with a contemptuous glance at Caresse. Then with a sweep of her elaborate skirts she allowed Lucien to help her into her carriage, which stood waiting with its four matched horses that were the talk of Nouvelle Orléans.

"So that was the governor's wife," Caresse mused as Lucien returned to her side. "She reminds me of a mule dressed up in horse's harness; no matter the fancy trappings she is still a mule."

"Caresse de Villier, I think we are going to suit each other splendidly," Lucien said with a laugh, holding the door open for her.

The cool gray and ivory of the shaded interior of the shop was a welcome rest for the eye from the blinding sun. Furnished with several white, gilt-trimmed French chairs it was an oasis after the dusty hot street.

"*M'sieur*, but you are early," the soft cadences of a slender, elegant woman greeted them from the silk-curtained portal on the other side of the room.

"We finished our *déjeuner* earlier than I planned," Lucien answered smoothly.

Why, he had intended to seduce me, Caresse thought with a sudden clarity, glancing at him with a bemused expression on her delicate features. I wonder why he stopped, she thought, remembering the marquise's description of him as a rogue and a devil.

"*Mam'zelle* if you would come with me to one of the fitting rooms we can proceed with your measurements. My assistant will show you the material I have in stock, and a few gowns already sewn that need only a few alterations to fit," Madame Cecil instructed her after the introductions had been made by Lucien. She drew the gray curtains aside revealing a narrow corridor.

"I shall await you out here, *ma chère*," said Lucien, sitting down on one of the fragile chairs. His long lithe frame seemed to overpower the spindly chair, for his masculine presence only accentuated the femininity of the room.

Trying to hide her nervousness, Caresse allowed the woman to show her into one of the small fitting rooms decorated with three long pier glasses angled so that she was reflected from all sides. Undressing with the help of one of Madame Cecil's maids, she insisted that she would keep on her plain linen chemise with its elbow-length sleeves. Clad in the garment her scar was concealed, but her stomach fluttered as the graceful Madame Cecil entered carrying a lavender silk gown brocaded with sprays of violets in a deeper purple edged with gilt. It was a lovely gown, but in a style that was at least five or six years old.

"*Mam'zelle*, M. St. Amant wishes that we alter this gown so that you may wear it on your wedding day," Madame Cecil explained, her features arranged in a carefully neutral expression, though her eyes contained something that looked strangely like pity.

"The material is lovely. Perhaps with a few alterations we could make it more up-to-date," Caresse mused, forgetting that she was supposed to be a simple country girl who would not be aware of what was fashionable in Paris. "Where did you find it, Mme Cecil?"

"M. St. Amant brought it to me, *mam'zelle*," the woman replied, avoiding meeting Caresse's gaze. "I believe it has been in his family for quite some time."

"I hopes you be happier marrying in that gown than the first Mme St. Amant," the young maid murmured in her West Indian patois, as she helped Caresse don the exquisite gown.

"Silence!" Mme Cecil exclaimed to the young maid.

Caresse met the pitying gaze of the older woman in the mirror as her stomach turned to ice. Suddenly she remembered the words of Soeur Xavier on that first afternoon as they walked to the Ursuline Convent. "He is a widower," she had said. How could she have forgotten that fact? Staring down at the gown she realized what the other two women were thinking. The gown fit her as if it had been made for her. The wedding gown of his first wife fit her, and he wanted her to wear it on their wedding day. *Mon Dieu,* she thought, her mind reeling with confusion, what kind of man had she agreed to marry?

Five

The deep rich sound of the bells from the parish church of St. Louis on the Place Royale chiming the hour echoed down the corridor of the Ursuline Convent. Within her small bedchamber, more like a nun's cell, Caresse stood at the narrow window staring down into the walled garden remembering the day three weeks before when she had been fitted for the gown Lucien had wished her to wear at their wedding. It had almost been her undoing when she had learned that the exquisite gown had belonged to his first wife. The courage that had enabled her to withstand the prison in Paris, and the long hard voyage to Nouvelle Orléans, had threatened to desert her, but as she stared into the pier glass in the fitting room of Mme Cecil's, that tiny essence deep within her that wanted to survive had grown from an almost-extinguished ember to a flame of resolution.

Lucien St. Amant was her only chance for a life in La Louisiane anything like that she had known in France, and it was only by having a certain position in the colony that she might be of some help to her father imprisoned in the Bastille. She would become Lucien's wife, despite her reservations, but it would be on her terms from the start. Her wedding gown would not be that of her predecessor.

Taking a deep breath to help strengthen her resolve, Caresse had requested to see any other gown that could be made ready by her wedding day. With a nod of understanding, Madame Cecil had one of her maids bring in an ivory silk taffeta gown with just a blush of peach, brocaded with sprays of lily of the valley in metallic silver gilt in the style known as *robe à la française*.

"The Marquise de Vaudreuil ordered it, *mam'zelle*, then she decided she did not want it, for the color did not flatter her. It will require much taking in for she is a plump woman, but it can easily be done in three weeks' time," Madame Cecil explained, with perfect understanding in her gentle sable eyes.

"*Très bien*. This shall be considered one of the gowns in my trousseau," Caresse had replied, her eyes meeting the older woman's gaze in the long silvered glass. "*Monsieur* need not be informed on which occasion I shall choose to wear it."

"*Oui, mam'zelle*, our lips are sealed," Mme Cecil had said with a slight smile while the two maids giggled their agreement.

The secret gown now hung on a satin, padded hanger from a hook on the plaster wall in her spartan room. It had been delivered along with the lavender gown that morning. The rest of her trousseau, except for a few undergarments, shoes, and accessories, had been sent to the St. Amant town house where she and Lucien would retire after the ceremony. In a few short hours, Caresse thought with a sigh as she gazed down at the garden slumbering in the late afternoon sun, she would be married. She would be Lucien's wife.

In the tradition of Nouvelle Orléans the wedding would take place in the early evening so the bride and groom could, after a brief reception, retire to their bedchamber to consummate their marriage. It was considered embarrassing for the newlyweds to spend too much time with their guests, and they were not expected to be seen in public for two weeks after the wedding.

Caresse gave a slight shiver even though the humid heat pressed down unrelentingly on the convent. She had seen very little of Lucien after her one afternoon with him. There had been some trouble with Indian raids at Sans Regret necessitating his presence. He had left Nouvelle Orléans as soon as he had escorted her back to the convent from Madame Cecil's. Word of a raid had been sent on to him from the town house while he awaited Caresse. He had been preoccupied on their ride back to the convent, which was just as well, she thought, for she had still been shaken by the idea that he had wanted her to wear the wedding gown of his dead wife.

Putting the carriage and Pascal at her disposal for trips to the dressmaker for the rest of her fittings, he had kissed her chastely on the brow at the convent gate before bidding her good-bye. Her first contact with him in three weeks was the note that arrived that morning with her bridal bouquet and a *corbeille de noces,* the traditional basket of bridal gifts sent by the groom. It contained a flat leather jewelry box displaying pearl-drop earrings and a pearl necklace with a gold heart-shaped locket suspended from it. In flowing script across the front of the locket were the words, *Tout est plaisir quand on aime,* all is pleasure when one loves. Prying it open, she had found on one side a miniature oil on ivory of a plantation house in the French colonial style. Facing it the words Sans Regret were engraved in the same flowing script as on the cover, with a tiny *fleur de lys* drawn underneath. She stared down at the picture realizing that this must be the St. Amant plantation. Studying the locket and soft glowing pearls Caresse knew that they were quite old, and wondered if the necklace had been created for Lucien's mother, or for his mysterious first wife. She chose to think that they had belonged to his mother, the woman in the portrait with the sad soulful eyes, and closed the worn leather case till she was ready to dress for the ceremony.

"Are you ready for me to help you with your hair?" the cheerful voice of Yvonne inquired from the open portal.

"Yvonne, you came," Caresse cried out with relief and happiness. Her friend had been married for two weeks, but as the Indian raids upriver made travel risky, she and her new husband had remained in Nouvelle Orléans at a boarding house. They would stay there till Pierre felt it was safe to make the journey to his small plantation up the Mississippi on what was known as La Côte des Allemands, the German coast, for the many German settlers who had small prosperous farms along either side of that part of the river.

"Of course I came as I promised," Yvonne said with a bright smile, obviously pleased that her friend was so glad to see her. "This is your special day, and I will help you dress as you did for me. Pierre and I will be at the church so you will feel that there is someone to represent your family, *ma chère*. I understand from the gossip that all of what passes for society in Nouvelle Orléans and the river plantations will be attending at your fiancé's invitation, even the governor and his wife, the Marquis and Marquise de Vaudreuil no less, will be there," Yvonne told her excitedly.

"*Mon Dieu!*" Caresse exclaimed, her hand to her lips in horror before dissolving into laughter thinking of the Marquise's expression when she saw Caresse's wedding gown. There would be several startled people in the church when she walked down the aisle, she thought, including Lucien when he realized she had discarded the idea of wearing the castoff gown of his first wife.

"What is wrong?" Yvonne asked in concern as Caresse laughed with nervous strain till the tears rolled down her cheeks.

Hurriedly, trying to regain control, she told her friend the story of the two gowns and her determination to start her marriage without the shadows of her predecessor, the first Mme Lucien St. Amant.

"But I do not blame you, *chère*. How awful to wear the first wife's wedding gown," Yvonne gasped, giving a slight shudder. "The gown you have chosen instead is lovely, even if it was originally sewn for the Marquise. You will wear it with such beauty your Lucien will forget all about his strange wish once he sees you coming toward him in the church," she reassured her with a loyal smile, thinking how lucky she was to have the kind, uncomplicated Pierre as a husband.

Helping Caresse to dress her hair high on the back of her head in a chignon under a lace coif, caught with two clusters of silk lily of the valley, Yvonne realized how delicate and refined was her friend's bone structure. With the pearl drops in her ears, and the necklace about her throat, she looked like she could preside over the court at Versailles, the young woman decided, wondering once again what Caresse's real identity was back in France.

"Such fine silk," Yvonne sighed as her friend stood up in her delicate chemise. Caresse wore ivory silk stockings with sprays of lilies embroidered upon them, held up by silver garters with tiny rosettes, and upon her feet were ivory silk shoes with slender hourglass heels, all of the finest quality from Paris. "Your Lucien has spared no expense, but then Pierre tells me he is the wealthiest man in Nouvelle Orléans after the Marquis de Vaudreuil."

Slipping the ivory gown over the pannier hoops encased in a silk petticoat, and the taffeta petticoat that lay over the pannier, Caresse, for the first time since that cold November day when she had been taken to La Salpêtrière prison, felt like her old self. The aura of another time and place seemed to slip around her shoulders with the lace-trimmed bodice. She only wished she had a long pier glass like that at Madame Cecil's to see how she looked, but she really didn't need it for she could see the wonder on Yvonne's face.

"Oh, Caresse, you look like a *princesse!*" She exclaimed.

"Merci, ma chère Yvonne. I do not need a looking glass, for if I look half as lovely as you say I shall be happy," Caresse said with a sigh, allowing herself to think for one moment about her father and this strange wedding where she would have no family members, no aunts, no uncles, no cousins. Her mother and brother had died of the smallpox years before, in Paris, while she had been away at convent school in Lyons, but her father should have been at her side to walk her down the aisle to give her hand to Lucien. Brushing a tear away, she pushed the thought down deep. Today she would begin a new life with a new name. She would not dwell on the past.

Touching the glass wand from the bottle of lily-of-the-valley perfume, another gift from Lucien, to the pulse point at her throat and at her wrists, before pulling on her fingerless lace mitts, she resolved to allow nothing to spoil this day. She had endured so much just to arrive in this strange exotic land. The fight for survival had proved to her that she was strong, that she could handle anything that came her way in her marriage. In spite of any obstacles thrown in her path after the ceremony,

80

she would not be a helpless *fille à la cassette* at the mercy of outrageous fortune. She would be Mme St. Amant. Later, Caresse would remember these thoughts and shake her head in despair at her naiveté, but on this afternoon, as she picked up her bridal bouquet of white rosebuds, jasmine and rosemary, she rushed out to meet her future with the joy and hope of an innocent young girl.

Twilight, the time known as *l'heure bleue,* the blue hour, softened the streets of Nouvelle Orléans as Caresse rode in the open carriage, bedecked with bouquets of white roses, to the church of St. Louis. The gray doves that were everywhere in the city cooed in the rafters of the galleries of the passing houses and shops as the sultry night air was filled with the scent of the night—blooming jasmine and the blossoms of the moonflower vine.

From the covered basket beside her on the seat came a tiny meow. "Hush, Blanchette," she whispered to her pet. Then calling to the coachman she said, "Pascal, please remember to take my kitten to the town house as soon as I enter the church. Put her basket in the master bedchamber, but leave it closed. She will feel safer within the confines of the basket till I arrive."

"Oui, mam'zelle," he replied, touching the handle of his whip to his tricorn hat in deference.

There was a crowd of people in front of the church. The rabble of the waterfront had been attracted by the well-dressed guests who had already entered the sanctuary. Sailors, fur trappers, whores, and beggars, as well as the ever-present street vendors, all watched as the St. Amant carriage drew up in front. Murmurs of appreciation floated on the sultry air as Caresse was helped from the carriage by Pascal. A few feet away a fur trapper from Canada began a lilting Canadian song on the concertina about a *jolie blonde.* Having heard Pierre play the catchy air, Caresse flashed the musician a happy smile.

Two aides-de-camp to the governor opened the heavy double doors of the church as she climbed the several steps to the portal. For a moment she was stunned by the sight of the filled sanctuary, the flickering light of the many tall tapers in the iron candelabra festooned with white roses, jasmine, and the feathery green cypress boughs. The heavy perfume from the guests crowded into the pews, the scent of burning candles, the wilting overripe fragrance of the flowers in the suffocating heat threatened to make her light-headed as she paused in the doorway, feeling avid eyes all turned in her direction. Transfixed by the number of people, Caresse stood unmoving. Then she looked down the long aisle to where Lucien stood waiting, dressed in a gold silk velvet-sleeved waistcoat heavily embroidered with metallic threads of blue and green, his white linen shirt with a fine silk cravat at the neck setting off his dark visage. His sinewy legs were encased in matching breeches and ivory silk stockings, and there were silver buckles on his shoes. Dressed as fine as any courtier, he had, however, left his hair unpowdered. Pulled back in a queue, it gleamed blue-black in the glow from the tapers.

Perhaps it was some trick of the glow of the myriad candles, but it seemed as if Lucien's dark, luminous eyes were willing her to come to him. Drawn by that piercing ebony gaze that held her to him, she moved slowly down the aisle toward the tall lithe figure who totally captured her attention as if they were the only two people in the church of St. Louis. She heard the rustle of the gowns as the guests rose to their feet in respect for the bride. Nothing mattered, however, but the man waiting for her in front of the altar at the end of the long aisle.

Lucien seemed to stiffen as she approached him, a shadow first of anger, then of respect, and finally of amusement curving his sensuous mouth, his dark eyes gleaming as she came to stand in front of him. "Your gown is a surprise," he whispered, staring down at the tiny figure clad in the ivory silk that surrounded her like a cloud, the silver-gilt lilies sparkling as if they were made of diamonds.

"I prefer lilies to violets," she replied as they turned toward the altar and Père Dagobert, the superior of the Capuchin friars, who would perform the marriage ceremony.

Caresse seemed to drift in a daze through the sacrament that joined them as man and wife. As Lucien slipped on her finger the gold band engraved with some design she could not see in the darkened church, Caresse wondered for a brief moment if this ring too had once been worn by her predecessor, then she dismissed the thought from her mind as they were declared man and wife. His lips were warm on her own as he claimed her in a brief kiss before escorting her down the aisle framed on both sides by the smiling faces of their guests, some not bothering to conceal their curiosity about the new Mme St. Amant.

The full ivory sphere of the moon was rising over the Place Royale as they left the church to climb into a flower-bedecked carriage. Cheers and a few ribald comments from the crowd greeted them as the carriage pulled away toward the town house. The strains of the Canadian's concertina following them as he once more began his serenade.

"I believe I married a very strong-minded woman, *ma chère*," Lucien said with amusement, taking her hand in his.

"Do you regret it?" she asked, turning toward him with a teasing glance.

"Remember the St. Amant motto, *ma chère femme*.

We live our lives *sans regret,*" he reminded her, but for a moment there was a shadow in his dark eyes as he looked away from her to stare at something she knew was a memory from the past.

The town house was aglow with light shining from the long windows. From behind their carriage they could hear the rattle of the carriages of their guests and their excited laughter. Lucien St. Amant was known as a generous host, so the wedding reception promised to be a lavish affair.

"*Mes félicitations m'sieur, madame,*" Dominique said, with guarded eyes, opening the front door. She stood back so they might enter the foyer, lit now with tall ivory candles in the gilt sconces on the plastered walls. "Everything is ready, *m'sieur.*"

"*Bien,* Dominique. Our guests are right behind us," Lucien told her with a nod, leading Caresse toward the dining room.

"Dominique, did Pascal take my covered basket to my bedchamber?" Caresse asked, hesitating a moment.

"*Oui, madame,* I took the liberty of putting a small bowl of milk inside," Dominique answered, a slight warmth in her eyes for the first time since Caresse had met her.

"*Merci,* 'twas kind of you," she said with a smile for the moody woman who made her even now quite uneasy.

Dominique inclined her *tignon*-clad head, then turned to answer the knock on the door.

" 'Twould seem our first guests have arrived," Lucien commented with a sigh and a grimace. Before Caresse could answer, he moved with a charming smile to greet their guests as if he was especially delighted they had come.

Caresse sighed as yet another elegantly attired couple swept inside the foyer to be presented to her. Yvonne had been right, she thought, 'twould seem that most of Nouvelle Orléans had been invited to their reception. She had not realized how involved Lucien was in the society of the colony. For what seemed hours she had smiled at face after face as their guests filed past them and into the dining room for the delicate flutes of champagne that had been brought from France. The sound of conversation and laughter floated throughout the house as it filled with people. They were finally forced out through the open French doors into the garden where tall flaming torches stuck in the ground lit up the dark velvet of the night.

The marquis and marquise arrived as the last guests, to Caresse's relief. The icy blue gaze of the governor's wife swept over her gown and then the woman's thin lips curved in a frosty smile. "You have excellent taste, Mme St. Amant."

"Merci," Caresse replied with a slight incline of her head.

"You have surprised us all, *mon cher* Lucien, but now I understand the compulsion," the Marquise de Vaudreuil said, her eyes still on Caresse. "I must confess that day at Mme Cecil's I was quite mystified at seeing you with what appeared to be a child, a *jeune fille à la cassette*. But seeing your bride come down the aisle in that magnificent gown, it all became clear to me. You continue to amaze me, for I would never have thought of you as a sentimentalist, but this is the mad gesture of a romantic," she commented in a voice that softly mocked him.

"Solange, 'tis easy to see why Lucien married this beauty," her husband, the marquis, broke in with a smile that contained more than a hint of lust. "Lucien, with your permission, I claim a kiss from the bride." Then without waiting for a reply he leaned over to place a lingering kiss on Caresse's lips.

Stunned to see that the handsome marquis was

a great deal younger than his wife, Caresse could only give a thin smile as he stepped back. She felt Lucien stiffen at her side as he looked at the Marquis de Vaudreuil with ill-concealed dislike.

"Shall we see to our guests, *ma chère*," Lucien said tersely, holding out his arm to follow the governor and his wife into the dining room. "I believe there is a cake to cut, and I could use a glass of champagne."

The rest of the evening passed in a blur of champagne and too many strange faces for Caresse. It was as she was speaking with Yvonne and Pierre out in the garden, Lucien seeing to the other guests in the salon, that Dominique came to her side. The woman was so quiet Caresse did not realize she was there until she spoke.

"*Madame, m'sieur* has requested that you retire discreetly to the bridal chamber as is considered proper in Nouvelle Orléans," the dignified housekeeper reminded her. "There is an outside staircase to the second-floor gallery, if you will follow me."

"*Oui,* Dominique," Caresse replied, giving a Gallic shrug to the amused Yvonne and Pierre.

"May you find as much happiness with your Lucien as I have with Pierre," Yvonne whispered in Caresse's ear as she embraced her friend in farewell.

If any of the guests realized where Dominique was leading Caresse they were too polite to mention it, or too drunk with wine to care. She looked for Lucien, to catch his eye before leaving, but he was inside the house, his tall form visible, silhouetted against the wall in the dining room. Turning away from the guests, and with a racing pulse, Caresse followed the graceful Dominique across the flagstones to the staircase in the shadows of a huge magnolia. The perfume of the large alabaster blooms, glowing like votive candles in the moonlight, engulfed her as she swept up the stairs to the second-floor gallery.

Inside the masculine bedchamber that had been Lucien's until this night, Caresse was touched to see that he had made some changes to give it a more feminine romantic look. White roses in crystal vases stood everywhere, on the dressing table, the marble mantel, the tables beside the bed. Jasmine vine, with the rich perfume from the tiny white flowers, was entwined around the bedposts under the mosquito *barre*. Over the headboard was hung a wreath of rosemary, jasmine, and white rose buds. The ivory silk sheets gleamed in the glow of the tall myrtle tapers in silver candelabra.

"Madame, your *chemise de nuit,"* Dominique said, lifting the gossamer night rail of ivory pleated silk, trimmed with a deep edging of delicate lace at the low bodice, the cap sleeves and the swirling hem, from the burgundy damask counterpane.

Checking first to make sure Blanchette was sleeping in her basket, Caresse stood nervously biting her full lower lip as Dominique helped her to disrobe. It was awkward, but she made sure to keep her back turned away from the woman, shy to reveal the scar that branded her a felon. The thought of Lucien entering through the now-closed portal to claim her as his wife made her tremble with a myriad of emotions, including the fear of seeing revulsion in those dark expressive eyes when he saw the scarlet lily branded on her shoulder. In her young life she had known little of men; however, it was not only the physical joining with Lucien that made her tremble, but the thought that she could no longer keep the secret of her shame from that perceptive gaze.

Taking the cloth dipped in cool perfumed water scented with lilies from Dominique's hand, she gestured that she would wipe the heat from her body, reluctant to allow the woman to get close enough to discover her secret. Quickly, she brushed her nude form with scented powder from a glass jar, as the serving woman fetched the *chemise de nuit*. Caresse stood silent and trembling, her back turned away from the woman's gaze, as Dominique slipped the gown over her head. Her shame veiled, she sat down before the white-and-gold dressing table Lucien had brought in for her use, so the woman might brush out her hair.

As the woman brushed out her long ash blond tresses with firm relaxing strokes, Caresse remembered that Dominique had worked for the St. Amants for years. She would have known the first Mme St. Amant. What devilish twist of fate made her ask, she would never know. She would only remember later how much she wished she had not inquired.

"Dominique, did—did you know the first Mme St. Amant?" Caresse's voice stammered slightly as she looked into the looking glass, shadowy in the candlelight, to stare at the reserved woman who brushed her hair with authoritative strokes.

"*Oui,*" she answered quietly, not meeting Caresse's eyes.

"What was she like?" Caresse persisted.

"*M'sieur* Lucien's *maman* was a sad yet lovely lady," Dominique replied quietly.

"*Non,* I mean M. Lucien's first wife," Caresse corrected her.

"You know about her?" Dominique asked in startled tones, meeting her eyes in the looking glass for the first time.

"*Oui,* but I wondered what she looked like," Caresse explained with a flush to her cheeks. "There are no paintings of her."

"Not here, *madame,* but at Sans Regret there is one," Dominique replied carefully.

"What was her name?" Caresse persisted, determined she would know something about this woman who seemed so elusive.

"Aurore, *madame*," Dominique answered, obviously struggling with some inner turmoil.

Suddenly Caresse was struck with a flash of intuition, of understanding so terrible she flinched from the knowledge of it. She had to ask, had to know. "Who was the woman you thought I was that first day we met, Dominique? The woman you thought had returned from the dead."

The older woman stared into the mirror, her eyes filled with a sadness and something that was almost regret as she whispered, "Do not ask that, I beg of you, *madame*."

"I must know," Caresse answered, her face as white as the roses in the crystal vase on the dressing table. "Tell me, Dominique."

"Aurore St. Amant, *ma pauvre petite*." There was a deep sadness in her voice as well as relief that the terrible words had finally been spoken.

"I see," Caresse answered, a cold sinking feeling in her stomach at the confirmation of her worst suspicions. It explained so much, why Lucien, a wealthy man who had his pick of the women in Nouvelle Orléans, had been attracted to her that first day on the docks, his pursuit of a *fille à la cassette*. It had been her resemblance to a dead woman, a woman whom he must have deeply loved to seek her replacement in one who would bring her back to life, at least in her physical appearance.

The knock on the closed bedchamber door startled them both. Placing the silver-backed hairbrush on the dressing table, Dominique said quietly, "Speak of nothing that I have told you, *madame*. 'Tis not the time, if you wish to make a success of your marriage." She met Caresse's eyes in the silvered glass for one long moment, then turned to open the door.

"You may leave us, Dominique," Lucien commanded in a husky voice as he entered the chamber, his dark eyes reflecting the fiery glow of tapers in their silver holders as he drank in the sight of Caresse rising to face him from her bench in front of the dressing table.

Stunned by Dominique's revelation about Aurore St. Amant, Caresse was torn by conflicting emotions. She was fiercely drawn to this magnificent man, but whom did he see as he stared with such smoldering fire in his midnight black gaze? Was she only the reflection of a ghost?

Six

"You are breathtaking, *ma chère*," Lucien's voice was throaty with barely controlled passion. "Come here to me." He held out his hand, not moving from where he stood, halfway between Caresse and the four-poster clad in its ethereal cloud of mosquito netting.

She stood frozen, unable to move. His mere presence in the darkened chamber caused a warm giddy feeling to flow through her, making her light-headed. Unable to look away from those eyes that ensnared her from across the room, holding her to him as if by bonds of steel, she knew that she could not fight the magnetism he held for her. This attraction to him, the desire to feel his mouth on her own, to be enfolded in those strong arms and held against that powerful masculine form was consuming. She glided to him as if in a dream, walking as a sleepwalker walks, unaware of anything, her large gray eyes fixed on his own piercing gaze.

"*Ma chère femme,* my dearest wife," he whispered against the silk of her hair as he swept her, weightless, into his arms. "How I have longed for this night."

Wrapping her arms around his neck, molding her soft contours to the lean strength of his body, she could feel the warm caress of his uneven breathing on her cheek as he enfolded her into the sanctuary of his embrace. The strangest feeling of having come home overwhelmed her as he held her to him, kissing lightly, first her temples, then down to her closed eyelids, the tip of her *retroussé* nose, and finally the trembling hunger of her moist waiting mouth.

He moved his lips over hers, devouring their softness, drowning in the scent of lilies that rose from her warm, yielding body to tease and tantalize his senses. The combination of her awakening passion and her shyness drove him wild with desire. He, who had known many women, experienced a myriad of unfamiliar emotions as he held this delicate child-woman to him, wanting both to ravish and cherish the woman he had been drawn to because of her resemblance to another.

Why had he asked her to marry him? He was still not sure he could give the answer. Had he wanted her only because she resembled Aurore, or because she struck some chord within him that was hers alone? Did he do it out of some sense that he was avenging the past, trying to right an old wrong? It did not really matter what drew him to her, but when she entered the church in a gown of her own choosing he had known that she was no pallid ghost of Aurore, although the resemblance was startling in the right light. In the shadowy bedchamber, as she rose from the bench in front of the dressing table, he had for a moment been transported back in time. But as she came into his arms he had known that this lovely woman was real, and that she was his present, his future. Then past and present merged as her mouth opened under his, and the night became aflame with his hunger that would not be appeased until he made her his body and soul.

Succumbing to the passionate domination of his

kiss, the strength of his embrace, Caresse sank against him in a surrender to his will—his intense ardor allowed her senses no refusal. It was wonderful after so much loneliness to be wanted, so she curled against him, willing herself to allow no thoughts to intrude on the sense of completion she felt when held against Lucien's lean hard form.

With the poignant perfume of the roses and jasmine swirling around them in the soft sultry night air, Lucien guided Caresse to the waiting bed with the husky murmured words, *"Ma chère,* I can wait no longer."

Her body ached for his touch as she sank down on the silk sheets, the back of her hand pressed to her trembling lips as she watched him swiftly strip his clothes from his lean sinewy form. She had never seen the nude beauty of a man's body before this night, only the marble perfection of the statues of Greek gods at the palace of Versailles. Lucien, her husband, was as wondrously formed as the finest sculpture.

Slipping in beside her, he gave a pull on the tasseled rope that lowered the mosquito *barre* around the bed, surrounding them as if in a mist. The four-poster, with its silk burgundy canopy, became a small hidden chamber, the fragrance of the jasmine blossoms entwined around the bedposts stronger, more sensual, inside the cavern of the enclosed *barre.*

A hot ache grew in her throat as he turned toward her, gently touching her hair spread out on the pillow around the pale flower that was her face. Her gray eyes implored him to be gentle, yet urged him to show her the rapture that she instinctively desired.

"We have all night to discover one another, *ma petite,"* he murmured, leaning down to kiss her trembling mouth, stroking her hair, the line of her cheek, the slender length of her throat, as his tongue teased and traced the fullness of her lips.

With a sigh, she opened her mouth to him. As his tongue swept inside, she met him, touching, tasting him, as her senses vibrated with the life force.

His hand gently caressed the taut nipple of first one breast, then the other, through the thin silk of the nightgown. The sensitive massage of his knowing fingertips sent currents of desire racing through her till each and every nerve seemed to be at its peak of tension.

"I wish to touch the silk of your own lovely skin, *ma belle femme,*" he whispered as his mouth traced down her neck with light kisses till he reached the pulsing hollow at the base of her throat. "Allow me the privilege of seeing all of your beauty." He began to slip her gown from her shoulders.

Lost in the cloud of her own aroused passion, her lips curved in a sensual smile as she looked up at him through the heavy-lidded eyes of desire. Reaching up to stroke the raven's wing satin of his hair she thought once more how glad she was that he had left his hair unpowdered. It was only as the gown slipped from her shoulders and down her arms to expose the throbbing coral peaks of her ivory breasts that she remembered her secret, remembered the scarlet lily that she wore branded on her left shoulder.

"*Non,* I am shy, truly shy," she pleaded, placing her hands over his to stop him from lowering her nightgown any further.

"But, *ma chère* Caresse, you are exquisite. As your husband I am to teach you the joys of love between a man and a woman, and one of these joys is the sight, the feel, of the beloved's body. I appear before you unencumbered by clothing, hiding nothing. Can you not grant me the same trust?" His eyes, appearing enormous in the dim light from the tapers, stared down at her mesmerizing, challenging, consuming her with their intensity.

Suddenly, she knew that she could not continue this night without revealing her secret, but she dreaded seeing the disgust she knew would appear in those expressive eyes. She looked up at him with all the torment and conflict that was warring inside her heart.

"What is it, *ma pauvre petite*? I see a fear, a great sadness in you," he said softly, taking his hand from her gown and cupping her chin so that she could not look away from him.

"Are you a clairvoyant?" she mused, trying to put off the moment of revelation that she knew was only seconds away. She wanted to bask in this wonderful warmth for a few moments longer before it was withdrawn from her when he saw the scar that branded her as a felon. When he realized she had tricked him, that his wife was not a country girl, a simple *fille à la cassette*, but a correction girl from the dregs of La Salpêtrière prison, he would be at the least repulsed, at the worst furious. But wasn't she Mme St. Amant according to the law of France and in the eyes of the church? It would not be enough, she suddenly realized in the depths of her heart, if he looked at her with disgust.

" 'Tis not necessary to be clairvoyant when I can see such sadness in those windows to the soul, your beautiful gray eyes. Tell me, *ma chère* a sorrow shared is a sorrow lightened," he insisted, willing her with his intense gaze.

" 'Tis this," she said, pulling away from him so the long lovely line of her spine was toward him. Sweeping the silver-gold of her hair to the side and over her chest, she pulled her gown down to her waist exposing the delicate planes and hollows of her back, her peach-ivory skin, and the scarlet *fleur de lys* on her left shoulder.

The sound of his intake of breath seemed to fill

the small enclosure of the four-poster, as he stared at the lovely rigid back with its puckered scarlet-wine scar on her shoulder. The sight of such a disfigurement on her exquisite skin tore through him like a knife. He was stunned by the emotions evoked by that symbol on this delicate woman, and the knowledge of what she must have endured when it was burned into her flesh. Never had he admired her more than at this moment when she revealed herself to him, unable to keep hidden from him what he knew she considered her disgrace.

She waited, as tears of despair ran down her cheeks. Once more she would be alone, so alone, as she had been throughout her brief life. Her parents had always been cool and remote, like gods on Mount Olympus. She had seen little of them, for children were not encouraged at the court of Versailles. They were sent away as soon as they were born, to be raised by wet nurses, governesses, and then at boarding school. Caresse had been no exception, having lived since the age of five in convent schools, as did the other daughters of the wealthy and powerful. Their parents preferred to be sycophants to the King of France at his splendid court at Versailles than to be with their children at their estates in the provinces.

"Ma pauvre petite," he whispered as his lips tenderly touched the scarlet *fleur de lys* on her shoulder.

Her fingers clutched the silken sheets as she felt his lips kiss the dreadful scar, his fingertips tracing down her spine, giving her comfort when she had expected only revulsion. Then his hands were on her shoulders turning her to face him.

" 'Twas not easy what you have borne. I admire your courage as much as I admire your beauty. This has only confirmed to me how right I was to ask for your hand," he told her, his voice firm but full of a gentleness that she would never forget as long as she lived. He took her face between his hands, bending down to kiss the tears from her cheeks.

"You understand what it means?" she asked through trembling lips.

Ma mère also wore the scarlet lily on her shoulder," he replied softly, tracing her lower lip with the tip of his finger. "She was one of the infamous correction girls, but Jacques St. Amant did not care from the first moment he saw her on the wharf, as I saw you, *ma belle femme*. I told you one day I would confide in you the significance of your betrothal ring. If it had not been for the scarlet lily *ma mère* wore, he would never have met her, for she would not have been sent to La Louisiane." Lifting her hand with the ring to his lips, he kissed it tenderly. "The gold *fleur de lys* with the ruby baguettes is a symbol of what brought them together. He made her promise to never be ashamed of it again. And tonight as we join as man and wife I ask that you, too, never be ashamed to show this to me, my beautiful scarlet lily," he said with a tenderness that reached down inside her aching heart and began to heal some of the pain that had devastated her pride, her sense of femininity.

"I never shall again," she whispered as his mouth came down on hers in a slow caressing kiss.

Gently, he eased her back down on the bed, held within the circle of his embrace, his burning mouth never leaving hers. She moaned softly as he pressed her back against the silk of the sheets, the softness of the feather pillow. He lay beside her so that he could caress her throat, the fullness of her breasts, tracing first the outline, then teasing the tiny peaks that hardened at his touch.

She gasped as his lips slid in a fiery series of kisses down to the hollow of her throat where he circled the throbbing of her pulse with his tongue. When she thought she could not bear the pleasure, he moved down again to circle first one rose pink nipple, then the other with his burning mouth, as she turned to offer herself up for his delight and her rapture.

"Mon coeur," she murmured, stroking his hair with her fingers, as he kissed her gently, lingering over each breast, then down to the soft ivory silk of her belly, as his hands caressed and slowly moved apart her thighs.

This rapture between a man and a woman was more than she had dared to hope for even after the whispered confidences of Yvonne, and the few stories she had heard in the weeks she had been with her father at Versailles. Caresse had known what to expect, but it had been filtered through the giggling stories of the girls at her convent school, and the mating of the animals on their country estate outside of Lyon. Nothing had prepared her for the beguiling sense of abandonment she felt in his arms, and the hot rush of desire.

When his mouth kissed the silken untouched skin of her inner thigh she thought she would faint from the pleasure that was centered in her loins. Never had she experienced the rush of sensation that had taken over her body. She arched and moved under the knowing touch of the tapered fingers with their slightly callused tips so unusual in a gentleman. And, she realized through her heated daze of desire, that is exactly what Lucien was—a gentle man controlling his own needs that she might be fully awakened before their joining. It was not so with all men, she knew, for she had heard the jaded remarks of the courtesans at Versailles who had enjoyed the opportunity to shock an innocent young woman with stories of how their different lovers gave them pleasure.

The perfume of the jasmine and roses seemed to fill the enclosure of the four-poster in its cloud of netting. The flickering golden light from the tall tapers, burning lower in their silver holders, cast a mellow light across the two bodies entwined on the silken sheets. The bronzed masculine form stretched in counterpoint to the soft feminine peach-ivory curves. Sleek ebony hair loosened from its queue flowed into the silver-ash blond curls on the pillow, then those blue-black satin waves were against the mound of her belly as the two graceful bodies moved to a silent melody that sang through their veins.

Caresse gave a soft moan as her pleasure grew under his tender assault of tongue and touch. She had become a wanton creature of sensation and deepening hunger. Her fingers reached down and threaded through the ebony silk of his hair, pressing his mouth to those more intimate blond curls, so wild and overwhelming was her desire to experience all the joy, all the rapture he could teach her on this unbelievable night.

The soft moist inner petals of that most intimate part of her felt their first gentle invasion of a masculine touch. She felt her thighs, her hips tighten and quiver with the wondrous new sensation. It was glorious, she thought through a golden haze of arousal, as she soared higher and higher, freed from all earthly restraint by the swirling, building mysterious sensations that left her spellbound. He held her in his thrall of ecstasy till she reached the pinnacle, crying out his name as she experienced sensual fulfillment for the first time. Trembling, her breath coming in gasps, she collapsed into his waiting gathering embrace.

"I . . . I did not know," she murmured, turning her face·into the soft fur of his chest.

A husky chuckle came from deep within Lucien's throat as he held her to his chest, stroking the waterfall of her tresses, his erection pressed against the thigh she had thrown over him. "That was only the first lesson, *ma chère,* in the joy that can be between a man and a woman." Gently he turned and lay her back against the pillow. "Now we shall begin the second," he murmured. He reclaimed her lips with his slow drugging kisses as he covered her soft body with his lean sinewy form.

She felt the tide of desire once more sweep over her and carry her out on that languorous sea of rapture where time ceased to exist—where all that mattered was the circle of Lucien's embrace, the burning sweetness of his mouth on her lips, her skin. The hot molten honey of passion flowed through her veins as he prepared her for the ultimate invasion, the total consummation of their joining as husband and wife.

"Look at me, *ma chère* Caresse," he commanded huskily as he rose over her, parting those moist throbbing petals that he might finally enter and claim her as his own. "Forgive me but 'twill be painful for a moment, then we shall find our ecstasy together."

For a brief heart-stopping moment she felt her resistance to his entry, then one quick burning pain as he penetrated her. The discomfort soon turned to a wondrous swelling rapture that banished all memory of pain. *"Mon coeur! Mon amour!"* she cried out as her arms wrapped around him, digging the pearl of her fingernails into the hard planes of his back as he took her higher and higher in passion's spiral. Arching up against him, she urged him deeper, and deeper still, as her hips found his rhythm and together they danced that wondrous dance of thrust and counterthrust, the dance of man and woman. They moved bodies entwined, mouth on heated mouth, till they reached the crescendo in one soul-shattering merging of two into one.

The shadowy chamber was still and hot, without a breath of air stirring. They separated briefly only to lie in a loose embrace amidst the tumble of the

100

silken sheets. Neither broke the silence, for they were both shaken by the depth of emotion they had experienced. Even in her innocence, Caresse somehow realized that their lovemaking had reached a plane of intensity that many were never lucky enough to experience.

Lucien held his wife to his chest, lightly stroking the tangle of her hair shimmering silver in the dim candle glow. He was shaken to the very core of his being. He had long enjoyed bedding a lovely woman, but he had thought his heart had so hardened after Aurore that never would he love again. Tonight, however, there had been no thought of Aurore, no fear of feeling too much, for his heart had followed its own path that had nothing to do with logic or self-preservation. When he had looked down into those wide innocent gray eyes, filled only with wonder and trust, he had felt his heart surrender to this fragile woman. In his act of conquest he had been the one to capitulate, for she had found a way around the carefully erected barrier that he had built around his innermost being.

Staring out through the mist of netting into the shadowy chamber, he saw back through time to another beautiful woman who had driven him almost to the brink of madness, the madness he had always feared he would inherit from his poor broken mother. He had loved Gabrielle with every fiber of his being, as had Jacques St. Amant. In the end that love had destroyed the good strong man he considered his father. He knew firsthand what love could do to a man, he thought, narrowing his eyes, as he stared above the beautiful head of Caresse, who was curled up beside him in complete trust. She must never guess how much she meant to him, for it would be a weapon she could use to make him miserable. He never stopped to think, to wonder if Caresse was even capable of such manipulation. Life had taught him only too well what women were capable of when it came to their relationships with men.

Caresse did not know if it was the noise that awakened her, but suddenly she was awake and lying in the huge four-poster alone. From outside the windows facing the street came the sound of music and singing interrupted here and there by a few masculine shouts. Sitting up in the tumble of the silk sheets, Caresse reached for her night rail draped across the foot of the bed. Slipping the garment over her head, she pushed aside the mosquito *barre* to see Lucien standing in a long burgundy silk dressing gown at the French door leading out onto the front gallery, the wooden louvered blinds tilted open, the curtains pulled back.

"What is that awful noise?" Caresse asked, slipping on her ivory satin mules with their high hourglass heels.

" 'Tis a custom here on the wedding night. The *charivari* is a mock serenade of discordant music and rather ribald jokes by a crowd of some of the more intoxicated of the male guests and rabble from the wharves. The bridal couple has to appear and furnish them refreshments and small gifts," Lucien explained as he looked down at the growing crowd in front of the town house. "As a widower taking a new young bride I expected it," he added in wry tones.

"And why is that?" Caresse inquired softly, coming to stand beside him.

"A widow or widower is always serenaded. Sometimes the comments can be *grossier*, crude," he said tersely. "Hold your head up, *ma belle femme*, and pay them no mind. Don your peignoir. We must make our appearance on the gallery while

102

Dominique and Pascal serve them and distribute the gifts or they will never leave."

Giving her hair a quick brush, Caresse slipped on the cream silk peignoir brocaded in silver gilt bouquets of lily of the valley. Joining him at the French door, she was welcomed by the look of admiration she saw in his eyes before they turned and, hand in hand, walked out onto the gallery to the roar of the crowd's approval.

Flaming torches clutched in some of the men's fists sent sparks up into the indigo velvet of the night sky. Beneath them the front doors opened and Dominique handed out mugs of claret cup and a local pineapple ale brewed with brown sugar, cloves and rice called *bière du pays*. Pascal followed her, handing out pouches of tobacco. A cheer rang out again at the sight of the two servants.

"Merci, mes amis," Lucien called down to the crowd. "Share our joy on this our wedding night."

Caresse smiled, acknowledging their cheers and toasts to her beauty. They were a drunken, but good-natured, crowd. But as she looked down at them, clasping Lucien's hand, her eyes met those of a well-dressed man standing apart from the others. The light from a torch held by a man standing next to him had drawn her attention to the tall elegant figure. Her gaze was caught by the expression of disdain in his cold amber eyes that locked with hers. She saw the disdain turn to surprise and then a strange look of yearning. He wore an elaborate ice blue silk waistcoat and breeches, as if he were going to a court function, and on his head was a powdered wig caught back in queue with a wide silk ribbon. But there was nothing effeminate about this man, with his narrow aristocratic features. Rather a cold repellent strength seemed to emanate from him. Caresse gave a light shudder, looking away from his now insolent stare.

"May the second Mme St. Amant live longer

than the first," the bitter taunt cut through the laughter and singing of the crowd.

There was a sudden silence as the men turned toward the elegant figure in ice blue silk standing on the edge of the banquette. Even the concertina came to a stop as the stunned crowd looked from the bystander up to where Lucien stood with his arm now around Caresse's shoulders.

She could feel the terrible leashed fury within her husband as he stood at her side. A muscle flickered in his jaw, but his visage was a marble effigy of contempt as he locked eyes with the stranger, his black eyes blazing with his barely restrained anger.

The terrible moment was broken by the cry of *"Bonne chance!* Good luck!" from first one man and then another. The stranger was the only one not to join in as Lucien gestured down to Dominique to serve yet another tray of drinks, to the crowd's delight.

"Come, *ma chère,* while they are occupied, we shall slip back inside," Lucien commanded, leading her back across the gallery to the French door.

Caresse looked over her shoulder to see the cold bitter gaze of the stranger as he stood for a moment, then turned and strode back down the banquette toward the Place Royale. Out of the corner of her eye she saw Dominique staring after the stranger with a strange unreadable expression.

As Lucien shut the door and locked it, pulling the wooden louvered blinds closed so no light could penetrate, Caresse asked him, "Who was that man?"

"What man?" Lucien said in a clipped voice.

"The one in the blue silk, the one who shouted that rude comment," she answered, determined to find out the man's identity.

"Philippe Dubrieul," Lucien replied, coming toward her.

"Then he is known to you," she said with surprise.

"He was the stepbrother of Aurore, my first wife," he explained in a harsh bitter voice. "I wish never to hear his name spoken in our home." Placing his arm around her waist, he guided her back toward the four-poster. "No more questions. There is only time for love, *ma chère*," he whispered against the silk of her hair as they slipped into the waiting bed.

But even as Lucien pulled her into his embrace, Caresse remembered the stranger's words, and for a moment she thought she could smell the scent of violets, Aurore's scent. Entwining her body with her husband's, her fingers buried in his hair, her mouth returning his burning kiss, she thought she could hear the word Aurore echoing on the night breeze.

With a stab of despair, she wondered if her marriage was to be haunted by the spectral memory of his first wife, the woman she resembled so closely, Aurore St. Amant.

Seven

The humid heat was streaming into the bed-chamber with the morning sun as Caresse tossed and turned, still deep in sleep. But as her discomfort grew, she finally opened heavy eyelids to discover that Lucien was gone, and Dominique was gliding through the open French door that led out on to the gallery overlooking the garden.

"I bring you your *petit déjeuner, madame.*" The woman greeted her in her soft patois. " 'Tis stifling today. A cup of strong *café* and some of my warm sugared *beignets* fresh from the oven will give you energy to face such a morn." She swept inside the mosquito *barre* to place the woven bed tray, painted a sparkling white, in front of Caresse as she sat up, placing her pillows behind her shoulders.

"And my husband?" she asked, thinking how long it had been since she had breakfasted in bed.

"*M'sieur* has been unfortunately called away on business, but he requested that I tell you he will return before the church bells ring the midday hour. He also wanted me to convey his apologies for having to interrupt the seclusion of the *lune de miel,* the honeymoon, but it was of the gravest importance."

Caresse brushed the tangle of her hair from her face, and quickly poured a cup of the hot black *café* from the silver pot, adding the warmed milk from the other pot. Fatigue lay over her like a blanket, the humid heat adding to her languor. A few sips of the strong coffee would clear the cobwebs from her brain, she hoped. She even welcomed the chance to be alone. Caresse was really a solitary person. She had a feeling Lucien was too. Idly, she wondered if Aurore had liked to have her solitary moments. Taking a bite of the delicious *beignet*, she remembered Lucien asking if she minded staying out in the country at the plantation. He said some women were afraid of the isolation. Had he been speaking of Aurore?

"Please pour some of this milk into the saucer for Blanchette," Caresse instructed Dominique as she heard a tiny meow.

"I have already seen to the *petit chat, madame.* While you slept. I took her down to the garden. She has had a bowl of milk and a few fresh shrimp in the kitchen house. But as I could not look after her constantly, I brought her back up here and returned her to her basket," Dominique explained.

"Merci, 'twas very thoughtful of you," Caresse told her with a smile of gratitude.

" 'Tis good to have a pet in the house again. Mme Gabrielle had a dog as well as several cats. She seemed more at home with animals than with humans, but then her pets had never hurt her in any way and accepted her as she was. Of course there were no pets allowed in the house when Mme Aurore was mistress," Dominique confided, a shadow once more in her eyes. Then as if she realized that she had said too much she changed the subject. "I have had Pascal and the groom, Raymond, bring up canisters of water. I thought you might care for a bath, *madame."*

"Oui, 'twould be lovely," Caresse nodded. "And your *beignets* are as light as a feather." She wanted to ask why Aurore had not allowed pets in the

house, remembering that Lucien had said he had a dog, Bruno, at Sans Regret. But she was embarrassed to seem too curious about Lucien's first wife.

"Merci, madame." Dominique gestured for Pascal and Raymond to bring in the brass canisters of water. They entered with eyes averted from the bed that was draped once more in its tent of netting. Pulling the copper tub out from behind a screen, they quickly filled it with water, then left. Dominique poured a small amount of perfume into the tepid water and the chamber was soon filled with the scent of lilies. Linen towels and a bar of French soap were placed on the stool beside the tub.

"It looks wonderful," Caresse sighed as she slipped from the bed and then from the silk night rail without thinking of her scar. She felt Dominique's eyes fasten on it for a moment, then quickly look away. Well, it was bound to happen Caresse thought with a shrug, as Dominique draped her long hair over the edge of the tub so that it would not get wet. The woman was to be her personal maid, and now that Lucien knew about her scar, there was no longer any reason to keep it covered from Dominique.

"Were you Aurore's lady's maid?" Caresse asked casually as she soaped herself. She had resolved to hold her tongue, but she could not control her curiosity.

"Oui, madame, and his mother's as well, although I was very young at the time. M. Jacques assigned me to poor Mme Gabrielle when my own *maman* died of the smallpox," Dominique said as she poured a pitcher of fresh water over Caresse to rinse off the suds.

"Why do you always refer to his mother as if there was something wrong with her?" Caresse inquired, realizing that this was the second time the maid had made reference to Lucien's mother in such a way.

"Because she was *folle,* quite deranged," Dominique explained to Caresse's shock. "Mme Gabrielle hardly ever spoke, for often she was far away in a world all her own. A happier place I think, *madame,* where there were no bad memories."

"But how long was she like this?" Caresse asked in surprise.

"All her life, or as long as I knew her, and the gossip in the quarters was that she had been so since her arrival in Nouvelle Orléans."

"But how terrible for my husband," Caresse said softly, rising from the tub and stepping out onto the towel Dominique had placed on the wide cypress boards of the floor.

"M'sieur, like his father, was very protective of his *maman.* He would hear not a word against her. There were many fights he had defending her *honneur* when he was a young boy at the school of the Capuchins. Children can be so cruel, *madame,"* Dominique replied.

"Oui, indeed, they can," Caresse agreed, thinking sadly of a young boy fighting for his mother's honor against the taunts of the other boys. A pang tore through her heart as she dried herself on the linen towel. "So it was common knowledge that his *maman* was . . . disturbed?"

"Nouvelle Orléans is a small city, and it was even smaller when *m'sieur* was a child. M. Jacques tried to keep *madame* at Sans Regret, but there were times he had to come into town, and he would not leave his wife behind with only the servants to watch over her, even though one of those servants was my *maman.* We would come with them to Nouvelle Orléans."

"He must have been a wonderful man to care

109

so for a woman who was not quite normal," Caresse commented.

" 'Twas said that M. Jacques fell in love with his wife the first time he set eyes on her. He was a strong man, who always had a soft spot in his heart for the helpless, like poor *madame*. She was often more like his child than his wife." There was a strange note to Dominique's voice. She paused and stared out the window as if seeing something years before, something that was painful. Then pulling her attention back she continued, "I think that is where M. Lucien learned to care for those whom he felt needed him, like his poor *maman*. Unfortunately his compassion was misplaced in his first marriage," Dominique said almost angrily, a shadow coming into her sable-brown eyes. "And because of that tragedy, he became hard and lived, as the family motto says, without regret in everything he did the last few years."

"Whatever do you mean, Dominique?" Caresse asked, stunned.

"Your *robe de chambre, madame.*" Dominique held out the cream silk peignoir. "I beg you to disregard my last words. I have no right to comment on such matters." There was a tremor in the woman's soft voice as she slipped the robe under Caresse's long hair.

"Merci," Caresse said as the garment was draped around her nude body. "Of course I shall say nothing to *monsieur* if you wish me not too, but I want you to feel that you can speak freely to me. There is much I shall have to learn about the running of Sans Regret. I hope that I can count on your help." Sitting down in front of the looking glass over the dressing table, her eyes met those of Dominique in the reflection.

"You can, *madame,*" the woman replied as she began to brush out the long strands of Caresse's hair with the silver-backed brush.

"That will be all for now, Dominique. I shall brush *madame's* hair," the deep masculine voice, with its husky tone, interrupted them. "The men can come for the tub later."

Turning, Caresse saw the tall lean figure silhouetted in the open French door leading out onto the gallery that overlooked the garden. The sun was to his back, shading his face. She wondered how long he had been standing there, and what he had heard?

"Oui m'sieur," Dominique replied, placing the brush on the dressing table. With her gliding graceful stride she left the chamber.

"Non, ma chère," Lucien protested, as Caresse started to rise. "You look so lovely, and I promised to brush that magnificent hair."

In a few lithe strides he was standing behind her. Picking up the brush he began to pull it through her tresses with long strokes, as his eyes made love to her reflection in the silvered glass.

"Where did you go?" she asked in a throaty voice as she felt the beginnings of passion rise within her at every stroke of the brush.

"To arrange for our return to Sans Regret. I know it is against custom to leave our bridal chamber so soon, but there is fever in Nouvelle Orléans, and I want you safe upriver at the plantation," he explained.

"When do we leave?" she asked, with a shudder, as he put down the brush and began to massage her temples with his long fingers.

"In two hours, I am afraid. We must leave as soon as possible. There is already panic on the docks, with everyone who has a plantation or friends out of the city trying to hire any vessel that floats. As much as I wish it were possible, there is no time to spend the afternoon in lovemaking. Dominique must pack for you, and Pascal for me. Pascal and Raymond will stay here to watch over the house. The slaves do not seem as susceptible to fever as the French. All that will be left in Nouvelle Orléans will be rabble, house slaves guarding their master's house, and a few government officials, along with the priests and the good Ursuline *soeurs.*"

Caresse felt a pang of concern in her heart at the thought of the convent, which had been her refuge, becoming a charnel house of the sick tended by Soeur Xavier and her herbal medicines. The orphan children she had taught would also stay and face the fever's wrath, and wrath it would be, she knew from stories of previous epidemics.

"Do not look so frightened, *ma chère*. I will see that nothing harms you," Lucien insisted, gently turning her around so that she faced him.

" 'Tis not me that I fear for, but for the *soeurs* and the children staying with them," she replied with sadness in her gray eyes.

"They are in good hands with the Ursuline *soeurs*, for they have cared for many in these summer fever epidemics. I should have forced the priests to disregard the banns so we might have married earlier, *ma chère*. 'Tis folly to stay in Nouvelle Orléans during the fever months," he said with a frown, his handsome visage a grim mask.

Pulling her to her feet, he gathered her to his long lean frame, holding her tight against him as if the power and strength of his body could keep her safe from the illness that was crawling through the streets of Nouvelle Orléans like a deadly fog. His hands stroked the long silk fall of her hair down her back, his lips pressed her temple, as gently he rocked her back and forth. "I shall allow nothing to harm you again," he whispered against the wisps of hair that curled in the humidity.

Caresse felt a coldness grow within her at his words. What did he mean *again*? Despite their wondrous night of passion, they had known each other barely two months. Was he, in his mind, holding Aurore in his arms? She shuddered inwardly at the thought that to Lucien she might be only a substitute for the woman he really desired but could no longer touch.

"If we are to leave so soon then there is much I must do," Caresse said coolly, trying to pull away from his enveloping embrace. Her gray eyes darkened with the pain of her suspicions, her throat raw with unuttered shouts and protests.

"There is time, *ma chère,* for one kiss," he muttered, thickly, his hold on her tightening as his mouth sought the hollow of her throat.

A new anguish seared her heart as she realized that in spite of her suspicions she still wanted him. His kiss was igniting a fire in her blood. The knowledge that she could want his mouth on hers, his hands on her skin, even though he was using her, twisted and turned inside her. Tears moistened her eyelashes, as his lips moved slowly to her waiting mouth trembling with her need and despair.

With a surrender to her traitorous body she parted her lips, allowing his possession and entrance. A wild surge of pleasure swept away all thought as their tongues met. Her fingers stroked the silk of his hair, then the sinewy strength of his back. Arching against him she felt her nipples harden through the thin material of her *robe de chambre* as they pressed into his chest. How he wished she could feel the warmth and texture of his skin against her own.

"*Ma belle femme,* I cannot resist you. I must have you," his voice was a heated husky whisper against her throat as he swept her up in his arms and carried her to the bed.

A moan of anticipation tore from her throat as he placed her on the tumble of the silken sheets.

His dark eyes never left her own as Lucien stripped the clothes from his lithe, lean body.

He knew he was endangering them both by taking the time to possess her but he could not stop himself. He felt a dark, fiery obsession that was driving him beyond logic, beyond caution. The keelboat would wait for him, it was manned by his slaves, his captain, but there had been panic this morning at the docks, and it was not unheard of for a boat to be commandeered by a frantic family desperate to leave the disease-ridden city.

"There is no time for the play of love, *ma chère*. I apologize for this, but at Sans Regret there will long afternoons for all the nuances of lovemaking. Today I must have you quickly," he rasped as he lay down beside her, bending his sleek dark head so that he might take a throbbing nipple in his mouth.

He swirled his tongue around the erect rosebud. Her moans of hunger and aroused passion soared on the sultry still air of the chamber as he moved his mouth to her other nipple, sucking it lightly into a hard little peak. His fingers stroked through her intimate silken curls as he opened her woman's lips, arousing, preparing her, for his more forceful invasion.

"*Mon coeur!* My heart!" Caresse cried as the heated honey of rapture moved through her, overriding all inhibition, all reluctance, all doubt. Her body, her very soul, cried out for complete surrender to him. She ached to feel him inside her, remembering their ecstatic joining when she had felt so complete, no longer alone, but wanted, desired, by this splendid man who was her husband.

As he rose over her, her thighs opened and, instinctively, her hips moved in a sensuous invitation. Her arms lifted up so that her hands could grasp the sinewy muscles of his upper arms. "Now!" she begged.

With a moan of possession, that was in reality more a surrender to his obsession, he thrust inside her honey-moist waiting depths. Her body opened to him, responding to every thrust with a counter-thrust of her own.

There was no pain this time, only the wondrous rapture that seemed to build within her till she was all sensation. Her fingernails dug into his skin as her passion soared out of control, higher and higher. Nothing existed, nothing mattered but their two bodies giving and receiving the rapturous joy of exquisite sensation.

They abandoned themselves to their spiraling climax as the first chime of the midday bells rang in counterpoint to their moans of rapture. Their moment of total ecstasy reached its pinnacle as the church bells finished ringing out across Nouvelle Orléans signaling the rapid passing of precious time.

They lay loosely entwined, their breath still rapid as they savored for a moment the satisfaction and gentle afterglow of their lovemaking. The intensity, the sense that their passion was out of their control, even when they should have been preparing to leave, had only added to the exquisite rapture they had experienced.

"Ma chère, we must arise and dress," said Lucien with a sigh, lifting her hand to his lips as concern shadowed his expressive eyes. "We have tarried longer than we should have, but I must confess it was worth the risk," he murmured against the fragrant skin of her soft palm.

" 'Tis so dangerous?" Caresse asked, not really concerned, for she was still basking in the warmth of satisfaction. Held in Lucien's embrace, she felt immortal, as if nothing could ever harm her as long as she had this man with his great inner strength beside her.

"Oui, and I have added to it by prolonging our

115

departure. But do not worry, I shall take care that nothing happens to you," he replied, pressing her to him, giving her a swift kiss on the forehead. Then he was rising to dress, urging her to do the same.

The next hour seemed to pass in a blur of dressing, and packing the few clothes that had been taken from the trunk sent with her trousseau from Mme Cecil. Lucien was directing Pascal, as Dominique saw to Caresse.

"Why are you taking that?" Lucien asked, puzzled, as Caresse handed Raymond the *cassette* she had brought with her from France. "I would think that your new trousseau should be ample for your needs."

"There are a few belongings I do not wish to part with," she explained softly. The thought of the man's cape that lay in the bottom of her *cassette* flashed across her mind. She felt foolish, and worse, somewhat disloyal, for keeping another man's cape now that she was married, but it had been her talisman during the worst time of her life, and she wanted it with her. Besides, she thought with a frown, as wonderful as their lovemaking had been there was still a slight cloud on her happiness. Was Lucien's ardor truly for her or for the living image of Aurore?

The afternoon sun beat down on the open carriage as they made their way through the throng to the docks. Blanchette's basket was on the seat beside Dominique as she faced Caresse and Lucien. Their trunks and portmanteaus were strapped on the back. It was only a short drive to the wharf from the house on the Rue Chartres. As they turned onto the quay from the Rue St. Pierre, Caresse was startled to see the figure of Philippe Dubrieul striding toward the levee. It seemed that

Lucien was right, she mused, everyone who could afford it was trying to leave Nouvelle Orléans.

Fear was a palpable presence in the stifling, humid August air that lay over the city like a wet smothering blanket. French soldiers from the barracks on either side of the Place Royale tried to keep order on the wharves. German farmers and their families, in town to sell their fruits and vegetables at the market tried to launch their keelboats and pirogues to escape fever-ridden Nouvelle Orléans. The rumors of the arrival of the disease in the city had spread like a wild fire, sending the citizens into a panic. *Voyageurs* and *coureurs de bois* from New France in Canada some of whom had come down the Mississippi to trade, and some to settle in the swamps and along the bayous outside the city—they also were leaving. They had come into Nouvelle Orléans to escape the rash of Indian raids that had recently occurred along the river, but they preferred to take their chances with the Indians rather than succumb to the ravages of the fever. Friendly Indians, who sold sassafras root and game at the market, were swarming into their pirogues as well.

Two-masted brigantines, three-masted merchant ships, as well as single-masted sloops and keelboats, all crowded the waterfront. Drunken men swarmed in and out of the riverfront taverns, pothouses, and gambling dens. Not all could leave Nouvelle Orléans, and they found their courage to face the deadly fever in a bottle.

The smell of rancid wine, brandy, and cheap rum hung in the air, adding to the pervasive scent of decaying vegetables, fruit and other more unsavory odors. Tobacco, indigo, and myrtle wax candles, waiting for shipment to the West Indies and France, added their own more fragrant perfume.

Pascal pulled up in front of the steps leading up to the levee and the wharves. As Lucien helped

Caresse out of the carriage, she saw two familiar figures climbing the steps to the levee. Yvonne and Pierre carrying baskets, with two African men following them carrying trunks, were striding toward where the pirogues were pulled up on the muddy bank of the Mississippi.

"Please, Lucien, could we not allow my friends to ride with us on the keelboat to their plantation? I believe it is located just down river from Sans Regret," Caresse asked, her hand on her husband's arm as he helped her up the steep wooden steps. Dominique followed behind carrying Blanchette in her basket.

"If you wish, of course. Traveling up river in a pirogue is hard work and dangerous for a woman," he agreed as they reached the top of the levee. "Wait here. I shall ask Pierre."

As the St. Amant keelboat pulled away from the dock into the rushing ochre waters of the Mississippi, Yvonne and Pierre stood with Caresse and Lucien in the bow of the sixty-foot-long boat. They watched the St. Amant slaves, standing on the gangplanks that ran on either side of the keelboat, push long poles into the river's mud and drew the boat forward while they strained until they reached the end of the pole. Then they pulled it up and walked to the stern, and began the monotonous business all over again, propelling the boat upriver against the strong current.

" 'Tis such a relief, *chère*, to be here with you instead of in that tiny hollowed-out log of a pirogue," Yvonne confided to Caresse in a whisper so that Pierre would not overhear. "Perhaps our small plantation's name is appropriate after all. Pierre told me he called it Bonne Chance, and it was certainly good fortune that allowed us to be leaving at the same time as you and Lucien. I was surprised to see you, *chère*, so soon after your wedding, but then the fever has changed everyone's plans."

" 'Tis my good fortune that you and Pierre will be living so close. You must promise to come and visit often," Caresse said with a hint of desperation in her voice, as the straining slaves pushed the keelboat upriver away from Nouvelle Orléans. The dense swamp and canebrake soon blocked out any sight of the town, only the spire of the church of St. Louis silhouetted against the azure sky suggested civilization in the vast forbidding wilderness.

"Are you frightened of going to Sans Regret, *chère?*" Yvonne queried in surprise.

"Uneasy I should say, not frightened," Caresse explained thoughtfully." 'Tis just a feeling, but now that I know you will not be far away I feel much better."

"I thought perhaps you were allowing the gossip about the place to frighten you," Yvonne said with concern.

"What gossip?" Caresse asked, surprise widening her gray eyes.

"Forgive me, I thought you had heard, and that was what was bothering you," Yvonne sighed, an expression of chagrin on her usually cheerful features. " 'Tis just silly legend spread by the slaves, and somehow it reached Nouvelle Orléans. People like to gossip about someone as handsome and wealthy as your husband. You know how envious people can be."

"Yvonne, please tell me," Caresse insisted, placing her hand on her friends arm.

"They . . . say that Sans Regret, the house, the grounds, is haunted by the ghost . . . the spirit of Aurore St. Amant," Yvonne admitted with reluctance. "There is probably nothing to the story. The slaves are superstitious and when someone dies un-

119

der mysterious circumstances, everyone's imagination is stimulated."

"Aurore died at Sans Regret?" Caresse asked softly, biting her lower lip.

"*Oui*, that is what everyone says," Yvonne replied, concern for her friend in her sympathetic blue eyes.

"How? How did she die?" Caresse inquired intently, in a low voice that could not carry to where Lucien stood talking with Pierre.

"She fell off the second-story gallery when the railing gave way, breaking her neck on the bricks below. 'Twas ruled to be an accident, but some say she committed suicide, because she was so unhappy and frightened at Sans Regret. Others . . . hint at another story," Yvonne murmured, looking over her shoulder in Lucien's direction.

"What other story?" Caresse continued to insist.

"That Aurore St. Amant was murdered. 'Tis said that is why her ghost, her spirit, is restless. She cannot find peace till her murderer is punished." Yvonne wrung her hands. "I should not have told you, but sooner or later someone would have been only too happy to frighten you with the old legend. And that is all it is, a legend, a ghost story made up by superstitious slaves and people jealous of Lucien's wealth and handsome appearance. Oh, *chère*, forget it, do not let it interfere with your happiness with Lucien," Yvonne pleaded, touching her friend's arm as if to reassure her, regret for her words in her blue eyes.

"Do not worry, I shall not let it interfere," Caresse promised, looking away to stare at the wild verdant swamp, but she knew she was lying to Yvonne.

Aurore, always Aurore. The woman had been haunting her since the moment she walked into the town house on Rue de Chartres. What would she find at Sans Regret, the house in which Aurore

120

had met her death? Suddenly she remembered Dominique's words that Lucien's first marriage had made him hard. Why? What had happened to make both of them so unhappy that it was rumored she had taken her own life? That Aurore had been murdered she would not even consider, Caresse decided. She could not even think of it, for if she did she would be alone at an isolated plantation with a man who might have killed his first wife. No, she thought, it was impossible, remembering Lucien's gentle, yet passionate, lovemaking. Staring out at the haunted landscape of the swamp, she knew he was not capable of murder. Not Lucien.

Eight

"Is the shadow of unhappiness I see in your lovely gray eyes because your friends have departed for their plantation?" Lucien asked. He stood next to Caresse watching the cypress dock of Bonne Chance disappear from sight as they rounded a bend in the wide twisting brown ribbon of water that was the Mississippi River.

"Perhaps a bit," Caresse replied, raising her hand to shade her eyes under the wide brim of her straw hat that she might catch a last glimpse of Yvonne. She gave a light shudder in the breeze from the water, even though the air was warm and humid.

Yvonne and Pierre had disembarked with their slaves carrying the two pirogues, then returning for their two small trunks. The small house in the raised cottage style was barely visible through the thick branches of the giant live oaks. There had been a moment when she embraced Yvonne that Caresse had experienced a momentary panic. She quickly covered it up and bade her friend a cheerful farewell, extracting a promise that they would come visit at Sans Regret in a month's time.

"I hope you are not finding the landscape frightening, *ma chère.*" Lucien commented, his dark eyes glistening with some unreadable emotion in the long golden rays of the setting sun.

"Non, why would you think that?" she questioned, looking away from him across the water to the eerie festoons of gray moss that hung from the gnarled trees like cobwebs in a deserted house.

"I'll warrant that at home you never saw anything like our Spanish beard," he said with a gesture at the hanging moss. "I thought you might find this strange land, that looks so different from France, rather unsettling."

" 'Tis different from France, that is true," Caresse replied slowly, "but it has a wild beauty about it. I do not frighten easily, you will find." There was a light bitterness to her soft voice as she thought of La Salpêtrière prison.

"I am glad to hear it, *ma chère,*" he said, and there was understanding in his deep voice as if he knew she was thinking of her days in prison. "A man needs a wife who is strong within herself to stand beside him in this wilderness." There was a strange tone to his words as if there were another meaning behind them.

Caresse thought of Aurore. Had she been strong? She realized with a sudden flash of insight that there had been something strange about the first Mme St. Amant. Dominique had allowed her dislike of Aurore to show in her comments, and Yvonne had heard rumors that she had taken her own life. Perhaps, once she was living at the plantation she would be able to find answers to the questions she had about Aurore St. Amant.

"You are lost in thought," Lucien said softly, caressing her cheek with his thumb. She seemed so remote that he wanted to bring her back to him. What regrets was she having about accepting him as her husband? The memory of another who had stood beside him on their wedding trip from Nouvelle Orléans haunted him.

"How much longer to Sans Regret?" she asked, instead of responding to his comment.

"About another half-hour. 'Tis not far," he replied. "I am afraid you will see it at twilight, for we are losing the light."

"There are no more plantations on this side of the river, between Bonne Chance and Sans Regret?"

"A few German farms on the other side, but only one plantation, Chêne Vert, Green Oak, the Dubrieul plantation," he replied briskly, dropping his hand from her cheek to stare out across the rushing water.

"Dubrieul . . . but is that not the name of—" Caresse stammered, then broke off the rest of her sentence.

"*Oui*, 'tis the name of Aurore's step-brother. He stayed on to run the place after his father and step-mother, Aurore's mother, left for Saint-Domingue to tend his sugar plantation there. Her mother hated Louisiane from the first day she and Aurore's father came to Nouvelle Orléans. He was a representative of the king. Four months after Aurore's father was killed in an Indian raid, her mother married Edouard Dubrieul, a widower with one son. Some say that Dubrieul had been her lover for many months before her first husband's death," Lucien explained in a dispassionate voice. "I never cared for the man, nor do I care for his son. We shall see little of Philippe Dubrieul, for his dislike of me is as strong as is mine for him."

"He is unmarried?" Caresse persisted, her curiosity roused by the knowledge that Aurore's step-brother was living so close to them. She realized that he had been seeking transportation to his plantation when she saw him down on the docks.

"*Oui*," Lucien said, his lips curling in disgust at the thought of Philippe Dubrieul. "There is Chêne Vert, and now let us not discuss him again."

Caresse looked across the river to where the outline of a house could just be seen through the dark shadows of the trees in the pearl-gray twilight. The structure was in the style of the raised cottage, like Bonne Chance, only somewhat larger with a high roof that extended over the gallery. A torch flared on the dock that extended out into the river, and a pirogue could be seen tied up to one of the cypress posts.

Caresse mused that Philippe Dubrieul had arrived at his plantation before them. Had he passed them as they stopped at Bonne Chance?

"Soon we will be at Sans Regret. I sent word ahead—with one of the supply boats leaving before us—that I would be returning with my bride this evening," Lucien told her in a gentler tone of voice, pulling his gaze away from the river to face her. "I can only hope they received the message, and Zoé was able to ready the house for our arrival. Although the drums probably sounded the message from plantation to plantation long before the keelboat arrived. We French pretend not to notice that news travels faster on the slave grapevine than by any other method."

His mood had once more made the kind of abrupt change that Caresse had begun to notice was typical of her husband. It was always disconcerting to her, but she tried not to show how it unnerved her.

"I am anxious to see Sans Regret, for the miniature in the locket you gave me was lovely. It seems impossible that such an elegant house could exist out here in such wilderness," Caresse replied, as her heart skipped a beat at the touch of his hand on her waist. The long shadows of twilight falling across the river gave them some privacy which Lucien was quick to take advantage of. He held her in a loose embrace as they watched the alabaster sphere of the moon cast a wide silvery beam across the dark waters of the Mississippi.

"My father contracted with a master builder, a free man of color, to construct the house on the

125

land grant he had been given along the Mississippi River. With the help of slaves, it took him three years to build the house that was intended as a sanctuary for my mother. We lived in Nouvelle Orléans till it was ready, although I remember little of that time. I was four years old when we moved to Sans Regret. It has always been home to me, as strong and enduring as my father seemed to me as a child."

Remembering what Dominique had told her of Lucien's childhood, and his poor mother's deranged mind, Caresse was filled with sadness for the young boy, and the strong caring Jacques St. Amant who had built a beautiful refuge for a woman he loved, a woman who could never be a complete companion to him despite his loving care.

Then, as if conjured up by her melancholy thoughts of its past history, they rounded a bend in the river and saw the flambeau of the dock of Sans Regret plantation. From somewhere a bell began to toll as the slaves fought the river's current to push them toward the cypress wharf.

Strong dark hands were reaching out for the ropes of the keelboat as they moved close to the wharf. A tall raw-boned white man dressed in rough clothes stood giving orders to the slaves in German-accented French. Through the arching branches of the giant live oaks, lights could be seen through the open French doors of the house that led onto the second-story gallery.

"Helmut, may I present my bride, Mme Marie-Caresse St. Amant," Lucien said as he helped Caresse from the gangplank of the keelboat to the wooden boards of the dock. "*Ma chère*, this is our overseer, Helmut Zweig."

"*Enchanté*, Mme St. Amant," the tall sandy-haired man said, removing his battered tricorn and giving a stiff bow. But as he raised his head to look into her face, illuminated in the flare of one of the flaming torches, his ice blue eyes widened and his ruddy face whitened.

"How kind of you to arrange a welcome for us, M. Zweig," Caresse said, giving him a slight smile, as she felt a knot form in her stomach. She knew what caused that expression of shock, and then confusion, on the overseer's rough features. He had been here when Aurore was alive, and he had thought for a moment that she was Aurore returned from the grave.

"Dominique, Zoé says that she has everything in order," the overseer said, turning with relief to the slender housekeeper as she stepped off the gangplank carrying Blanchette in her covered basket.

"I will put the basket in the kitchen house so the *petit chat* can have something to eat, then I will bring her to your chamber, *madame,*" Dominique told Caresse as she stopped beside her.

Caresse nodded her thanks, then turned toward her husband as he held out his arm to escort her down the levee and up the crushed shell path through the trees to her new home. The moon shone down through the interlaced branches of the gnarled oaks, turning the shells alabaster and gilding the hanging festoons of moss till they appeared to be silver lace sweeping down to the long grass. The heady perfume of tea olive and jasmine drifted on the sultry night air to surround them like an embrace. It only added to the sensuous, strange atmosphere that was Sans Regret in the moonlight.

"There is all the long glorious night ahead of us to savor what was so hurried this morning," Lucien said in a low composed voice, with just an edge of uncontrolled passion, as they approached the imposing structure that was Sans Regret.

Caresse looked up at him with a shy smile, before turning her attention to the elegant house where she would now be the *chatelaine*. It was built in the style of the French West Indies, with the main floor raised, and the ground floor used for storage rooms, warming kitchen, wine cellars, and summer dining room. Thick pillars reached to the second floor where narrow colonnettes soared to the high roof that extended far out over a wide gallery to provide shade. Small doll-sized dormers, in front of tall brick chimneys, peered out from the high massive roof, the moonlight reflecting in the many-paned windows, making them appear to glow like the eyes of wild creatures of the swamp.

" 'Tis lovely, *mon cher.* I can understand why you enjoyed growing up here. There is a sense of enduring strength as well as elegance about the house," Caresse told him as they reached the first-floor gallery with its carefully laid brick floor. She did not say what else she thought about the house. There was also a sense of isolation, with the forbidding cypress swamp waiting at the edge of the cleared fields. She felt a slight shiver run up her spine as she stepped on the bricks of the first floor gallery. Was this where Aurore had fallen from the gallery above to break her neck on the moss-covered stones?

"What is it?" Lucien demanded, a sharp edge to his voice, as his arm tightened about her waist.

"What do you mean?" Caresse answered lightly, realizing that she had allowed her uneasiness to show on her face.

"For a moment you looked frightened," he replied, watching her intently in the light from the open door of the warming kitchen.

"Nonsense," she said, giving a slight shrug of her delicate shoulders. "Did I not tell you I am not easily frightened? I have experienced terrors you would never comprehend," she continued, and this time there was bitterness in her soft voice.

"Forgive me, I did not mean to cast a shadow on our first night at Sans Regret," Lucien apologized as he guided her past the warming kitchen

128

to the back of the house, where an impressive double stairway rose to the second floor.

The side of the house facing the river was considered the back, allowing an unimpeded view of the Mississippi from the rooms opening onto the gallery. Close to the house she could see it was built of plastered masonry over brick tinted a pale yellow, the long shutters at the French doors and windows a gleaming dark green.

There was much activity in front of the double staircase for this was where the kitchen gardens were located, neatly planted rows behind picket fences, as well as the *dépendances* located a distance from the house, containing the kitchen house, slave cabins for the house servants, a wash house, smokehouse, stables, sheds for storing indigo, and a cabin where the slaves' clothes were sewn and household mending took place. Lucien explained the purpose of each building as they paused at the foot of the curving staircase. Further away through the trees, Caresse could see the fires from the slave cabins.

It was as Lucien escorted her up the graceful curving staircase to the second floor, where the family living quarters were located, that Caresse heard the murmurs from the house servants, and felt their eyes staring at her back. She knew what they were saying, could feel their stunned surprise as they stared after her. In the dim light of the moon her resemblance to their former mistress must be all the more remarkable. Their uneasiness, their fear, was palpable in the still humid air. What were they seeing? Was it the ghost of their former mistress, Aurore St. Amant?

Reaching the top of the staircase and the wide gallery, Caresse turned in surprise to Lucien, for there was no central hall in the house. Each chamber seemed to open into the next, and those along the gallery all had French doors that opened to the covered walkway.

" 'Tis typical of planter's houses in the West Indies, and in La Louisiane, to have no central hall, but to have rooms arranged *en enfilade*, one leading into another. The arrangement does not waste space, and allows circulation of air, although it does not always guarantee privacy," Lucien explained, a wry twist to his sensuous mouth.

"I am sure I will get used to it," Caresse replied with a wan smile. It all seemed so strange and exotic, like the land of which it was a part. Fatigue seemed to descend upon her in waves. The day had been long, and all the activity in the humid heat had drained her of energy. And while Sans Regret seemed an unusual and elegant house, its very strangeness was just one more element in a tiring day of new experiences.

"You are exhausted. Forgive me, *ma chère*, we shall go immediately to our bedchamber where you can rest till we are ready to dine," Lucien said, sensing that she could not cope with anything more. With his arm about her waist, he led her firmly through the large high-ceilinged *salle de compagnie* or parlor. Long French doors opened to the gallery that faced the river.

Caresse was aware of an elegantly furnished chamber that might have been in a chateau in France, before Lucien swept her into their bedchamber that opened off of it. This room also faced the river. Through another open door she could see a *cabinet de toilette*, a dressing room, and beyond that an even smaller room, a *salle de bain*, with a wondrous marble bathing tub in the center.

"I see you have discovered the talk of La Louisiane, Sans Regret's famous white marble bathing tub," Lucien commented, a sparkle in his midnight black eyes.

"The queen does not have such a magnificent bathing chamber," Caresse said with a light laugh, deep dimples appearing beside her smiling mouth.

"I know now I shall enjoy our sojourns at Sans Regret."

"I hope you will find even more reasons to enjoy staying here with me." His voice was a husky promise of sensual delights to come.

Suddenly there was a clicking sound on the wooden floors and a large dark object hurled through the open French door. Caresse turned to see the largest, most ungainly creature she had ever seen come bounding across the threshold. The dog threw himself against his master, his long pink tongue lolling out of his fierce-looking mouth.

"This has to be Bruno," Caresse laughed, holding out her hand so the curious canine could smell her scent. The dog circled her, sniffing as if to make sure who, and what she was, as Caresse stood still speaking in a low voice to the wary dog. Finally, the creature lay down at her feet, looking up at her with soulful dark eyes that seemed to beg her to pet his shaggy head. With gentle, yet firm, strokes, she rubbed his head and then behind his floppy ears, and down his chest. Slowly the dog relaxed and rolled over so she could stroke his stomach.

"Wherever did you learn that? He took right to you, and Bruno does not take to everyone. I traded two copper cooking pots for him when he was a pup at a Choctaw village on the other side of Lake Pontchartrain. He has always been a bit wild, but I have never seen him take to anyone like he has to you," Lucien said in amazement.

"Let us pray he feels the same about Blanchette," Caresse said wryly, wondering how the kitten was taking to the kitchen house. She had seen nothing of Dominique since they had reached the mansion.

"Perhaps she can charm him as his mistress has done. If the slaves see how easily you tamed him they will think you have special powers," he joked, not realizing that one of the maids stood in the

131

doorway carrying a copper jug of water for washing.

Caresse, however, saw the young woman, and also saw the expression of fright in her large dark eyes as she stared back at her. She knew that the girl had seen her taming of the dog and that she also was stunned by her resemblance to her former mistress. Once more fatigue swept over Caresse as she remembered the reason Lucien had married her, and why he took such delight in seeing her at Sans Regret.

"Come in, Fantine. This is your new mistress," Lucien told the frightened young woman as she walked with hesitant steps into the chamber. *"Ma chère,* this is Fantine, the housemaid. She is Zoé's daughter.

" 'Tis a pleasure to meet you, Fantine. If you would, put the water in the *salon de bain,* and fetch me some towels. I would like to freshen up before dinner."

"Oui . . . madame. There are always linen towels kept in the armoire in the *salon de bain,"* she answered, walking in an odd stiff gate across the bedchamber and through the dressing room to the small bathing chamber.

"Why do they stare at me so?" Caresse suddenly asked Lucien, determined to hear her husband admit that she resembled Aurore.

She was tired of all the pretense and could not help but feel angry that he had not told her the truth after their marriage. But why? She had not expected him to be in love with her. She had been reared to expect an arranged marriage where her husband was selected by her father for reasons of wealth and family. If love occurred after marriage then they were lucky; if not, after several sons were born, she would be free to take lovers discreetly, and her husband would have probably already taken a mistress or two. But then, she thought, she had not expected to fall so in love with this man who had seemed in the convent to be only a solution to her predicament. And now somehow she had allowed herself to become obsessed with the long-dead Aurore. What did it matter if he had married her because she looked like another, as long as it enabled her to escape her bleak future? She was Mme St. Amant of Sans Regret plantation. No one from France could reach her in this God-forsaken wilderness, even the king and his courtiers did not care what happened in the colony of La Louisiane.

"What is it, *chère*?" Lucien had come to stand in front of her as Fantine left the chamber. He had cupped her tiny soft chin in his two fingers, forcing her to look up at him.

"You did not answer me," she replied.

"They are interested in the new mistress, the new *châtelaine*. They try to figure out what kind of mistress you will be, kind or not, strict or not. 'Tis only curiosity," he reassured her, but he could see in those trusting, sad eyes that she did not believe him.

He could never tell her the truth, never admit that he was capable of such weakness. How could he confess that he had been drawn to her because of her resemblance to Aurore before discovering that she was infinitely more intriguing? He sensed she had a strength that had been lacking in his first wife, a strength that made him uneasy. There were many secrets at Sans Regret, secrets he did not want discovered.

Lucien wondered what he had done in marrying a woman like Caresse, bringing her to the plantation. But he knew deep in his soul that he had been lost from the first moment he had seen her. He had never believed in love at first sight until now, until he met Marie-Caresse de Villier. His own sentimentality had filled him with disgust, but it had changed nothing. His obsession had grown

133

since that first day, and he feared it would only grow stronger with time. He must never let her know his feelings for her. Had he not learned what loving a woman could do? Never, he thought, would he allow that to happen again.

"Are you sure that is all?" Caresse insisted coolly, one arched brow lifted in question.

"What else could there be, *ma chère?*" he murmured, bending to kiss the throbbing pulse point at the base of her throat. A quickening of desire shot through her being.

"I . . . I think that is something only you could tell me," she managed to whisper, trying to fight her own traitorous body's reaction to his seduction. Always it was like this between them. The passion, the hunger, would wipe away all rational thought, all conversation that was not expression of desire and need.

The soft sound of slippers on the wooden floor of the gallery outside the open French door caused them to draw slowly, reluctantly, apart. A quick courteous knock on the opened door wakened them from the hazy dream of sensuality that had enfolded them.

"Pardonnez-moi, m'sieur, but the overseer wishes to see you," Dominique apologized, gliding into the room at Lucien's command. "He said 'tis serious trouble in the quarters."

"I see," Lucien replied, his voice short as his eyes met those of Dominique's for a brief glance of understanding. "Make your *toilette, ma chère,* and when I return we shall dine on the gallery. 'Tis cooler and the view of the river on a moonlit night is quite lovely," he told Caresse, lifting her hand to his lips for a brief touch. Then without a backward glance, he strode from the chamber, Bruno at his heels, his tall dark form silhouetted for a moment in the moonlight flooding the gallery—then he was gone.

"I shall unpack a gown of your choosing, *madame*," Dominique said to Caresse, crossing the room to where her trunk stood. "Then I shall pour water in the basin and you can wash away the heat of the journey as I take the gown to the laundry house for a pressing. The *petit chat* is having her dinner in the kitchen house."

"What is wrong, Dominique? I can feel the tension in the air," Caresse interrupted her as she opened the large trunk.

"*Madame*, the slaves . . . the slaves practice their own religion from West Africa, and from Saint-Dominigue. Your presence has upset them," Dominique explained, her back turned as she lifted a light blue silk gown from the trunk.

"Why would my presence upset them, Dominique?" Caresse insisted, knowing it would confirm what she had felt since she had walked up the curving staircase.

"Your resemblance, *madame*, to the first mistress—to Aurore St. Amant," she said softly, turning to look at Caresse with a strange look in her eyes.

"And this upsets them so that my husband must speak with them?" Caresse asked, her voice catching on the words.

"*Oui, madame*, they believe the ghost of Aurore St. Amant has returned to Sans Regret, or that your husband's power is so strong he has raised the dead from her grave."

It was as she stared back at Dominique in despair that she thought she smelled the faint scent of violets drifting in to the bedchamber on the sultry night air.

Nine

Silver streams of moonlight slanted through the arched boughs of the live oak trees, bathing the gallery of Sans Regret, and the man and woman seated at the elegantly set table, with a ghostly light. They watched in silence as a mosquito circled the glass hurricane chimney that protected the wavering light of the taper in the center of the lace-draped table. The sultry night air caressed them as they stared across the shadowy lawn that led to the rushing waters of the Mississippi. The soft air was perfumed with the fragrance of the jasmine bush that had grown to an enormous height beside the corner of the house. It was the perfect romantic setting. But the gallery was haunted by old memories, by the remembered presence of one long dead but somehow there still, watching the new mistress of Sans Regret.

Caresse lifted her long-stemmed wine glass to her lips. She was drinking more than usual, but the atmosphere of the house wore on her nerves. It was an elegant oasis in the middle of the wild swamp that pressed on all sides. But the beautiful house, like the swamp, seemed to Caresse like a living being, harboring secrets, waiting for her to make a false step. She felt a slight shiver at her foolish fantasy, and sipped the cool dry wine to quench her thirst and give her courage to face her first night as the *chatelaine* of Sans Regret.

"What is it, *ma chère?*" Lucien's deep voice inquired, startling her so that her hand shook and a few drops of wine spilled on the cloth.

"What do you mean?" she replied, placing the glass with care on the table.

"I am happy that you approve of my choice of wine, but I do not think I have ever seen you indulge quite as much as you have tonight. And as you have not eaten much of Zoé's delicious food, I sensed that something was bothering you," he replied, placing the heavy silver-embossed knife and fork on the delicate china plate. His penetrating eyes pierced the distance across the table, not allowing her to look away.

"The . . . trouble in the quarters . . . were you able to quiet their fears?" Caresse asked hesitantly, returning his gaze.

"This is what is bothering you?" he asked, reaching across the table to take her hand in his long slender fingers.

"There is much about living on a plantation that is strange to me, but I sensed the unease in the atmosphere about the house, and among the servants," Caresse told him. She was determined to make him realize she wasn't a foolish young woman who could have her head so turned by a display of elegance and wealth that she would overlook everything else.

"The Africans have their own religion, their own beliefs. They are very different from us, but you will come to understand them as you spend more time at Sans Regret," Lucien explained in quiet reassuring tones. He stroked her hand, his intense gaze mesmerizing her till she could think of nothing but the feel of his touch, the memory of what it felt like to have those knowing fingers caress the burning skin of her body.

"It seems I have much to learn," she managed to respond, despite the ache of longing that his touch was kindling in her veins.

"And how I shall enjoy instructing you," he said slyly as he lifted her hand to his heated mouth.

This time it was a delightful shiver of desire, instead of fear, that shook her slender form as he circled his tongue in her soft palm, then took one tiny finger into his mouth, sucking it in a light sensual motion that caused explosive currents of longing to race through her. Her sigh drifted on the soft currents of night air like the circling gray smoke from the taper.

The hazy cloud of desire was blotting out all fear, all questions from her mind. There was only the splendid sensation of awakening desire filling her mind and heart with the promise of delight beyond imagining. The moonlight through the trees that had seemed eerie before was now a lovely romantic glow.

"Come, we shall retire for the night," Lucien commanded, keeping her hand clasped in his as he rose to his feet. With a quick forceful movement, he pulled her up and against him.

She felt his lips move over hers, demanding a response as he clasped her against him, her silk gown swaying with the force of his embrace. Her arms lifted and wrapped around his neck as she sank into the warmth of his embrace. Within the circle of his arms, she could forget her fears. But as her lips opened under his, she felt a rush of cool air brush past them, and heard a low growl from Bruno sprawled a few feet away.

Lucien stiffened as the sound of a hand running over the keys of the harpsichord in the salon drifted out to them from the open French door. It was only a moment, then all was silent, but it was enough to pull him away from Caresse.

"What was that?" she asked, realizing with a start that she was whispering.

"Wait here," he ordered, moving swiftly past the now-alert Bruno toward the open door of the salon.

The atmosphere was once more heavy with mystery and hidden menace. The cool whirl of air had vanished as quickly as it had come. There was only the steamy heat of the night surrounding her as she stood waiting on the gallery, but for what she did not know.

Suddenly, she could not stand to be alone. It was too frightening. She moved quickly to the open French door of the salon and Lucien.

Pausing in the doorway, she peered into the gloom, for there were only two lit tapers on the marble mantel of the fireplace across the chamber from where she stood. Lucien stood, his back to her, at the keyboard of the gilded harpsichord.

He turned at the sound of her step and muttered one word in a voice raw with despair. "Aurore!"

"Non," she managed to answer through her pain, " 'tis Caresse, your wife."

He moved toward her, his eyes burning coals of some unreadable emotion. His hands reached out to clasp her head between them, tilting her pale visage up to him. His burning gaze traveled over her delicate features as if to reassure himself that it was, indeed, she who stood before him.

"Never leave me," he commanded, his voice a harsh rasp, his eyes glittering feverishly. "Swear it!"

"I . . . I swear I shall never leave you," she repeated as his fingers pressed into her soft skin. This was some frightening stranger who stood in front of her demanding allegiance.

With a swiftness that took her breath away, he swept her up into his arms and strode through the open door holding her tight against him. Her head buried in the hollow of his neck, she could feel the

139

rapid beating of his heart as he carried her into their bedchamber, Bruno at his heels.

The chamber was lit by a single taper on the delicate bedside table. Lucien's pace never slackened till he reached the bed. Carefully he placed her on her feet, stripping the gown from her body with a practiced hand that told Caresse she was not the first woman he had undressed. He had spoken not a word since his command in the salon, but his hands and mouth spoke a language all their own as each part of her body was revealed.

The moan that escaped her throat was a mixture of apprehension and desire. Never had Lucien seemed more of a stranger than he did as his mouth traced the path of his hands on her throbbing breasts, the planes and hollows of her back, as he stripped the garments from her trembling body. Her limbs obeyed the gestures of his firm insistent hands as he motioned for her to step out of her gown and petticoats, her corset and chemise following like leaves tossed in the wind.

He was a man possessed as he knelt down to slip the satin slippers from her feet. Her breath caught in her throat as he began to peel the silk stockings from her slender legs, his lips kissing, caressing, the tender inner thigh, the hollow of her knee.

A stream of alabaster moonlight shone in through the lace panels of the French door and fell across the long pier glass tilted in its rosewood stand. Caresse saw the figure of a woman standing in front of a kneeling man, his mouth pressed against the soft ivory of her belly. She was stunned to realize that those were her hands entwined in the ebony silk of his hair pressing him to her, that it was her nude form that arched up to him, seeking every nuance of his skilled seduction.

The reflection of the wanton woman in the silvered glass filled her with a strange inner excitement. It was as if a mask had been torn away to reveal a part of her that had been repressed, but now in this strange house was allowed to break free under the tutelage of the master of Sans Regret.

Then a cloud passed across the opal sphere riding low in the night sky, blotting out the tableau of passion in the pier glass. There was only the wavering circle of light from the tall taper in the darkened chamber, scented now with the perfume of lilies from Caresse's heated body. She was all fire and flame from the touch and taste of Lucien. Fears and questions had fled under the intensity of the desire he had aroused within her—all that mattered was sensation.

He rose to his feet, towering over her, and quickly stripped the clothing from his own lean form, holding her immobile by the power of his gaze. There was something savage in those burning, relentless black eyes that reached the hidden depths within her. It was this part of her that responded to the pure need she saw reflected in those dark depths.

Taking her hand, he drew her to the four-poster as the moon slipped from behind the cloud to stream once more into the chamber. The filmy netting of the mosquito *barre* surrounded the bed like a mist at Lucien's quick pull on the velvet rope. Then they were entwined on the soft linen sheets, sinewy masculine thigh wrapped around slender feminine limb.

Her delicate fingers pulled the ribbon loose from his queue allowing his hair to fall across her hands as she arched her breast up to his seeking mouth. A gasp of pleasure filled the sultry night as his tongue circled the taut rose peak that throbbed for his touch. His firm hands allowed her no escape from his heated mouth, from the intensity of his need.

Caresse did not seek escape, for she wanted to experience every sensation that Lucien was eliciting from her newly awakened body. The loneliness, the desolation, was gone, vanished in the splendid solace of his embrace.

"My beautiful wife," he murmured as his lips sought the hollow of her throat, then moved upward to claim her mouth in a deep drugging kiss that was balm to her aching heart.

Nothing could ever harm her as long as he was with her. Here in his strong arms she had found her refuge, her calm port in the terrible stormy seas of her life.

When his knowing fingers gently stroked open her thighs, she trembled with anticipation for the rapture yet to come. She wanted to join with him completely once again, finding physical release as her spirit soared to the pinnacle of life's sweetest mystery.

As he rose over her, his breath caught in his throat, for the moonlight shining on her hair seemed to imbue it with its silver glow. The soft gray of her eyes reflected such trust, such love, that it tore open the fortress that he had built around his heart.

"Mon Dieu!" he gasped as he fought for control.

"Mon cher, 'tis all right to feel," she whispered, reaching up to brush away the blue-black lock of hair that fell across his brow.

Her understanding of his emotion, her sweet tenderness, shook him to the depths of his soul. "I must have you, now. I can wait no longer," he told her, his voice full of such stark need that it almost frightened her.

Her eyes never leaving his, she wrapped her legs around his. Draping her arms around his neck, she arched her hips as his moan of conquest echoed in the perfumed air.

At his first thrust she flinched, frightened at his intensity. Then as he surged inside her moist depths she surrendered and gloried in her submission. Heated mouth on heated mouth, skin against skin, two hearts beating in harmony, they soared higher and higher, bathed in the light of the moon that had caressed so many lovers since time began, till they reached their summit. With mingled cries of fulfillment, they found their release and knew the peace of joined bodies and souls.

They slept in loose embrace, the deep slumber of the exhausted. So deeply did they sleep that the storm was long raging outside before the fury of the wind, and the driving of the rain, woke them. Bruno had moved under the protection of the high bed to escape the wind that had blown the French doors wide, allowing the rain into the chamber.

Lucien's heavy eyelids reluctantly opened at the crash of thunder and the flash of lightning. Caresse stirred from his chest, as he pulled the sheet up about her shoulders. Slipping from the bed, and out of the mosquito netting, he strode through the darkened chamber toward the French doors now swinging back and forth in the fury of the storm.

As he shut them against the rain, he saw a pale strip of light on the eastern horizon that told him, despite the darkness of the storm, it was near dawn. His rising from the four-poster had roused Bruno. With great reluctance the dog crawled from his dry sanctuary under the bed. It was then that Lucien saw something in his mouth.

"Here, give that to me, boy," he called softly to the dog. With a reluctant whine, Bruno dropped what appeared to be a chicken-leg bone on the straw matting that covered the cypress boards of the floor in summer. "Good dog," he muttered, giving the shaggy animal a scratch behind the ears.

A jagged flash of lightning lit the chamber with enough light to confirm to Lucien that it was the bone of a chicken that Bruno had found under the bed. His nostrils flared with fury, and his eyes were black ice as he stared down at the bone. He knew what it meant. Chicken bones were used to cast spells in the Africans' religion, spells that were meant to cause harm. Someone at Sans Regret had placed them under the bed to ward off the evil that they thought was Caresse.

"What is it?" the soft feminine voice inquired from the four-poster as if his thoughts had called to her.

"Nothing," he replied evenly, turning his back to her and crossing to an enormous armoire that stood against one wall. Pulling the carved door open, he quickly placed the dried bone on the shelf, determined not to raise any more questions in his wife's mind. Slipping a gold silk robe from the padded hanger, he wrapped it around his tall lean form. Then crossing to the fireplace, he struck a lucifer stick kept in a tin box and proceeded to light the two tall tapers under their glass hurricane globes.

"It appears your first day at Sans Regret will be a rainy one," he said, carrying one candlestick to the bedside table to replace the taper that had burned to a melted pool during the night.

"What is that fragrance?" Caresse asked, her delicate nostrils inhaling a scent that she had smelled only once before. It had clung to the cloak given her by the stranger who had visited her cell in Paris. Never would she forget it, for it still clung faintly to the cloak that lay at the bottom of her *cassette*.

"The scent of the myrtle candles comes from the berries used in making the wax. The bushes grow in great abundance at Sans Regret," he replied. "We use them to make the candles that we export to France. You will in time come to associate the scent with the plantation."

144

"Non, I know the scent of the candles. This is different, a woodsy fragrance," she insisted as he pulled the bell rope that connected with one downstairs in the warming kitchen. It was dawn. One of the kitchen maids should be adding wood to the small fireplace where food was kept warm when it was brought from the kitchen house at the end of the garden. The first pot of hot strong rich coffee should be dripping for the morning's breakfast. A pot would be maintained all through the day, for in the enervating heat and humidity the energizing effects of the strong coffee were often sought by both master and slave during the day's activities.

"There," she said as he pulled back the *barre* to sit beside her on the bed. " 'Tis clinging to your robe!"

"Ah, *ma chère,* I understand now," he gave a slight smile as he brushed a lock of hair from her cheek. "What you smell is vetivert. It comes from the vetivert root. The dried roots are put in the corners of the armoires to protect against mildew and to scent the clothing instead of lavender—'tis too hot and humid here to grow lavender."

"Then it is used throughout La Louisiane?" Caresse inquired, biting her lower lip as she thought of the significance of what Lucien was telling her.

"And the West Indies as well," he answered, pulling her into the circle of his arm as he reclined against the headboard. "But did not the good Soeur Xavier explain the use of the vetivert root to you when you helped her in the convent garden?"

"The nuns did not use sachet to scent their garments," Caresse reminded him with a wry twist to her mouth.

"Of course not," he said, with an answering smile at his error. But then, he thought ruefully, he was not too familiar with the lives of nuns. His experience had been with more worldly women.

"Have you ever been to Paris?" Caresse asked

145

softly, pulling back so that he was forced to look down at her that she might see the expression in his eyes.

"Paris? But why do you ask, *ma chère?*" he replied with an edge to his voice.

"I wondered if perhaps I might have seen you there. Perhaps passed you in the street, totally unaware that someday we would be husband and wife," she answered with a shrug, waiting with her heart in her throat to see if Lucien was the stranger who had been her savior that cold day in La Salpêtrière prison.

" 'Tis a romantic thought, *ma chère,* but were you not from Lyon?" There was a guarded look to his handsome visage, and distrust chilled his dark eyes.

"I . . . I have been to Paris several times with my father to . . . deliver special silk to the shops there," she stammered, flinching before his cool watchful expression.

"You have had many experiences for one so young," he continued in the cold, remote tone that chilled her blood.

"*Oui,* I have," she said with a catch in her voice.

"Forgive me, *ma pauvre petite,*" he told her softly, lifting her cold fingers to his warm lips. "I did not want to bring back any memory of past pain. 'Tis over, behind you. La Louisiane and Sans Regret are a new beginning. Let us put the past where it belongs. We shall never speak of it again, unless you wish to tell me. I shall always listen." His dark eyes were once more warm as he placed a tender kiss on the tip of her nose as if she was a child.

A brief knock on the door silenced her reply as Lucien called for the servant to enter. He pushed her pillow behind her shoulders as Fantine walked into the chamber carrying a white wicker tray, kicking the door shut behind her with her foot.

"*Alà vous café,*" she announced in her soft patois, her tignon tied with precision about her elegant

146

head, her spotless apron crackling from the stiff starch. She approached the bed with a shy smile. The rich scent of piping-hot coffee filled the air from the silver pot on the tray. *"Bonjour, m'sieur et madame,"* she greeted them as she pulled back the *barre*.

"Bonjour, Fantine," Lucien replied as she placed the large tray in front of them.

As he asked the maid a few questions about the weather and the grounds of the plantation, Caresse poured the dark hot coffee into the eggshell-thin porcelain cups. She realized suddenly that Lucien had never told her if he had been to Paris. Somehow he had turned the conversation around so that she had been distracted by her slip in revealing that she had spent time in Paris. He had outwitted her this time, but she was determined to find out the truth. If he had, indeed, been her mysterious stranger, why was he keeping it a secret? She gave a shiver in the cool damp, for since coming to Sans Regret she had found not a refuge, but a shadowy house full of secrets. Deciding the hot coffee would banish her fears, she lifted the cup to her lips. It was as she did so that she saw the tiny flowers painted under the gold rim. They were violets, Aurore's favorite flower.

She felt her stomach churn as she sipped the coffee. It was foolish, she knew, to let such a small detail bother her, but she could not help it. Everywhere she looked, there were reminders of Aurore.

"Are you all right?" Lucien questioned after requesting that Fantine have water be brought for bathing.

"A slight chill is all. The storm has cooled the air so after such heat," Caresse told him. "The coffee is delicious and so warming."

"You seemed far away, *ma chère*. I was concerned

147

that you were still brooding over the past," he said, clasping her hand in his firm fingers.

"The past is behind us, remember," she chided him gently as she slipped her hand from his to lift the cup to her mouth.

Today, she vowed, she would begin to put her mark on Sans Regret as Lucien's wife, and the new *chatelaine*. She had an uneasy premonition that the ghost of Aurore would be difficult to erase no matter how strong her determination. But erase it she would, for she was Lucien's wife, and she wanted to banish Aurore's ghost from the house and from his mind. With all her heart and soul she wanted him to forget her.

Part Two

I seemed to move among a world of ghosts,
And feel myself the shadow of a dream.
                    Alfred, Lord Tennyson, "Oenone"

Suspicion begets suspicion.
                    Publius Syrus, *Moral Sayings*

Ten

Sans Regret Plantation
October 1749

The long golden streams of autumn sunlight shone down on the kitchen garden through the spreading branches of the giant live oaks. Caresse stood next to a carefully cultivated bed of vegetables pointing out to a small African boy which peppers and herbs she wished him to pick for the evening's meal. Taking a scrap of linen and lace from the deep pocket in her skirt, she wiped the moisture from her upper lip.

"When does it get cooler?" she asked the boy as he carefully walked between the rows of vegetables and herbs, the handle of a split-oak basket over his arm.

"Not for many weeks, *madame*," he replied.

Caresse sighed, for he was only confirming what Lucien had already told her. In France the trees would be touched with color, and the mornings would be frosty, but here in La Louisiane the heat was as intense as summer. Dominique had reassured her that by the following autumn she would become acclimated to the heat and humidity. She had said it took most of the new French settlers at least that long to learn to endure the climate. Sometimes Caresse thought she would not survive another day, let alone another year.

"Sylvan, I think I shall sit on the bench for a few minutes," Caresse told the young slave as she felt one of her dizzy spells coming over her. Sinking down on the cypress bench under the low branches of the verdant oak, she sighed, realizing that she had still not regained her strength from the bout of fever that had struck the second day after her arrival at Sans Regret. Dominique and Lucien had taken turns nursing her through the delirium that she had thought, during her few moments of clarity, would kill her. Although she had recovered, it had left her weak and prone to light-headedness.

"You want that I fetch Dominique?" the young slave called out before bending down to pick the basil leaves.

" 'Tis not necessary," she reassured him, wiping her brow with the damp handkerchief. The depression that had been her constant companion since the fever broke, once more threatened to overwhelm her. Lucien had explained that melancholy was often a side effect of the fever, that it would disappear when she had fully regained her strength. How she hoped he was right.

Staring across the garden toward the twin curving staircase of the elegant house, she thought how all her plans of asserting her position as *chatelaine* had come to naught. It had been over two months since they had arrived at Sans Regret, and she had spent most of her days delirious with fever or convalescing slowly on the chaise placed for her on the gallery facing the river. But she had been luckier then many in Nouvelle Orléans. The news of the heavy death toll had traveled from the stricken city up the river to the settlements and plantations. Death always seemed close in La Louisiane. If not from disease then from Indian attack, poisonous snakes, or tainted food left to spoil in the heat. 'Twas a savage Eden, this Louisiane, Caresse mused. Had she the strength to live in this fierce wilderness? Somehow she had to find it, for she knew that despite everything her destiny lay here with Lucien. France was a half-forgotten dream.

"*Ma chère*, are you sure you should be out here in the sun?" Her husband's deep voice came from behind her.

"I am feeling much better," she said, turning to see him hand the reins of his stallion to a groom. Allowing herself the pleasure of watching his long lithe stride as he came toward her, she felt the pounding of her pulse and the familiar fluttering in her stomach that she felt seeing him even if he had only been gone a few minutes.

"I hope you are not pushing yourself because of our guests. Dominique can see to everything. If the Marquis and the Marquise de Vaudreuil were not his house guests, and now to be ours, I would have never consented to have Philippe Dubrieul. I detest the man, but there is business I wish to discuss with the governor, and when he requests a visit I can not refuse if I want to continue to ship indigo to France. I do not, however, want their visit to wear you out," he said tenderly as he sat down beside her.

"Although I would rather we were having Yvonne and Pierre as our first guests, it will give me a chance to play the role of *châtelaine* for the first time," she said with a smile that shone even out of her sad gray eyes.

"You need not play the role, *ma chère*, you *are* the *châtelaine* of Sans Regret," he told her, his voice husky with emotion.

"I wish to assume all my roles as your wife," she murmured, her silky voice a promise that set his heart pounding.

"How long I have waited to hear those words," he breathed, lifting her hand to his lips for a brief brush across her palm with his lips.

A flash of memory from the long days of her illness flickered at the edge of her mind. She seemed to see those burning orbs staring out at her from an overwhelming darkness, only the wavering light from a faraway candle behind them to lighten the blackness.

"You promised not to leave me," that magnetic voice had called to her. She had clung to that anchor in her sea of pain, and somehow she had found her way out of the darkness.

"I, too, have waited far too long," she murmured, caressing his face in a gesture that told him she hungered for more.

"If it was not so near to the hour when our guests are to arrive, I should carry you up those stairs to our chamber despite the eyes of the servants and the overseer," he told her, each word a sensual picture that sent a tingle of warmth up her spine.

"I shall remember that the boring evening ahead is a promise of what is to come," she teased him lightly, a shudder of delight running through her at the circle he made with his tongue on the sensitive palm of her hand.

Only the ringing of the wharf bell signaling an arriving boat broke the sensual spell they had woven around the cypress bench in the shadows of the live oak. They rose to walk around the house and down the *allée* between the oaks to the dock on the Mississippi River.

"I believe our guests are early," Lucien commented. "Philippe's note said that they would not arrive till sundown. Perhaps the governor and his wife have become bored with Dubrieul's company. Solange is notorious for her short attention span."

Caresse glanced at her husband from under the

wide brim of her hat. She had forgotten that Solange Vaudreuil, the governor's wife, considered Lucien an intimate of the elite social circle that made up the governor's court. How close had Lucien and Solange de Vaudreuil really been, Caresse wondered with a tinge of jealousy. She knew the dissolute Marquise de Vaudreuil was infamous for her flirtations with young handsome men, men often much younger than the middle-aged Solange. Had Lucien been one of those men the governor's wife called her *beaux cavaliers*? He had confessed his past was less than exemplary, but had that past included an affair with the dissipated Solange?

From down the *allée* came the hurrying form of Helmut Zweig accompanied by one of the male slaves. His pale face was flushed, and there was a strange look in his blue eyes.

"M. St. Amant, there's a pirogue of Choctaws landing," the German overseer gasped as he reached them. A renegade group of Choctaws, friendly to the British, had attacked the German settlements above them on the river only months before, driving some of the farmers from their farms and killing others who stayed behind.

"Did they give any sign why they had come to Sans Regret?" Lucien asked calmly.

"The leader could speak a little *français*," Helmut Zweig replied, trying to catch his breath. "He said he wanted to speak to Jacques's right hand. I swear that is what he said. I know it makes no sense, but I asked that he repeat it." The overseer shook his head, wiping his sweating brow with the back of his shirt-sleeved forearm.

"*Au contraire*, it makes perfect sense," Lucien said with a glow of warmth in his dark eyes. " 'Tis Nashoba, the son of my father's friend, a Choctaw chief. I am Jacques's Right Hand, and that is how I was known in their village," he explained to Caresse and the overseer. "Come, I wish you to meet

155

him," he said, turning to Caresse. "Do you feel like walking to the wharf? They will make their camp there, and will refuse to come up to the house."

"*Oui,* certainly," Caresse replied, intrigued at discovering yet another facet of her husband's life.

"My father would take me to the Choctaw camp when I was a young boy, and it was there that I met Nashoba," Lucien explained as they walked down the crushed-shell path between the enormous live oaks. "We became inseparable one long summer when I lived with him and his family as his brother. My father thought the only way I could understand the Choctaw was to live with them in their camp, as he had lived in an Indian camp in New France in Canada as a boy. He was a wise man, for my summer with the Choctaw taught me much about what was really important in life. Nashoba treated me like a Choctaw, and from him I learned how to live in the swamp, how to hunt, and later how to survive despair." There was a faraway look in his dark eyes as he stared down toward the river.

Caresse sensed that although he was walking beside her, his mind was seeing another time, another place. She felt a terrible loneliness wash over her. There was so much about Lucien's life that she knew nothing about. When he withdrew from her like this, she could only speculate on what pain there must have been in his life to have caused him to build such a wall between him and the rest of the world.

"Why will the Indians not come up to the house?" Caresse asked, trying to break the silence that had fallen between them.

"Aurore was frightened of them. She became so distraught at the sight of them landing at the dock that she made me promise they would come no further," he replied in terse tones. "She was hysterical until I agreed."

Aurore, it was always the memory of Aurore that

seemed to hang about Sans Regret like a shroud. The more she heard about the woman the more foolish she sounded, Caresse thought in irritation. It was no wonder Lucien retreated into himself. He must have learned to do it in self-defense while married to the shallow Aurore. How could he have possibly loved such a silly woman? She sighed in frustration as they climbed the grassy slope of the levee. Perhaps now that she was recovered, she could discover some of the answers to her questions about Lucien's first wife, and put to rest the melancholy ghost of the woman who threatened to drive a wedge between her and the magnetic man who walked beside her.

A tall well-built brave came forward to greet Lucien as they reached that stretch of land between the levee and the river called a batture. His dark eyes passed over his wife, but there was no recognition. Nashoba had never seen Aurore, Caresse realized with a sense of relief. She would not have to endure the stunned side-glances of those who had known Aurore and were shocked by the resemblance.

Lucien clasped the forearms of the Choctaw brave in welcome. The respect between the two men was obvious. Nashoba spoke rapidly to Lucien in his own language, completely disregarding Caresse as if she did not exist.

Lucien listened intently, interrupting several times with questions. He spoke the Choctaw language fluently, to Caresse's surprise. She watched the two men, seeing her husband in a new light. Where was the elegant, languid Nouvelle Orléans gentleman? The man who stood talking with such concentration to the Choctaw brave bore little resemblance to the courtier who made flirtatious conversations with the dissolute Marquise de Vaudreuil. Which man was the real Lucien St. Amant?

As they stood talking, the other three braves

157

stood at a distance with watchful eyes and expressionless faces. It was the closest she had ever been to such fierce looking warriors, but she could not help being impressed by their stalwart muscular forms, their well-proportioned limbs, the nobility with which they held themselves. This, then, was the noble savage talked about in the salons of Versailles. It was an apt term, for they had more grace and noble bearing than many of the courtiers surrounding Louis XV. Trying not to stare, she turned her attention back to the two men deep in conversation. She sensed that Lucien was disturbed by what Nashoba was telling him.

But the ringing of the bell on the dock by the young African boy whose duty it was to watch the river halted the men's discussion, drawing all eyes toward a keelboat approaching the Sans Regret dock. The jewels at the neck of the plump female figure standing at the rail were set aflame by the long slanting rays of the setting sun. Their guests from Chêne Vert had arrived.

"Come, we'd best greet them," Lucien said to Caresse with a grimace, leaving Nashoba's side.

The Indians watched in stoic silence as the keelboat tied up at the dock, but the occupants stared at them in stunned dismay. The governor's wife's cold blue eyes flitted over the braves, lingering on the muscular thighs displayed beneath their brief breechclouts. Solange de Vaudreuil really was disgusting, Caresse mused. She gave a sigh at the thought that they were staying till the cooler weather made it safe for them to return to Nouvelle Orléans. The fever always lessened, she had been told by Dominique, after the first cold weather came through the colony. Caresse could only pray it came soon.

Mon cher cavalier," the Marquise de Vaudreuil trilled, moving toward Lucien, who bowed over her hand.

Had he really been one of the disgusting So-lange's young men, Caresse wondered, or was it just one of the woman's affectations? She turned to greet the handsome marquis as he stepped onto the wharf, astounded once again that this man was really her husband. As he bowed over her hand she found herself staring into the narrow amber eyes of Philippe Dubrieul standing behind him.

"*Madame*, at last we meet," he murmured.

"*Enchantée, monsieur,*" she replied formally, ex-tending her hand to him with great reluctance. He was looking at her, but he was seeing Aurore. For a moment, she felt sorry that she was not the woman who must have meant a great deal to him. It was strange, she thought, but stepbrothers and sisters usually did not care for one another, espe-cially when they had not been reared together. Philippe Dubrieul seemed to be the exception, for she felt in every nerve of her body that this man had cared deeply for Aurore St. Amant.

Lucien greeted him coolly, and it was obvious the two men cared little for each other's company. After a formal bow in his direction, Philippe turned his attention, to her discomfort, back to-ward Caresse.

After speaking first with Nashoba, Lucien indi-cated that they would walk to the house. Extending his arm to the governor's wife as a proper host should, he led the way with the governor at his side, and Caresse with Philippe bringing up the rear.

"And how do you find Sans Regret, *madame?*" Philippe inquired. His question had an intensity about it that was more than good manners. He seemed to really want to know her answer.

"Please, you must call me Caresse," she re-quested, thinking that by calling her by name it would help to banish the sense that she was Aurore.

"*Merci*, Caresse, and you must of course call me

159

Philippe," he said, staring down at her with that strange intense gaze that seemed to look through her to something, or someone, that only he could see.

"To answer your kind question, Philippe, I find Sans Regret quite beautiful," she responded, her hand resting lightly on his silk brocaded sleeve as etiquette required.

"It does not frighten you to be here in this wilderness?" he asked, as they passed under the arched branches of the oaks draped with moss swaying in the slight breeze from the river.

"*Non*, although 'tis a wilderness out there just beyond the fields, it has a savage kind of beauty."

"You are a perceptive woman as well as a beautiful one," he said gallantly, but there was an intimate tone to his voice that disturbed Caresse.

There was something in Philippe's manner toward her, the way he looked at her, that was unsettling. It was more than the mild flirtation that was *de rigueur* between men and women in polite society. This was something darker, more intense.

"Has Dominique explained the significance of that particular tree?" he asked, gesturing to a massive live oak on which one enormous, gnarled moss-covered limb had grown into another. The two twisted limbs almost touched the ground.

"*Non*, she has not mentioned it," Caresse replied in puzzlement, for she realized she had not noticed how odd it looked till Philippe had pointed it out.

"The Africans believe that everyone, everything, has a double or a ghost, and when people, animals, even plants, die, the ghost or double remains close by the loved ones, caring or helping to meet their needs. As there are good spirit-doubles, there are also more malevolent spirits of the damned that can be called upon to do one's bidding. They believe that by the appropriate chants, or ceremonies, these spirits can be centered in special objects to

160

be called upon when needed. The preferred objects are those that have some unusual qualities. One limb of a tree growing into another is considered a powerful talisman of doubling. One who possessed such an object would be endowed with powerful magic to create either good or evil," he confided as they passed by the unusual tree in front of the gallery. Caresse noticed for the first time that one branch reached out to touch the railing of the second-story gallery.

"You seem to have enthralled my wife, Dubrieul," Lucien commented tersely as they climbed the curving staircase. Dominique led the way to show the governor and his wife their bedchamber so they could freshen themselves before dining.

"I was explaining the Africans' religion, and their concept of spirit-doubles," he replied coolly, and waited to see what effect his explanation would have on his host.

"Voodoo is not encouraged at Sans Regret," Lucien responded, his voice quiet, but with an ominous quality to it.

"You may not want it at Sans Regret, but it exists even here," Philippe said with a tinge of ridicule in his words.

"It is not a topic of conversation that I wish to discuss," Lucien answered, with a thread of warning in his voice.

"As you wish," Philippe said with a polite inclination of his powdered wig.

"We will excuse you, *ma chère*, as I know you wish to dress for dinner," Lucien turned toward Caresse as the de Vaudreuils followed Dominique down the gallery to their chamber. "Dubrieul and I will have a game of billiards before we dine." He lifted her hand to his lips in farewell, then turning toward Philippe said, "As I remember, you were a fair player."

161

She watched as the two men, as wary of each other as two strange swamp panthers, strode toward the billiard room at the other end of the house. There were uneasy currents in the house tonight, she mused as she entered her bedchamber. They had surfaced with the arrival of Philippe Dubrieul.

Fantine helped her disrobe and then step into the wonderfully cool marble tub filled with tepid water scented with her essence of lily perfume. It promised to be a long night, she thought with a sigh, picking up the cake of French soap.

The young maid went to get Caresse's gown of pale rose silk, with a stomacher of fine lace embroidered with pearls, and deep ruffles of lace as delicate as a cobweb at the sleeves. Dominique was to be the marquise's maid for the length of her stay as a courtesy. Fantine was to take the older woman's place as Caresse's maid.

The scent of vetivert drifted faintly on the soft humid air as the maidservant opened the armoire. The fragrance always triggered a memory of the stranger in Paris. Had he come from La Louisiane or the West Indies? Or had he bought the fragrance at a perfume shop in Paris? New scents from around the world were all the rage at Versailles. Caresse shrugged, soaping the heat of the day from her body. She had other more pressing matters to think about. France was in the past, almost another lifetime ago.

The night lay ahead of her, her first dinner party at Sans Regret as *châtelaine*, and she wanted to make Lucien proud of her in front of his friends. And there was the nagging need to drive the memory of Aurore from his mind.

Let her ghost return to her tomb, she thought and with the thought came realization that if Aurore had died at the plantation she must be buried here. But where was her tomb? It was not with those of Lucien's mother and father in the small family cemetery enclosed by the iron fence. There were only two white tombs made of marble in that small enclosure. Where had Lucien buried his wife? Why had she not been placed in a tomb with the other St. Amants? Caresse knew that if she found out the answer to that question, she might discover the key to unlocking the enigma that was Lucien St. Amant. She would begin tonight by asking Philippe Dubrieul about his stepsister.

Eleven

On the gallery facing the river, the flickering golden light from the two ornate silver candelabra on the dining table cast long shadows across the lace cloth. Caresse, sitting at one end of the table, stared down the length to where Lucien sat at the other engaging Solange de Vaudreuil in the light flirtatious banter that the woman adored. The seating arrangement with an uneven number of guests had been awkward. Caresse had solved it by putting the governor's wife and Philippe on one side, and the governor in solitary splendor on the other side. But she now regretted the arrangement for Philippe was seated on her left, and his continued intense scrutiny was disconcerting. She had thought that during dinner she might somehow tactfully bring the conversation around to his step-sister, but there was something in his yearning gaze every time he looked at her that stayed her tongue.

"Sans Regret is as lovely as I have heard, Mme St. Amant," the governor said with a gallant smile to Caresse.

"Please, you must call me Caresse," she replied, signaling to Antoine, the butler, to serve the gumbo. "I was not aware, M. Le Marquis, that you had not been to Sans Regret before today."

"Please, you do me such honor, you must call

me Pierre-François," he said with a slight bow of his head. The elaborate powdered wig he wore would be in the height of fashion at Versailles, but Caresse surmised it must be uncomfortable in the humid heat of La Louisiane.

"We always wished to visit, but Lucien never entertained at the plantation after . . . after Aurore's death," Solange de Vaudreuil interjected, then realizing her faux pas quickly took a long drink of wine.

There was a long silence as Lucien stared into the flickering flame of the candles in front of him. Philippe had paled at her words, clutching the napkin he raised to his lips so tightly in his fist the knuckles had turned white.

" 'Tis delightful then that you and the Governor should be our first guests since our arrival at Sans Regret," Caresse said in as pleasant a tone as she could manage, determined her first dinner party would not be a disaster, shadowed by the memory of Aurore.

Lucien raised his elegant head, the raven black hair gleaming in the glow of the candles, and although he remained silent, his brilliant dark eyes burned with admiration. There was something else in those expressive orbs that set her pulse pounding, and kindled a warmth in her veins. She saw the reflection of smoldering desire in their depths. Remembering his words earlier in the garden, Caresse quickly placed her wine glass down on the table. Her hand had begun to tremble with the intensity of her own aroused passion.

"I wanted to inquire about the reason for the visit of the Choctaw chief," the governor said to Lucien.

"Nashoba came to warn me that the British are stirring up trouble among some of the renegade groups of Choctaw who wish to join with the English allies, the Chickasaw, against the French," Lucien answered, turning his gaze toward the marquis. "I have put more guards at the edge of the indigo fields under my overseer's command."

"The British push us toward war. I do not have to tell you that the victor will dominate the North American continent," he commented thoughtfully. "The military defenses of this colony have been neglected far too long—although the lack of funds coming from France complicates any remedy I would have for the situation." He gave a sigh as he nodded to Antoine to refill his wine glass.

"And do you have any assurance that the funds that are sent to Nouvelle Orléans are dispensed to those fortifications to which they are intended?" Lucien's tone was cool, but there was an edge to his words that surprised Caresse and startled Solange.

"What exactly are you intimating, Lucien?" she asked sharply, her large blue eyes cold as ice.

"Why nothing, Solange. What did you think I meant?" Lucien gave her a slight smile that didn't touch his piercing eyes.

He was toying with her, Caresse realized, like a fierce jungle cat with its prey. This was yet another side to her husband's character. The fashionable rogue who had danced attendance on the governor's wife was gone, and in his place was a dangerous cynic. Solange was bewildered by the change in the man whom she had fancied was intrigued with her power and position. But even in the convent, Caresse had heard the stories that both the governor and his wife were engaged in an elaborate system of patronage, and other forms of corruption using their office and position to enrich their own coffers.

"But enough of this trying military talk. We have committed the worst of social faux pas gentlemen, we have bored two beautiful ladies," Lucien said smoothly, lifting Solange's plump beringed hand in his. "Can you find it in your generous heart to forgive me?" He lifted her fingers to his lips as she nodded in her garishly decorated powdered wig, simpering like a young girl.

Caresse watched the tableau in stunned amazement. Lucien had changed once more before their eyes back into the foppish courtier. Solange may be fooled, she thought, but she knew now that this was one of the many masks her husband donned at his whim. She could not decide which was the real Lucien, the rakish courtier, the wealthy concerned planter, the sometime *coureur de bois* who was the confidant of a Choctaw chief, or perhaps all three?

As Antoine brought in the dessert, and silver dishes of *dragées,* sugar-coated almonds, the conversation turned to the winter social season that would begin in November after the first light frost had made it safe for everyone to return to the city. Solange confided her plans for a masquerade ball. Lucien listened with the pretense of great interest, and the governor's wife was delighted.

As Solange prattled on, Philippe leaned toward Caresse. "Did we bore you, Caresse?" he asked quietly, his strange amber eyes seeming to devour every feature of her face.

"I do not find the talk of Indian attacks boring, I assure you," Caresse replied.

"Then you do find some aspects to living at Sans Regret frightening?" he persisted, those narrow amber eyes seeming to try to peer behind her cool facade.

"I would not say frightening. Perhaps they make me uneasy," she replied, trying to avoid that unnerving stare.

"Uneasy in what way?" His voice was low, intimate, his whole body seemed to be anticipating her answer.

"There is something here in the house and

about the grounds—" She stopped, seeing the intense interest in his narrow amber eyes. This was the time to ask him, to try and find out more about Aurore. "You will probably find this a foolish fantasy, but there are times . . . I almost sense an unseen presence watching me in the shadows."

"I would not find it foolish at all," he replied eagerly, lowering his voice so only she could hear him. "There are others who have felt this presence. I have felt it all evening. She is here with us."

Caresse experienced a cold chill run up her spine at his words, and the hairs on her forearms seemed to tingle as she forced herself to lift her wine glass to her lips. She drank the rest of her wine to give her courage to ask the rest of her questions. "Whom do you mean?"

"Why Lucien's first wife, of course. Aurore." His voice lingered on her name as if he enjoyed the feel of it on his tongue.

"I find her quite interesting," Caresse said through dry tense lips.

"*Oui*, I can understand that. You resemble her, but her hair was dark, black as night. She only powdered it white, and her eyes were a deep blue," he told her, his voice filled with a strange excitement. "And the beauty mark above your lip, she did not have one, but often she placed a patch in just that spot." He stared at her mouth, lost in thought.

Caresse gave a shudder, for the more she heard about Aurore the less she liked it. Did she look so much like the dead woman? Was that what Lucien saw when he looked at her with such hunger in his dark expressive gaze?

"Mayhap, you could resolve something that has been puzzling me," Caresse said in a low murmur, careful that Lucien could not overhear.

"I hope that I may be of some assistance to such

a lovely lady," he replied, never taking his eyes from her.

"Why . . . why is Aurore not buried in the family plot?"

" 'Tis ground consecrated by a priest from Nouvelle Orléans. Aurore committed suicide, thus was denied burial there. Her body rests in a marble tomb in a glade between two large oaks. It was a favorite place of hers," he told her with a catch to his voice.

As he spoke a swirl of wind seemed to come out of the still sultry night, causing candles to flicker and to go out. The leaves in the nearby giant oaks rustled like the silk gown of a woman passing by.

Philippe lifted his head at the touch of the wind like a skittish animal sensing trouble. His eyes darted about the shadowy gallery as if he expected someone to appear. His nostrils flared as he half rose in his seat, then, trembling, he sat back down.

"Mon cher, what is it?" Solange asked, staring at his blanched face. Making the sign of the cross, she muttered, "You look like you have seen a ghost."

"Not seen, Marquise, felt," he whispered.

" 'Twould seem a storm is blowing in from the gulf. Shall we retire to the salon," Lucien announced, rising abruptly to his feet and throwing his linen napkin on the table in a gesture of disgust. "Perhaps you could make yourself useful, Dubrieul, and play us a tune on the harpsichord."

Antoine lit the tall tapers, and numerous oil lamps about the chamber, as they walked in through the open French doors. There was a heavy atmosphere about the room that even Solange's trilling voice confiding one of her many scandalous stories about a love affair gone bad in Nouvelle Orléans could not lighten. They had all been unnerved by Philippe's strange utterance on the gallery, but he seemed unaffected. Striding straight to

169

the harpsichord, he seated himself and began to play a plaintive melody as the wind gusted stronger about the house and in through the open French doors.

"With Philippe engaged in his own pursuits, we have an even number for a game," Solange announced, gesturing toward the elegant walnut card table imported from France. It stood in front of the fireplace, filled this time of year with a large rose and blue-on-ivory porcelain vase containing an arrangement of sweet olive branches laden with hundreds of tiny white, intensely fragrant blossoms.

Seated across from Lucien, Caresse could almost believe she was back in France at one of the salons at Versailles. Only the soft humid air, so unlike that of the cool rainy autumns in France, reminded her that she was in the wilderness of La Louisiane. She found her mind wandering as Philippe played song after song, and Solange flirted outrageously with Lucien.

The storm that had threatened earlier struck with full force, buffeting the thick walls of the house with strong winds and a driving rain. It began to wear on Caresse's nerves as the card game wore on and on. An overwhelming fatigue made her eyelids feel as if they had weights on them.

"Are you all right, *ma chère*?" Lucien's concerned voice cut across Solange's babbling. He looked up from the cards he held fanned out in the long, bronzed fingers of his right hand.

"*Oui*, 'tis only that the storm is a bit wearing on one's nerves," she replied, trying to force her concentration back on the game.

"Is it true, *mon cher* Lucien, as I have heard, that 'tis during storms that the ghost walks at Sans Regret?" Solange inquired with a drunken laugh.

"Solange, really," her husband reproached her, but he too had drunk a great deal.

170

"Oh, Lucien knows that all of Nouvelle Orléans gossips about the infamous ghost of Sans Regret," Solange dismissed his rebuke with a wave of her plump beringed hand. Turning toward Lucien she asked eagerly "Will I see the ghost tonight, *mon cher*? I do hope so."

"If you continue to drink my brandy, *ma belle* Solange, you may see a great many things tonight," Lucien replied, his voice heavy with sarcasm.

She stared at him for a moment, then touching his arm, gave a ribald snort of laughter. "You are a very naughty man to tease so."

At that moment a strong gust of wind blew open the French door and extinguished all the candles in the silver candelabra Philippe had placed on the harpsichord. His fingers came to a discordant end on the keys, as even the drunken Solange seemed at a loss for words.

"Perhaps the ghost heard you," the governor said to his wife as Lucien rose to shut the door, for the rain was pouring in. "As the old saying goes, be careful what you wish for, you might get it."

It was as Lucien reached the door that they heard a loud sound as if something was being ripped apart. Another gust of wind blew in from the gallery, and with it a wispy gray-white apparition that whirled up toward the ceiling, then fell to the floor.

"Mon Dieu!" Solange's gasp spoke for them all.

Her husband strode to where it had landed as the others stared in horrified fascination. Reaching down, he picked it up and, holding it aloft in the dim light of the remaining tapers, said, "This is your ghost, Solange, a piece of Spanish beard."

There was a silence, then the high-pitched laugh of Solange filled the chamber as Lucien stalked out into the storm. Caresse hurried to the door, anxious to escape the atmosphere of the salon, even if she had to endure the fury of the storm to do it.

"Stay back!" Lucien called out from where he stood a few feet down the gallery. A flash of lightning showed what he was concerned about, for a gnarled branch of the live oak nearest the house had broken off and lay across the gallery railing, having knocked out a few panes of glass in the French door of a vacant bedchamber.

Caresse paused on the threshold, watching as her husband stood in the driving rain, staring down at the enormous broken branch. It was then she felt two masculine hands grip her shoulders, the warm breath on the back of her neck.

" 'Tis the oak, the doubling oak," Philippe hissed. *"Mon Dieu,* it broke the glass in the door to Aurore's bedchamber."

Caresse felt a shiver go up and down her spine at his words, as his hands clutched her shoulders. "Please," she said, giving a shrug, "you are hurting me."

"Pardonnez-moi," he murmured, releasing her.

She couldn't explain it, but she knew that she had to get Lucien away from that room. "Lucien!" she called into the fury of the storm, stepping out onto the gallery. The wind struck her in the face with its fury, whipping her skirt back against her legs. And again, when he did not move, "Lucien!"

Slowly, he turned around, the flash of lightning illuminating his tortured face, the burning anguish of his dark eyes, as the wind tore at his hair and his cravat. She held out her arms, feeling the rain lash her skin.

"Lucien, come away from there! Come to me!" she cried out.

Whether he heard her or not, she could not tell, but with the next flash of lightning he was in front of her, sweeping her into his arms. He held her to him so tightly she thought she could not breathe. But it did not matter, all that mattered was that she was in his arms, and he was safe from some terrible menace that she dared not name.

He was pulling her into the salon away from the storm. Inside, Solange and Pierre-François stood staring at them as Philippe fumbled with a decanter of brandy kept on the table by the fireplace. Water dripped from their clothing as Lucien latched the French doors, then strode over to where Antoine was picking up the cards that had been blown to the floor.

"When it is light, have several of the field hands saw off the rest of the branch, for it has split some from the tree. There is nothing we can do tonight," he told the African servant. Then turning to Caresse and his guests, he said in cool authoritative tones, "I think 'tis best if we all retire for the night. There are candles there on the table." He gestured to where single tapers stood in brass candleholders next to a lit candle from which they would light their wicks.

Without a word, they followed his advice, and even the talkative Solange was strangely quiet. Each carrying a brass holder like a talisman against the terrors of the dark, they left the salon for different wings of the house.

Caresse relished the comforting strength of Lucien's tall form next to her as they walked to their bedchamber. Never had the atmosphere at Sans Regret seemed more malevolent than on this stormy night, she thought with a shudder.

"That will be all, Fantine," Lucien said to the young maid half asleep in the chair next to the light of one wavering candle.

Struggling to her feet, she began to help Caresse with her gown, but at Lucien's shake of his elegant head, she nodded her understanding, and quickly lit the rest of the candles in their chamber. Turning toward the door she bade them a *bonne nuit* and left.

By the light of the tapers Caresse saw that Blanchette and Bruno were both asleep in their respective corners. Somehow during her long convalescence they had worked out an uneasy coexistence. A well-aimed scratch on Bruno's nose when he had come too close had taught him to treat the delicate-looking cat with respect. He had learned to stay out of reach of her nimble paws.

"Perhaps the storm will bring in cooler weather," Caresse said hopefully as she began to undo the intricate closing of her gown.

"And you are looking forward to cooler weather?" Lucien asked, seeming to be miles away as he stood behind her in Fantine's place.

"That dreadful woman and her husband will not leave till the first light frost. I was hoping that we would have an especially early frost this year," Caresse said with a sigh. " 'Twill be All Saints' Day, day after tomorrow. Dominique said that there is often a cool spell about this time."

"Ah, I agree that the sooner our guests are gone, the better, but I had not realized 'twas almost the first of November," he mused aloud, something troubled in his voice.

"And why does that bother you?" she asked, over her shoulder, as he unhooked the last of the hooks of her bodice.

" 'Tis not important," he answered tensely.

But she knew as she stepped out of her gown, and then her petticoats, that for some reason it mattered a great deal. She was just as certain that he would not tell her, for she felt the wall close around him shutting her out, the wall that came down whenever something had to do with Aurore.

"Ah, you are so lovely in the candlelight," he whispered into her hair from where he stood behind her.

She felt his hand come around and gently stroke the tips of her breasts through the translucent ma-

174

terial of her chemise. Desire began to flow in her veins even as she tried to fight the magnetic attraction he had for her. There was too much of Aurore in the house tonight. She did not want to be only the reflection of a dead woman. But he was like a drug that she craved with every fiber of her being. The need for his touch was stronger than pride, worth bending her dignity, just to feel him take her once more to that wondrous place of rapture.

"I need you tonight, *ma chère*, more than I have ever needed you," his voice was a harsh rasp as he circled each throbbing nipple with the palm of his hand, his heated mouth on the pulse point in her neck, beating as rapidly as the wings of a tiny trapped bird.

She gave up the battle, leaning back against him, allowing his lips and tongue to trace the blue veins in the marble of her throat. Her hand sought behind her the hard sinewy strength of his thigh, caressing its contours, relishing the memory of how it felt wrapped around her own. As he slipped the thin chemise from her shoulders, her nails dug into him through the cloth of his breeches.

The storm seemed to gather strength once more as he picked her up and carried her to the waiting bed. She watched from the soft enveloping feather mattress as he stripped his clothes from his body. His arousal was evident, sending a violent shiver of want through her. She sensed a difference in him tonight. A frightening, exciting difference. She didn't know where it came from, whether it was from the storm outside, or the emotional storm within him, but he had a leashed fury about him.

When he pulled her to him, he muttered against her burning lips, "I shall try to be gentle, but I can make no promises."

"Nor can I," she replied to his startled laugh. Then there was no more laughter as she bit his lower lip so sensuously that it set his blood aflame.

His mouth came down on hers hungrily, hard and searching. She answered his bruising kiss with her own tongue capturing his, swirling around that moist velvet invasion, then sucking him, tasting him with a wildness she didn't know she was capable of feeling.

Strong masculine hands cupped the soft mounds of her buttocks, pressing her to the powerful length of him. Her delicate fingers entwined in the locks of his hair as they kissed and embraced like two wild animals that had found their mate. Rolling back and forth on the soft feather bed, first he was on top, then she, in a dance of passion.

With the French doors shut against the storm, allowing none of the cooling air to penetrate, the chamber was warm, close, like an embrace. Their bodies were soon slick with moisture, only adding to the sense of wantonness that seemed to have caught them in its spell.

It was as if they could not get enough of the taste, the smell, the feel, of each other. Moans and gasps of hunger and delight filled the chamber like the sweetest music, a counterpoint to the sounds of the power of the storm.

"Oui, mon coeur!" she cried out as he thrust inside her hard, conquering, filling her with his need. Her hips arched to meet him, moving, returning his thrust with her own wild abandon.

They sensed, for they were too aroused to think, to reason, that they were searching with their passion for a way to forget their own tragic pasts. The torment of their life before they met was burned away, for a few precious timeless moments, when they communed in the primeval rapture that consumed all memory.

Later, as they lay in each other's arms, exhausted but fulfilled, Caresse felt a strange melancholy come over her like a sickness. She sighed, pressing even closer to the refuge of Lucien's lithe form.

"What is it, *ma chère*? You sighed a heavy sigh," he murmured into the tangled silk of her hair, stroking it with his fingers, enjoying the sensual feel of it under his skin.

"I do not know, *la mélancolie* has come over me like a fog," she said, giving a wan smile, trying to shake the sadness that threatened to overwhelm her.

"Ah, this I think I can explain, 'tis called the *petite mort*, the little death. When lovers experience an especially close joining, where they communicate both body and soul, the separation after fulfillment is reached is difficult. There is the realization that they are no longer one, but must return to their individual identities. This is what you are feeling, *ma chère*," he explained with light reassuring kisses on her hair, the silken skin of her temples. "Close your eyes and slip into slumber. It is only part of life, part of love."

Caresse did as he advised, closed her eyes, wanting the escape of sleep. But the words *petite mort* kept echoing in her overtired brain. She did not want to think of the word *mort* in connection with their relationship, although she understood Lucien had only been speaking metaphorically.

Sleep, however, was a long time coming. She felt the quiet breathing of Lucien telling her he had fallen into slumber. As she heard the chiming of a clock in the hall striking one in the morning, she realized that it was *la vigile de la Toussaint*, Halloween, when the dead were supposed to walk the earth. Giving a shudder, she buried her head against the soft fur of Lucien's chest. Held in his strong embrace, nothing could harm her, not even the ghost of Aurore. Then, remembering the broken branch of the oak, she felt a chill. What had happened on All Saints' Day that still bothered Lucien? She had a premonition that it concerned Aurore, and its anniversary was only a day away.

Twelve .

A light fog swirled in from the river to wrap Sans Regret in an eerie mist. In the morning, the men had gone out to see to the cutting of the broken oak limb and then to check the fields and other trees, leaving Caresse and Solange together in the salon. Although the sun had not come out by afternoon, the day was rather warm, with a cloying dampness that made both women uncomfortable.

"I cannot believe the fog is so dense on the river Philippe dares not try to return to Chêne Vert," Solange commented, waving the broad palmetto fan scented with vetivert from the wrapping of the root on the handle. They stared out the open French door to where the river was hidden from view by the fog.

"*Oui,* 'tis a pity," Caresse replied sincerely. His presence was disturbing, for he stared at her intently whenever they were in the same room. He saw the vision of Aurore, and she hated being reminded of her resemblance to the dead woman. She was thankful that Lucien had insisted he accompany him and the governor on their tour about the grounds.

"I, for one, am glad that he is staying the night. Please excuse my observation, but I find the atmosphere at Sans Regret oppressive. The more people to fill these chambers tonight the better," Solange said bluntly.

"Because 'tis All Hallows' Eve?" Caresse questioned, startled at the woman's frankness.

"If there ever was a house haunted by a ghost, 'tis this one," she said emphatically. "And then the woman's killing herself on *la Toussaint*, 'tis too macabre," Solange said with a shudder.

"Aurore died on All Saints' Day?" Caresse gasped, remembering Lucien's expression when she reminded him that it was only two days away.

" 'Tis when the servants found her, at any rate."

"And where was Lucien?" Caresse managed to whisper.

"He returned several hours later, having camped upriver on his way home from one of his many trips for Pierre-François," Solange told her, relishing the role of informant to the new Mme St. Amant."

"I see. He had been gone for quite some time," Caresse answered, hating her curiosity for it seemed tawdry discussing Lucien and his first wife behind his back. But she had to find the answers to the questions that had bothered her since the first day she discovered her startling resemblance to Aurore.

"So they say, but then he was gone a great deal of the time. He requested the assignments from Pierre-François. We, of course, found that quite odd. But then Aurore was quite odd as well, if you will forgive my choice of words." Solange gave a crude laugh, continuing to try to stir the air with her fan.

"What do you mean?"

"She thought she had certain powers," Solange explained with a shake of her elaborate powdered wig, "to foretell the future with her pack of cards. 'Twas her table, the one we played at last night. She had ordered it from France. It used to stand in the salon at the St. Amant town house in Nouvelle Orléans. There was many a night that they entertained everyone of any significance in the city during the *saison de visites*, and as one entered the salon, there would sit Aurore at her card table. Her cards would be spread out on the table with her *belle mignonne* to one side, and a crystal flute of champagne on the other." Solange gave a shudder.

"What pray tell is a *belle mignonne*?" Caresse inquired in puzzlement. She had heard the name before, but couldn't quite place it.

"They are out of fashion now, for which we should all be grateful. They were quite ghastly, Aurore's especially. A *belle mignonne* is a human skull. They were popular in the time of the old King Louis XIV. His queen had quite a collection, I understand. One was supposed to contemplate them in order to be aware of the vanity of worldly pursuits. Aurore used hers, however, strictly for effect. It was how she was," Solange explained with a shrug, lifting her glass of brandy to her lips. She had started drinking when the men left as if she needed the alcohol to give her courage to remain in the empty house.

"I remember my *maman* telling about them when I was a child," Caresse said thoughtfully. "She, too, thought they were macabre."

"Your *maman* knew about *belle mignonnes*, *chère*? 'Tis strange, they were known among the aristocracy at Versailles. But Lucien told us you were from Lyon," Solange commented, staring at her with narrowed eyes. "You are not what you seem to be, Caresse. Or perhaps I should say you are exactly what you seem, but not what you pretend."

"You were telling about Aurore and her belief in having special powers," Caresse quickly reminded her.

"Ah, *oui*, Aurore," Solange replied, her knowing blue eyes telling Caresse that she would give up the questions about her past for now, but that she would not forget her suspicions. "Well, her *belle mignonne* was all for effect as I said. She had it lit from within by a candle, and the skull was draped in one of her powdered wigs. I shall never forget that grinning skull with the light from the taper shining out through the eyes. It set a certain atmosphere, just as she intended. Everyone had to have their fortune told by her cards. It was quite strange, but she was usually right in her prophecy. Of course, this only added to her reputation, and to people's fear of her."

"People were afraid of her?" Caresse inquired in startled tones. She had known the Africans feared Aurore, but did not know that the French did also.

"Oui, very frightened," Solange answered, taking a long drink of her brandy before continuing. " 'Twas rumored in Nouvelle Orléans that she was a high priestess of the African religion that some call voodoo. I know the Africans were terrified of her. My own maid claimed Aurore had great powers that she could use for good or evil, depending on her mood, and it seemed her mood usually veered toward evil. And then, of course, she had been born on All Hallows' Eve, a sign to many that she had psychic powers. 'Tis strange but she might have died on her birthday." Solange gave a shudder, and reaching out for the bottle of brandy she had placed on the table and pulling the stopper from its neck, she filled her glass to the brim.

"Strange that she would take her own life on her birthday?" Caresse questioned softly, musing that Aurore did not seem like the type of person to take her own life.

"She always said that she had been born on All Hallows' Eve and that she would die on it," Solange explained, her florid complexion turning pale. "I had forgotten that prophecy of hers till this mo-

181

ment. She made it in her dramatic fashion on the birthday masquerade ball they gave the year before her death on All Hallows' Eve. *Mon Dieu!* If I had remembered I would never have agreed to this idea of Philippe's that we visit Sans Regret before returning to Nouvelle Orléans." She lifted the glass to her lips with a trembling hand.

"She said that she would die on All Hallows' Eve," Caresse mused aloud, wondering if the woman had been so deranged she had killed herself to make her prophecy come true.

"Lucien was furious at her theatrics, as he called it. They had a terrible argument right in the middle of their own party. When Philippe tried to side with Aurore, claiming that she must always be protected from evil forces on her birthday, Lucien called him a fool. He left the party for Sans Regret with Aurore's taunts ringing in his ears. She claimed that he did not want to face the truth that she had powers he was helpless against."

"How horrible," Caresse whispered, thinking of Lucien coping with a woman such as Aurore.

"She was a horrible woman, indeed," Solange agreed. "I think we all realized that she was somewhat unbalanced. Most people stayed away from her after that. She really began to frighten them, for one could sense that there were no limits for Aurore. I know many spoke of the St. Amant curse, that Lucien, like his father had married a madwoman."

"Was she deranged enough to kill herself in order to fulfill a prophecy?" Caresse asked, a cold chill starting at the base of her spine, as she realized that she resembled a woman who might have been insane.

"That always puzzled me, for Aurore seemed too self-centered to kill herself. She enjoyed the power she had over the Africans, and some whites as well," Solange said thoughtfully. "I could imagine her killing someone else, but never herself."

"From what you have told me about her, that was my conclusion," Caresse agreed. "Perhaps it was an accident?"

"You have stood on the gallery, have seen the thick posts of the railing. Could you have accidentally fallen over a waist-high railing?" Solange asked, cynicism etching each word.

"*Non,* I must admit it seems impossible," Caresse said with a sigh.

"There is another story about what happened that eve," Solange told her, lowering her voice so the servants couldn't hear if they happened to pass by the salon on the gallery.

"And what was that?" Caresse asked with a dry mouth. She knew she did not want to hear what Solange was about to tell her, but her curiosity was too great.

"The house servants claim that they heard a man and a woman arguing in the salon before midnight. They had been given the night off for their own celebration in the quarters; in fact, they said Aurore insisted she didn't need anyone to stay in the house with her. This was most unusual, for she always felt uneasy at Sans Regret. It is so isolated, and, as I said, Lucien had begun to make many trips to fortifications upriver for Pierre-François. But on this night she dismissed all the house servants, telling them that she expected her husband to return that night since it was her birthday. It seems he had made her such a promise. When the servants heard the arguing voices as they were returning from some religious rites they held in a clearing down by the river, they assumed it was Lucien. It was even rumored that they had seen the silhouette of a tall, lean man against the far wall of the salon in the light from the tapers. Later, of course, many wondered, who was this man? And the young African slave whose duty it was to sleep in a shack down by the dock to watch for visitors claims to have heard a lone horseman traveling the path by the river late at night. Could it have been Aurore's murderer? You must understand, *ma chère* Caresse, many people feared Aurore, and this fear could easily turn to hate, hate so strong it could become murderous. 'Tis easier for me to believe that she was murdered than that she killed herself," Solange said firmly, drinking the rest of the brandy in her glass in one swallow.

"I am tempted to agree with you, although I did not know . . . Aurore." Caresse paused. "But the alternative is frightening."

"What do you mean?" Solange asked sharply, sitting up stiffly in the fragile gilded chair.

"If she was murdered, the murderer was never caught. He, if it was a he, is still alive, still perhaps in Louisiane."

"Oh, I thought you meant something else," Solange muttered, waving the palmetto fan.

"What did you think I was going to say?" Caresse asked, puzzled.

Looking over her shoulder to make sure they were alone, Solange said in a low voice, "There were some that hinted the murderer might have been Lucien. I do not think anyone would have blamed him. It was said that she had taken a lover during Lucien's long absences, one of those who shared her belief in voodoo. There are many Frenchmen who, if they do not share all her beliefs, thought that she had special powers, sensual powers," Solange explained, her eyes avid now with the gossip she was confiding. "It is rumored that there were strange rites, orgies you could call them, in a clearing in the swamps on summer nights. People thought perhaps he couldn't take her behavior any longer, or had surprised her with a lover, then waited till the lover left, and killed her. He could have disappeared into the swamps, for he knows them like the back of his hand, and reappeared after her body was discovered, as if he had just returned home. No one knows what happened that night, nor will we, but people do like to talk about it. Aurore was that kind of woman. She is still discussed even though she has been dead these seven years tonight. It has given Lucien quite a reputation, I must tell you. There is nothing a woman likes so much as that hint of danger about a man."

Caresse felt sick to her stomach, both at Solange's words, and that she was listening to such gossip. It was preposterous, the very idea that Lucien could have killed Aurore. He would certainly not have married her, a woman who resembled Aurore, if he had killed her. No one would do that unless they were very sick, obsessed with a woman whom they had killed in a fit of jealousy, and wished to have come back to life. No, she thought, willing herself to bury such thoughts. He was not that kind of man. He was not!

"Are you all right, *ma chère femme*?" The deep familiar masculine voice brought her back from her terrible dark musings, but in doing so startled her so that she flinched away from him.

"Please . . . please, I am fine," she whispered, pulling away from his hands that gripped her shoulders with such strength, the strength to push a small woman over the gallery railing to the stones below.

"Solange, what kind of ghost stories have you been telling my wife?" Lucien turned, with fury in his dark eyes, to the plump woman who sat fanning herself with a satisfied look on her cruel visage. It was the glee of a satisfied cat who has moved in for the kill after tormenting its prey.

"I am sure I cannot imagine what you mean," she drawled, her blue eyes cold as ice. " 'Tis this house, *mon cher*, 'twould give anyone a fright."

185

There was, however, triumph in her voice. She had planted the doubt she wanted in Caresse's mind. It would pay him back for never taking her to his bed. He had married this delicate child-woman, instead of becoming her lover; for that he would pay. But she had only told Caresse what many had gossiped about for years in Nouvelle Orléans. The mystery of Aurore St. Amant's death would never be solved.

"You must not let Solange fill your pretty head with fears of our Louisiane," the governor cautioned Caresse as he followed Lucien into the salon from the curving staircase. His wife was up to her old tricks of stirring up trouble, he could sense it in the humid air. She had that predatory feline look about her.

"Where is Philippe?" Caresse asked to change the subject. Somehow she must put Solange's words from her mind. She could see now that the woman had wanted her to doubt Lucien for some twisted jealous reason of her own. Aurore had not been the only strange woman in Nouvelle Orléans.

"He has been acting as skittish as a new colt," the governor snorted, taking the brandy decanter from his wife's hands. "I think you have had enough, *ma chère,*" he murmured to his frowning wife. "I could use that more than you."

"Ah, here he comes," Lucien said in a tone that conveyed his dislike of Philippe.

"I could use some of that brandy," Philippe muttered, eyeing Pierre. "What ghastly weather."

"You will be staying the night?" Lucien inquired in clipped tones as Philippe poured himself a brandy.

"*Oui,* I would like to stay at Sans Regret tonight," he replied, lifting the glass to his lips.

"I could have our overseer escort you home on the path along the river. You could borrow a horse," Lucien continued, standing stiffly beside the seated Caresse.

"*Non, merci.* I wish to intrude on your hospitality one more night," Philippe replied, after taking a long drink of the brandy.

"May I ask why?" Lucien baited him.

"I wish to visit my stepsister's grave on the morrow. 'Tis *la Toussaint,* when one pays respect to one's dead. This, in case you have forgotten, is the anniversary of her birth, tomorrow the seventh anniversary of her death." He spoke calmly but there was a nervous tic to his left eye.

A silence, like the fog outside the salon, engulfed them at Philippe's answer. The subject that had hung over them was out in the open. No one, however, seemed to know what to say.

"I have not forgotten, although I believe the dead should stay in their tombs," Lucien said, breaking the silence. "This cult of remembrance can become macabre." His voice was cold and cutting as steel.

"I would expect such a response from you," Philippe lashed back, a vein in his temple throbbing with the intensity of his emotion. "You never loved her, never!"

"Enough, gentlemen, there are ladies present," Pierre-François reminded them, as he stepped between them. Then turning to Caresse he said, "I find I have worked up quite an appetite. Shall we be dining soon?"

"I shall see," she said, looking up at him with relief. "If you will excuse me I shall go down to the warming kitchen and see if the summer dining chamber has been prepared." With a quick glance at the thunderous expression in Lucien's eyes, she touched his arm in passing.

It was as if she had pulled him back from an abyss. He stared down at her for a moment as if he did not recognize her, then lifted her hand to his lips. "Do not be gone long. I have missed you," he murmured against her skin. There was no longer the burning anger in his dark eyes, only a curious deep yearning. She couldn't help wondering if the emotion she saw reflected in those onyx depths were for her, or for the memory of Aurore.

The fresh air, even though warm and muggy, was a relief to Caresse as she glided down the right side of the curving staircase. She inhaled deep breaths of the humid air as if to cleanse her mind from the terrible suspicions Solange had aroused with her gossip.

The early darkness of autumn, along with the fog, had cast the gardens in shadows. But sounds of the servants could be heard through the ghostly mist like disembodied spirits. She clasped her arms around her chest as if she were cold, but in the warm humid air it wasn't a physical cold, only one of the spirit, that threatened to engulf her. What a perfect night for All Hallows' Eve, Caresse thought as she entered the warming kitchen.

"Are we ready to dine?" she asked Zoé as the large, immaculately dressed cook directed two serving girls to take iron kettles carefully from the smoldering ashes.

"*Oui madame,*" the woman answered, her round face glistening with perspiration from working around the hot fire in the kitchen house, and then supervising the transport of the dishes to the brick warming kitchen on the ground floor of the mansion.

"*Madame,* may I have a word with you?" Dominique asked, coming into the kitchen from the dining room. She had been directing a serving maid in the setting of the long cypress table made especially in Nouvelle Orléans. The cypress wood was not affected by the humid air that was even more moist in the dark shadowy first floor chambers.

"*Oui*, Dominique. What is it?" Caresse replied.

"Perhaps we could speak out on the gallery," she requested.

"Of course," Caresse answered, walking out of the bustling warming kitchen. Dominique was right behind her, a worried expression on her usually serene features.

" 'Tis a most delicate situation that I must speak of, *madame*," Dominique hesitated, her soft brown eyes troubled.

"What is it?" Caresse asked quietly, giving a slight smile of reassurance. "As mistress of Sans Regret I should know of any troubling situation, Dominique."

"*Oui*, 'tis what I thought also, *madame*," the woman agreed. "I have spoken of this to M. St. Amant, but he simply forbade the ceremony, thinking that would be the end of it."

"What ceremony?" Caresse asked, trying to follow the distraught woman's line of thought.

"The ceremony the slaves have every All Hollows' Eve. M. Zweig agrees with me that to forbid it would only cause great unrest. There has been talk along the river of a slave uprising, but so far nothing has been heard from the quarters at Sans Regret," Dominique explained, clasping her hands together in distress.

"And you think if the ceremony was canceled this could incite a rebellion?" Caresse asked, remembering that Dominique was a free woman who chose to work as housekeeper for the St. Amants. A cold knot began to form in her stomach as she knew that Dominique spoke the truth. The fact of slavery, the very institution of one man owning another, was still hard for her to grasp even though it was a fact of life in La Louisiane.

"*Oui, madame*. I do not wish to see African *or* French blood spilled at Sans Regret."

"The slaves can have their celebration, if they

will keep it out of sight of the house. I shall take responsibility if *monsieur* should find out. And, Dominique, have the overseer and his men watch that nothing gets out of hand, and that all return to their quarters when it is over," Caresse said, biting her lip as she considered the ramifications of reversing Lucien's decision. She could only hope that he never discovered what she had done.

"*Merci, madame.* I think that is a very wise decision," Dominique said, with a look of relief.

"Oh, Dominique, why did *monsieur* decide against allowing a celebration that has gone on for so many years at Sans Regret?"

"Because . . . because 'tis been seven years since Aurore St. Amant died on this night," she answered with great reluctance, and a strange shadow in her sable eyes.

"I thought she died on All Saints' Day," Caresse corrected her.

"Her body was found at dawn on that day, but the slaves believe she died the night before, on her *anniversaire,* her birthday," Dominique explained. "And seven is an important number in their religion. They believe that she has been dead seven years from tonight."

"But . . . Aurore St. Amant was not a part of their religion," Caresse said in surprise.

"*Oui, madame,* she was very much a part of their religion," Dominique admitted. "She was the high priestess of voodoo at Sans Regret. They think she might rise from her tomb on this special anniversary of her death. They want to be waiting to placate her spirit so that she will cast no evil spells on any of them."

"This is ridiculous, Dominique," Caresse said, unable to keep the scorn from her voice, although she had felt the hairs on the back of her neck stand up at the woman's words.

"Perhaps, *madame,*" Dominique replied, a veiled

expression on her usually open face. "They were, however, afraid of her power during her life, and that has not lessened since her death. If you have nothing else, *madame*, I shall convey your instructions to M. Zweig."

Caresse watched as the graceful figure disappeared into the mist that hung like a shroud over the plantation grounds. What had she done? A wave of apprehension swept over her as she thought of Lucien finding out she had just given permission for the slaves to hold special rites to welcome the spirit of Aurore if she rose from her tomb on All Hallows' Eve. How was she going to endure the rest of the long evening that lay ahead of her, listening for any sound that would alert Lucien to her foolish decision?

Thirteen

Wisps of fog seemed to swirl around the lower gallery, an eerie sight through the open French doors of the summer dining room. Every sound seemed magnified in the stillness of the misty evening.

The atmosphere in the chamber was strained, for the gloomy weather seemed to have cast a spell over those seated at the elegantly set dining table. Conversation was in awkward spurts, when one of them could no longer bear the long heavy silence.

Caresse felt every nerve in her body vibrating with doubts over what she had done. She listened to every sound, afraid she would hear some indications of the Africans' ceremony. Lucien seemed lost in some dark thoughts of his own at the end of the table, she noticed with dismay. His dark smoldering gaze seemed concentrated on the flame of the tapers in the silver candelabra nearest to him.

"Will they be having their usual celebration in the quarters this evening?" Philippe's voice startled them all, but Caresse flinched at his question, knocking over her wine glass. She stared, unable to move as the red wine spilled across the white tablecloth like blood.

"*Mon Dieu!*" Solange gasped, making the sign of

the cross. "The spilling of wine foretells the spilling of blood."

"*Sacré!* Enough of this foolishness," Lucien warned, grinding out the words between his strong white teeth. "There will be no ceremonies in the quarters, and there will be no more superstitious talk tonight."

"Really, *mon cher* Lucien, you act like a man who has something bothering him," Solange observed with a thin smile, her drowsiness, brought on by the amount of brandy she had drunk that afternoon, vanished at the chance for verbal sparring with her handsome host. He continued to be attractive to her. Since he insulted her by never trying to bed her, she enjoyed seeking her revenge in baiting him.

"Why have you canceled the Africans' celebration?" Philippe insisted, not allowing the subject to drop, even as a maid cleaned up the spilled wine.

" 'Twas dangerous in this heavy fog," he replied his dark eyes not even glancing at Philippe, but staring down the length of the table at Caresse.

The effect of those piercing ebony eyes seemed to go right through her. In the shadowy chamber they seemed to glow in the light from the tapers like the fierce gaze of some predatory beast. Always he was the enigma, the mystery. Why did he stare at her so intently? That unwavering gaze was beginning to wear on her nerves, already stretched thin to the breaking point.

"*C'est dommage,*" Solange said scenting a secret. "We had all looked forward to seeing a real voodoo ceremony, and on All Hallows' Eve how exciting."

"I am afraid Sans Regret is quite unexciting," Lucien replied, allowing his eyes to glance at Solange for only a moment, before turning that magnetic gaze back to Caresse.

"Perhaps you will not have to miss your voodoo celebration, Solange," Philippe told her, his amber eyes narrowing with dislike as he gave Lucien a cold look. "No matter what you might have advised, the Africans will have their ceremony, although they might have to move into the swamps to hold it away from your knowledge."

This was so close to the truth, Caresse felt weak in the knees. She had to clasp her hands in her lap so no one could see that they were shaking.

"Could Philippe be correct?" Solange asked Lucien with a rising excitement.

Lucien gave an infinitesimal shrug of his broad silk-clad shoulders. "Perhaps. If you wish to wander about in the swamps in this fog I cannot stop you, Solange."

"You are not any fun, *mon cher*. You have lost that wonderful *très dangereux* aura about you," Solange gave him a flirtatious pout of her tiny mean mouth.

"I have responsibilities now," he said huskily, turning his gaze that was as intimate as a kiss to Caresse.

"You have become boring," Solange uttered as if that was the ultimate insult. "I do not know how you stand being married to such a boring man, Caresse."

"He is the most stimulating, exciting man I have ever met," Caresse replied, her throat becoming thick with desire.

He stared at her, his eyes seeming enormous in the pale frozen mask of his classic visage. They burned with his passion for her, as a slight smile curved those sensual lips and melted for a moment the remote marble effigy of his magnificent face.

Her hands ached to touch him, feel the satin of his hair like cool water falling through her fingers, feel the masculine roughness of the crisp curls on his chest and thighs. In her mind she traveled over the sinewy length of him, remembering the touch, the taste, the scent of his beloved form. She wanted to feel his hands on her skin, she ached for it like a physical pain. Those remote features should be softened with the intensity of his passion, those lips should be murmuring her name over and over in a cry torn from his soul. The honey of arousal began to flow through her veins at the mere thought of their bed, that islet of rapture in a house full of shadows.

"Ma belle femme," he murmured, his voice a husky rasp of emotion as he lifted his wine glass to her in salute.

"Well, really. I feel like we have intruded on your bedchamber, Lucien," Solange complained, with a moue of distaste about her tight-lipped mouth.

"Solange," her husband said. There was a warning in that single word.

"Well, I, for one, wish to see this voodoo ceremony. It will make such wonderful conversation this winter in Nouvelle Orléans." She rose to her feet, pushing back her walnut chair with a vicious kick of her satin slipper before any of the men could reach her.

"Ah, 'twould seem we are going for an after-dinner stroll in the fog-drenched swamps," Pierre-François de Vaudreuil sighed, rising to his feet as did Philippe and Lucien.

"It will do your digestion good," Solange muttered, slapping at the slight bulge that hung over her husband's blue silk breeches.

"You might want to change into riding boots. The ground will be wet in many places," Lucien suggested, taking pity on the governor, as he stared down at the man's elegant shoes with their silver buckles. "You, too, Solange."

"Nonsense, if I ruin these I have many others," the stubborn woman sputtered, determined nothing would deter her from doing what she knew Lucien did not want her to do.

"I can testify to that, and I think she brought

most of them with her from Nouvelle Orléans," her husband said with a wry twist to his mouth.

"Are you not coming with us, Lucien? After all, you are our host," Solange spat at him from where she stood with Philippe and her husband at the door.

"We will catch up with you, Solange," Lucien replied with exasperation. "I know where Philippe is taking you, but Caresse and I wish to change into more suitable footwear for such a trek."

"As you wish," Solange said with a shrug of her fleshy shoulders. "Come, Philippe, you lead the way."

"Let us leave them to their own devices," Caresse said, rising to her feet as Lucien pulled out her chair. Their guests had disappeared into the fog.

"Ah, you tempt me, little one, but God only knows where that fool Philippe will lead them," he replied, placing his hands on her shoulders, his warm mouth seeking out the pulse point at the base of her throat. The tip of his tongue teased her by making a sensual circle on her silken skin.

Caresse felt her heart pound an erratic rhythm as he stood so close behind her she could feel the heat from his body reaching out to singe each vibrating nerve in her skin. Her fingers gripped the back of her chair to fight the weakness that was flooding her limbs. Suddenly, nothing mattered but that Lucien's mouth was caressing her throat, his hands were holding her against the hard length of him. The world began and ended for her within the circle of his embrace.

How long they would have stood lost in the myriad sensations that overwhelmed them they would never know, for the harsh bark of Bruno startled them from their reverie. The dog had risen from beside Lucien's chair and was staring out the open French door into the fog. The fur on his back rose, as he lifted his great shaggy head and howled the primitive lamentation of his wolf ancestors. He then moved swiftly to the portal where he stood like a sentry barring all entry, his lips curled back, his teeth bared in a savage gesture of warning to any who would dare to trespass.

"What does he see?" Caresse asked, in a shocked murmur, as she felt the hairs on the back of her neck rise at the primeval warning.

"I think 'tis more what he senses," Lucien replied tensely. He gave her shoulders a brief squeeze of reassurance.

" 'Tis all right, boy, all right," Lucien spoke in a low soothing voice to the animal, bending down beside him, stroking him gently.

Caresse came to stand beside the man and beast. This was not a night when she wanted to be by herself, even across a room. Staring out into the fog that swirled around the roots and low-hanging branches of live oaks she could see little. Whatever Bruno saw or sensed was beyond human comprehension. She almost turned away when she saw it, a ball of light that seemed to dance across the lawn from the direction of the swamp obscured from view by the mist.

"*Mon Dieu!*" she gasped, feeling Lucien rise beside her. "Do you see it?"

"*Oui,* 'tis called a *feu follet,*" he explained, but his voice was strained.

"What is a *feu follet?*" Caresse's words were a horrified whimper for the dancing light seemed a capricious apparition.

" 'Tis a mysterious fireball that comes from the swamps, caused perhaps by the decaying vegetation that is found in such abundance there. It can often be seen in the swamp at night, and sometimes it escapes into a cleared area such as the lawn of a house at the edge of the marsh." His voice this time was firm as he pulled her close to him within the circle of his muscular arm.

197

She welcomed the solid warmth of his body next to hers. They watched as the apparition disappeared in to the fog. Bruno, as if losing interest, turned his back on the scene and walked over to the table where he began to search the floor for tidbits of food.

"Even Bruno has decided a *feu follet* is not worth pursuing," Lucien joked, trying to ease the fear he saw in her eyes. What had that vindictive witch, Solange, been telling her whilst they had been gone this afternoon? He sensed that she was uneasy around him, and it sent a pang through his heart to think that she could fear him.

"If Solange sees it she will be thrilled thinking that at last she has seen a real ghost," Caresse tried to treat it all as a joke as Lucien seemed to want her to, but there was still a cold knot in her stomach.

"I should follow them, *ma chère*. Philippe does not know his way around these swamps as well as I do. They could be lost even as we speak. It would be better if you waited in the salon while I go after them. 'Tis not a place for you. There is a macabre atmosphere about the clearing that I do not wish to expose you to, for it is unsettling even in the daytime. I think only Solange would find such a trek appealing at night. She is always searching the next exciting experience, but then she has so few inner resources one can see why she is easily bored," he said, his voice etched with contempt and sarcasm.

"You are not leaving me in this house alone," Caresse corrected him. "I do not care how eerie the atmosphere is, it could not be worse than staying here. Come, let us go upstairs and change into more suitable clothing." There was a firm resolve in her voice that told him there was no use arguing.

"Remember, *ma chère*, that I warned you," he said cryptically, with a flash of something that could have been despair or resignation in his dark eyes as they left the dining room.

By the time she had changed with Fantine's help into her gray linen riding habit and leather boots, Lucien had also donned knee-high boots. A slight wind had come up, dissipating some of the fog, although it still clung to the dense bottom vegetation of the swamps. They had dismissed Fantine for the night, and the last they saw of her she was hurrying across the garden toward the kitchen house where the female servants' quarters were located.

"This way," Lucien told Caresse as they followed a path barely visible from the light of the pierced tin lantern he carried in one hand. The path left the stables and outbuildings behind, skirting the edge of the dark swamp.

Caresse felt the wind seem to gather force as it brushed her skirt, and caused the great branches of the oaks to creak and rub against each other in a mournful sound. As they passed by the African quarters she could see that all was quiet, but she sensed this was not because all were asleep, but rather because the cabins were deserted. Were they all at this celebration that she had given permission to hold?

"For once in his life Philippe was right," Lucien commented ruefully, as he too saw that the quarters were empty.

Caresse hesitated only a moment as Lucien gestured for her to follow him into the tunnel of oak and cypress trees draped in moss that was the beginning of the swamp. Sensing her fear, he held out his hand—glowing bronze in the light from the lantern. Feeling those tapered fingers clasp hers, some of his strength flowed into her and she was no longer afraid. With this magnificent fearless man beside her, who knew the swamps like the

199

back of his hand, as Solange had said, she had nothing to fear.

"We shall follow along this path till we reach the *chênière* where I believe they are holding this so-called celebration."

"What is a *chênière?*" Caresse whispered, although she did not know why she whispered. The swamp seemed an eerie forbidden place that they should not try to invade.

"A *chênière* is a mound of shells, quite a large mound, that has built up for eons in the swamps. There are usually several live oaks on them as there are on this one, but there is something else as well." He stopped on the narrow path, holding up the lantern so she could see his visage. "There is a tomb located on this *chênière*, the tomb of my first wife, Aurore."

Caresse felt as if her breath had solidified in her throat. She looked up into those black eyes that did not waver from her gaze. She saw a sad regret in them, a sense of the inevitable, and then a cool withdrawal, as if by recoiling from her he would not give her the chance to reject him.

" 'Twas why I did not want you to come with me. I wished to keep the secret of Aurore's death from you a while longer, perhaps till we knew each other better. She was a suicide. 'Tis why she is not buried in the consecrated ground of the family plot. Philippe insisted this was her favorite place at Sans Regret. Of course it was only later that I discovered she had joined with the Africans in their religion. She had become a leader of the group at the plantation. Philippe says that it made her feel less frightened for them to consider her their priestess. I did not realize how afraid she was to stay here alone till it was too late."

Some say it was murder, the words ran round in her mind as she stared up at Lucien, his pale face all that was visible in the flickering light from the lantern in the dark oppressive swamp. She licked her lips, for her mouth was so dry she didn't think she could speak. "I know," she managed to answer.

"When?" he asked, his gaze holding hers with the intensity of his emotion.

"That day on the flatboat coming from Nouvelle Orléans," she replied, "Yvonne told me of the gossip she had heard. She thought I should hear it from her rather than from a stranger. She begged me not to be frightened or let it interfere with my marriage to a good man."

"And has it?" his voice rasped.

"*Non*, for as I told you I do not frighten easily. I have known terrors others cannot even imagine," she said simply. "And she said you are a good man, and you have been good to me."

There was a flash of such naked pain, so intense in his dark eyes, Caresse flinched from it. He stared down at her as if he wanted to speak, but was weighing all the ramifications. "I stand in awe of such courage, such loyalty. Perhaps some day I shall feel worthy of it," he said in a voice full of strange emotion, then lifted her hand to his lips. Lowering the lantern, he turned, still holding her hand, and led her deeper into the swamp towards the *chênière* and Aurore's tomb. Caresse could not see how he knew where they were going, for the wild landscape seemed like a nightmarish dream, but Lucien seemed right at home within the unearthly luxuriance of forest and marsh. Twisted vines, as thick as a man's wrist, wrapped around ancient tree trunks and hung in tendrils from the branches, their green tentacles reaching out to the passerby like hands. The air as they ventured further into the swamp was heavy with decay and the fragrance of flowering vines. Underneath their boots, even on the path kept clear from the soles of the many African feet that transversed it, there was a soft vegetable mold, the result of falling foliage. And Caresse everywhere sensed moisture, drops of water from the leaves, the coiled vines, the feathery leaves of the cypress.

As they followed the twisting, turning path around a huge cypress tree, Caresse stumbling over the exposed roots reaching up for air in the suffocating waters of the swamp, she saw a red glow ahead of them and heard the beat of drums, a sensuous nerve-tingling beat that both lured and frightened her at the same time. She knew without being told that it was the sound of Africa. It spoke of tradition, of sensuality, of freedom.

Lucien stopped at the edge of what she knew must be the *chênière*, but they were both still hidden from view in the dense foliage, in the intense darkness of the swamp. "The smell is from a kettle of tafia they have boiling over the fire. We shall move quietly forward. I can only hope Zweig is keeping an eye out as he usually does on these nights. No matter what you see, you must make no sound. The tafia is a crude rum they make themselves, we do not know how long they have been drinking it. Not a sound," he cautioned her, not moving till she whispered her understanding.

As they moved forward cautiously, a grotesque sight out of Dante greeted them. An old African stood near a white tomb built of marble like a small, macabre, child's playhouse, sawing away on a two stringed fiddle covered in what looked like a snakeskin. Standing next to the old slave were three young men beating upon drums made out of huge dried gourds, and a skull that appeared to have come from a cow, and one strange instrument made from the skull of an alligator. Hides had been stretched across the weird drums, giving them their strange deep vibration. On top of the tomb rested a large cage from which came an ominous rustling sound. African men and women danced around the tomb in rhythm to the music.

The men were clad only in red loincloths, the women in short garments made of scarlet handkerchiefs sewn together in a definite pattern, brilliant calico *tignons* on their heads. The glow from the fire cast their long shadows over the white marble of the tomb.

As Caresse and Lucien stood watching, concealed from the dancers' view in the dense foliage of the swamp, the moon came out from behind the indigo black clouds. The moon glow only added to the eeriness of the scene, silvering the moss that hung from the branches of the oak that arched over the tomb that gleamed phosphorus in the sudden light. It seemed to excite the dancers as they began to writhe and twist convulsively, the air filled with their hoarse cries. Others joined them, coming from the trees, several who were house servants well known to Caresse. They all joined in the strange serpentine circle that moved around the tomb glowing in the alabaster light of the moon.

"*Sacré*" Lucien muttered, holding tight to Caresse's hand. "I see the others on the other side of the *chênière*. Look through the trees, you can see part of Solange's gown in the moonlight," he whispered to her. "The fools! They are not even trying to stay hidden. I don't like the atmosphere tonight, it is savage, not a place where Frenchmen are welcome."

Turning to where he pointed, she saw the flash of silk through the trees highlighted by the moon now directly above them. She wondered if they also found the scene as frightening and macabre as it appeared to her. If Solange wanted a new exotic experience she was not being disappointed.

As the moon shone down on the white shells of the *chênière*, bleaching them till they appeared like bones, the drums began to accelerate their beat. The dancers opened their circle as through the dark shadows on the east side of the clearing came a procession, several of the largest field hands carrying a crudely constructed sedan chair with a seated figure. When they moved into the moonlight Caresse felt her breath catch in her throat, for the seated figure holding herself like a queen was Dominique.

"Is Dominique now their priestess?" Caresse asked Lucien in a stunned whisper.

"*Oui,* and I told her I did not want this going on tonight," Lucien said tersely. "I made a special request of her, and she disregarded it. 'Tis not like her, but then 'twould seem voodoo is more important than old loyalty. She is a free woman, and can do as she wishes. But I did not realize she still feared Aurore's power."

Caresse couldn't control the spasmodic trembling within her at the knowledge that Dominique had tricked her with the story of rumors of a slave uprising to achieve her own ends. The ceremony to appease Aurore's spirit was so important she had to lie to make sure it was carried out. What kind of woman had Aurore been, to cause such fear even seven years after her death? And what would Lucien think if he knew that she had allowed herself to be tricked, had in her naïveté given her permission for this ceremony to take place against his wishes.

"Are you all right?" Lucien asked in a concerned voice as he felt her trembling beside him. He knew he should have insisted she stay back at the house. Caresse had not lived long enough in Louisiane to understand what she was seeing.

" 'Tis so strange, I must confess it disturbs me that a woman I thought I knew, a woman who has served as my maid for several months, is a voodoo priestess," Caresse answered with a shrug of disbelief. "And I believe I see Fantine over there on the far side of the circle. Are all the Africans at Sans Regret believers?" Her voice wavered at the realization that it was obvious that they were all here, dancing, moving to the primitive beat of the African drums. Never had La Louisiane seemed so foreign, so frightening.

"They mean you no harm," Lucien reassured her. "Their religion is very important to them, as ours is to us, but perhaps even more important, for we have taken everything else from them—'tis all they have that is their own," he admitted ruefully.

The field hands had lowered the sedan chair to the chalkwhite shells of the *chênière* so that Dominique could alight. With a regal grace she stepped out onto the shells clad in a scarlet silk garment wrapped around her slender form from right above her breasts to the middle of her thighs, a gold silk *tignon* on her head, the ends pointing stiffly into the air. Her legs and feet were bare, but around her ankles were bracelets of tiny bells that made a tinkling sound as she walked toward Aurore's tomb.

Caresse felt Lucien tense beside her as they watched the graceful figure approach the sepulcher. It was as she stopped directly in front of the engraved door that they heard the chant begin.

"Dansez Calinda! Badoum! Badoum! The chanting sound of the African voices drifted up into the sultry humid night like the gray smoke from the bonfire. The haunting sound seemed to permeate the swamp, coming from every direction. It surrounded them.

"Mon Dieu, non!" a hoarse male voice cried out above the chanting as Dominique slipped a long curved knife from her garment, and lifted it high in the air.

Fourteen

"What does he think he's doing?" Lucien muttered, as they watched the tall slender figure of Philippe dash across the shells to Dominique's side. He ran like a madman shouting to the stunned Dominique, intent on some wild purpose known only to him while the others watched in fascinated horror.

The drums had stopped at his shouted words, the dancers stood confused as if awakening from a deep sleep, still groggy. Dominique faced Philippe without flinching, her slender arm still holding the raised knife. She stood defiant and without fear.

"It must be done. She cannot return to Sans Regret." Dominique's words rang out in the stillness of the warm night. She stared up at him with her lip curled in disgust at his foolish behavior.

"If she is strong enough to return, then so be it," Philippe exclaimed, reaching out to wrap his hand around her slender wrist holding the handle of the knife.

They stood, a frozen tableau in the moonlight, as physical strength overpowered strength of will. Slowly, she lowered the knife to her side, dropping it on the ground.

"You will regret this, *m'sieur.*" Dominique hissed

as the Africans moved uneasily, unsure what she wanted from them.

"Is he in any danger?" Caresse asked, clinging unashamedly to Lucien.

"*Non*, although they would like to kill him for what he has done. He is a Frenchman, and they know he has not come alone. They sense us in the shadows," Lucien explained tersely. "And they know Zweig is not far away. Their freedom is unfortunately an illusion on this night, and they are aware of it. But Philippe shall have to look over his shoulder from now on. There are other more secretive ways to kill, than in front of a witness, if one is determined."

Caresse bit her lower lip as she couldn't help but anxiously search for the meaning behind his words. Suddenly, there seemed no safety in the swamp on this terrible night, even held against the lean strong body of her husband. "Some say it was murder," Solange had said.

"I'd best signal Zweig," Lucien said firmly. "The celebration is over for this All Hallows' Eve. Come, we shall walk out with authority. They will understand that it is over."

Taking from the top of his boot a small pistol that Caresse did not know he carried, he held it up and out to the side, firing once. Then taking her hand, he walked calmly to the middle of the *chênière*.

The Africans stood stunned both by the gunshot and the appearance of the St. Amants. Then Caresse heard their low frightened murmur as they moved back a few steps. Dark eyes went from Caresse and Lucien and then back to Dominique. It was as if they were looking for some signal, some acknowledgment that what they were seeing was true. The twin of Aurore St. Amant stood at her tomb, or perhaps it was her apparition.

The armed overseer Zweig appeared from the

shadows, as did the sheepish looking Marquis and Marquise de Vaudreuil, a small pistol in the governor's hand. Solange was as white as Aurore's tomb in the moonlight, all talk of exotic experience gone as she stood mute at her husband's side.

" 'Tis over, *fini,*" Lucien announced in a strong cold voice that allowed no dissent. He turned to Dominique. "Tell them to go back to their quarters. Neither of us wants anyone to get hurt."

The woman stared at him for a long moment as time seemed to stand still. Her almond-shaped eyes stared at him, then through him. "If you wish, *m'sieur,* but I would think that you, of all of us gathered here, would not want the return of Aurore St. Amant."

"She is gone. All that is left are her bones baking in that tomb under the sun of La Louisiane." He barked as he pointed toward the silent alabaster sepulcher.

"Perhaps, *m'sieur,*" she said, allowing her eyes to slide over the figure of Caresse at his side. Then she raised her hand and pointed behind her. As if of one accord, the Africans followed her stately lead from the *chênière* and back toward their quarters.

"A remarkable woman," the governor said as they all stared after the retreating figures. As the last two men picked up the cage from the tomb, they all realized, with a flicker of primeval fear, that it contained a snake.

"Remarkable!" Solange snorted. "The woman is *très dangereuse.* I cannot believe I allowed her to help me dress. No more Dominique as my maid," she said with an expression of distaste to Caresse.

"Of course, I quite understand," Caresse replied, wondering with a sinking heart how she could stand to have Dominique around her. Even though Lucien seemed to put up with her strange ways, because of how well she handled the slaves, she would have nothing else to do with the woman. She had tricked her, and it was obvious from the events of the evening that she was still obsessed with Aurore. Fantine would continue to be her lady's maid, she vowed.

"I do not mean to give offense, *mon cher* Lucien, but fever or no fever, the marquis and I leave on the morrow for Nouvelle Orléans. I have seen all the macabre events that I want to see," Solange told him as she took her husband's arm. "Put that pistol away, Pierre-François, you look foolish. Take me back to the house, I could use something strong to drink."

Philippe stood with his back to them, lost in some private reverie in front of Aurore's tomb. There was such a sense of forlorn sadness about his figure that Caresse pitied him. He must have loved her very much, even if she had only been his stepsister, she mused. Without thinking, she left Lucien's side to walk the few steps to where Philippe stood lost in contemplation.

"We should return to the house now, Philippe," she said softly, touching his sleeve.

He turned, his face pale, as he stared down at her as if she had awakened him from a sound slumber. "You are here," he breathed.

" 'Tis Caresse," she reminded him. "Come, you need to rest."

"We are all leaving now," Lucien said loudly in a cold hard voice, his black eyes smoldering with anger, as he came to stand beside Caresse. "My wife and I have had enough of this foolishness."

"Your wife," Philippe raised his head, his lips curled in contempt. "*She* was your wife in name only," he spat nodding his head toward the tomb, then turned and strode without waiting for the others back to the house.

"Leave him alone, he brings only trouble," Lucien ordered Caresse as he took her hand in his like she was a misbehaving child. "I have had enough of Philippe Dubrieul for one evening." They were his last words as the two couples made a silent retreat back to the sanctuary of the mansion. Although he continued to keep her hand clasped in his, he seemed far away, lost in some private musings where she was not welcome.

A great weariness came over Caresse as they reached the gardens in the back of the house. All was quiet, even in the quarters of the house servants. It was as if it had all been a vivid nightmare, but the images that played over and over in her mind were too real.

"What was that woman going to do with the knife?" Solange asked Lucien, suddenly breaking the long silence.

"If Philippe had not stopped her, she would have signaled for them to bring her some animal, probably one of the doves from the dovecote in the garden. She would have slit its throat, sacrificing it to appease the spirit of Aurore so that she would not return and walk the earth on All Hallows' Eve," he explained.

"How awful," Solange gave a shudder. "How can you stand to have her around?"

"She has always been very loyal to the St. Amant family, doing what she thinks is best for *la famille* even if it is not always immediately apparent." There was a finality to his voice that even Solange decided to respect.

But as they climbed the stair to their bedchamber, Caresse found herself agreeing with Solange. She could not understand why Lucien did not dismiss Dominique from his household staff. But then, she thought with a great weariness, there were a great many things she did not understand since coming to Sans Regret.

"I am sorry that you had to witness that debacle," Lucien said as they walked into the dark chamber. "Remember, I wished for you to stay here. Until one has lived here a long time 'tis hard to understand the ways of the Africans."

"And the masters as well," said Caresse with some bitterness.

Lucien turned from where he stood at the mantel lighting the tapers kept under glass hurricane globes. "What is it about me you do not understand, *ma chère*?" There was a curious expectant quality to his deep voice.

"Everything," she said in exasperation as she pried off one boot then set to work on the other. The fecund scent of the decay of the swamps still clung to the soles. "Your whole life has been a secret from me from the start."

"What do you mean?" His voice was stiff, defensive.

"Aurore, you never told me about Aurore," she replied flatly, taking off her jacket, then loosening the waistband of her skirt so she could step out of it.

"A suicide is not something one discusses," he answered with an edge to his words.

"You should have told me, not let me find it out from others," she said wearily, slipping off the men's-style shirt worn with her riding habit. Turning her back to him as she placed the shirt in the armoire, fatigue enveloped her. She swayed for a moment in her chemise and petticoat.

"Perhaps you are right, but we both have our secrets, do we not, *ma chère*?" He crossed the chamber in a few lithe strides till he was behind her, his strong hands on her shoulders, steadying her.

"You talk in riddles again." She brushed a strand of hair from her face, feeling his warm breath on her neck.

"Allow me to help you with the rest," he murmured, unlacing her stays, then casting them aside. With a few deft strokes, he had slipped her petti-

211

coat to the floor, but it was as he placed his hands on the shoulders of her chemise that she knew what he had meant.

The scarlet lily on her shoulder burned for a moment as it had in the cell at La Salpêtrière prison. He was right, she had her own secrets that she could not bring herself to tell him, at least not yet. Not till she could be sure that they would not come from France seeking her. When she knew she was safe from ever being sent back to prison she could confide in him, but for now she would say nothing. Whoever had persuaded the king to issue the *lettre de cachet* against her and her father could still be seeking their ruin. No, here in La Louisiane she felt safe from those who wished to hurt her. It was not time yet to remove the mask, not even for Lucien. He, as she was beginning to realize, wore a mask as well.

"Forgive me if I brought up painful memories," she whispered, as his hands slipped the chemise from her ivory shoulders. "I know what 'tis like to not be able to speak of something that has caused a great deal of suffering."

"*Ma chère femme*, when we are alone together in our bedchamber there is no past, only the present moment where all that matters is the rapture between us." His voice was a seductive caress as his mouth tenderly kissed the scarlet lily on her shoulder.

If only that were true, she thought with a pang of sorrow that was quickly softened by the gentle touch of knowing hands, the sensual feel of warm masculine lips on her skin, adoring her, arousing her. The near-tropic air kissed her nude body, as did his lips, as the last of her garments fell in a forgotten pool at her feet.

"Ah, *ma belle*, the sight of you takes my breath away," he murmured, turning her gently around so that she faced him. His intense dark eyes caressed

212

the length of her ivory form, awe and passion burning in those midnight black orbs. "Let us put the foolishness of the evening behind us. There is only room in our chamber for enjoying one another." Placing his hands on either side of her lovely face, he gently kissed first her forehead, then the tip of her nose, and then brushed his lips across her trembling mouth.

The wonderful warm sense of belonging once more flooded through her as his lips gently covered her mouth, his arms lowering to surround her, to press her against the length of him. Fatigue and anxiety seemed to vanish under his tender seduction.

As he led her to the four-poster in its cloud of mosquito netting, she thought with a sigh that if Aurore's ghost walked the chambers of Sans Regret she stopped at the threshold of their chamber. Here, even though the room was full of shadows, she felt free of the invisible specter that she often sensed in other parts of the house.

She thought no more of Aurore as he joined her on the feather bed. "Let me release the tension of the day," he said in a husky murmur of passion. Brushing her long silken tresses to one side, his long slender fingers stroked down the exquisite length of her spine, rubbing the knotted nerves that she had not even been aware carried tension. Slowly, she felt a warmth flow through her as she sighed in wonder. Then his amazing touch was on the backs of her thighs, kneading, stroking the tension from her muscles, till she felt as pliant as a willow in the wind.

" 'Tis wonderful," she sighed. "You have stroked away pain I did not even know I had."

A rich low chuckle was her answer as he bent down and kissed one perfect ivory mound of her bottom, before continuing his massage to the muscles of her calves and slender ankles, even caressing the soles of her tiny feet.

Suddenly, she began to giggle lightly, then developed a full-throated sensual laugh as she rolled over to face him. "You are tickling me," she protested as he moved up beside her, tracing his fingers up the curve of her body till she felt the blond silky hairs stand up where his hand had touched. "You are, you devil," she protested, dissolving against him with a husky musical laugh.

"So I have been called," he agreed, pressing her to him, looking down at her with a gentle smile as he captured her with his strong arms. "Now 'tis better, you are laughing, perhaps enjoying yourself just a little."

"*Oui*, a little," she teased, looking up at him with a seductive gleam in her gray eyes that set his blood aflame.

"There are many ways to make love, *ma belle femme*, and tonight we shall explore several of them," he promised as he pressed her tight against him, then with a swift lithe move was lying on his back with her stretched on top of him.

"What are we doing?" she gasped, with a stunned laugh.

"Wait, you shall see," he teased, his dark eyes glowing up into hers. "I want to see all of you as we love."

She felt his hands caress her buttocks, and then lower between her thighs, spreading her apart, preparing her with his knowing touch for that more passionate, intimate invasion. Her moan of arousal told him that she was almost ready to receive him.

Slowly, he stroked inside her with one tapered finger, feeling the moist warmth of her, gently rousing the fire within her loins. He wanted to drive all doubt, all the terrible images of the night from her mind, and replace them with the rapturous joy of their lovemaking. She had a wonderful natural sensuality about her that he wanted to bring fully to bloom.

"You shall make me wanton," she whispered, as his tongue circled the inside of her ear.

"I certainly hope so," he chuckled as he suddenly placed his hands at the slender indication of her waist and lifted her up so that he might enter her waiting depths.

"Oh, *oui,*" she sighed with a wonderful sense of completion as he thrust inside, filling her with his erection, with his love.

"Sit up, *ma belle,* that I might see you," he instructed her, helping her so that she was astride him, her tiny hands stroking down his chest, slipping the dark fur through her fingers as he drank in the sight of her in the glow of the tapers.

Her ash blond hair was a glorious silvery tangle about the pale flower of her face. The hard coral rosebuds of her nipples teased him from her full ivory breasts as she arched her back, glorying in the awe that was almost worship in his smoldering eyes.

"Like a beautiful lily bending in the wind, you are *ma belle fleur.*" His voice was full of love and joy. He knew that he would never forget this beautiful moment when she was all silvery light and awakened passion, returning his rapture with her own uninhibited movements. His heart was full of gratitude to fate for allowing him a second chance at love, at life, with this splendid woman as his beloved. The memories of the past could finally be put to rest. Whatever happened to him on the rest of life's journey, he had the memory of this moment of perfect joy when he had felt renewed in her arms.

She felt no shame before his adoring gaze, for such an emotion was totally wrong in such an atmosphere of love and acceptance. This experience was on a plane where such thoughts did not exist.

There was only a sense that they had finally found each other after such a long lonely time. How she could explain such a feeling she didn't know, but it was so strong, the sense of belonging, as if all of their life had been merely a prelude to this moment. As did most young girls, she had dreamed all of her life of the man who would come to her and love her one day. But how fortunate she was to have found her other half, the mate of her soul. Fate had somehow allowed them to find one another in the midst of personal sorrow and despair.

She smiled down at him lovingly as she moved gently with her hips, wanting to prolong the wonderful feeling of his sex inside her, joined with her in their love knot. "How fortunate we are that fate has been kind to us," she said, thinking for a moment of all those who would never know what they had been given.

"What is it, *ma chère?*" he asked softly, caressing her breasts, down to the indentation of her waist. "A shadow crossed your lovely face."

"Only a sadness for those who have not been blessed with such happiness," she replied, arching under his touch, her long silky hair falling over his hands like cool water.

"Ah, you feel it also, this sense of destiny between us," he mused, his handsome features somber for a moment. The lightness was gone, replaced with the depth of his wonder at the mystery of their finding each other when so much had been against them. He remembered his father telling him that if something was meant to be it would happen. But how strange were the workings of fate that they would come together, find each other in such a way. That this lovely woman, who resembled his greatest defeat, should show him the way out of the despair of the past.

"*Oui,*" she whispered, looking down at him with

her heart and soul in her soft gray eyes. *"Je t'aime,* Lucien."

"Je t'aime, Caresse," he replied, his voice so husky with emotion he could hardly speak. His control almost gone, he lifted her gently from him and was over her, his dark eyes blazing with a wild yearning. *"Je t'aime,* Caresse." His voice was a cry against the pain of living, as he took her again and again.

Tears streaked her face as she responded with all the repressed emotion of a lifetime. He had said he loved her, and she realized through her ecstasy that it was the first time in her lonely life that anyone had ever said those words to her.

Then there were no words, nothing but the music of shared cries of fulfillment, as he took her to that special soaring place of rapture. And together they reached the pinnacle in exquisite harmony finding their peace and contentment.

Entwined in the comfort of each other's embrace they slept, as the wind rose in swirls about the solid corners of Sans Regret. The rain came lashing at the windows as the wind bent the boughs of the enormous live oaks. But they slept, locked in the security of beloved arms, and unaware of nature's fury.

Suddenly, Caresse was awake, her heart beating so loud and fast she thought she could hear it above the storm. Her breath was coming in gasps as if she could not get enough air. What was it? What had frightened her? Then, slipping from Lucien's sleeping embrace, she remembered.

She couldn't breathe, was suffocating in that small horrible place. Somehow she had to get out, they had to let her out. The thin strip of light, she could see that outside there was light, the scent of rain, the feel of the wind. She couldn't stand it any longer, the darkness, the terrible desolation of the tomb.

A shudder shook Caresse's slender frame as she

217

remembered the nightmare. Aurore's tomb, she had been locked inside that marble sepulcher. The horror of it lingered with her still.

A gust of wind blew in through the open French door carrying the fresh scent of the rain. She took in deep breaths trying to cleanse her mind of the macabre dream. She went cold remembering that she had thought she was Aurore, trapped forever in the marble tomb on the *chênière* in the swamp. It was then that she smelled it, the scent of flowers on the rain, the scent of violets in November.

"What is it, *ma chère?*" Lucien called to her in a sleep-filled voice, his hand reaching out to stroke her arm.

"Hold me!" she gasped. *"Mon Dieu,* hold me!"

He pulled her down against him, almost aslumber once more. But Caresse, even resting her head against the safety of his chest, could not sleep. She was afraid to close her eyes lest she be once more transported to that horrible place in the swamps. But she knew with a strange dread that even awake she could not erase the presence of Aurore. Her haunting presence was here, in the chamber, as the scent of violets blew in with the wind and rain on the first of November, All Saints' Day, the day to remember the dead.

Fifteen

"Where is Philippe? I am anxious to start for Chêne Vert before the rain starts again," Solange de Vaudreuil stood dressed in her riding habit, slapping her leather whip against her skirt in impatience. "You were kind enough to lend us horses and a mule wagon for our bags so we might return to the plantation. And now he keeps us waiting."

"I believe he wished to place flowers at Aurore's tomb," Lucien said quietly as they stood at the foot of the twin curving staircases. Three saddled horses, held by the grooms, pawed the ground, as the driver of the mule wagon, an old trusted slave with a young boy beside him, piled Solange's hatboxes and several portmanteaus into the back of the wagon.

" 'Tis All Saints' Day, Solange," her husband reminded her, a warning in his soft voice.

"How he can go back to that macabre place I shall never understand," the Marquise de Vaudreuil said tactlessly, giving a shudder of her plump shoulders.

Caresse could understand her feelings even if it was rude of her to speak of them in front of Lucien. She would be glad to see them leave on the first stage of their trip back down river to Nouvelle Orléans. Their boat was moored at Chêne Vert.

She could only hope for Philippe's sake that the weather would be better on the morrow so that they could resume their voyage downriver.

Solange had refused to stay another night at Sans Regret. When the men told her that because of the overcast weather it was not the best day to navigate the treacherous Mississippi, she had become livid and then almost hysterical. Lucien had gallantly offered to lend them mounts so they might take the path along the river to Chêne Vert to everyone's relief. Philippe had, however, slipped away as the horses were being saddled in the stables.

The cool wind rustled the arching branches of the live oaks overhead, causing a flock of red-winged blackbirds to take flight and circle above them. In the moisture-laden air the scent from the sweet olive bushes was almost overpowering, reminding Caresse of awakening in the night and thinking she smelled violets on the rain coming in through the open door. She had been overtired and half asleep. It was no wonder she would have such strange fantasies after watching the voodoo ceremonies in front of Aurore's tomb. And that is all it was, she told herself firmly, nothing more.

" 'Tis about time you returned, Philippe," Solange called out angrily as his figure appeared at the edge of the swamp.

He appeared weary and preoccupied, with dark circles under his eyes. In his hand he carried a strange object, a black ball made of wax with feathers sticking out of it, and what appeared to be a cross drawn in the soft wax with a pointed instrument. Stopping in front of them, he threw the ball at Lucien's feet.

"This was in front of Aurore's tomb. I want no more such fetishes left there to dishonor her memory," he said through clenched teeth, his strange amber eyes ablaze with anger and something that looked almost like fear.

"She still frightens them," Lucien said tersely, a muscle flicking in his jaw, "even though she has been dead for seven years."

"They know that she is not at peace. Her spirit is restless," Philippe said with a sigh, wiping his face with the linen handkerchief he had taken from his pocket. Then he turned away to grab the reins of one of the horses from a groom's hand. "I shall return them on the morrow. My overseer will see then to my flatboat." He politely doffed his tricorn to Caresse as he said with a sad smile, *"Adieu, madame."*

The de Vaudreuils hurried to mount the last two horses, Philippe's odd behavior necessitating a hurried farewell. Caresse and Lucien, with Bruno and Blanchette at their heels, walked to the beginning of the crushed-shell path to see them off down the way that curved through the dense foliage along the bank of the Mississippi.

" 'Tis a relief to see them leave," Lucien commented as they vanished from sight into the dense vegetation.

"Solange can be trying on one's nerves," Caresse agreed as they walked back toward the house. She thought, however, that now they were gone, Sans Regret seemed to have such an air of isolation about the grounds, as well as the elegant house. How ridiculous she was being, afraid to be alone with her own husband. But the uneasy sensation stayed with her as they strolled past the giant oaks.

The wind was blowing the gray moss that hung from the trees back and forth in an eerie display, and far away across the river could be heard the sound of thunder. Passing the tree Philippe had pointed out as the doubling oak, Caresse wrapped her shawl tighter around her shoulders. The cooler weather had come the previous night with the rain, but the chill that ran through her was not physical. Rather it was spiritual.

"What was that awful ball Philippe carried?" Caresse asked, remembering the fetish he had thrown at Lucien's feet.

"A voodoo hex, black magic," he said in exasperation. "As I told you last night the Africans have their own ways. We will not stop their beliefs simply by forbidding them. But they have become too bold. They must know what the limits are at Sans Regret."

When they reached the spot where Philippe had thrown the black ball of wax they were both startled to see that it was gone. There was only one small feather to show where it had been thrown to the ground.

"Who would have taken it?" Caresse asked Lucien, glancing about the kitchen garden aware that even though there was no one in sight, dark African eyes were watching them from the shadows of the various buildings. Someone had removed the fetish, and the only people at Sans Regret were the overseer and the numerous servants.

"I do not know, but Philippe's presence here was disruptive. The servants always were uneasy when he came to the plantation," Lucien mused. "Now that he is gone everything will settle back to normal. You shall see." His deep voice was reassuring as he led her toward the house.

Why was Philippe disliked by the Africans? Caresse wanted to ask, but something held her tongue. She sensed that Lucien was shielding her from some deeper truth, something he did not want her to know. It made her feel so lonely when the old secrets between them surfaced, revealing that no matter how passionate the bond between them was, the past had a way of driving a wedge into their relationship. Suspicions once raised were

222

hard to dismiss, no matter how great their sensual attraction was.

"I must have a word with Zweig out in the fields. We shall meet at noonday, and take a long relaxing time to dine," Lucien promised her as they reached the first-floor gallery. "Do not tire yourself. Remember, you were very ill not long ago." He kissed her brow in farewell, leaving her beside the door to the warming kitchen, as he strode with lithe grace out to the stables.

Catching sight of Fantine as she helped stack the dirty dishes, Caresse called to her, determined to impose her own mark that very day on Sans Regret. Today would be her first step in keeping the past where it belonged, buried in a tomb in the swamp.

"Oui, madame?" Fantine glided to her side, with a gentle expression, her soft brown eyes, like those of a fawn, carefully lowered.

"Send Dominique to me in the salon. I wish to discuss the running of the house." Caresse's voice was polite but edged with authority. She was now Mme St. Amant, not Aurore. She would no longer feel like an unwanted guest in her own home.

While waiting for Dominique in the salon, she shut the long French doors that opened on to the gallery. The wind had strengthened, heralding the cooler weather of late autumn. Lucien had told her the winters were short in the colony but could be cool and damp. She thought of her departed guests who were riding toward Chêne Vert. If the rain began again it would be a miserable trip.

"Madame, you wished to see me." The soft voice of Dominique, with its slight patois lilt, caused Caresse to turn around from where she stood staring out the panes of the closed door at the swaying branches of the live oaks.

"Oui," she replied coolly. Keeping her expression aloof she faced the housekeeper, who was immaculately clad in blue gingham with a starched white

apron and *tignon* on her elegant head. There was no sign of the voodoo priestess about her person on this cool overcast morn. "I have quite recovered from my illness, and shall now take the *châtelaine* with the household keys." She held out her hand for the silver chain worn about Dominique's waist to which were attached the keys to the chambers of the house, and the storehouses, as well as the tea and coffee containers, the liquor cabinet, the medicine cabinet, and the gun case. The *châtelaine* was the badge of authority of the mistress of the plantation.

"The housekeeper for the St. Amant family has always worn the *châtelaine*," she protested, her almond eyes narrowing, as she made no move to remove the chain.

"I am sure that was true in the past because there was not a mistress who was well enough to take over the running of the houses. I am very capable of being *châtelaine* of Sans Regret as well as the town house in Nouvelle Orléans. You must understand, Dominique, I am Mme St. Amant now and as such I am in charge. The keys," she repeated once more holding out her hand, her eyes never wavering from Dominique's narrowed gaze.

"You are stronger than the others, I sensed it from the first moment I saw you," Dominique mused aloud. Then giving a slight shrug of her slender shoulders, she unfastened the silver chain and handed it to Caresse. There was a grudging respect in the depths of her dark eyes.

"There are to be no more tricks, Dominique," Caresse said in a low composed voice, each word edged with a steel warning. She fastened the chain about her waist.

"*Pardonnez-moi, madame?*" Dominique asked with an arched brow of injured shock.

"I am referring to the threat of the slave uprising if I had not given my permission for that ghastly

224

MORE PASSION AND ADVENTURE AWAIT... YOUR TRIP TO A BIG ADVENTUROUS WORLD BEGINS WHEN YOU ACCEPT YOUR FIRST 4 NOVELS ABSOLUTELY *FREE* (AN $18.00 VALUE)

Accept your Free gift and start to experience more of the passion and adventure you like in a historical romance novel. Each Zebra novel is filled with proud men, spirited women and tempestuous love that you'll remember long after you turn the last page.

Zebra Historical Romances are the finest novels of their kind. They are written by authors who really know how to weave tales of romance and adventure in the historical settings you love. You'll feel like you've actually gone back in time with the thrilling stories that each Zebra novel offers.

GET YOUR FREE GIFT WITH THE START OF YOUR HOME SUBSCRIPTION

Our readers tell us that these books sell out very fast in book stores and often they miss the newest titles. So Zebra has made arrangements for you to receive the four newest novels published each month.

You'll be guaranteed that you'll never miss a title, and home delivery is so convenient. And to show you just how easy it is to get Zebra Historical Romances, we'll send you your first 4 books absolutely FREE! Our gift to you just for trying our home subscription service.

BIG SAVINGS AND FREE HOME DELIVERY

Each month, you'll receive the four newest titles as soon as they are published. You'll probably receive them even before the bookstores do. What's more, you may preview these exciting novels free for 10 days. If you like them as much as we think you will, just pay the low preferred subscriber's price of just $3.75 each. *You'll save $3.00 each month off the publisher's price.* AND, your savings are even greater because there are never any shipping, handling or other hidden charges—FREE Home Delivery. Of course you can return any shipment within 10 days for full credit, no questions asked. There is no minimum number of books you must buy.

ceremony last night. I may be new to La Louisiane, to Sans Regret, but I learn quickly." She knew that there was a struggle of wills going on as to who would be the real *châtelaine*.

"There could have been an uprising, *madame,* if their *voodooienne* had ordered it," Dominique answered, her head held high like a queen as she stared unblinking at her.

For a moment the hairs stood up on the back of Caresse's neck. By some trick of the light, the lovely elegant Dominique had appeared almost reptilian. "You have that much power over them?"

"I am very strong, *madame,*" she said with a silken thread of warning in her voice.

"*Oui,* I can believe that, Dominique, but I, too, am strong." Caresse never let her gaze waver, although she felt a sick feeling in the pit of her stomach. It was as if they were having some eerie duel, but their weapons were words. Some instinct told her that if she wanted this strange woman's respect, if she did indeed want to be *la châtelaine,* she must show complete confidence in her own power as mistress of Sans Regret.

"*Peut-être, madame,*" she answered softly, her dark eyes glistening. "Is there anything else?"

"M. St. Amant will be returning to the house for *le déjeuner.* I wish it served up here in the winter dining salon. The weather is too damp and cool to dine downstairs. And I shall be spending the rest of the morning exploring the rest of the house. Now that I am recovered I wish to familiarize myself with every chamber."

"*Oui, madame,*" Dominique answered with a slight bow of her head. Gliding from the salon, she stopped at the portal and turned to face Caresse. "Will *m'sieur* wish to place the *immortelles* I fashioned for him on the tombs of *la famille* after you finish dining?" Her visage was impassive, but there was a gleam of triumph in her dark eyes.

"The *immortelles?*" she questioned.

" 'Tis a wreath of mourning that I fashion from wire and black linen rosettes to place on the tombs of his *mère,* his *père* and Aurore on All Saints' Day."

"I shall inquire," Caresse replied tersely, knowing that Dominique had not given up their silent duel for power at Sans Regret. "That will be all." She dismissed her, thinking that it was going to be more difficult than she thought maintaining her position as mistress of the houses and plantation. Dominique would fight her every step of the way. The mask of politeness had slipped from the woman's face the moment she realized that Caresse was not someone she could intimidate with her talk of voodoo.

Turning back toward the scene outside the French doors, Caresse bit her lower lip as her fingers touched the keys at her waist. Staring out at the swaying boughs, she knew there was something she had wanted to do ever since her arrival at the plantation, and with Lucien out with the overseer this was the perfect time.

Opening the French door, she stepped onto the gallery. The wind tore at her hair and at her skirt, but she fought against the gusts as it swirled around the corner of the house. She knew where she had to go to satisfy the curiosity that had been gnawing inside her since the day she walked up the path from the dock. Then she was there, in front of the door with the broken glass, a board nailed across the opening until a new pane could be brought from Nouvelle Orléans. Trying the knob she found it locked as she had expected. Methodically, she tried each key on her *châtelaine* until she found the one that turned the lock. Then she was inside, inside the chamber that had been Aurore's.

The lace curtains at the French doors, along with the overcast skies, made the room full of shadows.

Caresse paused with her back to the closed doors, her pulse pounding, every nerve alert as she stared about the chamber. It was foolish, but she could not help feeling like a trespasser. Someone dusted the room, for it was clean, but there was an empty melancholy atmosphere about the chamber as was often felt in unused rooms.

She moved away from the doors, determined that somewhere in this bedchamber of Aurore's she would find some clue to what kind of woman she had been, what had been her frightening fascination for so many people. It was obvious her favorite color had been lavender for the walls were tinted a pale orchid, the bed-curtains and the counterpane were of violet silk. A *lit de repos,* a day bed, was upholstered in lilac with bouquets of violets in a deep purple brocaded upon it. And permeating the chamber was the faint musty fragrance of violet perfume.

It was somehow morbid keeping the bedchamber exactly as it had been when she was alive, thought Caresse, for she realized that this was what had been done. A purple silk *robe de nuit* lay across the foot of the bed, and beneath its trailing hem were two small satin mules with hourglass heels worn a little at the edge. It seemed as if they were waiting for their owner to return that night.

Wrapping her shawl tight about her, she turned away from the bed to see a wig form holding a white powdered wig on the delicate inlaid walnut *poudreuse.* Amethyst earrings shaped like dangling violets shone in the dim light from an open lacquered box next to the wig stand.

It was horrible, she thought with a shudder, a chamber kept for a dead woman. Startled, she thought she saw a white face staring at her, then realized with a half laugh, half sob that it was her own reflection in the wavy mirror above the table. How many times had Aurore sat on the delicate stool with its purple velvet cushion, and stared at her visage in the silvered glass? What had been her thoughts? Had she waited impatiently for her husband's return, or had his arrogant handsome face also appeared in that mirror as he stood behind her stroking her ivory neck?

Fighting to remain in control, fighting the jealousy that filled her at the thought of those fingers caressing another's skin as he did her own, she turned away. A soft gasp escaped her as she found herself staring at another reflection of her own visage, but this was not a mirror. Rather it was a portrait in oils above the marble fireplace. But it could be a mirror, she realized, stunned, the face was so like her own. Aurore had been painted wearing a white powdered wig, so the hair appeared blond. The eyes, however, were a dark cold blue with a hint of despair or madness in their depths. There was even a beauty mark above her upper lip, but Caresse could see that it was a heart-shaped patch she had stuck on rather than one from nature like the one above her own lip. The ring on the finger in the painting was an amethyst surrounded by diamonds, she saw with relief. She could not wear the same ring that had been on Aurore's finger. *Mon Dieu*, she thought, that would be too much.

Staring up at the portrait, Caresse could understand the frightened looks she had received from the slaves, and the stunned expressions on those faces in what passed for polite society in Nouvelle Orléans. The resemblance between the two of them was amazing. Perhaps they were some distant relation. It happened sometimes that second or third *cousines* looked very much alike.

But why would a man marry two women who could be twins, unless he was trying to replace the dead woman he still mourned. She was filled with an overwhelming despair as she stared up at the portrait of Aurore. She pressed her hand over her mouth convulsively as she faced the reality of her marriage to Lucien.

As she stood before the portrait stunned and sickened, the French door she thought she had closed blew open with a gust of wind. Feeling the cool damp air on her back, she turned with a sigh to leave and close it behind her. It was then that she saw him standing on the threshold, his tall lean form blocking out the wind.

"What are you doing here?" he asked, spacing the words evenly as his burning black eyes seemed to impale her from across the room.

"I wanted to try and understand everyone's fascination with your first wife, and if it was true, as they said, that I really looked so much like her. 'Twould seem I have my answer to the last part of my question, but perhaps you can enlighten me to the first part," she said, her features cool, remote, and unsmiling.

"The first time I saw you, I admit I was stunned by the resemblance. It was what attracted me at first, but that is long over," he insisted, with a slight shrug of his broad shoulders, his arms folded across his chest.

"I wish I could believe it meant as little as you say, but as I have found since coming to Sans Regret that nothing is quite what it seems here. This is a shrine to a dead woman," she gestured her hand toward the bed and the dressing table. "If what you say is true then you will not mind my having the servants pack all this away, and put it in the attic where it belongs with other keepsakes of the past."

"I agree that 'tis time this shrine is dismantled. I do not care how you redecorate the chamber, but you may have trouble with Dominique," he pointed out coolly, not moving from where he stood on the threshold. It was as if he did not want to come into the room.

"Dominique is housekeeper to the St. Amant family, but I cannot understand why you allow her to have such power," Caresse said with a frown.

"Dominique is not a slave, as you know. She chooses to work for me as she did for my parents. She and her *maman* were sent to Sans Regret many years ago by a man whom Jacques owed a great favor, a man who had saved his life when he was a youth in New France. That man's name was Edouard Dubrieul, Philippe's father. He sent them to Nouvelle Orléans, at his wife's insistence that he get rid of them, because Dominique was his daughter. Her *maman* was Edouard Dubrieul's mistress. After Edouard gave them their freedom he sent them to Sans Regret where my father promised they would always have a home with the St. Amant family. Later when his wife died in Saint-Domingue he came to Nouvelle Orléans looking for Dominique's *maman* but she had died. Dominique refused to go to work in a household where she would be a servant to her own half brother. 'Tis a decision I think you can understand. Edouard Dubrieul was not alone long, for he met Aurore's mother soon after arriving in Nouvelle Orléans. The rest I believe you already know."

"Dominique is Philippe's half sister?" Caresse asked, stunned. It seemed the lives of those at Sans Regret and at Chêne Vert were as intertwined as the jasmine vine that wound around the trunk of the live oaks.

"Exactly, and as such she was close to Aurore after our marriage, although their relationship was often marred by disagreements. I realize now that they both wished to be the *voodooienne* at Sans Regret. But despite everything there was a strong bond between them, stronger than between many sisters, for when . . . Aurore became agitated only Dominique could calm her."

"Aurore was prone to hysterics?" Caresse in-

quired, surprised at this new facet to her predecessor's personality.

"She was what some people would describe as high-strung, nervous, and given to strange fancies," he replied with reluctance as if he did not wish to discuss anything about her.

"I see," Caresse answered softly, realizing that Lucien had thought to protect Aurore as he had his *maman*.

"What is it?" Lucien asked as she pulled her shawl tighter.

"I want this room dismantled regardless of what Dominique thinks. I am mistress of this house now, and it shall be done," Caresse said with determination, walking toward where he stood on the threshold of the open door, her head held high.

"Where does so much strength come from in such a fragile form?" he asked, stopping her with a firm hand cupping that soft yet stubborn chin.

"From the cells of La Sâlpetrire prison," she answered, wide gray eyes staring up at him, challenging him. She was tired of secrets, even her own. Suddenly she wanted to sweep it all clean, including this macabre room.

"Was that meant to shock me, *ma chère?*" The attentive dark eyes stared down at her with tenderness, a slight sad smile curving his sensuous lips that seldom showed any emotion.

"I am tired of secrets," she murmured.

"Have you not yet realized that there is nothing about you that could ever change what is between us?" he said softly, pulling her out of the chamber onto the gallery and closing the door behind him.

"And I you," she answered in a low voice, knowing that what he said was true. No matter what had happened between him and Aurore it did not change the desire, the passionate ache she felt whenever he appeared. It was a revelation to her to know that deep down she did not care about

231

anything as long as she continued to feel those hands on her skin, the heat of his mouth on her own hungry lips. She had heard of obsession, but now—when she stood on the gallery where she knew Aurore had met her death—she knew that she did not care what happened as long as she could have this magnetic man's touch. Now she understood the true meaning of the word obsession.

"Come, I want to discuss something with you," he said, guiding her, his hand at her waist, toward the salon.

"What is it?" Caresse asked with a weary sigh, hoping that it was not more about Aurore. The woman's presence was like a fog that surrounded her, interfering with anything that she wished to do.

"I have received a message from Nashoba. He wishes me to come to his village on the far side of Lake Pontchartrain. 'Tis important, *ma chère*, or I would not think of leaving you alone here at Sans Regret. But I have seen what a strong woman you are and I do not think a few days alone will bother you," he said with a low deep chuckle.

"It would not, but I have no intention of staying here when I have the chance to see a Choctaw village," she replied with a stubborn tilt to her chin.

"But *chère* this is no trip for a woman, 'tis through the swamps," he protested, frowning with exasperation.

"But I am not just any woman," she chided him, a look of implacable determination on her face.

"So I am finding out," he answered dryly. " 'Twill be a hard journey with little luxury, even after we arrive at the village."

"I do not mind that, but I would like to see how the Choctaw live, what Lake Pontchartrain looks like. I want a little adventure, *mon cher.* After our tiresome guests I could use simplicity," she said. There was no way, she thought, she was going to stay at Sans Regret with its haunted rooms and the hostile Dominique. She would not admit it, but she was frightened to stay alone at the isolated plantation. Had not Aurore met her death alone and frightened at Sans Regret? No, she would rather face the dangers of the swamp and the Indians. They were dangers one could see, rather than the invisible phantoms that haunted the house and grounds.

"I think I have little choice in this matter," Lucien commented in amusement as they reached the salon.

"You do not," she replied, giving him a saucy smile. "I am riding beside you, or following behind you, but I am coming. Nothing will stop me."

His fragile kitten had turned into a wildcat with sharp claws, he mused with confusion. He did not need the complication of Caresse accompanying him to the Choctaw village. There were secrets there that he did not wish discovered, but he realized, with amusement and dismay, that for the first time in his life he had met a woman like no other. She would do as she wished, and somehow he was going to have to adjust to it. But wasn't that part of her allure, he thought wryly, he never knew what she would do next. It was going to complicate everything. Yes, he thought with a sigh, his beautiful wife was certainly going to complicate his trip to Lake Pontchartrain.

Sixteen

"I am ready," Caresse called down to Lucien from the top of the staircase, the gray linen skirt of her riding habit caught up in one gloved hand.

"You are still determined to do this," he said in amused exasperation, standing arms akimbo, looking up at her in the early light of dawn.

"I heard you get up, and knew you thought to leave whilst I was still aslumber. You obviously do not realize that when I say I am going to do something, I intend on doing it," she replied, gliding down the curving staircase to where he stood.

"What is that you have in your hand?" he gestured to the small tapestry bag she carried.

"I thought we would be spending the night, so I brought along a few necessities," she said, staring at the man she thought she knew but who had taken on yet another disguise. Gone was the elegant courtier, the well-dressed gentleman planter; in his place was a *coureur de bois,* one of those rugged Frenchmen who ranged the woods from the south of the Mississippi to New France far to the north in the land the Indians called Canada. Soft leather breeches clung to his muscular thighs and were tucked into high boots of a darker worn leather. He wore a coarse linen shirt open at the neck and a plain gray waistcoat with horn buttons. An unadorned tricorn rested on his sleek black hair worn tied back with a leather thong. In his hand he carried a flintlock musket, and over his shoulder a powder horn and leather satchel. Somehow he was even more impressive clad in the simple garments.

"We are going to the village by pirogue," he pointed out. "If you can fit that bag in the prow you can take it."

"How generous of you," Caresse drawled, taken back both by his appearance and by his abrupt manner.

"This is not a pleasure sail, *ma chère*. If you insist on going I want you to understand what you are up against."

"My voyage from *la belle* France was not a pleasure sail either, and I managed to survive it very well. I think I can manage a trip on the bayous to Lake Pontchartrain with equal grace." She glared up at him like an angry kitten who refused to be cowered. It was this combination of courage and fragility of face and form that touched his heart.

"*Touché, ma belle* lily," he said with a slight bow of his arrogant head. "Have you broken your fast, for we shall be traveling far before we eat again?"

"*Oui*. I also brought along one of Zoé's calas and an orange, in case I became hungry. I know the village is a great distance away," she answered, touching her slightly bulging pocket.

"I see my worries were needless. You are obviously quite resourceful," he replied in a serious voice, but there was a ghost of a smile about his stern lips. She was like a delightful child, this lovely wife of his, with her valiant spirit and intense interest in all of life. Suddenly he couldn't wait to share the swamp with her, curious to see how she would react to it. Would she understand its strange beauty? If there was ever a Frenchwoman who could see it as he did, feel it deep in her soul, it would be this tiny porcelain doll with the fierce courage of a wildcat.

"Soeur Xavier said that I was a gentle soul, but a survivor," Caresse confessed as they began their walk down the path to the bayou. "I think she was right, for I have found I have been able to endure much I would never have thought possible a few years ago."

"Do not think of the past, 'tis over." He reminded her gently.

"And today I will be seeing more of this strange wonderful land," she said with enthusiasm. " 'Tis like an adventure one only reads about in books."

A silk weaver's daughter who reads novels, he thought, but did not comment on the strangeness of her statement for he did not want to bring up the past. It was amazing that she could still have such a zest for life after what she had been through in France. If he did nothing else worthwhile in his life he could at least make up to her for the pain and torment she had suffered. And today his heart lightened slightly as he saw how much she was enjoying this adventure, as she called it. She was sunshine and fresh air blown in by fate to lighten the darkness of his life. To see life through her enthusiastic eyes, her sense of joy and wonder at it all, made him feel more alive than he had felt in many years. Had he ever felt this way before in all his life, he mused, for even as a young boy it seemed the dark shadows were there waiting for him.

"Will Bruno be coming with us?" she asked as the huge dog trotted at their heels.

"*Oui*, he enjoys returning to the village whenever I go to *parle*, as the Choctaw call meeting with any Frenchman. His litter mates live there, and I think, like a person, he enjoys showing off for the relatives," he teased. "And of course there are canine females as a drawing card as well."

"Blanchette will enjoy her solitude, no offense

intended, Bruno," Caresse called back over her shoulder to the lumbering dog who had his nose to the ground investigating the numerous fascinating scents of the forest path.

The trail led past the family graveyard, and Caresse saw that someone had placed the *immortelles* in front of the tombs of Lucien's mother and father. Was there one in front of Aurore's tomb as well? Had Lucien visited that solitary resting place in the swamp yesterday on All Saints' Day? If he had, what had been his thoughts, she wondered, with a stab of jealousy, as he stood in front of that marble sepulcher.

When the path forked, Lucien gestured that they take the trail to the left. Caresse remembered dimly from All Hallows' Eve that the right one led to Aurore's tomb. Biting her lower lip, she looked away and lengthened her stride as she followed Lucien's lithe figure deeper into the dark shadows of the swamp.

Gray moss, like cobwebs, hung from the myriad branches of the trees as the forest closed around them. The spongy layers of moist vegetation were a fertile medium for growth of all types of semi-tropical plants entirely new to Caresse. Never had she seen such a landscape. A palette of gray and green tones was interrupted here and there by the burnished gold of clumps of goldenrod, and the tiny yellow flowers of the jasmine vines clinging to the thick trunks of the soaring oaks, cottonwoods, and the great towering cypress trees rising from their smooth stumplike roots reaching out of the murky water for air. Caresse could understand why the swamps were called *cyprières* by the settlers, for these soaring trees with their feathery green leaves were so numerous that they crowded out the light of the sun high overhead with their spreading branches.

The path came to an abrupt stop in a small clearing along the mossy banks of the waters of a slow-moving bayou. The murky olive green water seemed still and reflective, only a few circling leaves floating on its surface evidence that there was any current beneath those dark waters.

Caresse watched as Lucien moved with sure strides to where a pirogue lay with its hull in the air under the spreading branches of an enormous cypress. Bruno circled excitedly at his feet, as Lucien turned it over and gestured for her to join him.

"Get in and sit about three quarters of the way forward. Place your bag in the prow. Balance is everything in a pirogue. A fact Bruno has yet to learn," he commented with a smile as the dog jumped in the canoe eagerly, running back and forth sniffing out all the swamp creatures that had left a scent in its hollow bottom.

Picking up the skirt of her riding habit, Caresse stepped carefully into the rocking craft. At a sharp command from Lucien, Bruno also settled down on his haunches in the pirogue. Pushing her bag as far forward as possible, she realized this part of the canoe was already in the murky olive green water. Then with a swift push from Lucien, after which he leapt with sure-footed grace into the craft, they were launched into the opaque green bayou.

A flock of milk white egrets took off in startled flight as the pirogue skimmed across the water under Lucien's expert paddling. Caresse watched as they soared down the winding, twisting bayou deeper into the *cyprière*. A primeval stillness surrounded the gliding craft, and its occupants, in an unearthly quiet, adding to the sense that they were entering another domain, another dimension, where time moved at a different pace.

To Caresse it seemed almost an enchanted land where trees in larger-than-life shapes, sculpted by time, wind, and the seasons, towered over them, seeming to blot out the normal sunlight of an autumn day. Here and there a stream of golden light managed to break through the canopy of intertwined branches like the light seen through the clerestory window of one of France's magnificent cathedrals.

"Look to your right, *ma chère*," Lucien directed in a low voice, never breaking the rhythm of his paddling.

"Where?" she asked, seeing nothing but what appeared to be a log. Then as she watched the gray-green log moved, opening a cavernous mouth with rows of wicked-looking teeth to snap at some unsuspecting creature of the swamp. The alligator then slipped beneath the dark, still water, vanishing from sight. "I thought at first 'twas a log," she called to Lucien, looking back over her shoulder.

"Many a Frenchman new to La Louisiane has made that deadly mistake," he replied.

"I was thinking the *cyprière* was like one of the beautiful cathedrals in France, a natural cathedral, but now I am not so sure," she told him with a slight shudder. Then as a stream of mellow sunlight broke through ahead of them to strike the alabaster blooms of a wild magnolia and setting them aglow like votive candles, she turned back to him and said quietly, *"Oui,* 'tis like a cathedral."

"I, too, have thought the same, *ma chère*," he replied, his black eyes brimming with surprised delight.

"Then you have been to France," she exclaimed, turning around so that her wide dove gray eyes confronted him in sparkling triumph.

"A long time ago," he said tersely, avoiding those innocent feminine eyes. "I could not wait to return to Nouvelle Orléans and to the swamp."

Sensing his reluctance to speak about France, and not wishing to bring up her own life there, Caresse turned back so she faced the endless twisting bayou that lay ahead of them. When had he gone there? she mused, staring out at the passing scene, but not really seeing it. Perhaps he and Aurore had gone there on their wedding trip. Always it came back to Aurore. She did not like to think of their being together, she realized with a pang that cut deep. She had left instructions that Aurore's bedchamber be stripped and everything be put up in the attic while they were gone. When she returned she wanted no more reminders of Lucien's first wife. The stark white tomb on the *chênière* in the swamp flashed across her mind, and she knew that there would always be one monument that she could not erase.

Although they stopped once to rest and eat the food that Lucien had packed in his satchel along with the contents of Caresse's pocket they spoke little. With a few sips of wine from the bottle also in the satchel they finished their repast and once more Lucien took up his paddle. They skimmed silently across the still, reflective water of the bayou for what seemed like hours, each lost in his own thoughts. Even Bruno sat in an alert posture, his nose scenting the air, but he made no sound. He watched, as they did, the shifting patterns of light and shade, the occasional movement in the thick vegetation on the bank, listened to the bird song in the heavy warm air. As they penetrated deeper into the dark *cyprière* the air seemed to warm as if they were burrowing under a heavy wet quilt that surrounded them with its smothering layers.

Lucien drank in the sight of Caresse sitting with such erect posture in front of him. She had taken off her tricorn riding hat as the temperature rose, and her ash-blond hair curled in profusion over her slender shoulders and down the planes of her graceful back. Knowing how strange it must all appear to her, he marveled at her complete lack of fear. There was only an alert interest about her, almost awe. His desire for her was so strong, it continued to amaze him that this tiny child-woman had broken down the barriers of indifference he had created to protect his soul from being touched. She was in his blood, for the scent and the satin feel of her skin was imprinted on his brain, on the tips of his fingers. When he was not with her his mind and body ached for her.

As if she could feel his eyes devouring her, or could hear his thoughts, she turned around and gave him a sweet questioning smile. "What did you say?" she asked, puzzled.

" 'Twas nothing, *ma belle,*" he replied softly, knowing he had spoken not a word, but understanding that somehow she had heard the silent lament from his heart. In her youthful innocence she did not realize the uniqueness of their relationship. But Lucien had known many women, had bedded many, yet with Caresse he felt emotions that he had not known he was capable of experiencing. It disconcerted him that she could tear down with one sweet smile all the carefully erected barriers he had spent a lifetime developing.

There were so many different facets to her husband's character, Caresse mused. Today she was seeing another side to him. Handling the pirogue with ease and grace, he could have been one of the French trappers who came down the long length of the Mississippi on the last leg of their journey from New France. She could believe that he had spent time with the Indians learning their ways, as did many of the *coureurs de bois.* This was a part of his life that she knew Aurore had never shared. She relished the thought. She wanted their marriage to be unique, and it was starting today with their trip to the Choctaw village.

The air seemed a bit cooler as they turned yet another bend in the bayou under the branches of the moss-hung cypresses, the gray tendrils sweeping the murky water. The banks receded as they reached a wide stretch of water so covered in a fine green weed as to appear to be a well-kept lawn, but the pirogue cut right through the gently moving water weed that appeared at first glance to be solid ground.

" 'Tis *terre tremblante*," Lucien explained at her expression of surprise. "It looks like solid earth but is not. 'Tis thick clumps of duckweed growing in the water. 'Twill not be far to the Choctaw village."

"What an amazing land," Caresse sighed, transfixed by the exotic beauty of the *cyprière*. A flock of snowy white ibises feasted so intently on the far bank that they hardly noticed that they were not alone on the bayou.

Bruno, however, noticed the elegant birds and gave a short, deep bark. The sound startled them from their complacency and they rose in one alabaster cloud to soar to another more private part of the swamp.

"They know we are here now," Lucien said in wry tones, "Bruno has announced our arrival, although I think they were aware of us much earlier."

"Who knows we are here?" Caresse asked, turning around slightly to gentle the great dog with a few strokes to his shaggy head.

"The Choctaw," he replied in a low voice. "Nashoba's scouts have been watching us for some time."

"But how can you tell? I have seen no one," Caresse answered in surprise.

"The low whistle of a bird that was not really a bird. A rustle in the vegetation of the bank that was not made by a small animal. We have entered their domain, and their domain is carefully guarded. It is their way," he explained.

"You learned how to recognize the signs, to think

as they do during those summers you spent with Nashoba and his family," Caresse said.

He nodded, then his intense, aware dark eyes turned from her to stare down the bayou. His strong even strokes stopped, allowing the pirogue to drift on the opaque olive green water. "They are coming, *ma chère*. When we reach the village, keep your eyes low and do not look a warrior in the eye, for a woman to do so is considered rude. And do not speak unless spoken to. Let me do the talking. You will be required to sit with the women when I speak with Nashoba and his warriors. Be prepared—a Frenchwoman has never come to their village so you will be quite a curiosity."

Caresse felt a flicker of apprehension in the pit of her stomach at his warning, but she did not regret her decision to accompany Lucien. She wanted to know his world, understand what was important to him, and in doing so come to know this mercurial man who had become the center of her life.

Just as Lucien had predicted, a huge pirogue came around the bend of the bayou carrying four Choctaw warriors, their bronzed backs gleaming in a stream of sunlight through the trees. Nashoba, however, was not one of them, Caresse realized, for the fierce faces were those of strangers. They moved with a rhythmic grace till they were several yards away, then in response to Lucien's one shouted word they turned their craft around and led the way down the bayou toward their village.

A wind came up as they made their way through more *terre tremblante* and sailed into a great body of water that Caresse realized must be Lake Pontchartrain. The sun touched the water with gold as they moved between cypress knees near the bank, then struck out across the vast expanse of water. Caresse stirred uneasily in the pirogue for she had not realized how large Lake Pontchartrain was.

243

From her seat in the narrow canoe the lake seemed as vast as the ocean, and just as dangerous to cross in such a small craft.

"Do not fear, *ma chère,* I have transversed this lake many times," Lucien called to her as if he sensed her anxiety.

She turned to give him a tense smile as the wind came up over the water and blew wisps of hair across her pale face. Her small hands clutched the edges of the pirogue till her knuckles turned white, but she sat erect with her chin raised, staring straight ahead into the immense, boundless water, where there was no sign of shore.

Never had he admired her more than he did at this moment, thought Lucien, as he strained to battle the wind coming across the water. He had never known a woman who had such strength, such courage, inside such a delicate form. But then, he thought with a pang of sad compassion, what was crossing a lake no matter how large, when she had already left everything behind in France, friends, family, country, to start a new life in a strange exotic land? But no matter how strongly the winds of outrageous fortune blew, his lovely Caresse would bend gracefully with them to rise again. The twists and turns of fate had not broken her. He sensed that she trusted him, and because of that trust was willing to throw caution to the winds. If this was part of his life then it would be hers as well. But there was so much in his life that he had concealed from her, and these secrets would destroy that trust he saw shining out from her gray eyes. His bronzed hands tightened on the handle of the paddle as his gaze narrowed against the light of the dying sun. She must never find out, he vowed. Never.

The blue haze of smoke rising from a fire was the first sign of the village on the dark rim of land that finally appeared on the horizon. As they neared the shore, they sailed once more through marsh grass, cypress knees, and cattails. The scent of meat cooking over a fire drifted out with the blue smoke to tantalize Caresse's appetite.

The people of the village were expecting them, for as the pirogue drifted through the cattails toward the heavily forested shore, Caresse could see the tall forms of the braves, and the smaller graceful figures of the women and children. They stood a few yards from the shore in front of the trees watching their arrival with avid dark eyes.

"Remember what I told you," Lucien cautioned her as two warriors waded out into the water to pull the pirogue to shore. "Put on your hat—the color of your hair will cause enough comment as it is."

A wave of apprehension swept over her as she placed the gray tricorn riding hat on her head. The people of the village pushed forward to have a better look at their visitors.

"Come, *ma chère,*" Lucien's hand was reaching out to help her from the beached pirogue as she rose unsteadily to her feet. Bruno bounded out, seeking the village's canine population.

Caresse felt the dark eyes of the Choctaw staring at her from the shadows of the trees. Picking up her skirt, she tried to maintain as much dignity as possible as she walked with Lucien to where Nashoba stood waiting.

The tall imposing figure only glanced once at Caresse as they approached, then his fierce gaze was turned toward his friend Lucien. Dressed only in a breechclout, and with a pouch of leather decorated in a bead design about his chest, his dark hair long, he conveyed immense dignity. Caresse had seen King Louis several times at Versailles, and he had held himself that same way, sure of his right to rule.

But it was not Nashoba who captured her attention but the small graceful figure that moved to stand beside him. Lovely as a young fawn, the Choctaw maiden was clad only in a soft deerskin skirt, with her full breasts bare, her long ebony hair hanging to her waist. She glared at Caresse. Glancing up at Nashoba to make sure he was involved in his greeting to the visitors, she flung back her long hair as if in defiance. Then with a soft giggle, she threw herself with abandon into Lucien's arms. To Caresse's stunned dismay, he chuckled, with amused delight, lifting the young woman up into the air, as the people of the village laughed and shouted their encouragement.

Seventeen

The orange and blue flames shot into the indigo velvet of the night sky from the bonfire in the center of the Choctaw village. Dark silhouettes moved around the flickering light as the women placed dishes heaped with food before the men sitting on the far side of the leaping flames. The smell of roasting meat rose with the blue haze of wood smoke on the cool night air toward the twinkling diamonds of the stars. Over the lapping dark waters rose the burnished opal sphere of the autumn moon, casting its cool glow in a stream across the opaque surface of Lake Pontchartrain. The feasting to celebrate a successful hunt, and to honor their French guests, had begun at sundown.

Caresse sat with her back against the solid trunk of a live oak apart from the circle of Choctaw women. Placing the clay bowl on the ground beside her, she took a handkerchief from her pocket to wipe her hands. The venison stew had been delicious, flavored with unusual herbs, and she had eaten her fill apart from the others. She could feel the other women's dark eyes glancing at her as they chatted in their musical tongue. For the last several hours she had been the main topic of conversation. She did not have to understand their language to sense the meaning behind their words.

"You finish?" inquired the soft voice of the woman known as Isi.

After seeing Caresse's stricken expression when the lovely young woman had thrown herself into his arms, Lucien had explained that Isi was Nashoba's youngest sister. Her name meant deer because she had always run after them, even as a tiny child, as quick and graceful as a young fawn. He had watched her grow up those summer days he had spent with the Choctaw. She was like his own younger sister, he insisted as they followed Nashoba to his lodge at the north end of the plaza. But with a woman's intuition, Caresse sensed that Isi's feelings for Lucien were more than those of a sister. She had seen the flash of passionate interest in the young Choctaw woman's flashing dark eyes as they followed Lucien's every movement once they were inside Nashoba's lodge. Now Isi stood in front of her, the first time that the young woman had even glanced her way.

"*Oui*, I am finished," Caresse answered, looking up at the graceful young woman who had thrown herself into Lucien's embrace. " 'Twas very good." She gave a tired smile as she handed her the empty bowl. The day had been long and all she wanted to do was sleep. She wondered with a weary sigh how long the evening's festivities were going to last.

"You come watch," Isi replied, with a quick gesture of her head toward where the women sat away from the men.

"*Merci,*" Caresse said, rising to her feet, for she realized that to refuse would be considered rude. Lucien had explained quietly as they left the lodge for the feast that she could not eat with him. It was not done among the Choctaw. The men and women ate apart, but later he and she would be allowed a separate dwelling from the others, one of the rectangular, gable roofed summer houses that stood under the trees on the shore of the lake at the edge of the village. After leaving her beside the spreading branches of the oak, he had joined the circle of men on the far side of the blazing fire.

Curious, feminine eyes looked up from their conversation as Caresse approached with Isi. Several of the women were bare-breasted like Isi, but others wore chemises made of cloth traded from the French for furs. Children darted between the women, playing tag, and babies rested in a curious board wrapped in deer skin, only their small faces with shiny black button eyes visible. There was a happy atmosphere about the women's circle that made them all seem like one large family. Caresse envied them their sense of belonging, of community. It was a feeling foreign to her, and she realized with a pang that these people—whom some in France, even in Nouvelle Orléans, would call savages—exhibited a warmth and caring toward one another she had never seen in that supposed monument to civilization, Versailles.

Caresse sank down on the ground, in the space made for her beside an older woman with fine features and gray streaks in her ebony hair. A thin hand, bronzed by years in the sun, lifted and touched Caresse's ash-blond curls, then stroked her cheek. She sat quite still sensing that this gesture had great importance.

"You are lovely, *mon enfant*, and quite real," the older woman told her in French, "and come with only love and kindness in your heart."

"*Oui . . .*" Caresse paused for she did not know the older woman's name although she had seen her in Nashoba's lodge.

"I am called Luyu, wild dove in your *français*," she explained, her kind eyes staring intently into Caresse's own wide gray gaze. "Nashoba is my son, and I look upon your husband, Jacques's Right Hand, as my son as well."

"What did you mean that I was quite real?" Caresse asked as the sound of drums and the high-pitched sound of cane flutes filled the smoky night air.

"There has been much talk about you up and down the river, as well as from village to village. They say that you are the ghost wife of Jacques's Right Hand, but seeing you I can tell all that is foolish talk," Luyu answered first in French, then louder in Choctaw. The women listened intently to what she said. It was obvious she intended that they hear every word.

"I do not . . . understand," Caresse stammered, stunned that even here in a remote Choctaw village she was haunted by her resemblance to Aurore. "They believe that I am a ghost?"

"*Oui*, because of your likeness to the first wife, but I can see that you are nothing like that one. The goodness shines out of your eyes not like the other one with the eyes of ice," Luyu reassured her.

"You knew Aurore?" Caresse inquired in surprise, remembering Lucien's statement that she had never accompanied him to the village, had been in fact quite frightened of the Choctaw.

"She was known as Ice Eyes, feared by many along the lake, for she was a witch. This was known by everyone," Luyu assured her in low tones, although Caresse did not think anyone but Isi understood French. "I feared for Jacques's Right Hand married to that one. When she was killed I felt at peace," the older woman confided as they watched the men through the flickering flames of the bonfire smoking a long clay pipe which was passed from one to another.

"You said when she was killed, Luyu. I thought she was supposed to have fallen or committed suicide," Caresse said, trying to draw the woman out. Isi sat on the other side of her mother, her almond-shaped eyes staring often across the bonfire at Lucien. She once more seemed oblivious to Caresse's presence, intent only on watching Lucien seated beside her brother.

"*Non*, that housekeeper, Dominique, saw a man in the house with that witch the night she died. The story along the river is that she saw him on the gallery arguing with her that night only hours before she was found dead on the stones below," the Choctaw woman told her quietly. "She was killed by that man, all the Africans know that is how she died, the Choctaw as well. She deserved to die for she was evil, but the French they cannot admit this so they tell the foolish story that she fell or jumped," Luyu scoffed.

Caresse felt a cold knot form in the bottom of her stomach. She remembered asking Lucien why he put up with Dominique when she seemed to defy him. Was the real reason because she had seen something that All Hallows' Eve—something she was not supposed to see? Had she seen him argue with Aurore, then leave the grounds to return late the next morning as if he had just returned from a trip upriver?

"Are you cold?" Luyu asked in concern as she saw Caresse tremble.

Caresse shook her head as she wrapped her arms around her chest. Was that lithe figure who sat with such casual grace among the other Choctaw warriors really a murderer? But why would he have killed Aurore? Could it have been an accident? Perhaps during an argument she had leaned too close to the railing and somehow had fallen over. But if that were true why would he have chosen to marry a woman who looked so much like her? She began to shake once more as terrible images of that night came to her mind. Those masterful hands that elicited much rapture when they stroked her skin, could they have shaken Aurore with such rage that she was pushed or fell to her death below?

"Watch, little one, the dancing will begin," Luyu interrupted her terrible musings, pointing to where the musicians began moving nearer to a clearing in front of the fire. The night was suddenly filled with the deep, bloodstirring beat of drums, the rhythmic beat of gourd rattles, and the high, piercing trill of cane flutes.

The young warriors began to dance, first in lithe movements that told, Luyu said, of their successful hunt of the deer that had been served in the stew. Slowly, the women began to rise and join with the men, dancing inside their circle counterclockwise. Above them on the branch of an oak tree an owl, silhouetted against the moon, hooted his mournful cry, adding to the strangeness of the scene.

Caresse rose to her feet as the other women joined in the dance, even Luyu. Soon she stood alone, the Choctaw women all moving gracefully to the strange music. The primeval beat stirred something inside her.

It was as she watched the moving silhouettes that she saw through the flickering flames another man who was not Choctaw, but neither was he French, for he wore the scarlet coat of a British officer. Startled by what she saw, for she knew there had been talk of war between the French and British, she stood transfixed, her interest in the dancers banished by the sight of Lucien talking intently to the British officer. She knew the British had been urging some of the renegade bands of Choctaw to leave their French allies and join with them against any British foe. It had been one of these renegade bands that had attacked and killed French and German settlers along the Mississippi River.

As if the intensity of her gaze communicated something to Lucien across the clearing, he looked up, his black eyes blazing with some indefinable emotion, before he turned away to speak a few more words to the British officer. Their conversation, although brief, was intense, almost as if they were arguing. A group of dancers moved in front of her cutting off her vision for a moment. When they passed, she saw that the British officer had vanished. Lucien was striding toward her, his expression cool and remote. When he was only a few yards away, a slim feminine form reached out and grabbed his arm, pulling him into the circle of dancers.

A flash of frustration crossed his handsome features for a moment like a shadow across the moon, then he allowed himself to be pulled into the dance. He moved with Isi as they circled back and forth to the primitive beat in front of the flickering flames.

Caresse was filled with a great weariness, her muscles screamed from the strain of the day, and her spirit was exhausted by trying to adjust to the myriad new sights of this exotic land. France seemed very far away, almost as if her life there had belonged to another, but this new life was so full of questions and doubts she felt overwhelmed. Turning away from the sight of her husband dancing with the seductive Isi, whose serpentine hip movements spoke a language all their own, Caresse wandered down toward the lake shore. She was tired also of Lucien's women, the real and those who were only a haunting memory.

The lake shimmered with streams of silver moonglow as Caresse walked along its shore. Gray tendrils of moss swayed in the wind as it touched the lapping water like a kiss. Dark eerie silhouettes of dead trees in the water added to the lonely atmosphere as the solitary cry of a loon broke the silence of the night.

What was she doing in this strange wilderness so unlike anything she had ever known? Hiding, a voice inside her reminded her of the terrible reason she had come to La Louisiane. Those who wished her and her family ill would never find her in this forgotten colony. The memory of the tall mysterious man who had visited her in her cell flashed across her mind as it often did when she was alone and feeling a tinge of homesickness for France. Who was he?

"*Ma chère,* 'tis not safe for you to be walking down here alone," the familiar voice startled her, so lost had she been in her reverie of times long gone.

"Is the dance over?" she asked, without disguising her annoyance.

"For me 'tis over," he replied quietly.

"Isi must be quite disappointed that you left early. She seemed to so enjoy your company," she countered, each word edged with sarcasm. Lifting her delicate chin high, she stared up at him, her eyes shards of gray ice.

"Do I detect jealousy in those lovely eyes?" he murmured, catching her chin with the callused tips of his fingers. His piercing dark eyes glowed like coals in the light of the full ivory sphere that hung over Lake Pontchartrain.

"Is there a woman in La Louisiane who does not know you?" she retorted.

"Perhaps a few," he said with a shrug, his sensuous lips curled in a slight smile. "I told you I have not always led an exemplary life."

"*Oui,* and Yvonne warned me you were a rogue," Caresse admitted ruefully, a chagrined smile dimpling her cheeks.

"Even a rogue can reform, *ma chère,* with proper guidance," he teased, moving one tapered finger to trace the outline of her full lower lip.

"What if he is beyond redemption?" she whispered with a catch in her voice. The feel of his touch on her mouth, the heat from his body standing so close to her sent the slow, hot honey of desire through her veins.

"No one is beyond redemption, *ma belle*. Perhaps they just need to find the right person to show the way," he contradicted her gently. Then bending down, he brushed his lips across her hungry mouth in a caress that sent her moving against him, impelled involuntarily by her own uncontrollable passion.

He caught her to him, held her against the long hard length of his lithe form, as his mouth claimed hers in a deep narcotic kiss that banished all doubts, all thoughts from her mind. She flowed into him and he into her like the surging river into the welcoming embrace of the sea.

"Come, there is a quiet place for us," he whispered, into the silk of her hair as he guided her, his arm encircling her waist, up a path barely visible through the silent sentinels of the towering cypresses.

They left the clusters of circular plastered houses of the main part of the village behind. The sound of the music and dancing carried on the light breeze from the lake. Reaching a clearing of moss-hung live oaks where a rectangular Choctaw summer house stood with a roof of cypress, the walls of plaster mixed with moss, Caresse was relieved to see that they would be alone. Tonight she wanted to make love with Lucien, find that rapture with him that soothed, if only for a brief time, the doubts and fears she had about this man who held her to him with some strange invisible bond.

Streams of moonlight shone down through the intertwined branches to silver the long grass. But from inside the rectangular summer house could be seen the tiny glow of a light through the open door.

"Is there someone there?" Caresse asked, in a strained voice. She knew the Choctaw lived communally in their houses. Tonight she had no desire to share her privacy.

"*Non,* Luyu left an oil lamp burning that we might find our way," he replied pulling her tighter against him. "We shall be quite alone tonight, *ma chère,* with only the owls and Bruno for company."

" 'Tis what I desire," she whispered as they walked through the long grass to the open door.

"And you, *ma chère* are what I desire." His husky voice was filled with passion only waiting to be released.

Inside, the summer house was an intimate one-room retreat, with an earthen floor beaten down to smoothness, the walls plastered and white-washed with powdered oyster shells brought up from the gulf. A crude bed with a mattress of woven reeds, a doeskin sheet, and a luxuriant black fur blanket lying across it, stood almost in the middle of the single chamber. Caresse could see now that there were several small clay oil lamps hanging from the rafters. It was primitive, but clean, and filled with the scent of the wild jasmine vine that climbed outside the door and up and around the open gable ends.

Bruno whimpered a greeting as they entered, then rolled over and fell back asleep. He was not alone; beside him were two other dogs of rather mixed lineage. They all sprawled together in a friendly pack near the door.

" 'Twould seem Bruno has brought his lady friends home with him," laughed Lucien.

"What fools we females can be. A handsome rake who woos us with such skill can make us forget everything, even our dignity," Caresse mused ruefully.

"Methinks thou dost speak from the heart, fair lady," Lucien teased, pulling her against him.

She could not look away from the passionate tenderness of his gaze, the silent expectation in those liquid eyes. The doubts and fears were like smoke blown away by the fierce force of his desire. She could not fight against her need for him, that wonderful sense of belonging, of being desired, the sanctuary from all the uncertainty of her life, she found in his embrace.

"Oui, mon coeur, when I am with you I forget everything but the joy," she whispered as his mouth came down on hers.

His tongue traced the softness of her full lower lip as he groaned in delight at her soul-wrenching words that penetrated all the barriers erected around his heart. Slowly, with a sensuous joy, he entered the sweetness of her mouth that she offered up to him like a gift.

Clinging to him like the jasmine vine to the enduring oak, she tasted, caressed the coral ribbon that was his tongue entwined with her own, with a total abandon that was all consuming. She molded her soft contours to him, seeking to somehow lose herself within the wonder of his embrace.

"I have waited all day to touch you, *ma chère,* to show how proud I am of you, the courage you have." His voice was a husky whisper as he tenderly kissed the corners of her mouth, the opal perfection of her eyelids, the soft skin of her ivory throat.

Her breath was a sigh of welcome as his hands gently unbuttoned the jacket of her riding habit. Her tiny fingers moved to his shirt. Then there were only the fervid movements of their passionate need, as they stripped the clothes from each other's body that were a hindrance to the wondrous sensation of masculine skin against the satin of her body.

Then they were both nude, each standing unashamed before the other's adoring gaze, the glow from the lamps above them bathing their bodies with a mellow light so they appeared in their perfection to be bronze sculptures of the ancient gods.

Lifting her hand to his lips for a brief moment, he then led her to the waiting bed.

The seductive scent of the jasmine vine outside, and the lily perfume that clung to her skin, surrounded Lucien as he lay down beside this amazing child-woman who seemed only to desire to be with him. She asked so little of him that it tore at his heart, for at that moment he would have wrenched the stars from the sky to decorate her beautiful form.

Their mouths met with an aching tenderness as he pulled her against him on the soft doeskin, her legs wrapped around his, her fingers stroking the sinewy planes of his back. His lips seared a path down the elegant length of her throat, then moved down to capture one perfect rosebud nipple and caress it with the moist velvet of tongue and lips as his heart filled with the music of her moans of aroused delight.

From somewhere outside came the plaintive trill of a Choctaw flute, the rustle of the wind through the palmettos and the leaves of the live oak. But inside their hidden bower, away from the rest of the village, there was only the sound of a moan of ecstasy, the sigh of reunited lovers.

His burning mouth sought out each lovely curve, each silken hollow, as his fingers caressed the sensitive inner satin of her thighs till she opened them for his heated kiss, his wondrous touch.

"Beautiful, so beautiful, *ma belle femme,*" he murmured, rising up a little that he might drink in the sight of her beneath him.

She was breathtaking, woman incarnate, her blond hair a white-gold aura surrounding her. Looking up at him from under heavy lids, her smoke gray eyes showed both wonder and desire, the soft rose petals of her lips were swollen from his demanding mouth. There was no memory of another, for never had he been with a woman who showed with every nuance of expression and touch her love for him. It was such a new experience for him, this innocent acceptance of his desire, and her own overwhelming yearning. He had known sensual arousal with others, but never before had he known this deeper need, to join with another both body and soul.

Bending his head, he tenderly kissed the soft ivory mound of her belly, murmuring against the fragrant silkiness of her skin, " 'Tis as if I have never loved before, *ma chère femme.*"

"Mon coeur, I tremble for you," she gasped, his words having seared her soul.

"And I for you my beloved," he replied. Tenderly parting her delicate throbbing inner petals, he sought entrance to that moist honeyed cavern. He could not control his white-hot hunger a moment longer. With a moan that was both conquest and capitulation, he thrust his throbbing shaft inside her burning, welcoming body.

"Oh, *oui* 'tis what I need, what I must have!" she cried out, her arms wrapping around his back as she arched up to meet him, to welcome him with thrusts of her own. The depth of her hunger, the wild abandon that overwhelmed her, stunned her, as she met thrust with thrust, moan of rapture with echoing cry. She felt the tears flow down her cheeks, as breaking all restraint, they abandoned themselves to the dizzying, spiraling dance of love in an exquisite harmony of movement, sensual sensation, and merging of spirit.

"Caresse, *je t'aime,*" the words were torn from his throat as he reached the peak of rapture.

"Lucien, *mon coeur, je t'aime!*" Her cry echoed his, and together they joined, sounding like one voice, one exclamation of complete joy, as they found together their fiery release and melded two bodies, two souls into one.

* * *

259

The cool velvet night surrounded them as they lay under the luxuriant black bear-fur blanket, strands of her white-gold hair across the dark fur of his chest, his arm holding her to him. The tiny oil lamps had been extinguished, and there was only the stream of moonlight through the door and open gables to touch her silken tresses with silver. Her slow even breathing told Lucien that she slumbered, exhausted by the long day.

Although weariness threatened to envelop him, he could not sleep. For he was beset by feelings of remorse, strange alien thoughts for him. If he could, he would change the past, but that he knew was impossible. And if it had not been for the tragic mistakes of the past he would not hold this splendid woman in his arms. The conflict that tormented his soul, and robbed him of sleep, was that if she ever knew the truth about the past he could lose her, and *that* he would resist with every fiber of his being. But he knew secrets had a way of being discovered. There were others who would be only too happy to enlighten her to the other facets of her husband's character. Tightening his arm around her, he vowed silently to the lonely night that he would protect her from the truth as long as he could. The thought of those soft gray eyes staring at him with hatred and revulsion tore through him like a knife. No, she must never be allowed to know the truth. Never.

Eighteen

The opaque olive green water stretched out ahead of them in its serpentine path under the overhanging boughs. Silence was their constant companion after leaving their Choctaw escort behind them. Only the sound of the rhythmic dip of the oar in and out of the bayou broke the stillness of the afternoon.

Caresse stared out at the passing wilderness scene from her seat in the prow of the pirogue, every now and then her hand stroking the small leather bag in her pocket. Luyu had drawn her aside as Lucien had made his farewells to Nashoba and his men.

"Take this, *mon enfant,* the older woman had murmured in a low voice, placing a small doeskin bag in the palm of her hand. "Hide it on your person," she directed as the startled Caresse slipped it into the pocket of her riding habit. "Do not let anyone ever see it, but if you feel threatened, take the crystal from the bag and let the sun warm it in your hand. 'Tis a charm against those who would wish you harm at Sans Regret," she explained, touching Caresse's cheek once more in a gesture that was like a benediction. Before she could ask who Luyu thought wished her harm at the plantation, Lucien was at her side insisting that they must leave.

Caresse's last glimpse of the Choctaw woman had been as the pirogue pushed from the mossy bank into the waters of Lake Pontchartrain. Nashoba's mother had stood apart from the others, facing east and the rising sun. She held something up in each hand. Caresse was too far away to see what it was, but she thought she could see the woman's lips move as if in a chant or prayer.

An armadillo scuffing through a pile of dead leaves on the bank caused Bruno to stiffen and bark, awakening Caresse from her musings. She turned to quiet the dog as they passed by. The rough feel of his shaggy coat and the antics of the awkward armadillo lightened her mood. Like the sun coming out from behind a cloud and banishing the shadows, Bruno's mundane actions dispelled her anxiety about their return to the haunted atmosphere of Sans Regret. Aurore's remains had slumbered under the subtropical sun of Louisiana in her marble sepulcher for seven years. There was no such thing as a ghost; the only spirit that haunted the chambers of Sans Regret was the one she had conjured up from gossip and the superstitions of the slaves.

"When we arrive home I am going to send a message to the Sonniers to come for a short visit," Lucien spoke for the first time in hours. Even at their stop for food at midday he had been withdrawn and preoccupied.

The sound of his voice startled Caresse. He had been so remote, so lost in thought, since their departure from the Choctaw village, she had felt confused and rebuffed after the passion in the summer house the night before. It had both angered, and confused her, that after their intimate communion he had once more pulled back into the hard cold shell he wore around his emotions like the armor of the knights of old.

"*Oui*, 'twill be good to see Yvonne again. I wonder how she has adjusted to her new home," said Caresse, hoping that it had been an easier adjustment than her own.

"They will be safer with us for the next few days. I learned from Nashoba that there will be another Indian raid on the settlements along the river. Nashoba's men will guard Sans Regret. I cannot, however, guarantee the safety of any of the other plantations. There are restless bands among the Choctaw who are dissatisfied with the quality of the goods they receive in trade from the French. Their loyalty is weakening, so they are drawn to the British. The king's involvement in the European wars has cut off the supplies needed to trade with the Choctaw. De Vaudreuil knows this, but even he can do only so much, although he and Solange are taking their share of whatever does come through from France. After they are done there is little left for the forts upriver to trade with the Indians. The French in La Louisiane will pay for the foolishness and indifference at Versailles, and for the corruption in Nouvelle Orléans," Lucien said angrily.

"Did you find this out from the British officer you spoke with last night by the council fire?" Caresse asked with concern, trying not to let fear overwhelm her. She knew Indian raids were always a threat in the colony, but somehow with all the other more immediate dangers she had faced since coming to Sans Regret she had pushed it to the back of her mind.

"What British officer?" asked Lucien edgily.

"The British officer I saw you speaking with last night as the dancers began to form their circle," Caresse protested with a lift of her brows.

"You were mistaken, *ma chère*, there was no Brit-

263

ish officer at Nashoba's bonfire," he contradicted her, but his dark eyes looked away.

He was lying to her, she realized with a pang of shock and anger. She had seen the British officer, of that she was as sure as she was of her own name. "I saw him, Lucien. You cannot tell me that he was not there. 'Tis hard to mistake the red coat of a British officer," she insisted.

Above them a hawk circled looking for prey, and as if sensing his presence the creatures of the swamp came to a halt, trying to hide from the danger that flew above them. There was a stillness, a sense of anticipation, all around them. Lucien, too, paused for a moment in his steady maneuvering of the pirogue. He stared thoughtfully into the dense forest of the bank on their right. Bruno, his every canine instinct aware of the danger that vibrated in the heavy air, sat up on his haunches, ears lifted as if to discover the threat that hung like a palpable presence in the air.

"Perhaps you saw one of the braves who wore the officer's coat as a token of his kill in battle with the British and Chickasaw," said Lucien, an edge to his words. His distinguished features had become a remote mask, concealing any sense of the man she knew, the man who had held her to his heart. "I believe one of the braves did wear such a coat, but I had forgotten it till you spoke of it. 'Tis considered quite a badge of honor, for the British are hated by Nashoba's warriors. They have tried, along with their allies the Chickasaw, to close the Choctaw trade routes to New France. *Non,* a British officer would not be welcomed at the council fire of Nashoba," Lucien repeated in a tense, clipped voice that forbade any questions. He dipped the paddle into the bayou, and they resumed their silent slide over the murky water.

Caresse turned away to hide her confusion and fury. She knew that for some reason Lucien was lying to her. She had noticed the British officer's fair hair gleaming in the firelight, had seen the white linen ruffle about his neck. He had been no Choctaw brave dressed in stolen finery. Lucien's denial baffled her, causing strange and disquieting thoughts to race through her mind. Why, indeed, had a British officer been at Nashoba's council fire? Is that why they had come all the way through the twisting maze of bayous that led from Sans Regret to Lake Pontchartrain, so Lucien could meet with a British officer at Nashoba's council fire?

Suddenly the dark and primeval *cyprière* seemed frightening, full of unseen terrors and secrets. The security that she had found in Lucien's presence had been shaken by his insistence of what she knew was a lie.

Trade with the British was forbidden by French law in the colony, although planters from time to time had to smuggle their indigo crop to the waiting British ships at the mouth of the Mississippi to survive. Was it only such an arrangement that he was protecting, or was it something more serious? If he, a member of the Superior Council made up of prominent citizens who advised the governor, could meet a British officer at a remote Choctaw village, a meeting forbidden by French law, he was capable of any deceit. What other lies had he told her?

"We shall soon be at Sans Regret," he told her in gentler tones, observing that she had given a slight shiver that he thought indicated fatigue. The air was warm and heavy in the forested swamp, almost cloying in its humidity. No one could be cold in the muggy heat unless they were ill, and he cursed himself silently once more for allowing her to accompany him through the fever-ridden swamps.

Caresse gave him a slight smile, then turned her back to him. The plantation with its secretive atmosphere was no refuge, only another question in the turmoil of her mind.

A frown creased his brow as he sensed her withdrawal from him into one of the melancholy moods that had afflicted her at the convent of the Ursulines. He should never have allowed her to accompany him to the Choctaw village, but, he thought with a rueful grimace, he did not know how he would have stopped her. She could, despite her fragile appearance, be unbelievably stubborn. Perhaps a visit from her friend Yvonne would erase that sadness in her soft gray eyes, the withdrawal from him. It could not be helped; she had to be protected even if it meant that she no longer felt she could trust him. His expression was grim as he stared at the elegant line of her back. He knew now why he had always guarded his heart against love—the pain was too intense. But he knew deep within him that no price was too high to pay to keep her with him. He had to have her, for she was his destiny.

The autumn sun was setting as they reached the shadowed ground of Sans Regret. Bruno ran with joy toward the house at his release from the cramped quarters of the pirogue. The delicious scent of cooking meat was in the air, and the dog ran for the kitchen house.

"I feel as ravenous as Bruno," Lucien admitted, walking beside Caresse, feeling her cool withdrawal from him in her posture, her reluctance to look at him.

" 'Twill be good to soak in a bath," she admitted in polite tones as they walked through the kitchen gardens.

Both of their needs had to wait, for as they reached the shadow of the lower gallery they both saw to their dismay a familiar figure. Philippe Dubrieul stood speaking in what could only be described as an intense conversation with Dominique.

"Sacré! What is he doing here," Lucien cursed. "I thought we were rid of him."

Philippe and Dominique both turned at the sound of footsteps on the crushed-shell path between the neatly tended herb beds of the garden. Philippe looked resentful, then his expression softened as his eyes discerned Caresse. There was defiance in every line of Dominique's elegant posture, in her sable eyes.

"What, might I ask, gives us the pleasure of your company?" Lucien drawled, every word dipped in sarcasm as he stared at Philippe.

"A rumor came down from the river on a supply boat that a band of Choctaw attacked a French plantation north of here, not far from the settlement at Baton Rouge," Philippe replied coolly, but his narrow amber eyes gazed only at Caresse. "I was concerned about Mme St. Amant, for I had heard you were away."

"I thank you for your concern, but as you can see we have returned," Lucien said in polite tones of dismissal. "There are others along the river that need to be alerted to the danger."

"I believe the crew of the supply boat is stopping at every plantation to sound the alarm," Philippe told them as near the stables the huge bell used to summon the slaves from the fields began to ring. Its deep tones rang out in a rapid rhythm that Dominique and the two men seemed to recognize.

"Take Caresse inside," Lucien ordered Philippe as the garden in back of the house seemed to fill with house servants attracted by the tolling of the bell.

"Come, Caresse, upstairs," Philippe demanded, taking her arm, leading her toward the curving staircase that led to the second floor of the house.

"What is it? What is happening?" Caresse asked in a trembling voice. Then, as Lucien started across the herb garden where Zweig came running, a gun in his hand, she called out, "Lucien!"

He stopped for a moment and looked back over his shoulder at where she stood on the bottom step with Philippe at her side. He raised his hand and pointed to the second floor of the house, then turned and strode without a backward glance to the overseer.

"Hurry, 'tis the alarm. I think the Indians have been sighted," Philippe told her, pulling her up the stairs beside him.

"But they will not harm us," Caresse protested as she allowed herself to be led along the gallery into the salon. The sound of the huge bronze bell echoed throughout the empty chambers of the house.

"I am not as sure of that as you are," Philippe said, closing all the long French doors along the gallery, turning the bolt on each one. "Do not worry, *chérie*, I am with you," he reassured her, taking a small pistol from his pocket.

"But we have just come from the Choctaw village," Caresse protested. "They pledged to protect Sans Regret."

"He took you there?" Philippe said, stunned. "He has always spent too much time with those savages. *Par Dieu* let us hope that for once it will do some good." Philippe pulled out his powder horn and began to load his sidearm. "Can you shoot, *chérie*?"

"*Oui*, I have hunted," she replied, remembering the royal shoots she had gone on in the forest at Versailles. They had been more like a parade, or circus, than a hunting party, but her father had seen that she was taught to fire a hunting gun. He did not want her to disgrace him in front of all of his friends at court.

"And in the royal preserve, I should imagine," Philippe said, staring at her with comprehension in his narrow amber eyes. "Sometime you must confide the real story of how you arrived in La Louisiane, *chérie.*" Striding to the locked gun cabinet, he broke the glass with one knock of the butt of his pistol. Reaching inside, he pulled out a flintlock and powder horn. Quickly he loaded it and handed it to her.

"What do we do now?" Caresse asked, in a quivering voice, as the deep-throated bell continued to sound the alarm.

"We wait, *chérie,* we wait," he told her grimly, locking the doors that led into the other chambers opening off the salon.

As she stood holding the gun in her trembling hand, the elegant furnishings, the crystal chandelier overhead, the fine brandies in their cut-glass decanters seemed ludicrous for a stockade. The horrible ringing of the bell continued and it wore on her nerves till she thought she would scream.

Philippe stood near one of the long French doors, looking out toward the river as if to spot any warriors that might attack the house from the river. Caresse edged near him, as the bell abruptly stopped. The silence after such constant noise was even more frightening.

Staring out at the lawn filled with long shadows now as the sun set behind the house, it appeared to Caresse that there was something, or someone, moving behind each and every gnarled trunk of the four enormous live oaks. The imagination could play tricks on one's mind, she realized, when every nerve was stretched to the breaking point.

When the blood-curdling sound came from the direction of the swamp on their right it was almost a relief that the waiting was over. For good or for ill it had begun. The late-afternoon air was filled with the sound of guns, the cries of men dying, and then more frightening, the thud of feet on the stairs outside the locked door.

Philippe motioned for her to stand behind him as he moved to the center of the room. Then a single shot echoed off the gallery, silencing the thud of bare feet on the wooden floorboards.

Later, as she tried to recollect the sequence of events, it seemed that the raid had lasted a long time, but she could not remember how long, only the beating on the salon door and the wonderful sound of Lucien's voice demanding entry. She ran to the portal before Philippe and shot open the bolt.

"*Ma chère*, are you all right?" Lucien's voice was a harsh rasp as he swept her into his arms. She clung to him, the solid strength of his manly form.

"Is it over?" Philippe's question was a sharp intrusion.

"There were only a few of them, a renegade band, most of whom are now dead," Lucien explained dispassionately. "They picked up our trail in the swamps and followed us here, but they were not aware that they, too, had been followed by some of Nashoba's braves." He held Caresse in the curve of his arm leading her back into than salon and away from the door.

"Is this the same band who raided upriver?" Philippe asked, a strange look on his narrow features as he regarded Caresse clinging to Lucien's tall frame.

"We cannot be sure. The Choctaw are restless, unhappy with their treatment from Vaudreuil. The English take advantage of this fact. There could be more," Lucien said with a sigh of exasperation. "There is talk of civil war among the Choctaw. With Vaudreuil and the British manipulating the situation for their own gain, anything is possible."

" 'Twas foolish to take Caresse through the bayous to the Choctaw village. They could have attacked you when you were alone in the pirogue," Philippe sneered.

"I am well aware of what you say," Lucien ground the words out between his teeth. " 'Tis why I have decided we will be returning to Nouvelle Orléans."

"For once, I agree with you," Philippe replied. "Zweig can see to the rest of the harvest. Many plantation owners will do the same. The winter social season will start early this year. If I might intrude on your hospitality for one night, I too shall return on the morrow to Chêne Vert and leave instructions for my overseer. I find the muddy streets of Nouvelle Orléans call to me as well."

"How could I refuse my home to the man who defended my wife so gallantly," Lucien said formally, but stressing the words *my wife*.

"I think I should like to sit down," Caresse said faintly as the chamber seemed to move slowly around her. Moving toward the settee she saw through the open door the out stretched form of a dead brave, a knife clutched in his hand, blood seeping from underneath his prone body. He had almost made it to the door of the salon before being shot. It was Caresse's last conscious thought as she slumped to the floor.

"They are gone. Everything is all right," the deep soothing voice crooned to her from a far distance.

Her eyelids felt so heavy, her body as if there were weights on her arms and legs. But it was so safe in the darkness, she didn't want to leave it, to open those heavy lids and see such ugliness.

"I am here, *ma chère femme*, nothing can harm you," the voice was back entreating, luring her to open her eyes.

She felt warm lips on her forehead, the gentle touch of a hand brush the tangle of her hair from her eyes. A deep sigh was torn from her as she responded to that tender touch. She wanted to feel more, but it was gone. Weakly her eyelids fluttered open seeking the source of that soothing contact.

Dark eyes stared down at her, concern and tenderness shining in them. Long tapered fingers with their slightly square tips lightly stroked her hair. Above her she saw the canopy of the four-poster. Lucien had carried her into their bedchamber.

"Take a sip of this." He held a crystal glass half full of brandy to her lips. Lifting her shoulders as tenderly as if she was child, he allowed her to take a small drink of the golden liquid.

The warmth slid down her throat and into her stomach, relaxing the tense cramping and nausea. She lay back against the pillows with a sigh.

"Better?" he inquired.

"I . . . I think so," she stammered. "What about the others?" she asked, remembering that she was the mistress of Sans Regret and, as such, her first concern should be for the people of the plantation.

"No one was hurt but one of Nashoba's warriors and several of the renegade band. Nashoba and his men had the element of surprise with them. They drove what was left of the band deep into the swamps. For now they will stay away from Sans Regret. Zweig is seeing to the field hands, but the Choctaw have no quarrel with the Africans—often on a raid they will take them with them and give them sanctuary in their villages. 'Tis French blood they want to spill," he explained. "But the civil war that is escalating between the Choctaw makes it necessary that we leave for Nouvelle Orléans until it is resolved. I have spoken with Nashoba and he advised this is the best for now. Once we are gone from here the plantation will no longer be such an inviting target. They will move on to other, more vulnerable settlements where there are Frenchmen.

Dominique is supervising the servants in packing. We shall leave at first light on the morrow."

"I am glad," Caresse admitted. The crowded muddy streets of the small city would be welcome. There was strength in numbers, and the barracks of the French soldiers assigned to the colony lined the Place Royale only a few blocks from the house on the Rue de Chartres. "What about Yvonne and Pierre?" she asked remembering her friends.

"We shall stop and advise them to join us on our retreat to Nouvelle Orléans, *ma chère.*" Lucien reassured her, but seeing the worry in her dove gray eyes he held the glass once more to her lips.

The rustle of a woman's skirt told Caresse that they were not alone in the shadowy chamber. Turning her head, she saw the elegant figure of Dominique taking clothing from her armoire and placing it in an open trunk. "I should like to take Fantine with us to Nouvelle Orléans," she said to Lucien. She could tell Dominique had heard her request, for the woman paused a moment in her packing.

"If you wish, but Dominique can serve as a lady's maid as she did before we came to Sans Regret," Lucien reminded her.

"Dominique will be accompanying us to Nouvelle Orléans?" Caresse asked with an edge to her words.

"*Mais certainement,*" Lucien said, his heavy dark brows drawn together in a frown over his piercing black eyes. "As a *femme de couleur libre* she is considered French by the Choctaw. She would not be safe here." There was a dawning comprehension in those perceptive dark eyes that Caresse disliked Dominique.

"Of course she must accompany us to Nouvelle Orléans, but since her duties will be greater during the *salon des visites,* I shall keep Fantine as my personal maid," Caresse insisted in a tone that told him she had once more assumed her role as mistress of the St. Amant household.

"Whatever you wish, *ma chère*," Lucien replied with a shrug that plainly said the running of the household was up to her. "If you are feeling better, there is much I must attend to if we are to leave on the morrow. Rest here, and I shall have a tray sent up. I will join you later." His voice was lower on the last sentence as he lifted her hand to his lips. Turning her small cold hand over so it was palm up, he placed a lingering kiss on the soft inner mound.

She smiled up at him, amazed that in spite of everything, the feel of his warm lips on her skin could still kindle a smoldering fire in her blood. "Till later," he whispered against her mouth, as he bent over and brushed his lips in a teasing kiss, before he rose to his feet. As he turned to go he reached down and picked up delicate Blanchette from where she was hiding under the bed. "Company till I return," he told her, placing the cat beside her on the counterpane. Speaking a few words to Dominique, he left the two women alone as the lavender-gray shadows of twilight darkened the gallery outside.

"I shall be taking Blanchette with me to Nouvelle Orléans," Caresse told Dominique to break the tense silence that enveloped the room after Lucien's departure.

"*Très bien, madame*, I shall see to the basket," Dominique replied quietly, as she continued to pack the open trunk.

The words of Nashoba's mother came back to Caresse as she lay stroking the soft fur of Blanchette. She had said that Dominique had seen the man who had killed Aurore, that she knew the murderer. Was this the hold the enigmatic housekeeper had over Lucien? For she realized there was some bond that held them.

"Is there anything else, *madame?*" Dominique inquired, coming closer to the bed, her sable eyes enormous in the light from the tapers lit against the coming darkness.

"Just warm water for a bath, *s'il vous plaît.* I wish to wash away the heat and damp of our journey."

"*Oui, madame,* I shall have canisters brought directly from the kitchen house," she replied, turning to leave.

"Oh, before you leave, I wondered if the packing up of . . . of Aurore St. Amant's chamber is finished. If not, I would like it done tonight before we leave."

"That would be difficult, *madame,*" Dominique answered in a low composed voice, turning around as she paused at the French door.

"You mean nothing has been done," Caresse said sharply, sitting up, the rush of anger at her orders being deliberately disobeyed banishing her fatigue.

"*Non, madame,*" she answered. "The dead they do not like to be disturbed, you will understand this in time." She turned and glided from the room, leaving the French door open to the night air.

Furious, Caresse rose from the bed, suddenly realizing she was clad only in her chemise. Someone had undressed her when she was put to bed. Striding to the almost-empty armoire, she pulled out a silk dressing gown and wrapped it around her form. It was then that she saw in the corner of the armoire the black ball of wax Philippe had found at Aurore's tomb. Someone had placed the grisly voodoo charm in her wardrobe.

Gingerly, she reached down and picked it up. Turning it over in her hand, she saw a gleam from several strands of blond hair that had been wrapped around it. The glow from the tapers on the fireplace mantel made them shimmer against the dead black of the wax.

Shock yielded to fury as she remembered Luyu's words when she gave her the leather pouch. The Choctaw woman had said it was a charm against those who wished to harm her at Sans Regret.

Dropping the repulsive ball on the floor in a gesture of distaste, Caresse walked out on to the gallery. She needed fresh air to think.

Standing at the rail of the gallery she thought she saw something out of the corner of her eye. Turning to look down the gallery she thought she saw the flash of a white gown disappear behind the closing of one of the French doors. Then on the rising wind she knew she heard the light sound of a woman's laughter.

Caresse gasped, feeling a shiver of panic run through her. The door had been to Aurore's locked chamber.

Dominique's words throbbed in her brain, *the dead do not like to be disturbed.* Enough, she thought, I have had enough. Without a backward glance, she hurried back into her bedchamber, shutting the door against the night. But could you lock out a ghost? She started; catching her own frightened figure in the pier glass, for a moment she thought she was staring at the spectral image of Aurore. She had to hang on to her sanity till the morrow when they would leave this haunted abode for Nouvelle Orléans. But could she leave her doubts about her husband behind as well?

Nineteen

She didn't know what had awakened her, but one moment she was sound asleep and the next wide awake. Lucien's breathing was slow and steady beside her. The chamber was in darkness except for the light from the *veilleuse* on the bedside table.

It was then she heard it, what must have awakened her, the sound of music, the harpsichord playing in the salon. So faint she would have thought she had imagined it, but the longer she listened she knew that someone was playing the harpsichord.

Try though she might, she could not put it from her mind. Someone was trying to make her think a ghost haunted these rooms, and by doing so would drive her away. Well, they were wrong, she thought with a flash of anger. She would catch her in the act, for she was sure she knew who was directing this farce.

Slipping from the bed without awakening Lucien, she donned her *robe de chambre* and silently crept across the room. Opening the door into the study she could hear the music more clearly, and it did seem to be coming from the salon.

The moon shone in through the long French doors allowing her to cross the study easily to the door of the salon. Standing outside the door she could hear the sad music, a love song often played at Versailles. If the musician thought to frighten her away from Sans Regret, or make her as disturbed as the two previous mistresses, she was mistaken.

Taking a deep breath for courage, Caresse turned the knob slowly. With the door open a crack, she peered in trying to see if she could make out who was seated at the harpsichord giving the late-night recital. The chamber was, however, in shadows. She could see only a fold of some heavy ivory material, and the flow of dark hair.

Torn by indecision, Caresse stood in the half-open portal trying to gather the courage to confront the phantom musician. She had come this far, she reasoned. Now might be her only chance to unmask the person who seemed determined to make her think Aurore's ghost still inhabited these walls.

Opening the door, she slipped inside the salon, hesitating for a moment in the dimness. Someone had pulled the curtains at the French doors, blocking out the moonlight. The only light came from a three-branched silver candelabra on a table behind the musician. Moving quickly, she crossed the room to stand behind the tall figure with long flowing black hair dressed in some sort of ivory damask dressing gown.

"You came to me," the voice said quietly, startling her so she stood speechless. The voice was not feminine, rather quite masculine.

"Who . . . what are you?" Caresse gasped, as slowly the figure turned around.

"I knew if I played you would come to me."

"Philippe! 'Tis you," Caresse sighed in exasperation and relief.

He rose from the seat clad in a man's dressing gown, his powdered wig gone, his own hair flowing long and dark down his back. "I could not slumber, so I came here. But, *chérie,* I could only hope you would hear me, and come to me," he said, his narrow amber eyes filled with that strange lustful yearning that Caresse had seen before his gaze.

"Non, you do not understand," she protested as he came closer to her.

"You do not have to pretend, *chérie,*" he said, reaching out to touch her hair as it tumbled over her shoulders. "So rare, such a color."

"Please, I do not wish to hurt you, but I thought . . . I thought," Caresse stammered, unable to continue. What could she say? Should she tell him she thought he was a ghost or Dominique pretending to be the ghost of Aurore? It would sound insane.

"You are shy, I understand. She was shy too," he continued, stroking her hair, then down the side of her cheek.

"Non," Caresse objected, reaching up to push his hand away, but he caught it in his own, lifting it to his lips.

"Am I interrupting?" the cold, bitter voice questioned from the portal.

Turning, Caresse felt her voice catch in her throat. Lucien stood with folded arms watching them with blazing eyes that burned into her with the strength of his wrath. She took a few faltering steps toward him, the hand that Philippe had kissed outstretched in supplication.

"You seem to have a fascination for my wives, Dubrieul," Lucien said, and his voice, though low and controlled, was also cold and lashing.

" 'Tis not what it seems," Caresse protested, coming to stand in front of him.

"Go to our bedchamber," he ordered with a contempt that forbade any further argument. "I shall join you in a moment."

Suddenly his treatment of her infuriated her. He was judging her without listening for any explanation. The memory of his sensual dance with Isi at the Choctaw village somehow came to mind, only fueling her anger.

"You are being foolish," she sputtered, bristling with indignation. Then without a backward glance she swept from the room with head held high.

She could not know how much she looked like Aurore at that moment, or that this scene had taken place a little over seven years before. But to both men the sight brought back heartbreaking memories that tore through them like a reopened wound.

Caresse fled across the study into the bedchamber, slamming the doors behind her as she went, as if she could vent her fury at fate and Lucien. The events of the night had seemed out of her control, turning into tragic misunderstandings.

Throwing herself across the bed, she could only hope for first light when they would leave Sans Regret. Nothing here seemed to be what it appeared.

"Philippe has gone to his chamber. He says nothing was premeditated, that you only appeared when you heard his playing. Is he telling the truth?" Lucien's curt interrogation both angered and hurt something deep within her.

"Will you believe anything I say, or come to your own conclusions?" she asked wearily, turning over so that she stared up at him with reproachful eyes.

"You are mine, *ma chère,* never forget that," he said, an unmistakable warning in his husky voice. He reached down and grasped her by the shoulders, pulling her off the bed, pressing her against the long hard length of him.

She glared up at him, trying to fight the unwelcome surge of excitement she felt warring with her anger. The heat from his body, the hard sinewy feel of his chest, his hard abdomen, the length of his thigh spoke another language than that of anger.

"Mon Dieu, do not look at me like that," he groaned, pulling her into his embrace, his mouth hard and searching coming down on hers in a fiery ravishment.

Her arms came up around his neck as she returned his kiss with an equal aching hardness. It was as if they could burn out their anger in the savage intensity of their kiss. Heated mouth on heated mouth, they gave no quarter.

Then he was pushing her down, down onto the feather mattress, ripping the night rail from her body with one swift tear. A moan of arousal rose from her throat.

When he buried his mouth in the silky intimate curls at the V of her thighs, she pressed him closer, crying *"Mon coeur!"* The spiral of rapture began as she writhed under his heated mouth, her hands digging into his shoulders, urging him on. Arching up to experience each nuance, she was lost in the rapture only he could give her.

He could wait no longer to feel her hot sheath around him, to take her again and again. Lifting up his head, he spread her thighs wider, then with a groan he plunged inside her. Slowly, he savored each thrust. "You are mine now and always, Caresse," he murmured in a voice husky with emotion and desire as he moved faster and faster, plunging into her as if his passion could drive out any thought of another. "Tell me, say my name, and tell me!" he ordered with a groan that came from deep within him.

"I am yours . . . Lucien . . . *mon coeur!* Always!" The words were torn from her as he took her to the pinnacle. Then there was only the shuddering moan of ecstasy and release to rend the dark night, as he joined her in the shared fulfillment of lovers who have found the other half of their soul.

He held her to him with arms of steel as they finally slumbered, the depth of their emotions having left them exhausted in mind and body. They were unaware that not everyone slept at Sans Regret, that outside their chamber on the long gallery paced a lonely figure who could only envy their union from afar, and plot how to destroy it.

The first light of dawn awakened the slumbering household, and smoke soon came from the kitchen house where Zoé began the morning meal. Fantine, beside herself with excitement at the thought of her coming sojourn in Nouvelle Orléans, helped her mistress to dress while the master shaved at the shaving stand in his dressing room.

Lucien was anxious to depart. Although Nashoba and his men camped in the stable yard, he would only feel sure of Caresse's safety when they were in Nouvelle Orléans. Bruno circled at his feet seeming aware that this time he would be allowed to accompany his master.

Caresse had bathed quickly, anxious like Lucien to depart. The events of the night, as well as the Indian attack, had stretched her nerves to the highest pitch. She wondered if Philippe had already left for Chêne Vert. It would be awkward if he was still here. Telling Fantine to fetch Blanchette's basket, she pushed Philippe to the back of her mind, so occupied was she with the myriad details of their imminent departure.

The morning sun was streaming down as Lucien and Caresse walked toward the wharf with Bruno at their heels, and Dominique, with Fantine carrying Blanchette's basket, following behind. Philippe had left at first light for his plantation.

It all looked so tranquil, thought Caresse, as they stepped from the wharf to the waiting keelboat, looking back at the elegant house glowing in the light of the morning sun. The horror of the previous afternoon had vanished as if it had all been a bad dream.

The field hands were working under supervision by the overseer and his men, smoke curled from the chimney of the kitchen house, a maid carried dishes from the warming kitchen on the first floor to the wash house. It all looked so normal, but as her eyes swept the second-floor gallery they lingered on the twining oak and the branch that arched so close to the locked door of Aurore's chamber. For a brief heart-stopping moment, she thought she saw a figure at the French door, a flash of a white garment. She shook her head at such a fantasy, and turned away.

"Madame, is there something wrong?" Dominique asked in a soft knowing voice.

"Nothing, nothing at all," Caresse replied, moving down the rail to where Lucien stood speaking with the African who had been trained to captain the keelboat.

"We are ready to leave, *ma chère.* If you have forgotten anything now is the time to send someone to fetch it," Lucien teased, trying to lighten the mood between them. The excess of the previous night, the almost-devouring lovemaking between them, had left a certain awkwardness.

"Cast off, I am ready for the muddy crowded streets of Nouvelle Orléans," she told him with a smile.

Bruno ran from one side of the boat to the other as the African crew poled them out into the swift current of the Mississippi. The trip downriver was easy for the crew once the boat was caught in the current of the surging river. All that was necessary was to keep it on the right path.

As they sailed past a bend in the river Caresse thought she saw the figures of several Choctaw braves through the trees of the densely forested bank. Standing at the rail, she shielded her eyes against the sparkle of the sun off the tawny waves of the Mississippi. Had she really seen the war party, or had it been only a figment of her overactive imagination?

"What is it, *chère*?" Lucien asked, coming to stand beside her at the rail.

"I thought I saw something through the trees," she mused aloud. "But I cannot be sure."

"What was it you thought you saw?"

"It looked like a Choctaw war party," she told him with a frown.

"I pray that you were wrong," Lucien said.

"What of Yvonne and Pierre? I fear for their safety," Caresse confided, biting her lower lip in anxiety and frustration.

"Dubrieul said the supply boat was stopping at every plantation to warn the settlers. I am sure they alerted the Sonniers. Pierre is an expert *coureur de bois*, he would understand the seriousness of the situation," he tried to comfort her, but she could tell by the tense expression on his fine features that he too was concerned.

"*Miché* there be someone in the water ahead of us," Quito, the captain of the keelboat, pointed out to Lucien as he came up beside him.

They looked to where he gestured on the port side where a small pirogue containing one long figure was in danger of being hit by their much larger craft. As they gained on the narrow canoe the man at the helm looked familiar.

"*Mon Dieu*, 'tis Dubrieul," Lucien muttered. "There must have been trouble at Chêne Vert for him to try and escape in a pirogue. Have the men pull us out of the current and drop anchor so we can pick him up. I want to know what has happened at Chêne Vert."

The maneuvering of the keelboat from the strong current of the river was dangerous, but deftly managed by Quito and his crew. A relieved looking Philippe Dubrieul leaped aboard after catching the rope thrown to him. His pirogue was pulled on deck by the men.

"You'd best get under way, there are several Choctaw raiding parties roaming the banks looking for French blood to spill," Philippe warned them as he took his flintlock from the bottom of the pirogue resting on the deck. "And I could use a brandy."

Lucien gave Quito the signal to depart, then turned to Philippe. "The brandy and glasses are inside in the cabin. If what you say is true, 'twould be safer for Caresse to stay there till we reach Nouvelle Orléans."

Philippe nodded his agreement, his gaze lingering on Caresse's visage for a moment longer than was polite, before he turned toward the cabin. Lucien frowned, a muscle flicking at the firm line of his jaw, as he stared after their unwanted guest.

"We do not seem to be able to get rid of Dubrieul's company," he said tersely, holding out his arm to escort her inside the cabin. Placing her hand on his arm she followed him into the small cabin without comment, Bruno at their heels.

It seemed Philippe's warning was valid, for as the door shut behind them three arrows struck the deck of the keelboat. Hearing the shouts of the crew Lucien pushed Caresse to the floor. Grabbing a flintlock off the gun rack on the wall of the cabin, he moved to one of the small windows—the other was already manned by Philippe.

"Stay down, *chère*," Lucien's terse command rang out, as a rain of arrows seemed to strike the boat from the dense vegetation of the bank.

Caresse lay with her head on a bag of flour, her arms around the cowering Bruno, who sensed the danger. She tried to fight the sheer black fright that swept over her at the sound of the cries and moans of the crewman who were wounded and dying outside on the deck. The thought of Dominique and Fantine on that hellish deck was horrifying. She heard the frantic orders of Quito as he urged the remaining slaves to pole faster so as to reach the escape route of the river's current. She could only hope the women had taken cover that would protect them. The sound of the recoil of the men's muskets as they fired, then paused to reload the single-shot guns, echoed in the small cabin.

Suddenly, Caresse realized that she could fight her fear more easily if she were doing something, rather than cowering on the floor of the cabin. Leaving Bruno, she edged across the floor to the gun rack. Rising for a brief moment she took down the remaining gun and powder horn. Quickly she loaded it, and staying low, made her way across to where Lucien stood at the window. After he fired and bent down to reload, she handed him the gun she had taken from the wall. Taking the fired gun from his hand, she began to reload it.

"Magnifique, ma belle," he said, his grin of admiration flashing briefly, before he turned back to the window.

Loading and reloading as fast as she could, Caresse lost all sense of time in the midst of the battle for survival—and she felt her fear recede. A strange calm came over her, allowing her to attend to the required task.

After what seemed eons, the keelboat began to move faster and faster, telling them that they had caught the mighty current of the Mississippi. With its help they were soon beyond reach of the raiding party.

"Are you unhurt?" Lucien asked, turning from the window to where she sat at his feet, the powder horn in her lap, black streaks across her cheek, her straw hat crushed beyond repair on the floor beside her.

"Is it over?" she gasped, leaning against the wall.

"For now, but we dare not stop along the way. I am afraid that means we shall not be stopping at Bonne Chance," he told her with regret, but firm resolve in his dark eyes. "If they are under attack we could not help them. We are too vulnerable. We cannot even take the chance of slowing the boat to see how conditions are. We dare not leave the current of the river to sail close to the bank. I am sorry, *ma chère*."

"You are right, I know," she said with a sigh, brushing her hand across her eyes, determined not to give in to tears. She could only pray that Yvonne and Pierre had already left for Nouvelle Orléans.

"If I had not seen the tracks along the levee path on my way home from Sans Regret. If I had not taken the trouble to look closely for any clue, I would have walked into an ambush. I can only hope that my overseer and people are all right," Philippe mused aloud, sitting exhausted on an upturned barrel.

"I'd best see what we have on deck," Lucien replied, striding to the door.

"Wait, I am coming with you," Caresse struggled to her feet.

She followed him out on to the deck, to see the bodies of two slaves fallen in a pool of blood. Feeling the remnants of her breakfast rise, she ran to the rail and was sick into the swirling waters of the Mississippi.

"Go back inside, *chère*." Lucien stood at her side, then wiped her mouth with his handkerchief when she finished. Pulling a silver flask from his pocket he uncapped it, and held it to her lips.

"I am fine now," she muttered, after taking a long drink of the brandy, letting it warm and calm her stomach. "We must see that Fantine and Dominique are all right, and Blanchette."

"My brave stubborn lily, so much strength in such a fragile body," he murmured, brushing a tendril from her cheek with one tender gesture. His ebony eyes glowed his admiration, his desire for her. Never had she been more beautiful to him then at this moment as she stood, chin raised in determination, in a torn and wrinkled gown, her blond hair a tangle down her back, black smudges and tear stains on her cheeks.

"La Louisiane is only for the strong," she said with a rueful half smile. "You told me that once. You were right."

"*Madame, m'sieur,* help me," Dominique called from where she knelt behind several upturned barrels.

Hurrying to her side, they saw the outstretched form of the lovely Fantine, an arrow through her throat. The pitiful yowl of Blanchette in her basket beside the dead girl expressed Caresse's feeling. She wanted to howl like an animal at the waste of Fantine's young life, and at the guilt that surged through her, for the young maidservant had accompanied them to Nouvelle Orléans at her request. It was her fault that Fantine lay dead from the random shot of a Choctaw arrow.

"There is nothing we can do, Dominique. She died instantly," Lucien said softly, removing his jacket to cover the still form of Fantine.

"I thought as much, *m'sieur,*" Dominique said sadly. "She panicked. I told her keep down and nothing will happen, but she would not listen." The woman rose to her feet, coming to Caresse's side. "Come, *madame.* We shall go inside the cabin. The sun is hot and you have lost your hat."

Like a child, Caresse allowed Dominique to lead her away from the body of Fantine. She only stopped when she noticed they were passing the deserted dock of Bonne Chance. Walking to the rail she stared out across the water at the empty grounds, devoid of any sign of people. The house seen through the trees had a closed look about it.

"They have gone, *madame*, your friends have gone," Dominique reassured her. "Come, we go into the cabin and rest. You will see them in Nouvelle Orléans."

For the rest of the day, Caresse sat in the stuffy close cabin in a crude rocking chair, Dominique never leaving her side except to fetch the basket containing Blanchette. Lucien and Philippe told stories of other trips up and down the river, and the earlier times in the colony when Indian raids were more numerous. They continued to insist that this was unusual, a result of Vaudreuil's failure with his Indian policy.

Caresse stared dully at the dust motes caught in the stream of sunlight coming through the window. She had seen too much, witnessed too much violence. For the moment she wanted only to drift, not to think or to feel.

The sky had turned to the lavender blue of twilight, tinged on the horizon with violet and rose, when Lucien roused Caresse from her lethargy to accompany him out on the deck. Their nerve-racking journey was at an end. Ahead of them could be seen the spires of the church of St. Louis rising out of the violet-gray autumn mists.

"Look, *ma chère*, Nouvelle Orléans," Lucien pointed to the church spires as they made their way through the thronged waters of the port toward the wharf for keelboats near the market.

"How Fantine was looking forward to her stay," Caresse said softly.

"Try not to feel responsible for her death. 'Twill not bring her back," Lucien replied, putting his arm around her waist and pulling her into a loose embrace. "Life here is hard, *ma chère*, no one would deny that, so one must enjoy the short amount of time fate allows us. I do not mean to sound callous, but 'tis true. Perhaps that is why there is a sense of living for the moment in Nouvelle Orléans. In such a wilderness, in such a climate, death is never very far away, so live life to the limit. Each hour thus lived is an hour snatched from the abyss." There was a melancholy in his voice and in the expressive dark eyes that turned to gaze with tenderness upon her.

" 'Tis sad, but I think there is truth in what you say. I sensed it even when I was at the convent. And certainly the Vaudreuils conduct their life in such a manner," Caresse said with a shiver, even within the circle of Lucien's strong arm.

"What is it?" he asked gently.

"An old saying, something about feeling someone walk over your grave, or in La Louisiane in front of it," she mused.

"Enough of such morbid talk," he chided softly. "You are safe in Nouvelle Orléans. Remember last night," his voice was a husky whisper against her temple, "you are mine, and I refuse to allow anything, or anyone, to take you from me." He pulled her closer to him, as the long purple shadows of evening fell across the dock. They had arrived.

Despite Lucien's promise, Caresse felt a strange premonition that it was not so simple. Her hand slipped inside the pocket of her gown and touched the leather pouch from Luyu. The Choctaw woman had promised it was a charm against those who would harm her at Sans Regret. She wondered if it would work its protective magic in Nouvelle Orléans.

Part Three

What beck'ning ghost, along the moonlight shade?
Invites my steps, and points to yonder glade?
>   Alexander Pope, "Elegy to the
>   Memory Of An Unfortunate Lady"

Human blood is heavy; the man that has shed it
cannot run away.
>   African Proverb

Twenty

Nouvelle Orléans
February 1750

The cool damp February weather crept into Caresse's bedchamber on a draft under the closed French door. Walking to the fireplace, she took another log from the brass basket and placed it on the smoldering flames. Holding out her hands to the warmth she tried to ease the chill that seemed to penetrate right to her bones.

The delicate porcelain clock on the mantel struck five o'clock. Already the darkness of the early winter night had fallen, casting the chamber in shadows. Even the glow of the many lit tapers under their glass hurricane globes could not completely dispel the gloom.

"I should ring for Dominique, and begin dressing for the governor's *soirée*," Caresse said aloud to fluffy white Blanchette who had moved closer to the fire, rubbing against her mistress' ankles in a bid for attention. "But I should prefer to stay here and slumber before the fire like you," she crooned to the cat, picking her up and holding her to her cheek.

The *saison de visites*, the social season in Nouvelle

Orléans was now at its height, having been gaining in momentum since the beginning of the new year. Lucien being a member of the Superior Council, they had been invited almost every night to *soirées*, public dances, operas and plays given by players brought from France and Saint-Domingue, and the numerous card parties that the wealthier citizens held to while away the long winter nights.

Staring into the flames, Caresse thought of her friends Yvonne and Pierre who had made it to the city only hours before them last November during the height of the Indian raids. Living for the winter in a small raised cottage on the Rue du Maine, until Pierre decided it was safe to return to Bonne Chance, they did not have so busy a social calendar, but seemed cozy and content in their small house. Yvonne was carrying their first child, due in the spring, and was happy to rest by her fire, flourishing under Pierre's tender care.

Sitting on the floor on the hearth rug in front of the now roaring fire, Caresse stroked Blanchette curled up on her lap. Sadly, she had experienced no sign of carrying a child and now with Lucien often gone for days at a time on some mysterious business for the governor, there seemed less chance of her conceiving an heir. Frowning as she stared into the dancing blue and orange flambeau, she mused on her husband's long absences almost from their first days back at the town house on the Rue de Chartres in November.

There was a strain in their relationship and she could trace it almost to the day. Late one November afternoon, several weeks after their return to Nouvelle Orléans, Lucien had returned preoccupied from a meeting with the Superior Council and Governor Vaudreuil. There had been a tenseness and some other unreadable emotion in his dark expressive eyes. She had caught him looking at her strangely when he thought she was not aware of his circumspection. And that night he had made love to her with a depth of emotion, and almost desperation, that had left her spent with exhaustion. But on the morrow she had sensed something different between them, and Lucien's absences from Nouvelle Orléans began.

"*Madame,* I have brought you *café* and one of the calas you enjoy. The dinner at the governor's is not for some time," Dominique announced, as she deftly opened the door balancing the tray she carried on her other arm.

"*Merci,* perhaps 'twill give me the energy to face tonight, and one of Solange's interminable *soirées,*" Caresse said, with a sigh, rising to her feet.

"If you will sit before the looking glass at the dressing table, *madame,* I could dress your hair while you eat," Dominique said, placing the tray on the inlaid *poudreuse* imported from France.

Sipping the hot fragrant coffee, Caresse watched in the mirror as Dominique brushed out her waist-length tresses and began to pin them high at the back of her head. There had been a truce between the two women since their arrival back in Nouvelle Orléans. Since Fantine's tragic death, Dominique had served as her lady's maid as well as housekeeper. A free woman of color came every day to serve as cook in the kitchen house at the end of the enclosed garden.

"Will M'sieur Dubrieul be escorting you to the governor's *soirée* as usual, *madame?*" Dominique inquired, her eyes averted from the silvered glass so Caresse could not read the expression in those dark depths.

"*Oui,* since my husband is gone on official business to the settlement at Baton Rouge the marquise has asked that Monsieur Dubrieul serve as my escort, for the streets of the city are quite dangerous after dark," Caresse replied, taking another sip of the dark rich brew. She wished that she didn't feel she must make an excuse for Philippe Dubrieul being her escort.

Lucien wanted her to accept Solange's invitations while he was gone. It was important that she fulfill their social obligations. The marquise would provide an escort for her so he need not worry about her safety, he had explained in that new detached way he had of speaking to her. The first time he had returned from one of his long absences she had told him quite candidly that Philippe had been her escort at Solange's insistence. For a moment she had seen a flash of fire in his dark eyes, then he had given a shrug and said he was glad she was not traveling alone on the streets of Nouvelle Orléans at night.

"You will be wearing the ivory silk taffeta gown with the brocaded gold gilt, *madame*?" Dominique checked as she took two bouquets of silk lilies, with pearl drops on their petals, from a drawer to attach with a piece of lace ribbon to the completed chignon.

A fashionable lady always wore some type of lace cap, no matter how small, but for formal occasions the hair was dressed with pearls, ribbons, or tiny bouquets of artificial flowers. Solange's *soirées* were meant to rival those at Versailles—she and her husband tried to imitate the elegant life of the French court of Louis XV. Full court dress, or as elaborate costume as could be afforded, were *de rigueur* for the guests invited to the elaborate entertainments at the governor's house, and tonight was no exception.

"Lovely," she commented to Dominique.

" 'Tis rumored that the marquise's *coiffures* are only done once a week, since it takes her hairdresser over eight hours to achieve the desired effect. She is said to have a ruby-encrusted *grattoir* to scratch her scalp without disturbing her hairdo," the maid confided with a slight smile.

Caresse's eyes met Dominique's in the mirror. She grimaced and shook her head at yet another story of Solange's excess. Gossip flew about the narrow streets of the small town of the depravity and callousness of the governor's wife. 'Twas said that a purchase could not be transacted in Nouvelle Orléans without paying the extra fee attached by Solange de Vaudreuil. It was also rumored she controlled the flow of drugs into the city, and that anything could be purchased as long as Solange's henchman was paid his fee. Under the de Vaudreuils the city was beginning to resemble Versailles in more ways than one.

Standing so Dominique could help her with her gown, Caresse felt a pang that she would be going out to yet another function without Lucien. She did not care for the life of the social butterfly, yet her husband was forcing her into that role. Now that the Indian raids had ceased, she almost wished they could retire to Sans Regret, for at least there, despite Aurore, they had been together. Not that the town house was without its reminders of Aurore's presence. She would find them when she least expected. It might be a bowl decorated with violets on a table, the book of favorite menus written in a large careless feminine scrawl found in the study, a music box that played the same melody that Philippe had performed on the harpsichord that last night at Sans Regret, a chest or armoire opened to the faint scent of violet perfume. The memory of Aurore, even in Nouvelle Orléans, still haunted Caresse.

"I believe Bruno has heard a visitor at the front entrance," Dominique said as she straightened the folds of Caresse's skirt. The dog had risen from his place near the French doors to walk to the portal of the bedchamber with alert posture. In Lucien's absence he had become Caresse's shadow.

"Go see who Pascal has allowed entrance. I

would imagine 'tis M. Dubrieul," Caresse told the serving woman as she took one last glance at her appearance in the pier glass. "I shall be down in a few minutes."

"*Très bien, madame,*" Dominique replied, sweeping from the room.

Picking up her fan, silk muff, and gray velvet hooded cloak trimmed in white fur, Caresse left the chamber with Bruno at her heels. The long night stretched ahead of her, and only her promise to Lucien to fulfill their social obligations kept her from turning back to her bedchamber for a cozy night in front of the fire.

Starting down the stairs, she was surprised to hear the sound of voices raised in argument coming from the foyer below. She recognized Philippe's voice, but the other was more muffled and restrained. Could it be Dominique's? She remembered that the two of them were really half-brother and half-sister. The practice of some wealthy Frenchmen taking women of color as mistresses made for strange relationships in Nouvelle Orléans. A man might have two families, one white, one of mixed blood, living only blocks apart.

"I shall do as I please. Despite your power with some, do not make the mistake of thinking you can tell me how to conduct my life. May I remind you of your place," the angry voice of Philippe seemed to echo up the staircase as Caresse quietly descended.

"You would be well advised to remember yours," the controlled voice of Dominique interrupted him. Then both stopped speaking as they saw Caresse.

"*Chérie,* you look enchanting, as always," Philippe called out in a changed tone, coming toward Caresse as she reached the last step.

"*Merci,* Philippe," Caresse said with a brief smile as he bowed over her hand, holding it to his lips a trifle longer than was polite. From behind her Bruno gave a low growl. It was always Bruno's reaction to Philippe's presence.

"Please restrain that animal, *chérie*," her guest said with a grimace of distaste.

"He will not bite, he just seems to not care for your presence in the house," Caresse replied, bending down to give the animal a reassuring pat.

"An opinion I am glad to see his mistress does not share," Philippe said with a smile, turning his back on the dog. He took the cloak from Caresse's arm and placed it around her shoulders. His hands once more lingered longer then necessary on her shoulders, then he tenderly lifted the hood up about her elegant *coiffure*. " 'Tis cool and damp outside with a mist of rain. I would not want you to take a chill."

"I appreciate your concern, Philippe," Caresse said, moving away from his touch. "See that Bruno has some dinner, Dominique."

Caresse turned toward the woman as she slipped the high-heeled slippers from her feet and placed them in a silk bag to hang from the drawstrings on her wrist. Dominique then strapped the high wooden pattens on her silk-clad feet so that they would not become muddy walking the few feet from the house to the waiting carriage. This time of year the streets of Nouvelle Orléans were a revolting sea of mud and refuse. It was necessary to go through this routine every time a lady of fashion went out of the house. There would be maids waiting at the governor's house to help the ladies back into their elegant high-heeled silk slippers.

A heavy mist was falling as Philippe escorted her out into the fog-shrouded streets and the waiting carriage. Once inside, he rapped on the roof with his cane as a signal to the coachman to depart.

It was as if they rode through a cloud, only a light shining through a window making any dent in the gloom that surrounded the carriage. There were few people on the street—or else it was impossible to see them in the dense rain and fog. They reached the Place Royale and crossed in front of the Corps de Garde building containing the prison and courtroom. The door opened, throwing a stream of light out onto the gallery and the muddy street. Staring out the rain-streaked window to avoid Philippe's too intense gaze, she saw a tall lithe figure silhouetted in the portal. There was something about the figure, something familiar. She wiped the fog from the window with her gloved hand to get a better look. As the man stepped out to the gallery the light behind his cloaked figure reminded her of another cloaked figure, the man who had visited her in La Salpêtrière. Then they were past, and he was gone.

She sat back against the upholstered seat in dismay. Was she losing her mind or was her loneliness slowly driving her to fanciful imaginings? It had been so long since she had thought of him, that elusive stranger who had changed her life so totally.

"What is it, *chérie?*" Philippe asked with concern, sensing that something was wrong.

"I . . . I thought that I recognized someone, but I am sure 'twas just a trick of the light," Caresse finished in firm tones, determined not to dwell on her foolish fantasy.

"On such a night I do not see how you could recognize anyone," Philippe commented as the fog once more surrounded the carriage. "Only Solange could draw people away from their fireplaces in such weather."

"They are afraid not to come. Her power grows with each day in the colony. I heard that a planter cannot ship out of Nouvelle Orléans without paying her a fee, or import anything as well," Caresse commented.

"The colony has always been corrupt, but I must

say—just between the two of us—it has reached new proportions under Solange and the governor. He, of course, does whatever she wishes. She would make his life hell on earth if he didn't listen to her. Her family has connections at Versailles, the very highest one can imagine," he told her, his hand gripping the silver knob of his cane. "Do not ever cross her, *chérie,* I cannot stress this enough. She is not an enemy to be taken lightly." He gazed out the rain-streaked window, lost in some troubled musings of his own.

There was a crowd of carriages lined up in front of the governor's mansion on the corner of the Rue St. Ann and the Rue de Chartres facing the Place Royale. A lantern hanging on a post outside the entrance flickered in the misty fog. Here and there could be seen the lanterns on the carriages blinking in the rain as they moved up to the carriage block to discharge their passengers.

"They have all come, I see," Philippe said with an edge of sarcasm to his words. "As you said, *chérie,* they are afraid not to attend one of Solange's command performances."

A tall slave dressed in the de Vaudreuils' livery opened the door as they moved up in line to the entrance. Philippe stepped out to help Caresse alight on the high carriage block, then down to the boards of the gallery. The rambling two-story structure of brick covered in stucco was ablaze with light as they entered the long hallway that bisected the mansion.

Caresse retired to the salon on the right where the other women were changing into their shoes. Cloaks were removed and given to servants as elaborate hairstyles were checked in the numerous mirrors and pier glasses there for just such purposes.

"How lovely you look, so chic, 'tis a shame that Lucien cannot see you," Solange greeted Caresse as she reached the entrance to the chamber used for the formal dinner. "But then I am sure Philippe has seen that you are not lonely." The woman's voice carried down the receiving line to Caresse's chagrin. She felt several people turn and stare at her.

"No one can take my husband's place, Marquise," Caresse corrected her gently. She saw a cold hard gleam come into the woman's large, cold eyes.

"I can understand that, Mme St. Amant. Your husband is a man unlike any other."

"That is very true, Marquise," Caresse replied, her eyes meeting Solange's with perfect comprehension. Then she moved on into the elegant chamber.

The immensely long table was set with a lavish opulence of gold and silver, with Sèvres porcelain plates and delicate crystal flutes at each plate setting. Tall silver épergnes filled with camellias, the only flower in bloom now in Nouvelle Orléans, stood between silver candelabra every few inches on the table, draped in damask and lace.

"I see Solange has again outdone herself," Philippe's voice greeted Caresse as she reached the place where her name was written in elegant script on a small card by the gold-rimmed Sévres plate.

"We are seated together," she said with a wry smile. There was no doubt in her mind that Solange was deliberately throwing them together. And Caresse realized with a pang, she could be making sure that Lucien was being sent on missions for the governor because of her own twisted reasons. Solange liked to play with people's lives, it was another way of exercising her sense of power.

"Allow me, *chérie,*" Philippe said pulling out the fragile gilt-trimmed chair.

Understanding Solange's game and being able to do something about it were two different problems, Caresse realized with a sigh as the governor and his wife swept into the chamber and to their respective places at either end of the long table. All rose as the governor greeted them and motioned for all to be seated. After a footman seated the marquis and the marquise, the guests sank into their chairs with a collective sigh. The dinner had begun.

Course after delicious course was served with the finest wines, but it could have been sawdust as far as Caresse was concerned. She made polite conversation with the man on her right and Philippe on her left, and laughed at the jokes of the elderly gentleman across the table from her, but always there was the ache in her heart, the ache that was Lucien.

The gossip flew up and down the table. Who had fought in what duel over whom, the latest *affaires d'amour,* the terrible weather, the latest news from France, all were fodder for the mill of discussion. Caresse had heard it all before, but as dessert was served with a sparkling champagne, something new was thrown out for discussion.

"You mean you have not heard, Mme St. Amant, about the *voodooienne* who holds her rites every Saturday night in an abandoned warehouse down by the docks?" Mme de Mézières questioned from across the table.

"I fear I have not," Caresse replied, feeling Philippe stiffen beside her.

"Now, I personally have not gone," the woman gave an artificial trill, "but I have heard that even many of the French of Nouvelle Orléans have attended. She is supposed to be a remarkable clairvoyant."

"And what is this *voodooienne's* name, *madame?*" Caresse said with a sudden flicker of apprehension in the pit of her stomach.

"I do not know if I have heard it," the woman's brow wrinkled as she tried to think. "She is one of the *femmes de couleur libres,* but I do not think I have ever heard her name."

Caresse heard the light sigh of relief from Philippe at the woman's confession. She did not have to hear the name to give an educated guess that the *voodooienne* who was the talk of Nouvelle Orléans was none other than Dominique.

All gossip stopped as the governor rose to make the toasts holding a crystal flute of champagne aloft in his hand. The guests rose in unison at his signal.

The sound of the orchestra tuning up in the ballroom across the wide hallway beckoned the guests as the dinner ended. The governor, with his wife, led the procession into the high-ceilinged ballroom ablaze with hundreds of myrtle wax candles in the crystal chandeliers overhead, and in tall brass candelabra located in front of long mirrors in heavy gilt frames along the sides of the chamber between the French doors.

As the orchestra, made up of slaves borrowed from their masters for the occasion, began the opening melody, Philippe claimed Caresse for the first dance. They joined the other dancers whirling under the glow of the myriad candles. The damp air—heavy with the scent of the burning myrtle tapers and the perfumes of the guests—made Caresse dizzy as she followed Philippe's lead in the intricate steps.

The evening passed in a blur of polite partners, spirited music, and pauses for more of the dry delicious champagne circulated on silver trays by liveried servants. As the night progressed, the music became louder, the dancing more uninhibited, and several couples slipped from the ballroom with a swish of silken skirts and feminine sighs and giggles.

Caresse stood with Philippe, having insisted she needed to rest. A servant had immediately glided up with a flute of champagne. Snapping open her fan, she waved it in front of her flushed face as she sipped the golden sparkling wine.

"What do you know of this new *voodooienne* that all of Nouvelle Orléans is discussing?" she asked Philippe for it was the first chance they had to speak alone.

"She is supposed to be very powerful, or so they say," he said with a shrug, lifting his flute of champagne to his lips.

"You do not know her identity?" Caresse persisted.

"Leave it be, *chérie*. This is something you should not inquire about too closely," he replied, staring out at the dancers with a melancholy expression.

"Mme St. Amant," the high trilling voice of Mme de Mézières called to Caresse as she whirled by. "I remembered the *voodooienne's* name. Aurore, 'tis Aurore." The woman danced on by in a swish of black satin skirts.

Caresse felt the glass slip from her hand to shatter on the cypress floor. The name seemed to echo with the music, the dancers feet seemed to tap it out on the wooden floor. Aurore! Aurore!

"*Chérie,*" Philippe gasped, reaching out for her.

"*Non . . . non,*" she stammered, backing away from him. Her mind reeled with confusion and despair. She had to get out of here, the sounds, the lights, even the dancers seemed to be mocking her. Turning away from Philippe, she picked up her skirts and ran from the ballroom, bumping into one of the servants and causing him to drop his tray of champagne. The sound of breaking glass followed her as she weaved in and out of the startled dancers, making her way across the dance floor to where one of the French doors stood open to allow air into the stuffy chamber.

The cool damp air swirled around her as she ran out into the garden. From behind her she could hear the sounds of laughter. In her confusion and despair they seemed to be laughing at her. Aurore had won. Somehow she had come back from beyond the grave. She did not stop to think that Aurore was a common name in Nouvelle Orléans.

Running down the crushed-shell path of the garden through the grove of orange trees she reached a door in the wooden wall that encircled that garden. Without thinking she pulled it open, only wanting to escape the sound of the dancers, the frantic calling of her name by Philippe running after her.

Her satin slippers sank into the mud as she tried to stay on the *banquette* of the Rue St. Ann. The misty fog closed around her as she tried to remember how to get back to the town house. Her breath came in gasps as she realized how foolish she had been to panic, but the name Aurore on Mme de Mézières's lips had unnerved her.

Stopping for a moment beside the *presbytère* of the Capuchin fathers, she tried to catch her breath. Now that the first panic had receded she began to feel the cold damp as it seeped through her thin silk taffeta gown. Her feet were sodden and felt like ice. But she could not go back to the governor's house, she had to go on and try to get home. She had made a small spectacle of herself in her hasty departure; to return now, looking as she did, would mean complete disgrace.

The fog lay like a blanket over the city, but by keeping close to the wall of the *presbytère* she was able to find her way to the Place Royale. A right turn, and she was slipping and sliding on the muddy *banquette* in front of the church of St. Louis, then under the gallery of the Corps de Garde. Several masculine figures passed her, but so thick was the fog they were not aware of her presence. Stepping into the sea of mud that was the Rue St.

Pierre, Caresse gave up trying to hold up her skirts. The elegant gown was ruined.

Once across the street she knew it was only a few blocks to the sanctuary of the town house. Determined to make it, although her teeth were chattering from the cold and wet, she kept putting one foot in front of another. Passing storefronts barely visible in the fog she had no idea of how far she had gone.

It was as she passed the open door of one of the *salles d'escrime,* one of the numerous gambling houses, did she begin to wonder if somehow in the fog she had taken a wrong turn. Was she lost in the maze of muddy streets of the city, streets that were dangerous for a woman alone at night?

Exhausted, she stopped in the doorway of a closed shop. Resting her head against the glass display window she felt the hot scald of tears slide down her cheeks. She was so tired, so alone. What was the use of it all? Self-pity and despair filled her heart to overflowing.

"Looking for company?" a rough, male voice demanded as a figure moved out of the gloom. The smell of cheap rum served in the waterfront dives surrounded Caresse as he came forward into the doorway where she huddled.

"Non! Go away!" she said sharply, shrinking back against the locked door of the shop.

"I can pay," he leered, coming closer, the stench of him reaching out like fingers to gag her. "My money is as good as the next man's."

"Go away, I am not a *prostituée.* You will find them down by the docks," she said flatly.

"So who are you my lovely, out on a night like this alone—the queen of France?" he sneered, reaching out and grabbing her arm, pulling her against him. "You will do just fine. In fact this place will do just fine." He reached down with one hand to fumble with her skirt.

"*Non,*" she screamed, slapping at him with one hand as she tried to kick him with her foot. Then she felt his hand at her throat pressing her back against the door.

"Just be quiet and it will be over before you know it," he rasped, pressing her throat with one hand and lifting her skirts with the other.

With the last breath she had left, Caresse screamed again. His hand pressed on her windpipe and the foggy night blackened.

"Are you all right? *Mademoiselle,* are you all right?" A deep familiar voice seemed to come from some place above her.

"What happened?" Caresse managed to mumble as she slumped against her rescuer.

"He ran off the minute he saw my pistol," the familiar voice continued. "Come with me, my house is just a few steps away. You might be hurt."

"Lucien, oh Lucien, 'tis really you," Caresse sobbed, recognizing her husband's voice.

"*Mon Dieu!* Caresse! What in God's name are you doing out here? You are supposed to be at Solange's *soirée,*" the tall figure spoke, holding her against him.

"If you knew that, my beloved husband, why are you walking the streets of Nouvelle Orléans in the opposite direction from the governor's mansion?" she spat, all the despair and fury of the evening directed now at her elusive husband.

Twenty-one

"We shall discuss nothing out here on the street," Lucien replied, removing his cloak from his shoulders and draping it about her. "Come."

As the wool cloak draped about her shoulders, she was engulfed with the faint scent of vetivert, and Caresse was transported for a moment to a cell in La Salpêtrière prison. The sense of *déjà vu* was so strong she could not move.

"What is it? Can you not walk, *ma chère*?" Lucien asked with concern, all other emotions forgotten in his anxiety over her physical condition.

"*Non*, I . . . I can walk," Caresse said slowly, pulling the cape closer about her trembling form.

"*Mon Dieu*, then let us make haste for home and a warm fire," Lucien ordered, taking her arm and leading her down the wet slippery boards of the *banquette* toward their town house.

Pascal flung open the closed portal after Lucien pounded on the locked door, for there were no unlocked houses in Nouvelle Orléans at night. His arms were filled with Caresse's exhausted form, so he could not reach his key.

"I wish containers of hot water brought upstairs to our bedchamber," Lucien told the shocked Pascal as he half carried Caresse into the foyer.

"At once, *m'sieur*," the major domo replied, locking the door behind them.

"Where is Dominique?" Lucien asked as he led Caresse toward the stairs.

"She is not here, *m'sieur*," Pascal said, with an uneasy expression on his face. "Saturday night she usually leaves the house."

"For where?" Lucien continued sharply, looking at the man with a sudden alertness.

"I could not say, *m'sieur*," he replied, not meeting his eyes.

"That will be all, see to the water," Lucien said in dismissal.

"I know where she has gone," Caresse's voice was a harsh rasp from where the man had half strangled her before Lucien's intervention.

"Where?" he asked as he helped her up the stairs.

"They spoke tonight at dinner of a new *voodooienne* who holds ceremonies in an abandoned warehouse along the waterfront. I think she has gone there," Caresse answered, almost collapsing from the exertion of climbing the stairs, even with Lucien's help.

"Do not waste your energy, *ma petite*. We can discuss this later after we get you out of these wet clothes," he cautioned her, sweeping her up in his arms and carrying her the rest of the way to their bedchamber.

Bruno met them at the door, whining as if he sensed something was wrong. Even Blanchette woke from her place beside the fire and stared with enigmatic eyes, as Lucien quickly stripped the wet clothes from Caresse's shaking body. He wrapped her in a quilt until Pascal and Raymond could bring the heated water from the kitchen house for a hot bath. Seating her in a chair by the hearth, he stoked up the smoldering coals, adding more logs till the fire was a roaring blaze.

"Here, drink this," he commanded, handing her a crystal globe of cognac.

She took the globe in her trembling hands and held it to her lips, the rich, smoky liquid sliding down her throat with a spreading warmth. Huddled in the blanket in front of the roaring flames, she felt the ice inside her melt.

"Whatever were you doing out on the street alone, and in this weather, without a cloak or pattens for your feet?" Lucien asked softly, coming to sit beside her with his own glass of cognac. His dark eyes stared across at her as his hand reached out to clasp her own icy fingers. "Where was Dubrieul?"

"I . . . ran from the ballroom," she began, staring into the flame as if she could find an answer there. "Philippe was behind me, but I lost him on purpose. I did not want to speak to anyone, hear any more lies. Or perhaps I was running from the truth." She paused, staring into the fire, avoiding Lucien's intense gaze, afraid to see the reaction to what she was about to tell him in those expressive black orbs.

"But what truth did you fear?" he asked, puzzled.

"The *voodooienne* of whom everyone spoke, I found out her name was Aurore." She stopped, still not looking in his direction, although she felt him tense at the name. "I think I became for a moment a little crazed. I ran . . . ran from what I felt could not be. The dead they cannot return, even in Nouvelle Orléans. Of course, later I realized that the name is a common one, but it was too late, I could not return. My gown and shoes were ruined, so I tried to find my way back to the house." She lifted the glass to her lips, finishing the amber liquid, unable to speak of the rest of it.

"You think Dominique attends these voodoo rites," he said quietly, putting down his glass, taking her empty one from her as well, so he might clasp both her hands in his warm strong fingers, as if they could somehow transmit to her some of his strength.

"*Oui*, I do," Caresse admitted.

"I shall speak with her, but she is free. If she wishes to attend these voodoo ceremonies there is nothing I can do about it," he reminded her, continuing to rub her hands gently, his dark eyes serious as he sensed her withdrawal. "What is it about her attending the voodoo ceremonies that frightens you? I can assure you that Aurore is indeed dead, and has been so for over seven years."

"What is the bond between you and Dominique?" Caresse asked, unable to stop herself, her huge gray eyes filled with a kind of despair. " 'Tis more than a promise your father made to her father so many years ago. I sense that there is more to it. Please tell me, I must know." Her eyes pleaded with him, hoping against hope that there was something beside the awful suspicion that Dominique had seen him kill his own wife.

"*Ma chère*, this is not easy for me to speak of. My *maman* was not well, not well mentally. She had delusions, great fears, because of what had happened to her in France and on her way to La Louisiane. One morning at Sans Regret, after she had experienced a bad night, she simply walked down to the river. It was high from the spring floods and she walked right into the rushing water. I think she wanted to end it all, the memories that haunted her and gave her no peace. None of us had seen her leave, but Dominique. She followed her, and it was only her swift action and strong swimming that kept my *maman* from drowning. She saved her life. From that day Dominique has always had a home with the St. Amants no matter how odd her behavior."

"I see," Caresse answered, with a sigh. She

312

wanted to believe him with every fiber of her being, but always there was a question in her mind. She hated that small voice that said there was more, but could not silence it.

The rap on the portal signaled that the men were here with the canisters of hot water. Pulling the blanket closer about her nude form, she waited for Lucien to answer the door. She welcomed the respite from the nagging questions that threatened to destroy any trust she had in her mercurial husband.

"I shall be your lady's maid," he teased, bringing in the brass canisters the men had placed outside the door. "And I must say I am looking forward to bathing you." There was a sensuous gleam in his dark eyes.

Caresse gave him a wan smile. She felt cold and dead inside. There was no answering spark of desire, just numbness where her heart should have been. Was there enough hot water in all of Nouvelle Orléans to thaw the ice she felt in her veins?

Lifting the copper tub from behind the bathing screen, Lucien placed it in front of the fire on a straw mat. After pouring the steaming water into the tub, he crossed to her dressing table and picked up a jar of bath salts, and poured them into the water. It turned blue-green and filled the chamber with the scent of wild lilies.

"Ah, *madame*, have I forgotten anything? he asked, his smoldering eyes betraying his ardor. Taking her hand in his firm grasp, he pulled her from her chair before she could speak, then with a swift gesture stripped the blanket from around her shoulders. Picking her up as if she were a reluctant child, he gently placed her in the warm scented water.

With a sigh, she lay back, content to allow the water to hold her in its embrace. Closing her eyes, she could feel as if she were in a forest glade in

France in the spring, with the fragrance of the lily of the valley all around her. The world was fresh and clean, with no hidden shadows.

"Allow me to wash your back," Lucien's husky voice was in her ear as he began to stroke her tired cold limbs with a soft linen cloth.

As she moved forward slightly, he began to stroke down the length of her spine, the cloth discarded, his sensitive knowing fingertips taking its place. His gentle touch, the scent of the lily bath salts, the warmth of the water, all began to relax her tired body. The cold ice in her veins began to slowly melt under his tender ministrations.

"Ah, *ma belle*, you are so lovely, every part of you." His lips touched the scarlet lily on her shoulder, as his hands moved around to cup the soft alabaster mounds of breasts.

She shuddered as the icy numbness deep within her heart and soul began to melt, and the release of feeling surged through her. The wall she had built to keep from feeling the horrors of the night suddenly began to crumble.

"*Ma chère*, what is it?" he whispered against the silken nape of her neck, as he felt the deep shuddering sob well up from within her.

She leaned back against him, the sobs tearing out of her as he held her, not speaking, just providing a safe haven for her to find release. The tears, like the warm caressing water, washed away the cold despair she had experienced in her nightmarish wandering through the fog-shrouded streets of Nouvelle Orléans.

"Let it out, *ma belle*, all of it. You are safe here in my arms," he murmured into the silk of her hair.

Slowly the sobs stopped as he held her, rocking her back and forth gently, his lips kissing away the remnants of her tears. The gentle caring coming from such a self-contained man smote her heart and filled her being with love for him. He had replaced her despair with love and hope.

"Come, *ma petite*, the pain has been washed away, now is time for the joy," he murmured, standing up. Taking a soft linen towel he wrapped it around her as she too rose in the tub.

"Are you going to dry me?" She looked up at him with a shy sad smile.

"That, *ma chère*, is only the beginning of what I shall do with you tonight." His voice was a sensual promise as he lifted her from the tub.

Standing in the golden glow from the flames of the fire, he caressed the sensitive length of her spine with the towel, drying and arousing her in one sensuous sweep. Turning her so she faced him, he began to rub the linen gently over the mounds of her breasts, teasing the rosebud nipples till they throbbed with desire.

It was all calculated to stimulate her senses, the warmth of the fire on her bottom and the backs of her thighs, the stroke of the linen under her breasts as he lifted each globe and held its weight in the cup of his hand, circling the tiny hard coral peak. Then down across her hips to the soft blond curls at the V of her legs. Moving her legs apart he stroked down each silken inner thigh. The brush of the linen across her swollen woman's lips startled her with its erotic intensity.

Then the towel lay in a pile at her feet, his hands pressing her nude form against him as his lips found the hollow of her throat. "How long I have hungered for the taste of you, the feel of your skin under my hands," he murmured. "The nights I lay awake and thought only of how it would be to have you with me, to lose myself in the splendor of your beautiful face and form. Every stroke of the pirogue that brought me down the river was a stroke carrying me closer to you."

"The fire is so warm, too warm for so many

clothes," she murmured huskily, reaching out for the buttons of his waistcoat.

"I agree," he breathed, his pulse racing as he stripped the garments from his body. Then he too stood nude in front of her, gilded by the golden light of the flames.

"And I have wanted to touch you, *mon coeur,* all those long lonely nights without you," she whispered, reaching out to touch first the fur of his chest, then tracing down the V to that thicker, luxuriant nest. She felt and heard the shudder that tore through him at her touch.

His dark burning eyes radiated his joy as he reveled in her tentative yet arousing touch. Her trust in him was back, he could see it in the soft, dove gray of her eyes, the wondrous touch of her hand as she encircled his arousal.

"I too have hungered, hungered to feel you inside me, for without you I am empty and alone," she told him, unashamed to admit her need as she met his burning gaze. Her hand pressed his erection to the soft curls of her Venus mound.

"What more can a man desire than to hear such words from the woman who is a part of his soul?" he said, tracing the curve of her lower lip with his finger.

She opened her mouth to lightly circle his finger with the moist coral ribbon of her tongue, her hand continuing to tease his manhood.

"You drive me beyond endurance," he moaned, taking his hand from her mouth to sweep her up in his arms. With a few strides, he carried her to the bed.

Her hands caressed the satin of his back—her lips, the hollow of his neck. She drew in the warm masculine scent of him. Stroking his shoulders, her hand rose up to pull the cord from his queue so that the raven black satin of his hair spilled over her fingers.

"Ah, *chère*, turnabout is only fair," he gave a husky chuckle as he slipped her under the ivory silk sheet and heavy counterpane. Reaching up as she nestled down on the silk-clad pillow he pulled the pins from her chignon, the ribbons and bouquets long gone in her wild dash from the ballroom. Spreading her hair about her shoulders, he smiled down at her. "So lovely you take my breath away," he murmured. "I had forgotten the effect those eyes have on me."

"Perhaps if you were not gone so often you would not have trouble remembering," she chided him softly, but there was a sadness in the depths of those dove gray orbs. Whom did he see when he looked at her, Caresse or Aurore? Whose beauty took his breath away? Ever since she had viewed Aurore's portrait and seen the striking resemblance, the questions had burned in her brain. And now he was leaving her for weeks at a time, just as he had Aurore. Were they caught in some strange cycle of repeating the past?

"I wish that I never had to leave you, *ma belle femme,* but there are some things in life which we cannot control. 'Tis important what I do, or I would never leave you—this you must believe," he told her, his penetrating black eyes willing her to trust him.

Always there were the secrets, the hidden facets to his life and his past that would come between them, Caresse thought, as he lifted her hand to his lips, then slipped in beside her. As he turned toward her, cradling her face in one hand, that he might tenderly kiss first one high cheekbone then the other, she knew with a sharp pang that no matter whom he saw when he looked at her, she was lost.

"Do not look so sad, *ma petite*. There is nothing so bad that we cannot face it together," he murmured, kissing the tip of her nose, then the corner of her trembling mouth.

She sank into his embrace as his tongue slowly traced the tender fullness of her lips. Wrapping her arms around his neck, her fingers entwined in the raven satin of his hair as she gave herself up to the passionate seduction of his kiss. For a brief time she would become lost in the ecstasy, forget the apprehensions, the questions that plagued her with Lucien.

The rain slanted against the windows, the fire burned to a smoldering ember, but within the four-poster there was only the sigh of lovers enjoying the taste, the touch, the sight of the other's beloved form. Soft gray feminine eyes stared up into the burning masculine gaze that allowed her to see for a brief unguarded moment into the depths of his soul.

"Je t'aime, ma belle Caresse," he murmured with a catch in his voice as he entered her with one long shuddering thrust.

"Je t'aime, mon coeur," she moaned as he filled her honeyed cavern with the throbbing symbol of his hunger.

They lay for a heart-stopping moment when time stood still, savoring the ecstasy of life's sweetest mystery. In their passionate reunion they experienced the sense of discovering something fresh and new. In the deepest recess of their souls they felt that no two lovers had ever known such joy.

Suddenly it was as if they had spoken, for each knew that they could wait no longer. She arched up against him as he withdrew his shaft to the tip and poised for a moment to prolong the anticipation that would add to the ultimate rapture.

"I . . . I must have you," she gasped, staring up into the dark magnetic eyes that could look inside her lonely heart.

"Say you want me, *ma chère,"* he demanded, his

voice a husky rasp, holding himself back by some miraculous effort of will. "Say the words, Caresse, say my name!"

"Inside me! I must have you inside me! Lucien!" Her cry of his name was both a plea and a prayer of rejoicing.

With a shuddering moan he thrust inside her, his mouth coming down on hers. They were joined in one long elegant line of ecstasy, reaching the pinnacle of their rapture together.

"Even now I find I cannot stand to separate from you, *ma belle* Caresse," he whispered, rising up from her so his weight did not crush her, but remaining embedded within her.

"*La petite mort*, the little death upon separation after love," she murmured, smiling a sad smile up at him, her eyes moist from the depth of her emotion.

"Ah, *oui, la petite mort*," he sighed, slipping from her to lie back against his pillow. Reaching out, he pulled her to him.

She nestled down against him, her head on his shoulder. Exhaustion claimed both of them. Held in the safe harbor of his embrace, she could rest. The demons of the street, and of her own mind, were held at bay in the warm afterglow of the joining of their bodies and souls.

Bruno and Blanchette slept only a few feet away from each other in front of the smoldering fire. The rain might vent its fury against the window panes, but inside the bedchamber all slumbered secure in the warmth of each other's presence.

It was dawn when Caresse fought her way up through the mists of her nightmare. She had been running through the swamps surrounding Sans Regret, pursued by some unseen terror. Choking for breath, muscles crying out for rest, she finally reached what appeared through the fog to be a house, a sanctuary. One last superhuman effort and she was across the clearing. It was as she reached the small white structure, that she saw it was a marble sepulcher, the tomb of Aurore St. Amant. She could somehow see the letters carved in the marble even in the fog. The terror was all around her, with no avenue of escape. She was falling, falling into whatever waited so patiently for her return.

Gasping, her heart beating so rapidly she thought she could hear it, Caresse sat up in bed. Lucien was still fast asleep, turned away from her. Pressing her hands over her face, she could only repeat silently over and over, *it was only a dream.*

After regaining her composure, she realized that she was not imagining the sound coming from below in the courtyard. The gate had opened, creaking on its hinges, the sound carrying, now that the rain had stopped.

Seeing the pearl gray light of dawn outside the French doors, Caresse slipped from the four-poster. She feared after such a nightmare, sleep was over for the night. She picked up her *robe de chambre* from the foot of the bed and slipped into its velvet warmth.

Crossing to the window she stared down into the courtyard, quite visible in the early light. A figure was moving toward the *garçonnière* and the servants' quarters. Moving closer to the door, that she might see more clearly, Caresse saw it was a feminine figure clad in an amethyst velvet cloak. As the woman reached the stairs that led up to the servants' quarters, she stopped as if listening for something, then after a few seconds turned to go up the staircase. It was as she did so that the hood of the cloak fell back, revealing a white powdered wig, bouquets of silk violets pinned in the elaborate coiffure, the flash of dangling amethyst earrings. Then the figure vanished up the staircase out of Caresse's range of vision.

She stood staring out at the courtyard, wisps of fog still clinging to the corners of the walled garden. An icy fear twisted around her heart as her stomach churned in revulsion. The elaborate style of the powdered wig, as well as the amethyst earrings, had been familiar. She had seen them before at Sans Regret, in Aurore's room.

Her name is Aurore, the woman had said at the ball. What or whom had she seen dressed in the clothing of a dead woman? Could it have been Dominique? She has a home with the St. Amant family no matter how odd her behavior, Lucien had said adamantly. But in the cold light of dawn Caresse felt the old suspicions creeping back. Would Dominique still be welcome if she could prove the woman was involved in some macabre masquerade?

Looking back over her shoulder to where Lucien slept so peacefully, Caresse felt a shiver from the base of her spine. A man who had killed his wife could not rest so easily, could he? Then turning back toward where she had seen the gliding figure, another horrifying thought struck her like a knife to the heart. What if the tomb in the swamps was empty? What if somehow Aurore was alive?

Twenty-two

The air had a touch of spring in it as Caresse
bade Lucien good-bye at the gate of the courtyard.
There was a meeting of the Superior Council at
the governor's mansion, and on such a fine day he
had decided to walk.

"Give my respects to Solange and the governor,"
Caresse told him. "And thank them for their concern over the state of my health." Deep dimples
appeared in each cheek as she smiled up at her
husband, who responded with a wry curve to his
mouth, before brushing his lips across hers in farewell.

She stood at the open gate watching the lithe
figure stride down the *banquette* of Rue de Chartres. It had been three days since the disastrous
soirée and her horrible experience on that same
street when it had been shrouded in fog. Since that
night Caresse had not left the confines of the town
house or the walled garden. Lucien had sent word
to Solange that his wife had been taken ill, causing
her to leave the *soirée* without bidding them *adieu*.
In reply Solange had sent a basket of fruit imported from Saint-Domingue with her wishes for
a quick recovery.

Closing the gate with a sigh, Caresse walked
slowly back toward the house. Her peaceful idyll

322

was coming to a close, all too soon. Reality had once more intruded on their lives with the message from Government House that an emergency meeting of the Superior Council had been called for that morning. The last three days had been heaven, a brief second *lune de miel*. They had allowed no visitors; even Philippe had been sent away after a brief explanation that Caresse had left the ballroom because of illness. He had not believed Lucien—she had heard them arguing. Philippe had insisted upon seeing Caresse. When his request was denied, he stormed from the house, slamming the heavy front door.

When Lucien had come upstairs, she had made no comment on what she had heard. For a few precious days she had wanted to close out the world and its problems. Her doubts and suspicions about Lucien had been pushed far down in her mind under the spell of his magnetic presence. She wanted nothing to bring them to the surface. Although she knew she was living in a fool's paradise, she pushed it from her mind. It was this that had kept her from mentioning the strange figure in the courtyard at dawn. It was something she was determined to pursue on her own, without Lucien. He was still secretive about his work for Governor de Vaudreuil, so she did not know when he could leave on one of his excursions out of Nouvelle Orléans. Nothing must spoil the brief time they had together, certainly not an argument over Dominique.

The object of her musings appeared in the doorway of the kitchen house. Dominique carried a basket over her arm, and appeared to be about to depart for the open-air market along the levee.

"Before you leave, Dominique, I should like to speak with you," Caresse called to her. "I shall be in the salon." She could feel the woman's eyes on her as she walked briskly through the French door that opened on the long central hall.

Standing in front of the fireplace in the salon, Caresse stared up at the portrait of Lucien's *maman,* the tragic Gabrielle. Was she really the reason Dominique seemed to have so much authority? Lucien had turned this morning to his housekeeper, giving her the paper scrip de Vaudreuil had printed to be used for currency in the colony. When Caresse had interrupted him, saying that as mistress *she* would prefer to do the shopping, he had seemed surprised.

"Of course if you wish, *ma chère,* but Dominique does know the market and what ingredients to buy. The cook will require certain herbs and spices for her cooking that you may not recognize," he continued.

"I have done the shopping while you were gone, and I should like to continue," Caresse had replied with an air of determination, a steely glint in her usually soft gray eyes. "I am aware of the spices the cook requires."

"If you wish, then of course, but take Dominique or Pascal with you. 'Tis not safe on the streets for a woman alone without the accompaniment of a servant. You might be taken for one of the women on the docks. Nouvelle Orléans has always had an air of corruption about it, but since Vaudreuil and Solange have begun their reign the atmosphere has become poisonous. There is a sense that anything is allowed, any excess, that everything and everyone is for sale to the highest bidder," he told her, disgust in his dark eyes. "Go if you want, but be sure and take Dominique or Pascal," he continued over their morning coffee. "But I think, *ma chère,* perhaps not today. Are you not still supposed to be recovering from your unfortunate illness," he grinned. "Solange would be surprised to see you looking so well if you met her at the market."

"Oui, you are right," Caresse capitulated with a grimace. "Today Dominique may go, but on the morrow I shall accompany her. You may tell the governor I am making a rapid recovery."

Staring up at Gabrielle's lovely, half-mad countenance, Caresse felt a stab of irritation. The woman had made a hell out of her husband's life, and caused her son to be wary and guarded in his relationships. Then Caresse felt guilty for blaming the poor woman for something she'd had no control over. Gabrielle could not help her madness, but how many lives it had touched and harmed.

"You wished to speak with me, *madame?*" Dominique's low liquid voice startled Caresse.

"Oui, 'tis about something I heard, and something I saw at dawn Sunday morn," she said, watching the woman for any reaction. There was none.

"And how may I help you, *madame?*" Her voice was cool and polite, her visage a remote mask.

"I have heard that there is a new *voodooienne* in the city. Even some of French society is said to frequent her ceremonies and seek her advice. She is said to be an excellent clairvoyant. Do you know her?" Caresse asked, her eyes never leaving that remote face.

"Do you wish the services of a *voodooiene, madame?*" There was a flicker of interest in the woman's dark watchful eyes.

"No, but I wish to know her name." Caresse persisted.

"If you wish to visit her, I would be only too happy to accompany you," Dominique replied impassively.

"Her name?"

"She goes by several names, *madame,*" Dominique answered.

"And is one of those names Aurore?" Caresse asked, her tone hardened.

"There is much about voodoo you do not understand, *madame,* but I will be glad to teach you," she said softly, coming closer. "It intrigues you, I knew it would, in time. You have the mark, there." She came close to Caresse, reaching out and barely touching the beauty mark above her lip. "Together we could be more powerful than any *voodooienne* in Saint-Domingue. Join with me, let me be your teacher, your guide." There was a strange look in her almond-shaped eyes that stared down hypnotically into Caresse's own stunned gray orbs.

"I . . . I do not desire such power," Caresse stammered, floundering before the magnetic eyes. She knew the woman was trying to overcome her resistance, that she had a strange plan for the two of them.

"You say that because you have never experienced it," Dominique said in her dulcet tones with the accent of Saint-Domingue. Her intense gaze never left Caresse's pale, nervous face. "You are afraid of its power, and that is understandable and shows your intelligence. She too feared it at first, but later it gave her great peace."

"Whom do you mean?" Caresse asked, but deep in some inner recess of her heart she knew the name.

"The one who was your twin spirit, Aurore St. Amant," Dominique pronounced, her eyes seeming not to blink as she continued to stare into Caresse's eyes.

"I am not her twin spirit. I did not even know the woman," she retorted through dry lips.

"But you look so like her, perhaps a shade more beautiful, but that is because of your strength," Dominique continued with the same unwavering intensity. "Aurore was frightened of everything, she turned to voodoo out of fear." There was a twist of dismissal on her lips as she spoke of the dead woman. "With you 'twould be different. You would come to me as a student out of strength, not out of fear."

"I wish to have nothing to do with the practice of voodoo, Dominique. If you are going to be housekeeper here, then I would like you to stop your involvement with the voodoo activities as well," Caresse replied in as firm a tone as she could muster.

"You do not choose to become a *voodooienne*, it chooses you," she hissed, an expression of scorn contorting her lovely features for a moment. "But you will come to understand this in time, and then you will beg for my help as did Aurore." Dominique held her graceful head high and proud, looking at Caresse as if she were a foolish child.

The house seemed so empty, so still, that Caresse could hear the beat of her heart, the rush of her blood through her veins as she stood locked in a silent battle of wills with the elegant Dominique. The woman was one of the strongest personalities she had ever met.

The sharp rap on the heavy front door broke the spell Dominique seemed to have woven around Caresse. When the sound was repeated, she told the housekeeper, "Please answer that. I believe Pascal is helping Raymond with the horses in the stable."

"Of course, *madame.*" Dominique stepped back, her expression veiled, her manner once more that of a respectful servant.

Caresse let out a sigh of relief as the woman glided from the salon to answer the door. Looking down at her hands she saw that they were shaking, and burying them in the folds of her skirt, she tried to regain some semblance of control. It was going to be even harder than she thought dealing with Dominique. The woman seemed to have her own agenda, and the strength of will to carry it out. She felt a surge of anger at Lucien for putting her in such a position. Why couldn't he see Dominique for what she was, instead of through some mist of childhood? Then the small voice within reminded her that there might be some other reason for his indebtedness to the housekeeper.

"*Non,* I will not be put off, Dominique," a familiar masculine voice thundered from the foyer.

"What is wrong?" Caresse asked, coming to the door of the salon, glad to have some interruption of her terrible musings.

"*Chérie,* I have been so worried," Philippe called out, pushing past Dominique.

"Why are you not at the council meeting?" Caresse asked in surprise.

"I made an excuse and left early," he said with a shrug of his shoulders that dismissed the meeting as unimportant. "How worried I have been about you, *chérie.*" He lifted her hand to his lips in greeting.

"There is nothing to be worried about," she said, gently removing her hand from his firm grasp. "As you can see I am quite recovered from my touch of the fever, although the *mal de tête* was blinding, the night of Solange's *soirée,*" she lied, embarrassed by his concern.

"You should not have left so quickly. And coming home alone—'twas dangerous, *chérie,*" he chided, his eyes seeming to devour the sight of her.

"I am sorry to have worried you. Of course, you are right," she replied, searching her mind for some way out of the awkward situation, some other topic of conversation. "Perhaps I can apologize in some small way by at least having Dominique serve us *café* in the garden. 'Tis so warm out today, it makes one think spring has arrived."

"I should be happy to accept your offer, and to

have the chance to spend some time in your company," he replied gallantly.

Caresse sensed that there was more than polite manners behind his words. Every feminine instinct knew of Philippe's growing affection for her—or perhaps, she reminded herself, his affection for the woman who resembled Aurore. Leading the way outside, she was conscious of Dominique's scrutiny. Then she remembered that Philippe and Dominique were half brother and half sister. The strange uneasiness that she had felt in the salon talking to Dominique swept back over her. There was something wrong in all these tangled relationships, something wrong at the very core of it all, but she had no idea what it was that bothered her. There was only a primitive instinct that she was in danger from someone, or some ancient belief that had these people in its thrall. The question that raged inside her was whether Lucien was a part of it.

Seated at a table under the spreading branches of the huge live oak that dominated the garden, Caresse poured Philippe a cup of hot coffee from the silver pot brought by Dominique before she left for the French market. She had also brought a dish of that Nouvelle Orléans favorite, warm rice calas.

The garden had never truly been asleep in the brief winter of La Louisiane, for the camellias and jasmine vine continued to bloom in the subtropical climate. But there were still signs that the garden was casting off winter's blanket for spring rebirth. Someone had imported hyacinth bulbs from Europe and planted them in raised beds edging the flagstone walk. The delicate fragrant spikes of bell-shaped blooms perfumed the mild air, hinting at the spring to come, and the long hot summer.

"Are you planning on attending the event of Nouvelle Orléans?" Philippe inquired, stirring his coffee with one of the heavy silver spoons.

"And what would that be?" Caresse asked with a slight smile, pouring herself a cup of the fragrant brew.

"Why, Solange's masquerade ball to celebrate *Mardi Gras*," he explained. "I imagine you will be receiving your invitation on the morrow."

"And how do you know this before anyone else?" she teased.

"Let us say that Solange and I are very good friends—'tis all I can say and still remain a gentleman," he admitted, lifting the eggshell thin cup to his lips.

So Philippe was one of Solange's lovers, Caresse realized with a tinge of surprise. She would have expected him to pick someone of more delicacy, more refinement. Solange, while possessing a raw sensuality, could be coarse and crude when she chose to shock.

"You are surprised, *chérie*? Dare I hope that perhaps you are a trifle jealous?" He looked at her with such intensity it made her flush.

"Philippe, you are a good friend, and, as such, I certainly would not question your private life," Caresse answered, suddenly much occupied with pouring more coffee.

"But I would like to be much more than just a good friend," he protested, leaning toward her.

"Ah, so now I know what business was so pressing, Dubrieul, that you had to leave the council meeting early," Lucien's sardonic tone carried to them on the soft air from the open gate.

Looking up from the coffee pot at the sound of his voice, Caresse's visage came alive with a radiant smile.

There was, however, no answering curve to his sensuous lips. Instead his mouth was tight and grim, his jaw clenched, his eyes slightly narrowed with suspicion. Her stomach tightened, and she felt as if a cold shadow had come over the sun when she looked into his dark eyes that blazed with anger.

"I feel that I am intruding on your tête-à-tête," he drawled as he came toward them.

Caresse clenched the handle of the coffee pot until her knuckles turned white. Slowly she set it down on the silver tray. Rising to her feet, she said in a strained voice, "I shall fetch another cup. Dominique has gone to the market."

"If you are sure I am not interrupting," Lucien baited her. Reaching out he stopped her, his fingers clasping her arm. His gaze looked down at her with an expression that sent her temper soaring.

It had been his suggestion that Philippe escort her to the myriad social events he insisted she attend in his absence! And for him to act the injured husband when he had thrown them together at every opportunity infuriated her. He was spoiling the intimate mood that had existed between them since his return, and that caused her to feel an acute sense of loss.

"There is nothing to interrupt," she spat out the words with contempt, seething with anger and humiliation. Turning away, she pulled her arm from his grasp and headed toward the kitchen house.

"You should have more trust in your wife," said Philippe as Lucien pulled out one of the wrought-iron chairs.

"With you around, I would not trust one of the good Ursuline *soeurs,*" Lucien commented dryly. "I have a long memory, and remember your more than family concern for your stepsister."

"And I remember your callous treatment of Aurore. You knew she was afraid to stay alone at Sans Regret, yet you persisted in those long trips away for Vaudreuil. I know you were doing your duty for the crown and *la belle* France, but you did not care that Aurore was virtually alone, the only

331

Frenchwoman on a plantation of Africans except for that crude overseer Zweig," Philippe said heatedly.

"Was Aurore alone?" Lucien asked, the bitter edge of cynicism in his voice, one dark brow raised in contempt. "Strange, but Dominique told me another story. It seems Aurore had the comfort of your company for days at a time, whenever I was gone."

"So Dominique is your spy as well as housekeeper," Philippe snarled. "The woman always hated me. She couldn't bear that because I was the legitimate heir I inherited all the Dubrieul fortune, while she was not even recognized as my father's child. 'Twas the same reason she disliked Aurore. We had all the advantages of being members of the Dubrieul family, while she, with the Dubrieul blood in her veins, was a servant." He gave a shrug as he said, "Of course she would say anything to discredit both of us, even though she used Aurore for her own ends."

"What you say is true about Dominique, and who could blame her? The life of the *gens de couleur libres* is not an easy one. Free but not accepted as French citizens in Nouvelle Orléans. Always kept to a rigid stratum of society. I do not think we would find it an easy road," Lucien mused, staring out across the awakening flower beds of the garden.

"Yet, I have heard that she has a growing power among the Africans, as well as among some of our finer French citizens," Philippe said. "You know there is a new *voodooienne* who is said to command great respect."

"I have heard," he replied flatly.

Caresse stopped in midstride behind the tall sweet olive bush as she heard Dominique's name mentioned. Lucien's broad back was turned her

way so he could not see her. Shamelessly she eaves-
dropped on their conversation:

A soft gasp escaped her as she heard her husband admit that he had heard Dominique might
be the new *voodooienne*. She wondered, her hands
tightening on the small tray she carried, if he knew
that some of the source of her power was that she
was masquerading as Aurore. With her light skin,
and dressed in Aurore's clothes and powdered wig,
in a dim light she might pass as the dead woman.
How many had actually seen Aurore? Only a few,
and their memory would be dim, but all that was
needed was the legend of her return to be circulated about Nouvelle Orléans. Caresse knew suddenly why it was so important to Dominique that
she join with her. She resembled Aurore so closely
that even the French who were drawn to the voodoo
ceremonies would believe that Dominique had
raised the dead. And Lucien seemed unable or un-
caring enough to stop Dominique. Perhaps, that
small still voice within her whispered, it was because of what she knew, of what she had seen that
All Hallows' Eve over seven years before.

Taking a deep breath for courage, she left her
hiding place behind the sweet olive as she realized
Raymond was staring at her from the doorway of
the small stables. She must try and act as normal
as possible under the circumstances. Never had she
felt so alone, for there seemed nowhere to turn, no
one she could completely trust—even Lucien. No
matter how much she might love him, there were
still questions in her mind.

"Is there something wrong?" Lucien asked
sharply as the two men rose to their feet at her
approach.

"*Non,*" she replied in clipped tones, putting the
dishes on the table with a clatter, her hands shaking so that she had trouble controlling the heavily
loaded tray. She should have known that Lucien's

observant eyes would notice something amiss in her face. They were so attuned to one another, he might simply have sensed her distress.

Forcing a control over her emotions she had learned years before at convent school, she sat down on the chair Lucien pulled out for her. Then as the men seated themselves, she began to pour Lucien a cup of the fresh hot coffee she had brought from the kitchen house. The mundane everyday actions of serving coffee, cream and sugar, the passing of calas, all served to occupy her mind.

"Philippe was telling me that Solange is planning an elaborate masked ball for *Mardi Gras* before the beginning of Lent," Caresse said to Lucien as she passed him the plate of cakes.

"I heard all about it from the governor," Lucien said with a slight grimace. "You know Solange, she is determined it shall rival any *bal masqué* held at Versailles. But the dressmakers of Nouvelle Orléans shall benefit, so 'tis not a complete waste."

"And what shall you wear, Caresse?" Philippe inquired, sipping yet another cup of coffee.

"I have not really given it a thought," she admitted, relieved he had dropped *chérie* in front of Lucien. "Besides, is not part of the excitement of the masquerade that no one knows who is behind the *masque?*" She managed a slight smile.

" 'Tis a lot like life, *le bal masqué,*" Lucien commented, his black eyes fixed intently on Caresse, willing her to meet his gaze. "We never really know who is behind the *masque,* which emotions are real and which are false."

" 'Tis a cynical statement but true," Philippe agreed.

"And what do you think, *ma chère?*" Lucien continued, the dark watchful eyes that missed nothing staring at her with the same strange intensity. It

334

was as if he were expecting something from her, but she was at a loss to know what he wanted.

"I think 'tis true about some people. I find it cynical, as Philippe said, and very sad," Caresse replied thoughtfully.

"Why sad?" Lucien persisted, his dark eyes glittering.

"People wear *masques* to keep from being hurt, because they have been so damaged by life that they have become wary and guarded. And by donning the *masque* they close themselves off even further from the happiness and connection they really desire," she answered, her large gray eyes sad and tender as she met his gaze.

"*Ma belle* Caresse, you continue to amaze me. I know I married a lovely woman, but I did not know that I also married a philosopher," he replied in a voice husky with some indefinable emotion. Clasping her hand where it lay on the table, he lifted it and brushed it with his warm lips.

She felt her heart turn over at the gesture and at the smoldering invitation in his expressive dark eyes. A smile curved her mouth in reply. When he was like this, attentive and tender, she knew that her suspicions were ridiculous.

Philippe cleared his throat, stirring uneasily in his chair. Lucien seemed oblivious to their guest, but Caresse took pity on the man. She forced herself to look away from Lucien's magnetic gaze. "Perhaps another cake?" she asked.

"*Non,*" he said stiffly, rising to his feet. "*Merci,* Caresse, for a delightful morning. Lucien," he gave a slight bow in his host's direction. Picking up his tricorn and cane from the empty chair, he bowed stiffly once more and murmured, "Adieu." Then he strode rapidly toward the garden gate.

"I think we offended him," Caresse said with a sigh.

"I certainly hope so. Perhaps he will not come back," Lucien commented lazily.

"Until the next time you must leave Nouvelle Orléans and wish for him to serve as an escort," Caresse said with a touch of irritation, staring at the gate swinging back and forth from Philippe's abrupt retreat.

"But that will not be for some time," he replied, not denying that what she said was true.

She felt a quick flare of anger. If anyone wore a *masque* it was Lucien. When she was in his arms she felt that he was the other half of her soul, but there were times, like this one, when she felt she did not know him at all. He seldom spoke about himself, never about when he was married to Aurore, or where he went on his missions supposedly for the governor and France.

"And when exactly will you be leaving again?" she asked tersely.

"I am afraid I cannot tell you that, *ma chère*. When we are together let us live for the moment. The future will come soon enough," he said softly, stroking the palm of her hand with his thumb, as if gentling a wild creature.

"So I am supposed to wait, and never question," she said, not looking at him. "Never ask to peer beneath the *masque*."

"Do we not both have our secrets?" he reminded her.

"I . . . I do not think that they are quite the same," she stammered.

"Perhaps you wish to tell me, since you want us to have no secrets, why you keep a man's cloak in the bottom of your *cassette*," he said, feeling the shock run through her at his words. If she wanted the truth then it would have to start there.

"You looked in my *cassette*?" she gasped, her eyes two gray holes in the white sheet that was her face.

"Not I. Dominique. She thought to unpack as she

336

does all your clothing, but when she found the cloak, she came to me," he explained. "Because you insisted upon bringing it back with you from Sans Regret she thought it must have special meaning. Does it, *ma chère*?" His hand had tightened on hers as if to keep her from running away.

"Dominique! I might have known," Caresse spat out with revulsion. "So she is also your spy! I am tired of your excuses for the woman's behavior." She pulled her hand from his as he stared at her in surprise. Rising to her feet, she stared down at him, her gray eyes thunderclouds of rage and despair. "You refuse to see the woman as she really is, but then perhaps it is to your advantage to overlook her odd behavior as you called it. Enough! I have had enough of Dominique!" Caresse threw the words at him like stones, then turned and ran from the courtyard toward the outside staircase that led to their bedchamber.

Twenty-three

The curved heel of her satin slipper caught on the edge of the stair as she ran up the gallery staircase. As she reached out for the rail, Lucien's voice calling her name was the last sound she heard as she fell tumbling down the first five steps. When her head hit the brick gallery floor the blackness came up to meet her.

A wavering light and the sound of hushed voices drew her from the darkness. Opening her eyes she saw the light of a hurricane globe on the bedside table. The voices came from across what she realized was her bedchamber. She couldn't see. Struggling to sit up, the pain in her head was so great, and the dizziness so overwhelming, that she sank back against the pillow, closing her eyes against the light that now seemed too bright.

"*Ma chère*, are you awake?" The deep familiar voice of Lucien came from above her.

"*Oui*," she whispered, opening her eyes only a little, afraid of the light and the pain that had taken her breath away. "The glow from the lamp is so bright."

"Of course, I shall move it," he replied, gone for a moment from her side, then back again. "There 'tis on the far side of the table. Dr. Viel, the army surgeon, informed us that once you regained consciousness, light could bother your eyes.''

"How long have I been like this?" she inquired, opening her eyes completely so she could see Lucien in the shadowy room.

" 'Tis late, almost midnight,'' he answered, stroking her hair back from where it had caught on the small neatly bandaged wound on her temple.

"I have been unconscious all this time," she muttered in disbelief. Looking down she realized that someone had undressed her and slipped a silk night rail over her unconscious body. It seemed strange that she could remember none of it.

"We were worried, *ma chère*. I cannot tell you how much." His dark eyes caressed her face as he lifted her hand against his cheek.

"We?" she asked, turning her head to see the other figure standing in the shadows behind him.

" 'Tis Dominique, *madame*,'' the woman replied from where she stood behind Lucien.

" 'Twas Dominique who stayed with you while I went for the physician," Lucien told her quietly. "She has been very concerned about you."

Caresse closed her eyes, afraid they would show how uncomfortable she was in the woman's presence. She had been running away to the sanctuary of this room after her argument with Lucien. It all came flooding back. She had spoken about not having secrets. He had made the point that she was keeping her own past concealed from him. And he had asked about the man's cloak in the bottom of her *cassette*. She sighed deeply as she realized her own reluctance to speak of the past. How could she expect more from Lucien?

"You must rest, *madame*, till the doctor comes on the morrow," Dominique said in a low voice, a voice one used in speaking to the sick.

Somehow the woman's words only made Caresse

feel more helpless, more uneasy. Confined to her bed she was dependent on Dominique and Lucien. Her hand clasped her husband's tighter as she felt a momentary panic overwhelm her at the thought of being in Dominique's power.

" 'Tis going to be all right. Dr. Viel said 'twas most important that you regain consciousness, and once that occurred recovery would be swift," Lucien reassured her. His piercing dark eyes softened. Never would he lose the terrible image of her lying like a broken doll at the bottom of the stairs. The sight had awakened memories that he had tried for seven years to forget.

"If you do not need me any longer, *m'sieur*, I shall retire for the night," Dominique told him in a low voice.

"Please get some rest," he assured her. Turning back toward Caresse he said, "Excuse me one moment, *ma petite*." He released her hand with a pat as if she were a fretful child. Rising to his feet, he moved away from the bed toward the French doors, with Dominique at his side.

Caresse could hear the low murmur of their voices, though strain as she might she could not make out a word they were saying. Tears of frustration filled her eyes, for whenever she moved her head the pain was intense. She could not even sit up. The feeling of being as helpless as a newborn babe was terrifying, especially since she was so used to being independent. Trust did not come easily to Caresse after the tragic events in France. Her imprisonment at the whim of another had made her wary. She had good reason, she thought, to fear having to rely on the treacherous Dominique.

"I shall sleep on the *chaise longue* I had Pascal and Raymond bring from my *maman's* old room. Any thrashing about in the bed I might do would only disturb you and cause your head to ache," Lucien explained, coming back to the bed.

He bent down and kissed her first lightly on the tip of her *retroussé* nose, then on her lips. Turning, he blew out the lamp, and moved toward the fireplace where someone had lit a fire against the cool damp of the night.

With a deep sigh, Caresse closed her eyes, seeking release from the tumult of her emotions in the escape of slumber. Lucien, with Bruno and Blanchette stretched out on the floor beside him, were guardians against the terrors of the night. She wished that there were something that could protect her from the terrors she could conjure up from the turmoil in her mind.

The streams of morning sunlight were coming through the prisms that were the panes of the French doors when next Caresse's eyelid fluttered open. Miraculously, her headache was almost gone as she struggled to a sitting position. She could see where Lucien had slept on a faded blue damask chaise, but it was empty, a quilt thrown carelessly across the foot.

"Bonjour, madame," Dominique's liquid tones startled Caresse as the housekeeper pushed open the door from the hall with one hand, balancing a breakfast tray, without a tremor, in the crook of her other arm.

"Bonjour, Dominique" Caresse replied formally, pushing her pillows behind her so she could sit up without any fatigue.

"You are feeling much better?" she asked, placing the wicker tray in front of her.

"Oui, I am. The headache has almost gone," Caresse answered, lifting the small silver pot of coffee to pour a steaming black stream into the cup rimmed with tiny violets. She was determined not to mind the violets, although she made a mental

note to suggest to Lucien that they order new dishes from France.

" 'Tis good to see you looking so well, *madame*. *M'sieur* will be happy to hear it when he returns home. He has gone to the de Vaudreuil residence, but wanted me to assure you he will return before the doctor arrives," Dominique informed her, folding the quilt at the foot of the *chaise longue*.

"Did he say what business took him to the governor's house so early in the morning?" Caresse inquired coolly, adding cream and sugar to her coffee.

"A note was delivered by one of the de Vaudreuil servants. I believe his presence was requested by the marquise," Dominique told her, pulling back the curtains from the doors opening out on the gallery facing the street.

"The marquise, Solange? Are you sure 'twas not from her husband the governor?" Caresse questioned, unable to keep the surprise from her voice. Solange never rose and dressed this early in the day, although she had been known to receive her so-called *beaux cavaliers* in her boudoir while having her morning coffee on a tray in bed.

"Oui, madame, 'twas from the governor's wife," Dominique said, coming to stand by the bed. She stared down with an eager expression in her usually enigmatic eyes.

"I would like a bath, I think, before Dr. Viel comes," Caresse said in dismissal. There was something in the woman's expression that made her uncomfortable.

"The doctor said that if you woke up, you were not to get out of bed till he examined you," Dominique said firmly. "Although I agree that you are well, I promised *m'sieur* that I would do as he ordered. We shall humor them, *madame*, for what do they know of what really cured you? They do not realize that nothing can harm you," she mur-

342

mured in a low voice, the strange eager expression back on her delicate-boned visage.

"I am afraid I do not understand," said Caresse, leaning back from her tray against the pillows.

"This, *madame*, this is what cured you!" she said, bending down and reaching under the bed to pull out a plain red bag, with chicken feathers attached to it. Rising to her feet, she said, "There is one who does not want you to join with me. She has put a curse on you. 'Twas her spirit that pushed you down the stairs. But you must not worry, I have realized what she is doing, and have made *gris-gris* bags like this one. The bedposts have been rubbed with sacred oil, and I have sprinkled powder around the bed. She could not get through such protection. *Voilà*, you recovered," Dominique declared in triumph, holding the bag in her hand.

Caresse felt as if her breath had solidified in her throat as the fine hairs rose on the back of her neck. "You believe Aurore's spirit made me fall down the stairs and your voodoo charm saved my life?" she asked dully, knowing the answer.

"*Oui, madame,* I know so, for I have felt her presence in this house since our return from Sans Regret. She always was so happy when we returned from the plantation to the town house. How she loved to invite all of Nouvelle Orléans society to *soirées* here. She does not like you here as mistress in her place," Dominique replied, a warning in her soft liquid voice, her almond-shaped eyes fixed on Caresse's startled gray orbs. "She will try to harm you, but I can protect you from her power."

"I . . . do not believe in such things," Caresse said, trying to sound firm. The woman wanted to frighten her so that she would agree to join her at the voodoo ceremonies she held in the warehouse along the docks.

"You will come to believe in time. She will make

343

you," Dominique warned. "I can only hope by then 'tis not too late for me to help you."

"The door, there is someone at the door," Caresse told her woodenly. As Dominique turned to answer the rapid thud of the brass knocker, she said more firmly, "I do not like to be threatened. Do not think you can frighten me into joining with you as a *voodooienne.*"

"We shall see, *madame,*" Dominique had the last word as she paused at the door, a slight smile curving her lips.

Caresse shuddered, for she knew that the woman truly believed Aurore's spirit was threatening her. What was she going to do to try to convince her it was true? To what lengths was Dominique willing to go?

The arrival of the doctor and Lucien shortly afterward put a stop to her frightening and frustrating musings. Dr. Viel pronounced her on the road to recovery, although he cautioned her to rest the next few days. After seeing the physician to the door, Lucien returned to her chamber.

"Dominique tells me you were called to Solange's," Caresse said as they were left alone for the first time since he had returned.

"You know how Solange thinks everything she does, or wants done, is of the utmost importance," he replied drily. "She did give me an invitation for both of us to attend her *bal masqué.* The theme is to come as what you would most like to be if you were allowed another life, your most secret desire," he explained with a shrug. "I must say it opens some unusual possibilities for costumes."

"I shall be interested to see Solange's choice of costume," Caresse could not help saying, with a twist to her mouth. "But is that why she wished to speak with you?" she persisted, knowing that he was not telling her the complete truth.

"You know Solange, she likes to play the great

344

lady, with courtiers dancing attendance on her every summons. She calls people to her simply for the enjoyment of the exercise of power," he answered, enigmatically.

"You are not going to tell me what you discussed, are you?" she said, with a sigh, looking away from him. He had a way of soothing away her questions, and it was only later that she realized he had never answered her.

"There are some things, *ma chère*, 'tis better for you not to know. Solange is involved in some rather unsavory activities in Nouvelle Orléans. We have been friends for many years. She knows she can speak freely with me, ask my advice, and I will give her my honest opinion. When you are surrounded by people who only wish to curry your favor, an honest opinion is rarer then gold."

"I see," Caresse replied softly. They were old friends, he said. She wondered just how close they had been in the years since Aurore's death. it was a repugnant thought, Lucien and the corrupt Solange, but there had been stranger couplings at Versailles. Suddenly she felt rumpled and sticky. She wanted nothing more than to wash away the taint of sickness.

"What are you doing?" he asked, startled.

"Please have Raymond bring water for a bath," Caresse told her husband as she swung her feet over the edge of the bed.

"Are you sure, *ma chère*, that you feel up to it?" he asked as she slowly stood up.

"The headache is almost gone, nothing more than a slight pain," she assured him as he came quickly to her side.

"You must be careful on the stairs. Those hourglass heels, while all the fashion, can be quite dangerous," he told Caresse, gathering her to him in an embrace. "Promise me you will be careful."

"I promise," she whispered, relishing the cherished feeling she experienced in Lucien's arms. It would be so easy to pretend that everything was all right, to forget Dominique's strange warning. But she knew that she could pretend no longer. It was time Lucien knew the truth about the woman who had been so long a part of his life.

"I promise to be careful, although Dominique thinks that with the proper spell I shall not have to worry about falling down the stairs." She felt him stiffen slightly at her words.

"Dominique, like many of her people, believes in the power of such things. 'Tis harmless," he said in dismissal.

"I wonder," she mused with a sigh. "I wish I could be as sure as you that it does no harm."

"What do you mean?" he asked quietly, but she could tell he was not surprised.

"Dominique is so intense about her beliefs. She claims to have rubbed some sacred oil on the bedposts, and ringed the bed with some special powder. Oh, and she put a *gris-gris* bag under the bed. That, she claims, is what saved me from what she called a spirit that wished me harm." Somehow she could not bring herself to mention Aurore's name.

"I shall speak with her. But if you are going to live in Nouvelle Orléans and at Sans Regret, *ma petite*, you will have to get used to the Africans' belief in voodoo. She means only to help you, thinks she is protecting you. If you can, try and take it in the spirit in which it is offered."

"I fear that I understand only too well what is motivating her," Caresse murmured. Then raising her head and staring up at him, she said, "Dominique believes Aurore's ghost haunts this house as well as Sans Regret, and that she is jealous that I am now your wife. She believes that Aurore's spirit somehow pushed me down the stairs, and that she will try to harm me again." There, she thought, I have told him.

He stared down at her, some unreadable emotion in his dark intense eyes. His features were frozen into a remote mask that gave nothing away of what he was thinking or feeling. But she could sense that although he continued to hold her in his arms, some part of him had retreated deep within that wall he had built around his heart.

"I shall speak with her while you are bathing," he said, his voice hard. "The water will be up directly." Cool lips brushed her forehead, then he was gone. The sound of his boots on the wooden floor of the hall echoed throughout the house as he strode purposefully to find Dominique.

Caresse felt strangely let down. She should be relieved that this was one secret no longer festering between them, but somehow she sensed that it had pushed them further apart. He had been angry in a cold, controlled manner that was more unnerving than a passionate explosion.

Raymond brought canisters of hot water, carrying them to the bath at her direction. Once the tub was filled he quickly left. Alone in the chamber, for even Blanchette and Bruno had exited to seek out their feeding bowls on the gallery outside the kitchen house, Caresse enjoyed a long soak in the tub. She tried somehow to find that calm, centered place inside her that she would retreat to for solace whenever faced with turmoil in her life.

Several polite knocks on the door that opened onto the hall interrupted her musings. "What is it?" she called, wondering why—if it was Lucien or Dominique—they did not enter after the first polite rap.

" 'Tis Ninon, *madame*. *M'sieur* asked me to help you dress," the free woman of color who served as the cook called out from behind the closed door.

"*Entrez*, Ninon," Caresse called out in reply.

Ninon proved to be helpful, if reserved. She spoke little. She only inquired about what Caresse

347

wished to wear and how she wanted her hair dressed. The complicated costume of a lady of fashion required help just to don the voluminous petticoats, lace the stays that lifted up the bosom to the proper voluptuous roundness as well as fasten the elaborate closings.

Caresse appreciated Lucien's thoughtfulness, as it seemed he and Dominique were involved in a lengthy discussion, but she also realized, to her dismay, that it was his familiarity with women's clothing that made him ask Ninon to help her. What had Yvonne called him, a rogue *extraordinaire* in a city notorious for all manner of rakes and rogues.

The mild afternoon sun was warming the courtyard as she ventured out from the confinement of her chamber. This was her first spring in La Louisiane. She knew it came early, but in France this would be the dead of winter. A cloak was not even needed. There were some aspects about the colony she was finding were very much to her liking. Sitting on an iron bench at the end of the formal herb garden, she tilted her face up to the mellow rays of the setting sun, wondering where Lucien was, for he had not been in his study on the first floor.

She hoped his talk with Dominique had done some good, and the woman would stop insisting that Aurore's ghost was haunting the house, determined to do her harm. The only danger she feared came from someone very much alive.

As the sun sank slowly, coloring the western horizon rose and lavender, the garden became cool and full of shadows. Caresse rose from her sanctuary to stroll into the house. Her headache was gone, and she felt refreshed. She sought out Lucien, wondering once again what could have absorbed him so completely all afternoon.

She wandered through empty rooms on the first floor till she came to the salon lit only by the tapers in the sconces on either side of Gabrielle's portrait. Entering the chamber she felt a flicker of fear in the pit of her stomach. It was as if a sixth sense were warning her away. Then she saw it, the *belle mignonne*. The human skull sat on a small delicate table of the kind often used for card playing. A powdered wig dressed with bouquets of silk violets rested on the *belle mignonne*, which was lit from the inside by a flickering candle. Beside the skull was a deck of cards laid out in suits. On the other side of the cards stood a crystal flute half full of champagne.

Caresse stood staring at the tableau, remembering Solange's description of how Aurore would greet her guests at her *soirées* where she told everyone's fortune. Her heart thumped against her rib cage as every nerve vibrated a warning to leave. Someone wanted to frighten her, make her think that Aurore's presence was haunting these rooms.

Suddenly, it was anger, not fear, that flooded through her, giving her the energy to end it once and for all. Turning, she strode from the salon, calling "Dominique! Dominique!"

There was no answer in the house, so she hurried to the servants' quarters over the kitchen house. The scent of cooking wafted from the open door. She could see Ninon preparing the evening meal, but there was no sign of either Lucien or Dominique. Anger like a red haze came over her as she hurried up the stairs to the chamber she knew to be Dominique's. Pounding on the door, it swung open under her vigorous ministrations.

"*Madame, madame,* is that you?" Ninon and Pascal came out from the kitchen attracted by the sound of her knocking.

"Where is Dominique?" Caresse called down.

The man and woman looked first at each other,

then up at Caresse. "Dominique is at her house on the Rue St. Ann, *madame,*" Pascal replied.

"Her house!" Caresse gasped. She had no idea that Dominique owned a house in the district.

"Come, *madame*, I will bring a tray of warm food up to your boudoir if you wish," said Pascal. As she descended the stairs she could see the pity in his eyes from the light that fell across his face from the kitchen. *"M'sieur* was called away but he will return as soon as he can, I am sure."

She allowed him to escort her up to her bedchamber, Bruno and Blanchette trailing at her heels. He lit the tapers for her from the ever-burning *veilleuse,* the night light on the bedside table. Then he bent down to light the fire laid out that afternoon in case the night had a chill.

"I shall return with your tray, *madame,*" he said at the door.

"How long has Dominique had her own house, Pascal?" she asked suddenly before he could leave.

"A long time, *madame.* 'Twas her *maman's* before her. *M'sieur* Jacques gave it to her," he explained with a knowing look in his dark eyes. "If that is all?"

Unable to do more than nod and give him a wan smile of dismissal, Caresse dropped in a chair in front of the flickering flames. So Dominique's mother had been Jacques St. Amant's mistress. She could only stare into the fire, her heart breaking as she wondered if Dominique had carried on the family tradition and become Lucien's. Was that the reason he allowed Dominique so much authority? Had he married a *fille à la cassette* only to have legitimate heirs that could be considered French citizens?

There were no answers in the dancing flames as she sat in the shadowy chamber waiting for Lucien's return. Would he be coming from the embrace of his mistress, she thought with tears rolling down her cheeks. Suddenly, she wondered if, both Dominique and Lucien were gone, who had placed the *belle mignonne* in the salon. Strangely, she thought she smelled the scent of violets in the lonely room.

Twenty-four

"What are you doing sitting in the dark? And you have not touched your food on the tray," Lucien's voice startled her out of a light sleep.

Rising from where she had been curled up in the chair in front of the fire, she almost stumbled over Bruno as he also rose to greet his master. "I had no appetite," she said in a choked voice. Her emotions warred within her at the sight of him.

"You need not worry about Dominique. She has left our employ. We own a shop on Rue Royal that is at the moment vacant. She has decided to open a wig styling salon there with some capital I have provided," he explained. "All her belongings have been moved to a house her mother owned on the Rue St. Ann. Dominique would often go there on her days off." He had stopped in the middle of the chamber as if he realized something was wrong. His attentive eyes searched her pale visage from across the room as if trying to understand the source of her pain. "She will not frighten you again, *ma petite.*"

"Really, I wish I had your confidence," she said, showing her disbelief in the tone of her voice.

"What is it that has upset you?" he asked in a calm voice that still showed warmth and concern.

"Come with me, I want to show you something,"

she told him, picking up a hurricane lamp with a lit taper inside.

"Lead the way, *ma chère*," he agreed, opening the door so she could exit.

With a swish of her skirts, she led him down the hall to the staircase, holding the lamp high to light their way. The main foyer was dark, with only one lit taper in a hurricane lamp on the console table to lighten the gloom.

She felt him close behind her—the solid masculine warmth of him. She tried not to think of how much she would like to feel that sense of safety she always experienced when he was holding her. There was so much he had not told her about his past, about the intertwined lives of Dominique, her mother, Jacques and Gabrielle. What else had he neglected to confide?

"Here," she called over her shoulder as she swept into the parlor, "explain that." She held the lamp high in front of the table.

"What, *chère*, what am I supposed to explain?" he asked gently.

"It was here, the *belle mignonne*, the cards, the glass of champagne. They were all here on this table," she gasped, whirling around, holding the lamp high as she searched the corners of the chamber. There was nothing there, even the candles in the sconces beside Gabrielle's portrait had been extinguished.

"You saw these objects?" he asked, a wary look shadowing his eyes.

"*Oui,* they were here a few hours ago," she said, her arched brows drawn together in frustration.

"Perhaps it was a dream while you slumbered in the chair by the fire. You have been under a great strain. At such times dreams can seem very real," he said gently, coming to her and putting his arm around her shoulders.

"You do not believe me," she whispered, looking up at him with despair in her huge gray eyes.

"I think we are both tired. Shall we go upstairs?" he said in soft reassuring tones, taking the lamp from her trembling hand, and guiding her up to their chamber, his hand at her small waist.

Caresse allowed him to lead her, for she felt an intense desolation sweep over her. Had it all been a dream? No, she was sure of what she had seen in the salon. Someone had removed it without a trace, but who could it have been now that Dominique was no longer housekeeper?

Closing the door behind them, Lucien placed the lamp on the table beside the four-poster. Then turning to Caresse he gathered her to him, holding her in the sanctuary of his embrace. Her head against his shoulder, he gently stroked down the length of her spine to relax her and reassure her that the terrors of the night were locked outside their bedchamber.

"*Pauvre petite*, rest, nothing can harm you. 'Tis all over," he murmured, kissing her hair, the silken texture of her cheek.

Leading her to the bed, he pulled back the counterpane, then tenderly peeled the clothes from her exhausted form like the petals of a rose. His fingers pulled the pins from her chignon, allowing her silver blond hair to flow down over her shoulders.

She stood like an overtired child, not resisting, allowing him to undress her for she knew that she didn't have the energy. Her throat ached with defeat. She had seen the *belle mignonne*, she knew she had, unless she was going mad. But then Solange had said that the St. Amant men were cursed with having wives who were mad.

"Slip under the covers, *chère*, before you take a chill in this damp room." He helped her under the silk sheets and the heavy counterpane, pulling them up about her chin with a tender gesture.

She stared up at him with tormented eyes as he undressed in the glow of the tapers. How could she want him so much when she did not know if he had come to her from Dominique's bed?

"Do not look so sad, *ma pauvre petite*. It is like a knife in my heart to see such pain in your lovely eyes," he murmured as he slipped into bed, pulling her to his chest. "I told you once that there is nothing we cannot face and conquer together, remember?"

"Oui," she whispered against the soft dark fur of his chest.

"I do not know what you have heard about my past, what lurid stories Solange has been only too glad to impart. But believe me when I tell you that no one have I loved as I do you, *ma belle femme*, holder of my heart, twin of my soul."

She listened to his words that were a balm to her tortured mind with an overflowing sense of home-coming. No matter what had gone before, she sensed that what he was saying was from his heart. And she knew also that a man who was capable of such words was not a cold-blooded murderer.

"When I am with you, all the shadows vanish. 'Tis only when I am alone that they appear to make me doubt you, and indeed somehow to doubt myself," she admitted.

"What do you mean, doubt me?" he asked, tightening his arm around her.

"Tonight I found out from Pascal that Dominique's *maman* was your father's mistress after she arrived in Nouvelle Orléans. He bought her the house on the Rue St. Ann," Caresse explained, moving her head so she could look up into his beloved ebony eyes.

" 'Tis true, *ma maman* was, after the first few years of their marriage, often out of touch with the world for weeks at a time, lost in some secret place that she retreated to whenever the memory

355

of the past was too much. My father loved her very much, but he was a man, a vital, alive adult male, *ma chère*. He had needs, needs his mad wife could never fulfill. Dominique's *maman* was quite lovely and very lonely upon her arrival in Nouvelle Orléans. I think in her own way she loved my father, and he cared for her. He did not force himself upon her, she came willingly, I would say with great passion."

"And Dominique?" Caresse asked. "How did she feel about your father?"

"*Pauvre* Dominique, she was ten years old when they came from Saint-Domingue. Old for her age, I think children of mixed blood are forced to grow up faster than other children. She hated the position in which white men had put her and her *maman*. And I could not blame her. That is what I think brought us close—the bitterness at what the world had done to our mothers. Perhaps that is why I allowed her such authority for in my mind she was like a sister to me, and you know how often maiden sisters run the households of their widowed brothers. My father left her money upon his death, as did her natural father, Dubrieul. It would have set her up in business here in Nouvelle Orléans or in Paris, but she refused to touch it. Guilt money she called it, and mayhap she was right. She had been so long at Sans Regret, was so competent at running both houses, Aurore depended on her totally. It was easier to allow her to do as she pleased, but I think I should have encouraged her to take the money and make a life for herself that did not include serving the St. Amant family. It was a mistake that I do not want you to pay for, *ma chère*. Living in the house on Rue St. Ann, running her own business, perhaps Dominique can find happiness in her own life, and forget this obsession with Aurore," There was regret in his voice as he explained the tangled web of his and Dominique's lives.

"Then she has never been your mistress?" Caresse asked in a low voice, her eyes meeting his without wavering.

"Ah, so that is what is bothering you, *ma chère!*" he said with comprehension. "I swear she has never been my mistress," he said, kissing her lightly on the temple. "My life before I met you was not a monastic one, but my relationship with Dominique was never intimate. She was in some ways like a sister, and also a friend of my childhood. 'Tis hard to explain in words a relationship that was familial when there was no tie of blood between us. We grew up together, sharing the pain of watching our mothers live a shadowy life, although for very different reasons. I do not think Dominique would give herself to any white man. For many years she has taken Pascal for her lover, although both are so independent neither wishes to marry. It seems 'tis better for a *voodooienne* to remain single. And as you have come to realize, voodoo is what matters most to Dominique."

" 'Twould certainly seem that is true," Caresse replied. "But why did she agree to take money from the St. Amant estate now when she refused all these years?"

"I fear I told her what she wanted to hear," he said with a sigh of frustration, "that the money was to buy the strongest *gris-gris* she could conjure to keep Aurore's spirit from harming you. Of course she agreed that this would be an ongoing task, for Aurore's spirit was restless and jealous of you. I assured her I would pay a great deal to keep her protecting you."

"Mon Dieu, 'twill only encourage the woman," Caresse murmured uneasily.

"However we view it, 'tis necessary for Dominique and for you. She must get on with her

357

life and we with ours. The ghosts of the past need to be buried, forgotten. Our future stretches ahead and I think even Dominique realizes that there is room for only one mistress in this house and at Sans Regret." He touched her cheek, then tilted her face up for an urgent kiss full of passion and need.

Fatigue vanished as she opened her mouth with a moan under the insistent pressure of his burning lips. She met his invasion with a swirling surrender of her tongue as they intertwined, her slender ivory leg around his stalwart masculine limb.

He rolled her over in one lithe movement, his mouth pressing burning kisses down the slender length of her neck, holding himself so that his weight did not crush her fragile form. He marveled at her delicacy, trying to control his hot rush of passion.

"I shall not break," she whispered. It was as if she sensed his reluctance to unleash the hunger that he was finding hard to control.

In the exquisite act of love they celebrated life and the wondrous mystery of the bond between man and woman. Each sensation, each give and take, as he thrust inside her honeyed depths was a rebuke to the pain of the past and the terrible brush with death she had experienced. They had no need of spells or potions, for when he took her again and again, they were reaffirming the life force.

Then they were rolling over and over, till she was on top of him, his length still within her. Throwing back the tangled mane of her hair, she rose up till she was astride him, her gray eyes lit with a mischievous fire.

Placing her tiny hands on his chest, she bent down and kissed his mouth, tracing his lower lip with her tongue. When his mouth opened to capture the scarlet ribbon, she moved on, trailing her kisses down the side of his neck to bite his shoulder playfully. She felt his hands go to her waist as he began to move.

With a husky teasing laugh, she sat up, moving in wanton circles, her hands pressing down on his chest for balance. "Again, again, *mon coeur!*" She urged him on with her voice, with the abandoned movements of her hips, with the mesmerizing sight of her beautiful body wild and free.

When her shuddering climax began, he allowed himself to flow with her. Together they rode the crest of the wave, two moans of ecstasy and fulfillment merging into one cry of the celebration of life.

Once more toward dawn, they woke and sought out each other's body as if in reassurance. This joining was gentle, sleepy, almost languid in its movements, but no less enjoyable. With completion they fell back asleep still clasped in each other's arms.

The bright light of morning brought no regrets, only the sense of well-being that comes to lovers who know that even tighter bonds have been woven because of the previous night. They broke their fast late, the bells of the church of St. Louis chiming ten o'clock when Caresse managed to dress with Lucien's aid. The sun was warm in the walled garden so they requested that Ninon serve them outside.

"I was speaking with Ninon," Lucien told Caresse as she poured his coffee. "She has a sister who has worked in a dressmaking establishment, but who desires a change. Mariette is said to be skilled at hairdressing and would like to work as a lady's maid. Ninon says she is not sure if Mariette would want to leave the city for months at a time, but I thought till the time comes perhaps you could use her services. She could stay on as a housekeeper when we leave for Sans Regret.

359

"Tell Ninon to have her come by this afternoon," Caresse replied with a smile at his thoughtfulness. The house was a large one, they could use more help.

"And what is it you are planning today?" he asked, lifting the delicate cup of steaming coffee to his lips.

"I shall attend to the marketing, and then interview Ninon's sister," she answered with a smile as she realized, no longer would Dominique's shadow hang over the house. The constant battle over who was in charge had ended. "I cannot thank you enough for arranging Dominique's departure. It will make everything so much easier." She gave a sigh of relief, leaning back in her chair to enjoy the sight of a cardinal flitting through the sweet olive bush.

"If you are pleased, *ma chère*, then so am I," the warmth of his smile echoed in his voice. He covered her hand with his, the ebony eyes she loved meeting hers with a tender warmth. "Remember the doctor's warning to not do too much too soon."

"I will, but really I feel wonderful, no bad effects at all," she reassured him.

"I should hope not, *ma chère*," he teased, a smoldering look in his dark eyes as she realized the double meaning to his words. He had been referring to their night of love.

"You are just as Yvonne said, a rogue," she said with a smile, a sparkle in her gray eyes.

"Yvonne told you that?" he asked with a slightly chagrined look on his darkly handsome features. "When?"

"Before we married. A rogue *extraordinaire* in a city of rogues, I believe was how she phrased it," Caresse explained, two deep dimples appearing on either side of her mouth at his expression of discomfort.

"It did not appear to have frightened you off," he said drily.

"As I told you once, I do not frighten easily," she said softly.

"*Non, ma belle femme,* you are one of the most courageous women I have ever met." There was a strange note to his voice, a melancholy shadow in his dark eyes. It was as if a storm cloud had swept across the sun, so changed was his mood.

They sat without speaking for what seemed a long time to Caresse. Lucien was lost in thought, staring out across the courtyard as he drank his coffee. The somber silence began to wear on her nerves. What had she said to elicit such a reaction?

Putting his cup down in the saucer, Lucien turned to her as if he had made up his mind about whatever had made him withdraw into silence. "There is something I must see to, that cannot wait. Take Raymond to the market with you. Here." He handed her a pile of scrip notes that passed for money in the city. Rising to his feet, his tall figure loomed over her for a moment as he lifted her hand to his lips, and murmured, "Till this afternoon."

She watched, stunned, as he strode into the foyer to retrieve his tricorn and walking stick, which she knew concealed a thin rapier. No gentleman was without his sword cane on the streets of Nouvelle Orléans. She was used to Lucien's mercurial moods, but this had been stranger, more abrupt, than usual.

With a sigh she too rose to her feet, placing the sheaf of paper bills in the deep pocket of her gown, as she saw Ninon hovering in the doorway of the kitchen house, trying to appear not to be eavesdropping. Walking over to the woman she said, "*M'sieur* told me about your sister. If she is available I should like to speak with her at four this afternoon. After you finish with the morning's dishes, please take time to take her my message."

"*Merci, madame.* Mariette will be pleased," Ninon replied.

After a brief consultation with the cook as to what was desired from the market, Caresse went up to her bedchamber. While they had lingered over coffee, Ninon had made the bed, and Raymond had cleared away the water they had used to wash.

It was as she reached into the armoire for her reticule that she heard the rustling sound. Bruno had followed her upstairs and he too was drawn to the armoire. She heard the low canine growl of warning before she saw it, the brown coil in the bottom of the armoire. The flat reptilian head lifting up menacingly to strike.

A black primitive fright surged over her as she slowly moved backward. Mesmerized by the weaving head as the angry reptile reached out to strike, she felt only a horrible sense that she was going to die.

It happened so fast she never could quite remember how it all came about, but Bruno moved between her and the snake. With unbelievable quickness, he had grasped the serpent by the back of its flat head, swinging it around with one lithe movement and breaking its neck.

Caresse stumbled from the chamber. She did not even remember how she got to the courtyard. Bending over one of the flower beds she threw up her breakfast, sinking to her knees on the flagstones.

"*Madame!*" She heard the cries of Pascal, of Ninon, and of Raymond.

Gasping for breath, she told them what had happened as Ninon helped her to the chair by the table. Pascal ran for a long knife from the kitchen, and Raymond for a long-handled rake and empty cloth bag. Armed, the two men used the gallery stairs to approach the bedchamber.

"But how could such a creature get up to your bedchamber, *madame?*" Ninon mused aloud as she handed her a napkin.

Snakes are common in the muddy streets of Nouvelle Orléans, especially after a heavy rain when they slithered in from the flooding nearby swamps, but they were not found in the bottom of a closed armoire unless put there by someone. But why? Caresse looked away as the men carried the remnants of the reptile in the cloth bag. Bruno trotted at their heels.

"*Madame,* you were lucky. The dog broke its neck before it could strike. 'Tis a deadly viper that lives in and near the water," Pascal explained as Raymond left the house carrying the bag. He was heading for the canal at the edge of the city where refuse was dumped.

"Then how did it get in my armoire?" she asked tersely, reaching for the shaggy dog who stood beside her. Putting her arms around its great neck, she unashamedly hugged him. He had saved her life.

"I do not know, *madame,*" Pascal replied in a low voice, avoiding her eyes.

"Someone or something has put a powerful spell on you, *madame,*" Ninon whispered, making the sign of the cross. "Someone wishes your death."

The anger overcame the fear, as Caresse looked up at the frightened Ninon. She knew this was not the work of a spirit. This had been planned by someone quite real, quite alive. How she had managed it, Caresse could not know, unless someone who lived in the house had helped her.

Looking up at the two house servants Caresse felt a chill in her blood. She did not know whom to trust.

"Were there any callers this morning?" she asked

Pascal, for Lucien had given orders that they were not to be disturbed as they broke their fast.

"Several tradesmen, *madame,* with their usual deliveries of milk, cream, and eggs," he replied. "And M. Dubrieul left his card."

"I see," she said, but she was only more confused. There had been people in and out all morning, anyone could have done it. Even Dominique could have slipped in through the front door while they were out in the courtyard. "Ninon, if you will fetch my hat and reticule. I should like Pascal to accompany me on an errand. Please clean the bedchamber while I am gone," Caresse told the woman, rising to her feet. There was only one way she would know if what she suspected was true. She hoped she had the courage to do it.

Twenty-five

"Pascal, I shall need you to accompany me," Caresse told him as Ninon brought her the wide-brimmed straw hat that tied under her chin with pink silk ribbons, and her reticule. She had been unable to face going into the bedchamber so soon after what had just happened.

"*Oui, madame.* Will you be needing a large basket for our purchases?" he asked, turning toward the kitchen house to fetch one of the marketing baskets.

She nodded in the affirmative, then as he started for the kitchen, she turned and said to Ninon and Raymond hovering near her, "Raymond, go with Ninon to clean the chamber. Please check all corners, under the bed, and all drawers to make sure our reptilian visitor did not have a companion."

Ninon gave a shudder at her words, while Raymond agreed that it was a good idea. "I shall search thoroughly."

"*Merci,* and from now on I want all the entrance doors kept locked even in the day time," Caresse ordered, as Pascal joined her, the handle of a large woven basket slung over his arm. As they exited through the garden gate, Raymond latching it after them, she turned to him and said, "Before we go to the market, I wish to make another stop, but you must tell me the location."

"I . . . I fear I do not understand, *madame,*" Pascal said hesitantly.

"I wish you to take me to Dominique's house on the Rue St. Ann," Caresse replied as they started down the Rue de Chartres heading in the direction of the main square.

"Better, *madame,* if you let her be," he muttered, avoiding her gaze.

"She has to understand that this kind of harassment must end. It will not convince me to join with her in her beliefs. She is becoming desperate, and desperate people do not think clearly. I must convince her how serious this has become, how dangerous for everyone. Her obsession with Aurore St. Amant must end, for her sake as well as mine."

"Oui, madame, I shall take you there," he said with a sigh, giving in to her demands. He sensed that she was determined, but he also knew how determined Dominique could be when she wanted to achieve some objective.

The rays of the February sun were drying up some of the mud in the street, but with the warmth came the overripe smell of the refuse that had moldered there all winter. Wagons rolled past, lurching in the drying ruts, many carrying casks of rum and brandy for the taverns and gambling halls that were flourishing under the auspices of the governor and his wife.

Solange and Pierre-François would leave the colony wealthy, but they had set in motion a system of corruption and graft that would not be easily dismantled, Caresse thought. She knew Nouvelle Orléans had never been known for its law-abiding citizens, but the squalor and debauchery on the streets seemed even worse than on the day she had stepped off the boat from France.

Drunken soldiers straggled out of taverns, although it was only early afternoon. Some were retching into the muddy streets. There was little for the garrison to do in the city so the taverns did a brisk business, as did the brothels down by the wharves.

As they reached the Place Royale Caresse saw more fashionably dressed women heading for the open-air market that sprawled along the levee. Here the air was scented with the fragrance of brewing coffee, gingerbread cakes sold by strolling women from the large baskets they carried over their arms, and the sour smell of stale wine.

Ursuline nuns, in their gray robes, seemed to glide across the paths worn in the dirt of the main plaza as they too headed toward the market. Their heads were averted from worldly gazes, concealed by their soaring white headdresses that fluttered like the wings of a bird in the wind from the river. Caresse was disappointed she could not recognize them. Perhaps she knew one of those gliding figures. But there was no time to visit the convent, no matter how tempting the quiet refuge would be to her tormented mind.

Averting her eyes from the sight of two felons chained in the stocks in the plaza in front of the church, she followed Pascal's direction to turn down the Rue St. Ann, passing by Government House. Caresse tried to forget her terrifying escape from the gardens that foggy night when she first heard of the new *voodooienne* in Nouvelle Orléans. The woman seemed to want her dead.

Had the serpent been placed in her armoire not just to frighten her into seeking Dominique's help, but to kill her? Was it some mad revenge because Caresse had told Lucien of Dominique's warning that Aurore's spirit wished to harm her, and by doing so instigated her removal as housekeeper? If that was the case, then this was more than a fervent belief in voodoo; the woman was deeply disturbed.

She hoped she was not doing more harm by visiting Dominique, but the woman had to realize she could not frighten her. Carefully rehearsing in her mind what she would say, they made their way up the muddy wooden planks of the *banquette* of Rue St. Ann.

The houses became smaller, many one-story cottages, the further they walked from the Place Royale. Some of the structures needed paint, others were missing a shingle here or there, a shutter sagged at a window that contained no glass, only waxed paper, or heavy canvas. Tall weeds and clumps of palmetto grew in the small yards, giving places of concealment to venomous reptiles. Dominique had not had far to look for the serpent, Caresse thought with a slight shiver.

"That be her house, *madame*," Pascal stopped, pointing across the street to a small cottage with a front gallery.

Dominique's house was better taken care of than many they had passed, the walls freshly whitewashed, the shutters painted a dark green, and in the windows real glass, unusual in these small houses, and a walled garden to the side. The fronds of a tall banana tree as well as graceful waving stalks of bamboo grew high over the wooden fence. There was also an air of melancholy desertion about the cottage.

Caresse hesitated only a moment before stepping off the wooden *banquette,* her walking boots sinking into the drying muck of the street. Pascal reluctantly followed her. They had been lovers Lucien had said, and yet he was frightened of her. What kind of woman could hold such power over those who loved her?

Pushing fear to the back of her mind, Caresse walked through the gate into the small yard. A few sweet olive bushes and tangled jasmine vines softened the lines of the gallery as she stepped on its wooden boards. She heard Pascal breathing hard behind her. It was as if he had run a race, but she knew it was fear that caused his breath to come in gasps.

"It look like she be gone, *madame,*" he muttered, for there was a sense of emptiness about the place.

"I shall knock anyway, Pascal, to make sure," Caresse said, feeling a cold knot in her stomach as she raised her gloved hand. There was a malevolent atmosphere about the cottage, nothing visible, only felt by some primitive sense of warning.

As her hand touched the cypress door, it startled both of them by swinging open. The sense of dread, of danger, rose so thick inside her throat she thought it would choke her.

"We best not go in there," Pascal warned, a catch in his voice.

Caresse hesitated on the threshold. She had come so far, it was maddening to think that Dominique was gone. Confused by what to do she almost turned around and left in defeat when she saw in a stream of sunlight coming through the small windowpane the prone figure of a woman stretched out on the floor.

She did not want to believe what some primordial part of her brain warned her was true. She breathed in shallow, quick gasps, her hands clenched in fists at her sides. *Go in, you have to go in*—the words went round and round in her mind like the buzz of a bothersome insect.

"Let us leave here, *madame,*" Pascal whispered, although there was no one to hear their conversation.

"We cannot, something is wrong, I can feel it," she said in a low voice, not turning to look at him. She did not tell him that she could see a figure sprawled on the floor.

"I can feel it too, that's why we should leave. Bad

369

spirits here," Pascal muttered, making the sign of the cross.

Taking a deep breath, Caresse stepped inside the room she knew was the *salon*. It was furnished with elegant furniture from France: gilt-framed mirrors hung on the whitewashed plastered walls, tall tapers stood in silver candlesticks on delicate French tables, an Aubusson carpet in muted shadows of rose and blue lay on the cypress planks of the floor. Sprawled across the elegant rug was the figure of Dominique, her slender throat cut, her blood in a pool beside her.

"Mon Dieu!" Caresse gasped. There was no need to go any closer. The woman was dead. Nausea welled up and threatened to choke her as her body began to tremble.

"Ma chère, oh *ma chère!"* The sound of Pascal's cry of grief rent the melancholy silence of the house. He moved past Caresse to kneel beside Dominique's prone body, cradling her poor mutilated head in his arms, as he rocked back and forth.

Caresse's eyes filled with tears. She had prepared herself for every scenario, but finding Dominique murdered had not been one of them. Turning away from the intimate scene between Pascal and his lost love, she started for the door. He deserved some time alone to say good-bye.

"Mon Dieu, Caresse, what is going on?" Lucien's startled voice greeted her from where he stood in the doorway.

"Lucien!" It was both a prayer of thanksgiving and a cry of shock. She ran to him, to the safety of his embrace.

"Are you all right?" he asked, clasping her to him, her arms wrapping around the secure warmth of this chest.

"I . . . I am fine, but . . . Dominique is dead," she said with a long shudder, pressing her face into the velvet of his waistcoat.

370

"But how long have you been here, *ma chère?*" he asked, staring at Pascal weeping as he clasped the still form of his beloved Dominique in his arms.

"We just arrived," she confessed.

"Come outside, we can give him some time alone with her," Lucien said, sheltering her from the terrible sight with his arm, as he led her out onto the gallery.

"Who would have done such a terrible thing?" Caresse blurted out as they stood staring out at the small front garden only yards from the wooden *banquette*.

"I have no idea, *chère*, unless Dominique made enemies in her position as *voodooienne*. 'Tis possible. Voodoo is both sought and feared by many in Nouvelle Orléans." His voice was weary. "The police at the Corps de Garde must be notified, and the undertaker. Pascal should be consulted on the funeral arrangements, and Dubrieul should be told. She was his half sister even if from the wrong side of the blanket."

"I should like to leave as soon as possible," Caresse said with a shudder, thinking of the mutilated corpse lying just beyond the door.

"Wait here, I must speak with Pascal."

She nodded her agreement, leaning against the post of the gallery, trying to forget the terrible sight that seemed to be replaying over and over in her mind. When had it happened and why?

Suddenly a remembered fragment of conversation struck her and set the world to spin. She tried to keep control as she thought of Lucien's words the night before. Dominique will no longer bother you, he had said upon his return. The words took on a sinister quality after what she had found inside the cottage. What was he doing here? He had told her over their morning coffee that he had some business to attend to, something that could wait no longer. No, she would not even think such thoughts about Lucien, about her husband.

"Pascal will stay with . . . the body while I see you home," Lucien said, coming up behind her. She flinched at the sound of his voice. "Are you sure you are all right?" he asked.

"Please, I should like to leave now," she implored him. She had to get away from this horrible place, this house of death.

"Come," Lucien held out his arm.

She placed her trembling fingers in the crook of his arm, allowing him to lead her away from the melancholy cottage, guarding the secret of Dominique's murderer. "I am glad you came by, I would have been quite at a loss over what to do," Caresse told him through dry lips. There was a hard knot in her throat, her stomach churning as she fought to control the doubts and anxiety that had risen in her tormented mind.

"I thought to reassure myself that Dominique was resigned to our agreement," he said an edge to his words. "But I must confess I was stunned to see you there. I thought you were going to the market beneath the levee this afternoon?"

"Something happened to change my mind," Caresse said tersely, thinking of the other horror she had endured this long terrible day. "I, too, wished to make sure Dominique knew that I had no intention of becoming involved in her voodoo rites."

"I wished to protect you, *ma chère*, make your life easier after the terrors I am sure you experienced in prison in France. It does not seem that I have been successful," he told her with bitterness in his voice. She could feel the tenseness in his tall lithe form as she walked beside him.

"La Louisiane seems a savage Eden, with danger never very far away, I must admit," she confided. "But there are dangers in France as well."

"You are not sorry you came?" he asked quietly, his whole body seeming to wait for her answer.

She thought before she answered as they strode as quickly as possible on the sometimes broken boards of the *banquette* toward the Place Royale, and the Corps de Garde. If she had not come she would never have met Lucien, and despite her doubts, even fears, she knew that she would never regret the rapture she had known with him. It was what was tearing her apart, for she knew no matter what he had done, she loved him with a depth that frightened her.

"Do I take your silence for a yes that you have regrets?" he asked, the words teasing, but there was an edge in his tone. The wall was going up again, the mask slipping over his features in anticipation of her answer.

"I have no regrets about coming to La Louisiane . . . or marrying you," she said softly, pressing against him that he might know she meant every word. And strangely she knew she did mean it, murderer or not. She loved him with a desperation that was total and consuming.

"I am honored by such loyalty," he said, his voice husky with emotion, as he pressed her hand tenderly in the corner of his arm.

The late-afternoon sun was streaming across the dried grass of the Place Royale as they reached the police building. Soldiers lounged against the four massive square masonry-covered brick columns of the building's gallery. They stared with unabashed curiosity at Caresse. It was unusual for a fashionable lady to grace the doors of the Corps de Garde.

"Forgive me for subjecting you to such vulgar attention, *ma chère*, but 'tis important they know at once before someone sees Pascal alone with Dominique's body and jumps to the wrong conclusion," Lucien said as they entered the large main chamber of the building—a cavernous, sparsely furnished room with two enormous fireplaces at either end, it was a hive of activity. Uniformed men seemed to be everywhere. Crossing the brick floor under the huge exposed wooden beams of the ceiling, Caresse suddenly felt insignificant. Threading their way through the throng of men who turned and stared at Caresse, they quickly reached the small office of the officer in charge, in the rear of the building.

The young officer seemed to recognize Lucien, and ushered them into the small chamber, closing the door behind him. Caresse was relieved to be removed from the scrutiny of the soldiers, and sank gratefully into the chair the captain held for her. She listened as Lucien explained the nature of their business.

"There was no one in the house but the deceased, Mme St. Amant?" the captain questioned Caresse, writing down her answer.

"No one, Captain," she replied.

"Well, this happens all the time in Nouvelle Orléans, especially among the Africans. The woman being a *voodooienne*, she could have been killed by any one of her believers, perhaps someone who thought she had put a spell on them. We shall probably never know," he said, with a shrug, leaning back in his chair.

Caresse was outraged at his nonchalance. The atmosphere brought back unpleasant memories of another prison, another jailer.

"But you cannot just leave it at that, allow her murderer to go unpunished," she complained.

"Mme St. Amant, do you know how many dead bodies are found in Nouvelle Orléans every morning?" he asked in a patronizing tone. "If we tried to solve every case I would have no time to do anything else. Most are vagrants, felons, the flotsam and jetsam of the Caribbean washed up on the shore of Nouvelle Orléans, or Africans, like your former housekeeper, involved in voodoo. We do not look too closely at the voodoo rites. The Africans are allowed their religion within limits. It keeps them satisfied—less unrest, if you understand my meaning."

"I think I understand only too well, Captain," Caresse replied coolly.

"Très bien," he said, rising to his feet in dismissal. "I shall send a man to the undertaker, if you will bear the expense, M. St. Amant?" he asked, turning toward Lucien.

"I shall bear the expense," Lucien replied tersely, holding out his arm for Caresse.

She held her tongue till they were out of the Corps de Garde. "They will do *nothing* to find Dominique's killer because she was an African," she said with disgust.

"This is part of Nouvelle Orléans, *ma chère,* an ugly fact of life," he said, his voice hardened. "'Twas part of what drove Dominique to be what she was, consumed with assuming power through voodoo. She felt so powerless, walking that shadowy line between two worlds. I do not think we can begin to imagine the burden it must have been for her."

"You are right, it explains so much," Caresse mused aloud as they made their way down the Rue de Chartres to their town house. And it explained, she thought, why Dominique wanted to resurrect the dead Aurore in Caresse. It would make everyone believe she was the most powerful *voodooienne* in La Louisiane if she could show she had raised the dead.

"We shall soon be home, another block," Lucien told her, sensing the turmoil within her. "I think we could both use a brandy."

"Indeed," Caresse said, with a wry tilt to her lips. She would need several brandies to tell him about the serpent in the armoire, for she remembered he knew nothing about it. Suddenly she realized it had not necessarily been Dominique's doing. She could have been dead by the time the reptile was placed within the armoire, sometime while they partook of their leisurely breakfast in the garden. It didn't make sense, anyway, for she needed Caresse alive to masquerade as Aurore risen from the dead. It would have to be someone who had access to the house, and was deeply involved with voodoo. Who in Nouvelle Orléans wished her dead?

"You have taken a chill," Lucien said, his dark heavy brows slanted together in a frown. "I felt you shiver."

She looked up at him with a wan smile and a shake of her head.

The bells of St. Louis were sounding four chimes as they reached their garden gate. As Lucien tried the latch, he discovered it was locked.

"We had some trouble after you left, and I requested all the entrances locked," Caresse explained at his puzzled frown.

"What kind of trouble?"

Quickly, she told him as they walked to the front entrance. He pounded on the heavy door for admittance. She understood the vigorous knocking with his fist was also a release of his fury and frustration at what she had related. Raymond's opening the portal brought their conversation to a halt.

"*Madame*, Mariette is waiting for you in the kitchen house," Raymond informed her as they entered the foyer.

"I completely forgot I asked Ninon to have her sister come for an interview," Caresse said with an expression of chagrin.

"Raymond, have Mariette come to the salon. *Madame* will speak with her there," Lucien told the young man. "And Raymond, come upstairs after you deliver the message. I wish to discuss what happened there earlier this afternoon."

"What a terrible day," Caresse sighed as they walked into the *salon,* Lucien striding to the table next to the fireplace that contained the decanters of brandy and several crystal globe glasses.

"I agree," he said in a tense, clipped voice, pouring the amber liquid into one of the globes, then handing it to her.

She lifted it to her lips with a sigh of weariness. The liquid slipped down her throat, warming and untying the cold knot that was her stomach.

"*Madame,* I am sorry, but Mariette has left," Raymond announced, with an embarrassed expression. "She has decided to return to the dressmaker."

"I see," Caresse replied, lifting her glass to her lips. Who could blame the young woman, she must have heard what had had happened early that afternoon.

"Is that all she said?" Lucien asked abruptly.

"No . . . she said she's not working in a house with a spell on it," Raymond stammered.

"That will be all, Raymond. I shall meet you upstairs," Lucien dismissed him with exasperation.

"I hope Ninon does not decide to leave as well," Caresse shuddered.

" 'Twould seem poor Dominique managed to convince someone," Lucien said acerbically. Lifting his glass to his lips, he drank the contents in one swallow. Looking up at the portrait of the mad Gabrielle, he said softly, mockingly, "Perhaps Mariette is right and there is a curse on the house of St. Amant."

"Do not think such nonsense," Caresse said, coming to stand beside him. The torment she saw on his handsome features caused a pang in her heart. Her love and compassion for the young boy he had once been, as he watched his mother sink deeper and deeper into madness erased the terrible events of the day. "Do not torture yourself, *mon coeur*, with the pain of the past."

Flinging the glass against the marble of the fireplace, he turned to her, cradling her face in his hands. "I should never have married you, *ma chère*. Leave, leave now before you are hurt. Walk away from this house and me, and never look back." His burning eyes stared down into her soul, speaking different words, words of passion and despair. Those beloved orbs communed with the deepest part of her, devouring, consuming her as if he would never see her again.

"Non," she whispered, "I am staying."

"You are not afraid?" he asked huskily, his fingers burning into her skin as his gaze burned into her soul.

"I am afraid, but I am staying." Her words were both a declaration and a vow.

Twenty-six

A misty fog hung over the streets of Nouvelle Orléans the day of Dominique's interment in one of the small whitewashed brick tombs of the walled cemetery at the edge of the city. It was an eerie, lonely place with just five mourners and a priest following the coffin down the narrow path to stop in front of the open sepulcher.

Caresse shivered in the cool damp air, watching a flock of blackbirds take flight from the limbs of a live oak, startled by the intrusion of the living into the quiet city of the dead. Pulling the hood of her cape close about her face against the damp mist, she followed Philippe's tall form, Lucien behind her, Pascal and Ninon bringing up the rear.

The water was so close to the ground in the colony that the first French settlers had called it *flottant*, floating land. Most interments had to be in tombs or oven-like vaults built tier upon tier, usually into the cemetery wall. All this ran through Caresse's mind as the priest began to speak. The bouquet of blood-red camellias on the coffin was the only color in the muted landscape of gray, white, and black of the cemetery.

As the priest finished, Pascal stepped forward before the hired pallbearers could slip the coffin inside the tomb, and he placed something on the polished wooden lid. She saw Philippe give the man a cutting glance from his narrow amber eyes. Whatever it was, he had objected but not enough to stop Pascal. Caresse looked away, reluctant to peer too closely, for some strange premonition told her that it had to do with voodoo.

After speaking a few words with the priest, Lucien came to her side, touching her arm. "Come, there is nothing more we can do here."

Relieved it was over, she allowed him to guide her out through the maze of tombs, some as elaborate as small houses, to the entrance and the Rue de Toulouse. The carriage awaited with Raymond on the coachman's seat. Philippe lifted his tricorn to them in farewell, then started off, at a brisk pace, down the narrow street.

"I should have offered him a ride, but the thought of spending any more time in his company was more than I could bear," Lucien commented, helping Caresse inside the closed carriage. Ninon had climbed up beside Raymond. Pascal had asked for time to be alone and mourn beside Dominique's tomb. The priest was riding back with the undertaker and pallbearers.

"What a melancholy day for an interment," Caresse shuddered, looking away from the window as they left the cemetery.

"I told you that you did not have to attend," Lucien reminded her quietly. "After what you told me, no one would expect you to mourn her passing."

"She worked devotedly all her life for the St. Amants, and I am now a St. Amant. It was only proper that I pay my respects," Caresse replied carefully. She did not think Dominique had created the *belle migonne* tableau or put the venomous reptile in the armoire. There would not have been time for her to accomplish both feats before her death. But the question of whether they had, indeed, been done at Dominique's orders continued to torment her.

"Will you be going to Solange's this afternoon?" Lucien asked, for the governor's wife had invited Caresse for an afternoon of cards with several other prominent wives in the city.

"Do you wish me to go?" Caresse asked, staring out the window. The atmosphere between her and Lucien had been strained the two days since Dominique's death. Although that night he had made love to her with a passion and desperation that had taken them to the heights of rapture, in the morning, he was gone when she awoke and he stayed away till late in the evening. Hurt and angry, she had pretended to be asleep when he had returned home. They had spoken little upon rising except when he told her she did not have to attend the services for Dominique.

"Not if you do not care to go," he replied in that cool remote voice she hated. "I thought it might be a pleasant diversion after such a depressing morning."

"Perhaps you are right," Caresse muttered uneasily, but to her dismay her voice broke with her effort to remain calm.

"I shall leave the carriage for you. My business can be conducted on foot," he replied in the same remote tone.

Always he was leaving on some mysterious business. It was maddening, thought Caresse, biting her lip in frustration. Where did he go? Whom did he see? What would keep a man away from home so much, except perhaps another woman? Her eyes darkened with pain at the mere thought of Lucien with a mistress.

"Ah, we are home," he announced as they pulled up in front of the entrance. Helping her down, he strode to the door, as Raymond and Ninon went around to the back entrance.

Fitting the key in the lock he took from his pocket, he opened the door, allowing Caresse to precede him into the gloomy foyer. It was cold and damp in the house, sending Caresse to seek the warmth of the smoldering coals in the banked fire in the salon.

"Have you given any thought to your costume for Solange's *bal masqué?*" Lucien inquired as if to lighten the mood between them as he followed her into the shadowy chamber.

"I have not been in the mood for designing costumes," Caresse replied, allowing him to help her off with her cape.

" 'Twill be in just a week," he reminded her.

"Perhaps Madame Cecil has something already sewn. This *bal masqué* of Solange's seems to be an annual affair," Caresse answered absently, taking off her gloves and holding her hands to the mild warmth of the fire.

"Solange sent a costume home with me last night. It seems she had it imported from France several years ago. She claims she never wore it, for after seeing it, she decided it was not her style. She thought you might like it. I think 'twas because the size was too small, although I was diplomatic enough not to point that out to her," Lucien confided. " 'Twould look lovely on you, though, and I think she meant to be kind."

"You were with Solange last evening?" Caresse asked in a taut voice. She knew the governor was gone, inspecting the fortifications at Balize at the mouth of the Mississippi River.

"I promised Pierre-François that I would look in on her. You know how easily bored Solange can become, and when she is bored she can create havoc," he commented with an edge of distaste to his voice.

"And how are her plans for the *bal masqué?*" Caresse asked stiffly, keeping her back to him, as she

382

fought the jealousy that tore through her. Was the dissolute Solange the business that kept him out to all hours of the night?

"Elaborate as usual," he said, his voice heavy with sarcasm.

He didn't even like Solange. Why would he spend so much time with her? Perhaps she just didn't understand men, she thought, giving a heavy sigh.

"Have I made you that unhappy, *ma chère*?" he asked, coming to stand behind her, his hands on her shoulders, his lips in her hair.

"Why do you ask such a question?" she murmured, fighting the overwhelming need she had to be close to him, to turn around and crawl into his arms.

"You sighed such a heavy sigh," he answered, pulling her against him.

"The weather's turning cool after the touch of spring has added to my melancholy," Caresse answered, leaning back into the comfort of his lean frame, the feel of his hands on her shoulders.

"You should consider going to Solange's this afternoon. I do not like to think of you sitting home alone brooding in this large house."

"Perhaps you could stay and keep me company," she spoke in a whisper, afraid that she knew only too well what his answer would be.

"I wish I could, *ma chère*, but what I must attend to cannot wait," he told her, his tone apologetic, but firm and unyielding. He kissed her temple lightly, his arms coming around her form till he held her in a close embrace. "But there is time before I have to leave to slip to our bedchamber," he whispered in her ear, his breath a warm caress.

"Is there, now?" she murmured, a low husky laugh welling up from her throat. The sensuality of his words lightened her mood, captivated her imagination.

It was as Lucien turned her around to face him, that they heard the clatter of Raymond's boots on the wooden floor of the long hall. He was coming from the courtyard, having driven the carriage around to the stables. Quickly they moved apart as he reached the open door of the *salon*.

"Excuse me, *m'sieur*, but a manservant belonging to a M. Sonnier is in the back. He has requested I deliver this note to *madame*," Raymond announced, holding a silver salver containing a folded piece of parchment, sealed with a red wax seal.

"Yvonne," Caresse said, holding out her hand for the letter. Quickly, she slit it open with the help of the letter opener Lucien handed her from the desk.

"Is she all right?" Lucien inquired, noticing Caresse's brows drawn downward in a frown.

"Her time has come, 'twould seem the babe will not wait to be born," Caresse replied. "Pierre has sent for the midwife at the convent, but I promised Yvonne that when her time arrived I would be with her. Pierre says she is frightened with the babe coming so early. She was not due till the end of next month. I must go to her," she told him, concern for her friend in her large gray eyes.

"Of course," he said, turning toward Raymond waiting in the hall. "You shall have to bring the carriage around again, *madame* must go out. Tell the Sonnier servant that *madame* will return with him. He can ride with you."

"*Merci, mon cher,* I wish we could have our interlude as we planned, but I know Yvonne is frightened facing her first delivery without a single female relative to give her encouragement," Caresse told him, with the whisper of regret in her words.

"Do what you must," he said, with a slight tinge of wonder in his voice. "When it comes to such matters we men stand back in awe of a woman's courage."

"I must confess I know little about such matters myself, but I do remember hearing that one should always pray the mother's labor is short," Caresse said, with a sigh, as Lucien picked up her cloak from where he had draped it over the back of a settee.

He placed the garment around her shoulders, fastening it about her neck tenderly. Picking up her gloves from where she had laid them on a table, he took one hand and lifted it to his lips, turning it over to place a kiss in the sensitive palm. As she shuddered with arousal, he slipped the glove over her fingers and up to where it met the ruffled sleeve of her gown.

"You do not make it easy to leave," she murmured, her voice a husky whisper.

"I do not intend to ever make it easy for you to leave me, *ma belle femme*." He slipped the other glove on her hand. Leaning down, he brushed her trembling lips with his heated mouth. "Until later."

"*Oui*, later," she whispered, as he brushed a silken tendril from her cheek, then lifted her hood around the silver-gold halo of her hair.

"Give Yvonne and Pierre my regards," Lucien told her as he helped her inside the carriage. Before closing the door, he lifted her glove hand to his lips in farewell. There was a strange sadness in those dark eyes. Then he shut the door.

Leaning forward so she could look out the rain-streaked window of the carriage, she stared out at him standing without cloak or hat in the mist. A sudden foreboding filled her that she would not see him again for a long time. Lifting her hand, she wiped the fog from the glass so she might catch one last glimpse of his handsome figure before they turned the corner and he vanished from sight into the gray cloud that covered the narrow streets of Nouvelle Orléans. She leaned back against the seat, saying a silent prayer that her premonition was only a *crise de nerfs,* brought on by the melancholy events of the morning.

The Sonnier cottage, with its hipped roof and wide gallery on the Rue du Maine, was an oasis of warmth and light in the gloom of the February afternoon. Pierre had opened the door himself at Caresse's knock.

"How kind of you to come. I know Yvonne will be so happy," he told her, taking her cloak. "Come, she is back here with Soeur Xavier."

The raised cottage was like many in the city, four square chambers on the second story, opening into each other as at Sans Regret. The lower level was of brick and used for storage. Each room on the top floor also opened out to the front or rear galleries. Separate buildings or dependencies provided the kitchen and the servants' quarters in the rear of the walled garden.

Caresse could hear Yvonne's moans as she followed Pierre through the elegantly furnished *salle de compagnie* into the master bedchamber. Orange and blue flames danced in the fireplace across from the four-poster bed of cherry. The red-and-white *toile de Jouy* bedhangings and counterpane were a strangely cheerful counterpoint to the sounds of pain coming from the bed.

"Ah good, Mme St. Amant is here, *mon enfant,*" Soeur Xavier moved from her place beside the bed where she was spoon-feeding the flushed young woman sugar water to keep up her energy for her ordeal.

"How is she doing?" Caresse asked, glad her old teacher was here from the Couvent des Ursulines. The nuns ran the hospital for Nouvelle Orléans and for many years delivered all the babies born in the colony. The physician was only called if the delivery was especially difficult, for the nuns were more skilled in the birthing of infants. The doctor was chiefly a surgeon for the military. .

"Our Yvonne is doing quite well. She is a strong young woman, and one can see the babe is anxious to enter this world," the kindly nun answered, staring at the small clock beside the bed, timing the contraction that caused her patient to arch like a bow in the bed. Yvonne's hands clutched the linen sheets as she twisted and turned in the throes of her labor.

Caresse wrung out a cloth in a bowl of water to bathe her friend's flushed face as soon as the contraction ended. Yvonne lay exhausted, panting, resting for the next contraction.

As the nun walked out of the room for a moment to fetch more water, Yvonne looked up at Caresse with a hint of her old mischief in her bright blue eyes and whispered, *"Mon Dieu,* 'tis not as enjoyable pushing the babe out as it was putting him in."

"Oh, Yvonne, you must not let Soeur Xavier hear you say such a thing," Caresse said, grinning down at her friend.

"I shall never look at that again without a shudder," Yvonne said, pointing to the narrow couch with low scrolled arms that stood at the foot of the four-poster.

She would be moved to the *accouchement* bed when the moment of birth was near. The scrolled arm at the foot of the couch would unlock and slide to the side, and Yvonne would hold on to the other to help her push the baby out into the world. Every master bedchamber in La Louisiane had one at the foot of the bed shared by husband and wife.

Then Yvonne was unable to speak as another contraction began. Caresse held her hand as the nun hurried to time its length. It seemed to Caresse that they were lasting longer and coming closer together.

"You are doing magnificently, *mon enfant,*" Soeur Xavier told the panting young woman. " 'Twill not be long."

"He cannot come soon enough for me, *Soeur,*" Yvonne moaned, pressing Caresse's fingers in such a tight grip she winced.

The rain was coming down harder, as the three women, bound together by a ritual as old as time, waited for nature to take its course. Pierre would come to the door every few minutes to be assured everything was going as it should, then Soeur Xavier would return to the bedside to time the latest labor pain.

"Tell . . . tell me some gossip," Yvonne gasped to Caresse at the end of an extremely hard contraction. "Anything to keep me from thinking about the next one."

Caresse chatted about Solange's plan for a *bal masqué,* and they giggled over what would be her choice of costume despite the good sister's frown of disapproval. Then Yvonne was distracted by yet another long contraction.

"A few more of those, *mon enfant,* and you shall be ready to be moved to the *accouchement* bed," the nun told the exhausted young mother-to-be.

"Thank *le bon Dieu,*" Yvonne muttered, "I do not think I have much strength left."

"I shall fetch more linen, and speak to your husband," Soeur Xavier said, moving toward the door.

"Tell me quick before she comes back, and the pain begins again, about the murder of Dominique," Yvonne gasped. "Pierre heard about it at the market. Is it true she was a *voodooienne* and a tall white man was seen leaving her house that morning?"

Caresse stared down at her friend, stunned, but before she could question her the contractions began again. They did not stop till Yvonne's moans became deep guttural cries. She began to push as Soeur Xavier told her to do.

" 'Tis time, *mon enfant,* we shall move you for delivery," the nun told Yvonne, helping her, with Caresse on the other side, to the narrow *accouchement* bed.

Caresse stood helpless as Yvonne held on to the arm at the head of the couch and pushed with each merging contraction. Her moans were deep and constant, but Soeur Xavier seemed to see nothing unusual, encouraging her in a low voice. She forgot it all when the crown of the baby's head, with a slick of orange-red hair, appeared, then the tiny well-formed body slid into Soeur Xavier's waiting hands.

"You have a fine son," the nun announced as Caresse felt tears well up in her eyes and choke her throat. The child was crying lustily, his hair a red thatch like his mother's.

Later, after Pierre had seen his son, and was escorting Soeur Xavier to the door, Yvonne lay back in her bed, dressed in a fresh gown, the baby wrapped in a blanket in the crook of her arm. She looked up at Caresse and said, "He is mine all right, look at that hair. I cannot believe something so sweet could cause so much pain," she sighed. Then looking back up at Caresse she asked with a stricken look, "I did not say anything vulgar in front of the *soeur,* did I? With the pain and all I cannot remember."

"*Non,* although I would wager Soeur Xavier has heard language during a delivery that would make a sailor blush," Caresse chuckled, touching the baby's tiny fingers in awe.

"I am glad you were here, Caresse," Yvonne told her with a yawn.

"I am glad I was here too, but now I think both

of you could use some rest," Caresse said softly. *"Bonne nuit,* and sweet dreams."

Yvonne and her baby were both asleep by the time Caresse had closed the bedchamber door. Rising from his chair beside the fire, Pierre gave her a tired smile. "I shall ring for your coachman. He has been enjoying food and companionship in the kitchen house. But could I offer you some late supper? I have not eaten, and would enjoy the company."

"Oui, that sounds wonderful," Caresse agreed, realizing that she had not eaten since that morning. She also had an ulterior motive, wishing to question him about what he had heard about Dominique's murder. Yvonne's statement had teased the edges of her mind all the long afternoon and evening.

A maid brought them a steaming pot of gumbo, a fresh crispy loaf of French bread, and creamy butter, as well as a bottle of wine. The delicious food and wine served to restore Caresse's sagging spirits and energy. As they drank a toast to the new baby, and began the cheese and fruit from Saint-Domingue that the maid had brought for dessert, Caresse decided to ask Pierre what he had heard about Dominique's death.

"Really not too much, just a little gossip, in the *cafés* and at the market. She was a *voodooienne* of some power in the city, so *naturellement* there is gossip," he answered with a Gallic shrug of his broad shoulders. "But life is cheap here, and all too often murders are never solved in Nouvelle Orléans. The talk in the *cafés* is that someone killed her to silence her, that she knew too many secrets about important people in the city. It seems she had quite a large following among the governor's set."

"Yvonne said that you heard a tall Frenchman was seen leaving her house the morning she was killed," Caresse said, hoping against hope that she had misunderstood her friend.

"Some children playing in the street claim to have seen such a man, but you never know," he said, leaning back and sipping his wine. "I am going to give you some advice as a friend, Caresse, and I hope you will take it for your own safety. Forget about Dominique—'tis always dangerous when a Frenchwoman involves herself in voodoo. Leave it and walk away."

"I do not think I have any choice. The police are not interested in investigating her murder," Caresse replied with a grimace of disgust.

" 'Tis best, believe me," he said with authority. "This man, if there was such a man, will never be found, and if he was, nothing could be proved."

As Caresse rode home from the Sonniers', her conversation with Pierre went round and round in her brain. If there had been a man, he will never be found, he had said, but she had a terrible suspicion that she knew the identity of that man. She felt the nauseating sinking of despair in the pit of her stomach as she stared out at the narrow rain-lashed streets. Only a light here and there from a window, or open door of a *café*, lighted the blanket of darkness.

Her mind went back to the morning Dominique had been killed. Lucien had left that morning to take care of something that would wait no longer, he had told her. Had it been to silence Dominique forever? She could not help remembering Luyu telling her that it was rumored Dominique had seen the man who had been with Aurore the night she died. When Lucien told Dominique she would have to leave, had the woman threatened to remain silent no longer? Had her husband, the man she knew she loved with her heart and soul, killed two women?

Twenty-seven

The town house was shadowy and empty when Caresse arrived home. A flickering light from a single taper was her only welcome in the cold dark foyer.

Pascal had come from the servants' quarters when Raymond helped her from the carriage at the entrance of the stable. She had insisted he take her around to the back, not wanting to wait for Pascal to come all the way through the house to answer the door.

"I have dined. If you will light the fire in my bedchamber, I shall go directly to bed," she told Pascal as he accompanied her into the main hall. "*Monsieur* has not returned home?"

"*Non, madame,*" Pascal replied, allowing Bruno and Blanchette to enter behind him.

"Have they been fed?" she asked, bending down to give Bruno a vigorous pat and rub, then a gentle stroke down the silky back of Blanchette.

"*Oui, madame,* they ready for a warm place in front of the fire," Pascal said, with a slight chuckle, the first lifting of his melancholy since the death of his beloved Dominique.

"I think you are right," she agreed, sweeping up the stairs behind Pascal who carried an oil lamp to light the way.

After starting a roaring fire, he left the bed-chamber to Caresse and her two pets. She experienced a slight pang of anxiety as she opened the door of the armoire, but tonight she was almost too tired to feel nervous.

Donning an ivory silk night rail and garnet velvet *robe de chambre*, she poured herself some cognac from the decanter on Lucien's desk. Despite the roaring fire, and the heavy velvet robe, she could not seem to drive the chill from her bones. She knew that it was a pall of the spirit more than of the weather. Pierre's words would not leave her no matter how she tried to push them away.

Staring down at Lucien's desk, lost in thought, she at first did not notice the letter lying there. But somehow the crest on the wax seal of the parchment drew her attention through the fog of her musings. She had seen it before, in France. There was no mistaking the royal seal of the king.

Stunned, she picked up the envelope, turning it over in her hand. It must have come on the latest boat from France, perhaps in the diplomatic pouch for the governor, but it was unmistakably addressed to Lucien. He had already gone when it was delivered, so Pascal must have brought it up here and placed it on the desk.

Laying the parchment envelope back on the desk, she finished the cognac with one swift drink. Here was another mystery concerning her husband, a letter from the king. For a man who had not been to France, he certainly was on intimate terms with the king, something courtiers at Versailles schemed for years to achieve.

"Who is he really, Bruno? Can you tell me?" she murmured aloud, sitting in the chair by the fire, stroking his shaggy head as he lifted it to look at her with sleepy eyes.

"Why not ask him?" A deep masculine voice spoke from behind her with quiet emphasis.

She turned around, rising quickly to her feet. Lucien stood by the bookcase on the other side of the fireplace. She glanced at the French doors. They were still locked, and the door to the hall was closed.

"But . . . how?" she stammered.

" 'Twas something I meant to show you, *ma chère,*" he said, a strange enigmatic look in his dark eyes. Turning, he swept his tricorn from his head, placing it on the chair, then lightly pressed one of the scrolled leaves on the bookcase. To Caresse's amazement, the bookcase swung silently outward to reveal the top of a flight of stairs. A candle in a lantern flickered where he had left it on the top step.

"You came through there?" Caresse asked in amazement. "But why?"

"I thought to surprise you. I saw the light from the street, and I seem to have misplaced my key. It seemed foolish to rouse Pascal when I could so easily use the hidden entrance," he explained, picking up the lantern and closing the bookcase door.

Caresse watched, still stunned, as he removed his rain-sodden cloak. "But why is there a hidden staircase in the master bedchamber?" she inquired.

"When my father had the house built he included it in the plans, for he had lived in New France and had experienced Indian attacks. There is one at Sans Regret as well, in the chamber that belonged to Aurore. Fire is also always a danger in Nouvelle Orléans. The passageway is another escape route. It opens behind the large sweet olive bush at the side of the house next to the gate in the wall. Unless you were aware of its existence you would never know it was there, for the jasmine vine that crawls up the house conceals the opening that is flush with the masonry wall."

"I cannot believe you never told me of its existence," Caresse managed to reply through stiff lips.

"Forgive me, *ma chère*, I did not mean to frighten you," he apologized, coming to stand in front of her. Reaching out, he stroked her cheek with a gentle finger, then touched her hair that she had allowed to flow down her back. "Have I ever told you how much I enjoy seeing your hair free, tumbling down like moonlight?"

"Such honeyed words," she said, with a slight edge to her voice. He was hiding something, trying to distract her.

"Perhaps, but I mean them," he murmured, wrapping a silken tendril about his finger. "What a lovely sight you are, *ma belle*, on such a night. And how was the birthing? Does Pierre have a daughter or a son?"

"A son," she answered softly, remembering the babe she had held in her arms for a moment before handing it to Yvonne.

"And the mother?"

"She is fine, tired but happy," Caresse replied.

"When I saw the light from the street I knew you were home," he murmured, his ebony eyes searching her face as if he could somehow read her thoughts. "I could not wait to touch you like this." His hand stroked her hair, then touched her chin, tilting her pale visage, with its wary expression, so that she was forced to meet his gaze. "Could not wait to taste you like this," he murmured as his lips brushed hers. He felt her tremble and sigh, but her mouth did not open to him. "Hold you against me," he whispered, enfolding her in his arms, pressing her to his lithe, hard length.

"You . . . confuse me so I cannot think," she moaned as his mouth came down to caress her throat with burning lips that kindled a fire in her own blood.

"Do not think, *ma chère*, feel," he murmured,

circling the throbbing pulse he could see blue against the translucent ivory of her skin.

"If only 'twere that easy," she sighed, as though his words released something within her, allowing her soft feminine curves to melt against the hard insistent contours of his body.

"This is all that really matters. Everything else is but a prelude," he told her, his hands entwining in her long hair. His lips kissed her temples, her eyelids, then reclaimed her mouth. He crushed her to him in a kiss that was hard, searching. It was as if he could drive all other thoughts from her mind, but the hot drive of desire.

Her arms wrapped about his neck, her hands pulling the thong from his queue and gathering his raven black hair in her fingers. The touch, oh yes, she thought, the feel, the taste, the scent of him. She wanted to drown her senses in him, become a creature only of sensation that cared nothing for right or wrong. In his arms, she was home.

"Tell me that this is all that matters," he demanded, peeling the velvet robe from her body.

"This is all that matters," she gasped, knowing that for this moment in time he was right.

"How do you want me to love you, *ma belle?*" he asked in a murmur thick with desire as he slipped the silken night rail to her feet. "Like this?" He knelt before her, pressing his mouth to the satin of her belly, then lower to the ash blond intimate curls.

"*Mon coeur!*" she moaned, digging her nails into the muscles of his shoulders.

"This is life, *ma belle,* the very essence of life," he reminded her, his husky voice breaking with a barely checked passion as he rose to his feet. Holding her face between his two hands, ebony eyes burning down into her own, he said, " 'Tis why man and woman are on this earth, to celebrate this wondrous mystery that fate has been kind enough to allow us to find in each other. Always I sought something, someone to fill that empty place, to answer the question of why am I here. With you I know the answer."

"And I, too, have found completion with you," she said with all her love shining out from eyes that caressed him with tenderness.

"Come, there is heaven waiting only a few steps away," he said, the deep timbre of his voice breaking with the depth of his emotion and hunger.

Hand and hand they walked toward the four-poster, the anticipation rising inside like a fire burning out of control. She turned toward him, her hands moving swiftly at his waistcoat, unbuttoning the brass buttons to his delight. He gloried in her hunger for him as she pulled at his clothing with an eagerness that touched him to the core.

"I want to feel your skin on mine, and the silky fur of your chest, and . . . here," she said, with a mischievous smile, as her fingers traced down the flat stomach to his throbbing erection. "Ah, that is what I want also," she teased, circling him with her small hand as his groan filled her ears like the sweetest music.

"If you continue to speak such words, *ma belle,* I cannot be responsible for my actions. Every part of me cries out to ravish you," he muttered, his eyes burning black coals.

"Perhaps 'tis what I want," she glanced up at him, then turning her back began to climb into the waiting bed.

The sight of her long slender back, the wine-red *fleur dy lys* burned into that delicate vulnerable shoulder, tore at his heart. Somehow, he should have been there, should have stopped such a horror from ever happening. Then, as she looked back at him—with a sensual smile curving her mouth, and with a slight teasing wiggle of her saucy bottom— the challenge flung over her shoulder, was too much. She felt him grab her about the waist as they tumbled onto the bed. His hand spread apart her thighs as he thrust inside her honey moist depths. It startled her, then delighted her as she felt his body slide over her back, trapping her. But what a splendid entrapment, the long hard length of him embedded within her woman's cavern.

"Again! Again!" she cried out as he moved slowly in and out, thrusting his entire length, filling her till she thought she could take no more, then pulling out, leaving her empty.

"I cannot last like this," he gasped, withdrawing to roll her over so that they lay with his body curved around her back, the soft mounds of her buttocks pressed against his hips.

She lay turned away from him, but his hand was never still, caressing the length of her spine, the beautiful bottom he adored, the silken legs. The rough male hairs of his thighs against hers aroused every nerve. Then his hand was between her thighs, separating those intimate woman's petals, stroking, teasing, carrying her higher and higher.

"Let it come," he whispered, circling her ear with his tongue as she writhed against him, sensing he was taking her on a solitary journey to fulfillment. And she gave in to the sensations that were overwhelming her, as his hand teased the tiny bud of passion, then moving downward thrust inside, showing her nuances she had never known before. She felt a wanton abandonment to movement, arching against his hand. Head thrown back in the throes of ecstasy, she saw him above her watching her, reveling in the experience he was giving her. She cried out his name, high and long, with the exquisite joy of her release.

"Ah, *ma belle* Caresse, how wonderful you are. You have a natural sensuality that is like a flower unfolding to greater and greater beauty," he told her, with joy in his voice, looking down at her as she lay exhausted on the bed. He spread her hair about her like strands of silk. "I want to always remember you like this." His black eyes swept over the entire length of her, still breathing heavily from the rapture she had known, a thin sheen of moisture on her ivory skin. Those intense eyes smiled down at her, touching her everywhere like the caress of his square-tipped fingers.

"You speak as though you are leaving," she said with a catch in her voice, for despite the complete fulfillment she had just experienced she felt the desire building once more in her blood. How wanton she must be, that he could rouse her with just a glance.

"Life is full of partings and the more enjoyable reunions such as tonight," he replied, in cryptic tones that told her nothing. The words had been so lovely that he was moving his mouth over hers, devouring its softness, before she realized he had not answered her.

Her mouth trembled as he traced the outline of her burning lips, seeking the entrance that she so willingly surrendered to his insistent tongue. He slipped his sinewy length over her, his arms wrapping around her, lifting the fragile feminine body up against him.

The heat from his body burned into hers as she stroked the muscles of his back, then lower to the firm buttocks, pressing him to her. A moan escaped her throat as she felt the urgent press of his erection against her intimate curls and belly.

Desire flowed through her once more, banishing all thought in the languor of his touch, the drug that was his kiss. She hungered again for that ecstasy she found only with him, but this time she wanted to feel him inside her, filling her with his length, his need.

"*Mon coeur*, fill me, complete me!" she gasped,

arching up against him as his heated mouth seared a path down the elegant length of her throat.

His moan of capitulation echoed like a *chanson d'amour* as he rose over her, reaching down to separate her intimate petals for his invasion. She writhed under his touch, the pearls of her fingernails digging into the hard muscle of his buttock in the agony of her need.

He thrust into her waiting depths, losing all control as he felt this passionate woman beneath him, unashamed to communicate her hunger for him. How he adored her at this moment of conquest when she responded totally, holding nothing back. In her surrender she had made sure of his capitulation, for what man could ask more of his beloved than this passionate response, this complete acceptance of him in every nuance of her body and soul?

"Je t'aime, ma belle Caresse," he whispered as he began to move inside her.

"Je t'aime my husband, my Lucien," she sighed, vibrating with a liquid fire. She began to move with him, allowing the whirling exquisite sensations to build with her, feeling his hard throbbing shaft thrust in again and again. Catching his rhythm they moved in their rapturous dance to music heard only in their souls. Faster and faster they whirled higher and higher as he led her to that wondrous place of rapture that lovers experience in the spiraling climax of their ecstasy. Their mingled cries of rapture as they reached the pinnacle and plunged over into the sea of total fulfillment came as if from one voice.

There was no need for words, for there were no words for what they had experienced. Their bodies, their hearts, the deepest part of their beings had communicated in ways that were beyond speech.

They knew lying in each other's arms that no matter what else had occurred in their lives, they had been given a gift by fate, the gift of experiencing total communion with the mate of their soul. If their lives ended at this moment they had known perfection most people could only dream of. The knowing was worth any pain, any loneliness, fate had thrust upon them in their journey to this point in time.

The fog swirled around the darkened house as the bells of the church rang the midnight hour. Caresse and Lucien were oblivious, lost in sleep and each other.

A half-burned log fell to the bottom of the fireplace in a shower of sparks, then settled down in the smoldering coals. Bruno sighed, rolled over and stretched out deep in his canine dreams, while Blanchette, curled up in the chair, buried her nose with one elegant white paw as she too sank deeper in slumber.

Bright morning sun had vanquished the fog as it shone into the bedchamber and fell across the four-poster where Caresse slumbered alone. The stream of light finally awakened her. She lifted sleep-laden eyelids to stare at Lucien's empty pillow. Only the indentation and the faint scent of him on the pillowcase showed that he had been there.

Stretching out her hand, she touched the place where his head had been. She rolled over into his place in the bed, burying her face in his pillow. If she closed her eyes she could pretend he was still here beside her, holding her against his manly form.

The knock at the door that led into the hall pulled her from her romantic fantasy. Struggling to sit up she called out, "What is it?"

" 'Tis Ninon, *madame*, with your tray," the woman called out through the closed door.

"Please come in," said Caresse, pushing her pillow behind Lucien's, and pulling the sheet up under her arms, for she was nude. As Ninon opened the door she saw her night rail in a pile on the floor on top of her robe. Lucien's clothes were gone.

"Bonjour, madame," Ninon greeted her. "The sun has come out and 'tis a most lovely day."

" 'Tis what woke me, the wonderful warmth from the sun streaming in," Caresse replied as the woman set the tray in front of her.

"Is there anything I get for you?" Ninon asked as she poured a cup of hot coffee.

"Bruno may need to go out, although I see Blanchette like her mistress decided to sleep late on this lovely morn," Caresse said, seeing the cat still asleep in the chair by the fireplace. The fire was burned out to a cinder.

"I believe the dog went outside when *m'sieur* left this morning," Ninon replied with a smile. *"M'sieur* wanted me to give you this." She handed her a note folded in half.

"Merci, Ninon, that will be all for now. In an hour could you have Pascal bring me water for washing?"

"Très bien, madame." Ninon paused for a moment, then before leaving turned back toward Caresse. *"Madame,* Mariette has changed her mind about serving as your housekeeper and lady's maid. If you still wish to employ her she would come whenever you desire."

"I see, why has she changed her mind?" Caresse asked.

"Now . . . now that the *voodooienne* is dead, she is no longer afraid to work in the house."

"All right, Ninon, have your sister come this afternoon—I shall be at home all day," Caresse told her with a wry twist to her lips. So Mariette thought that Dominique had been behind all the strange events that had happened in the house. She hoped the woman was right, but some instinct told her it had not been Dominique. She hoped she was wrong.

"She will be so pleased, *madame*," Ninon replied.

Caresse was barely aware of her leaving as she concentrated on Lucien's message.

Ma chère,

Forgive me but I thought 'twould be easier for me to leave while you slept. I must leave Nouvelle Orléans for a week, but shall return to escort you to the *bal masqué*.

Je t'aime,
Lucien

Confused, she stared about the chamber as if she could somehow discover him standing there as he had been the previous night. She felt a scream of frustration well up in her throat. He had left again, and not a word about his destination. A promise to return in time to escort her to Solange's ball, and I love you scrawled in his bold handwriting. It was all she had of him, except for the faint fragrance clinging to his pillow, and the memory of the previous night.

Looking about the room, she noticed that the envelope with the royal seal was missing from the desk. He had taken it with him.

She experienced a gamut of confusing emotions. The man she loved with all her heart was an enigma, a mystery. When she was with him, his intensity, his passion, overwhelmed all sense, all reason. Nothing mattered when she was with him, but the joy of being in his presence, feeling that the whole world was in the circle of his arms. But when he left her, the doubts, what Yvonne would call common sense, came surging back to haunt her.

Remembering his startling entrance the night before, she realized that someone could have used that entrance to bring in the serpent that was placed in the armoire. She shivered with revulsion. She hoped Mariette was right and it had been Dominique or someone working for her. She was dead, and if Mariette was right, the voodoo spells should end.

She was dead, Caresse thought, her hand trembling as she lifted her cup to her lips, and a tall Frenchman had been seen leaving her house the morning of her murder.

Twenty-eight

"You are quite the most beautiful shepherdess I have ever seen," the deep voice cut through Caresse's concentration as she regarded herself, dressed in Solange's costume for the *bal masqué*.

"Lucien!" she gasped, seeing his reflection in the long pier glass. Turning around, she ran to him. "I thought you would not arrive in time."

Opening his arms, he pressed her to his cloaked figure. "I promised to return in time to escort you. I always keep my promises," he said, reaching down to hold her small heart-shaped face between his hands. With great tenderness, he pressed her lips to his, caressing her mouth with a gentle massage that sent currents of desire through her.

She reveled in the wonderful safe harbor of his arms, the taste and texture of his mouth, the slight roundness of his chin where a slight beard was beginning, the familiar masculine scent of him. How she had dreaded the coming evening, attending without Lucien, but Solange had made her promise to come even if her husband did not return in time. She had reluctantly agreed, knowing Lucien did not want her to do anything to offend the governor and his wife.

"I thought you were not coming, and so I was dreading the *bal masqué*," she confessed, as the long

405

heart-stopping kiss came to an end. "If we hurry there is time for you to change. I believe Pascal said you had a costume from last year. He has pressed it and placed it in your armoire."

"I could use a shave, *ma chère,*" he admitted, still holding her as if he could not bear to let her go. "On my way into the house, I asked Pascal to bring me some warm water."

"Where have you been? Your cloak is torn, and damp," Caresse said with concern, as she was able to study her husband more closely.

He looked tired, and the plain clothes he wore when riding out in the fields were smudged with dirt, as was the plain black felt tricorn he flung over the back of a chair.

"Travels for the crown," he answered tersely, pulling back from her so she was no longer pressed against him. "I must be more careful. I do not want to soil such an exquisite costume."

"This is Solange's idea of what a shepherdess would wear," Caresse commented wryly, glancing down at the gown. It was of rose-pink silk taffeta gathered in puffs at the side to reveal a rose-and-blue-on-white striped petticoat. A laced stomacher lifted her bosom high, and the low neckline of the gown revealed nearly all but the coral tips. An apron of silk gauze that no country girl would ever wear completed the gown. The short skirt, reaching only to her shapely ankles, revealed rose silk shoes with high curved heels, and ivory silk stockings with seams of tiny rosebuds climbing up the sides. "There is a most ridiculous wide hat loaded with silk flowers, and of course a white satin shepherd's crook. The mask at least is only a domino." She indicated a half mask of rose silk. "I feared it would resemble a sheep!" Caresse said in disgust.

Lucien's smile developed into a low chuckle as he listened to her describe the costume, which was in reality quite charming although he agreed no shepherdess outside the walls of a ball at Versailles ever wore such a thing. "You would make the most delightful lamb," he murmured, touching the ringlet that Mariette had carefully dressed to hang over her shoulder to complete the picture of an elegant country lass.

A knock on the door announced Pascal with water for Lucien's shaving, putting an end to their conversation. Caresse sat before her mirror at the dressing table while her husband stood at his shaving stand. She applied the finishing touches to the rouge high on her cheekbones and across her lips slightly swollen from Lucien's passionate kisses. Touching a wand of lily perfume to the pulse points on her neck and wrist, she then flicked the wand between her breasts raised so high by the tight lacing of the stomacher. For a moment she touched the necklace at her throat from which hung the locket with the inscription, *Tout est Plaisir/Quand on Aime*. How true was the sentiment, for the night was filled with pleasure now that her love had returned. It did not matter where he had been, all that mattered was that he was home.

"Are you ready, *ma belle*?" Lucien asked coming from the shadows of the far corner of the chamber.

"If you will help me tie my mask," Caresse answered, standing up and turning around with her mask in her hand. She stopped when she saw him, for his costume was perfect. A roguish pirate, from the scarlet silk bandanna tied about his head, to the wide sleeves of his shirt open at the chest, tight black breeches tucked into high cuffed boots, a scarlet sash about his trim waist, a wicked-looking sword at his side, a gold ring fastened to his ear. A black mask tied about his eyes gave him a mysterious air.

"Well, what do you think?" he asked, flashing an irresistibly devastating grin.

"It suits you so perfectly," she said, with a low husky laugh, "a rakish pirate."

"Should I take that as a compliment?" he asked, taking her mask from her hand as Pascal took the shaving bowl out to be emptied. "Turn around, *ma chère.*"

"I like roguish pirates," she replied softly, turning around so he could tie on her half mask.

"And I adore this particular shepherdess," he murmured, bending down to tenderly graze her neck with his warm lips. "Come, if we do not leave now I shall be forced to keep you here with me in this chamber all night," he said, straightening up with a sigh.

"Perhaps we could leave early," Caresse suggested, in a low husky voice, as he placed her cloak over her shoulders.

"Oh, most assuredly, we shall leave early," he murmured, his voice simmering with restrained passion.

She smiled up at him over her shoulder, as her hand pressed his fingers resting on her arm. " 'Twill make the tedious time at Solange's pass more quickly, thinking of coming back home to our bedchamber."

"Your flowered hat, *madame,* and your crook," he said in a voice breaking with emotion, touched by her open response of love and desire. Handing her the wide-brimmed hat and tall crook with the rose bow and fluttering ribbons, he had to fight to keep from taking her in his arms. He wanted to refuse to allow her to leave till he made love to her in all the wonderful special ways he knew would arouse the wanton passion that she kept locked inside her fragile form.

"I shall not wear that hat till we arrive at the de Vaudreuils," she said determinedly, staring down at the huge silk roses decorating the flat crown of the straw hat. "And I shall feel the perfect fool

408

carrying a shepherd's crook, especially one decorated with a rose pink bow as wide as the hat, but
I suppose Solange would be hurt if I did not wear
the complete costume." Caresse gave a sigh of frustration as she picked up the long crook.

"The crook is a bit much," he agreed, with a
grin. "I think Solange could stand the disappointment of not seeing the crook." Solange was getting
her way enough these days with him; Caresse did
not have to do her bidding as well. Although he
knew Solange was vexed with him, there was a limit
to what he would do to keep her silence. After
knowing the splendor of his *belle femme* there was
no way he would ever take Solange to bed, no matter how she badgered or threatened. Even if it
meant he saw Caresse's beautiful gray eyes staring
at him with revulsion, he had taken as much of
Solange's blackmail as he was willing to take. He
had told her so before he left on his trip upriver
with Nashoba. When his report reached France,
the de Vaudreuils' tenure in La Louisiane might
come to an end, if all went as he planned.

"Good, then I shall leave the crook," she said
with a silvery laugh, flinging the crook to the floor.
"I am now ready for the *bal masqué*."

Government House was ablaze with light as their
carriage pulled up in front. Tall flaming torches
were a beacon in the dark unseasonably warm
night, competing with the glowing ivory-gold
sphere of a moon that hung over the river low in
the blue-black sky like a burnished pirate's coin.

She really did not need a cloak on such a night,
Caresse thought as Lucien escorted her across the
banquette and into the governor's mansion. The
Marquis and Marquise de Vaudreuil stood at the
entrance of the white-and-gold ballroom greeting
each guest. They were the only guests allowed to
go unmasked. Solange was dressed as a Roman

empress, her husband as the Roman Emperor Caesar.

"How appropriate. They treat the colony as their own personal empire," Lucien murmured to Caresse as they joined the receiving line.

"How lovely you look, *chérie*," Solange drawled as Caresse moved into place in front of her. "I wish to speak with you alone after all the guests have arrived. Meet me in my boudoir when the hands on the hall clock point the hour." Her blue eyes glittered down at Caresse with an unreadable emotion in their shallow depths. "I have something to tell you about your family in France that is most important. Do not look so shocked, I have done some checking on you, for I know you were really wearing the country girl persona as a disguise. You were not a simple *fille à la cassette*. I knew that, the moment I met you, but I had no idea your real identity was so noble," Solange trilled, bending close to Caresse, speaking low so none could hear their conversation.

A momentary panic overwhelmed Caresse so that she could not move or speak. Then realizing people were staring at her, she gave Solange a thin smile and moved on into the ballroom. She heard Lucien speak a few terse words to the marquise, then come to stand beside her.

"Is something wrong, *ma chère?* You look like you have seen a ghost," he commented in a low concerned voice.

"*Non,* I think 'twas only the shock of Solange's costume. I cannot imagine where she got the idea that Roman empresses wore red wigs. The style might be authentic, but that color is terribly unflattering," Caresse managed to say, using any explanation for her expression. She had in some ways seen a ghost, the ghost of her past, reflected in Solange's strange glittering blue eyes.

"The woman enjoys creating a sensation, but I

agree the color is both startling and unflattering," he replied.

As the Marquis and Marquise de Vaudreuil entered the ballroom the orchestra struck up the first minuet. Sweeping on to the floor, the guests watched them move through the stately steps for several bars, and then when the governor nodded, the other dancers joined them on the dance floor.

Lucien held out his hand to Caresse. She gave him a wan smile as she placed her cold trembling fingers in his warm grasp.

Her body and years of training responded almost automatically to the music, for her mind was whirling with fearful images elicited by Solange's words. She knew her identity, the position of her family in society, and she must also know she had been confined by a *lettre de cachet* to La Salpêtrière prison.

Caresse accepted partners for the next few dances, but her attention was always on the tall clock in the hall she could see from the dance floor. Her anxiety began to build as the time slowly, agonizingly crawled by until the hands pointed to the hour. She fled the ballroom, after sending Lucien for a glass of champagne, hurrying past a late arrival. All were still masked, so she could not tell who the tall man was that she passed so close her gown swept against his sleeve.

Up the wide staircase she ran, brushing past slave footmen dressed in the de Vaudreuil livery complete with powdered wigs. Solange was determined to turn the governor's mansion into a miniature Versailles, she thought, wondering if she was as determined to copy the intrigue of the French court as well.

The door to Solange's boudoir was closed as Caresse reached it, leaning against the wall to catch her breath, her lacing so tight it made it difficult to breathe. Memories of La Salpêtrière had tortured her through every step on the dance floor. What game was Solange playing? What news did she have of her father, and why had she gone to such trouble to find out Caresse's real identity?

The door was wrenched open as if Solange could sense her standing outside, sense her fear. "Come in, there is much I have to tell you. I think you will be most interested." Her cold blue eyes stared down at Caresse with a gleam of triumph in their icy depths.

Elegant and formal in shades of blue, gold, and ivory, the chamber could have been one in Versailles. Everything must have been imported from France, Caresse mused as she moved with caution into Solange's boudoir. Every instinct warned her that she was the prey walking into the trap of the hunter.

"So you are the daughter of the Marquis de Villier. How low your family has been brought by one man, a bastard born on the wrong side of the blanket. 'Tis one of life's little ironies, is it not, *chérie*? I marvel at how fate has played with you. But I forget you do not know just how ironic your life has become, do you?" She stared at Caresse, prolonging the agony, toying with her like a cat a mouse.

"What is it you wanted to tell me, *madame*?" Caresse asked through dry lips, determined to bring the woman to the point.

"The man who convinced the king to issue a *lettre de cachet* against you and your father, do you know his name?" she demanded, a cruel smile curving her lips.

"*Non*," Caresse answered in almost a whisper. "What is his name?" A terrible sinking feeling in the pit of her stomach warned her that she did not want to hear the name.

"Lucien St. Amant," Solange hissed in triumph.

"I . . . do not believe you," Caresse stammered

in bewilderment, giving a choked desperate laugh. Every nerve in her body screamed that it could not be true.

"Perhaps this will convince you," she said, walking to the ornate *bureau* and picking up a piece of parchment with a broken official seal. Striding over to where Caresse stood she handed it to her.

Looking down, Caresse read the letter from the warden of La Salpêtrière prison. He stated that she had been arrested on order of a *lettre de cachet* issued by the king's own hand at the request of a M. Lucien St. Amant. Tears clouded her vision till she could no longer see the terrible words. Opening her fingers the parchment fluttered to the floor.

"But why would he have married me if he knew who I was?" she asked through trembling lips.

"The ultimate revenge on your father, mayhap. He hated him, of that there is no doubt. Lucien went to a great deal of trouble to arrange the *lettre de cachet,* and spent a great deal of money, I wager," Solange said with some amazement that anyone could spend so much money on such an undertaking. "And then there is your remarkable resemblance to that bitch Aurore. She was truly evil, that one, but the men flocked to her like flies to honey. I asked him myself why he married you," Solange admitted, "but he would only say that fate was playing with him. Quoted some nonsense from Shakespeare about his only love come from his only hate." She gave a shrug of her plump shoulders.

"He knew that you had this information?" Caresse asked, stunned.

"I must admit it was enjoyable watching his anger, knowing he could do nothing about it or I would tell you everything," Solange confessed, her blue eyes reveling in the memory when she could make Lucien St. Amant suffer. He had the bad taste, the gall, to turn away from the most brazen invitations to her bed. He had danced attendance on her when she blackmailed him with the information she had, but he drew the line at bedding her. She would make him pay for it. He was not the only one who could seek revenge.

"But you have told me—why?" Caresse asked, puzzled. She realized it had been jealousy that had motivated Solange to investigate her past. She desired Lucien and he had turned away from her, so she had sought revenge. It was an old story, but why had she tired of her game?

"When Dominique was murdered I realized that if I did not want to be next I should tell you. There would be no reason for Lucien to silence me as he did your housekeeper," she said uneasily.

"You believe Lucien killed Dominique," Caresse said, feeling the ice of fear and despair spreading through her stomach.

"A tall Frenchman was seen leaving Dominique's cottage the day she was killed, a tall dark-haired Frenchman. But he will never be questioned. The police, the Superior Council, they would never hang a Frenchman for killing a woman of color, never," Solange spat out the words. "He killed Dominique because she knew he killed Aurore. It was part of his lure, for everyone knew he killed his wife in a fit of passion. She was said to have taken a lover during his frequent absences. To think he was capable of such passion was quite exciting to the more jaded women of Nouvelle Orléans." Solange gave a weary sigh. She was growing bored of the game. The little chit had not even broken down in tears. "I must return to the ballroom. You may stay here and collect your thoughts. 'Twould be better if we were not seen entering together."

Caresse stared at her, too miserable to speak, only nodding her head. She looked down at the parchment lying on the Aubusson carpet. What was she to do? Was she married to a man who was

414

mad? Had his lovemaking all been part of his intricate plan of revenge against her father?

"Oh, my condolences, *chérie*—your father died in the Bastille three months ago," Solange said matter-of-factly, pausing at the door. Then pulling it open, she swept out, leaving Caresse staring after her.

She floundered in an agonizing maelstrom as she realized that the man she had married, given herself to with all her heart and soul, had been responsible for her imprisonment in La Salpêtrière—and for her father's death in the Bastille. Her anguish almost overcoming her control, she swallowed hard, fighting back the sobs that threatened to consume her. It was useless to cry, it would solve nothing, she thought over and over in her tortured mind.

What to do? She could not see Lucien, not till she had somehow come to terms with what he had done. But why? What had her father done to incur such hatred that Lucien would go to such lengths to harm him and his family? Pulling her mask from her face, she threw it on the floor. She had had enough of deceit and false faces.

"Excuse me, I thought Solange was in here," the late arrival murmured, standing in the open portal. He was dressed as a musketeer in the time of the Sun King, Louis XIV. A broad-brimmed hat with a flowing plume obscured his hair and face, as did the black mask he wore about his eyes. "What is it, *chérie*?" He strode into the room, coming to stand in front of her.

"Monsieur?" she asked, looking up at him, her eyes still wet with unshed tears.

"Forgive me, 'tis Philippe," he answered, pulling his mask from his face.

"Philippe," Caresse said with sigh of relief. "Perhaps you could help me." An idea was slowing forming in her mind. She would go to Yvonne and

Pierre. They would take her in, give her sanctuary while she sorted out the turmoil in her mind about Lucien.

"I am at your service," he said, sweeping the hat from his head in a parody of all the plays she had ever seen featuring a musketeer as hero.

"This is serious, Philippe," she replied, in a choked voice.

"Of course, forgive me, but I am at your service in any way I can help," he apologized, his narrow eyes looking at her intently, his lean features somber.

"I must leave here without anyone seeing me, especially Lucien," she explained. "If you could escort me to the Sonniers' town house, I would be grateful."

"The Sonniers? But did they not leave today for their plantation Bonne Chance? I saw them board the supply boat with their slaves and baby," Philippe said quietly, watching her intently.

"Of course, how stupid of me. There is sickness in the city, and now that the Indian raids have stopped, they thought it would be safer for the baby at the plantation," Caresse muttered in a low tormented voice. Where would she go? What could she do?

"If 'tis that important to you, *chérie*, I could take you to Bonne Chance on my keelboat. It has been packed with supplies for my journey on the morrow to Chêne Vert. 'Twas time I was returning to my plantation, and with Lent beginning on the morrow the social season in Nouvelle Orléans is over till Easter," he explained, a strange eagerness in his narrow amber eyes.

"But I must leave here tonight, now, before Lucien finds where I have gone," she said in a desperate voice. She had to get away from him. If he was mad, what might he do when he found out she knew he was responsible for her father's death?

416

Now that his revenge was complete, might he decide she was expendable? If what Solange said was true, he had killed twice before.

"If it is that important to you, *chérie*, we can leave tonight. My crew sleeps on board. There is a full moon, we can leave as soon as we arrive at the docks. Put on your mask, I know a back entrance. We can slip out without anyone seeing us. By first light you shall be at Bonne Chance."

"Philippe, how can I ever thank you," she murmured, tying the mask about her eyes with clumsy fingers. "My cloak." She stopped. How could they retrieve her cloak without someone seeing them?

" 'Tis quite warm, but if you desire a cloak, I am sure Solange has one in her armoire," Philippe said coolly, walking to the large armoire that stood against the wall. Opening it, he searched for a moment, then pulled out a velvet cloak in a deep wood violet shade.

Taking the wide-brimmed shepherdess hat from her head, Caresse threw it carelessly on a chair. Slipping on the violet cloak, she mused that she seemed doomed to wear Solange's clothes tonight. Then she dismissed the thought with a shrug. The woman had deliberately hurt her. She cared not what she thought.

" 'Tis a lovely color on you, *chérie*, really your color. You should wear it more often," Philippe commented with a strange unreadable expression on his foxlike visage.

Caresse gave a slight shudder as she realized she was wearing Aurore's favorite color. Well, it could not be helped, but she would return the cloak to Solange on the first boat to go down river from Bonne Chance.

"Come, *chérie*, we should leave before Lucien comes looking for you," Philippe urged, pulling the hood of the cloak up about her hair.

Giving a nod that she was ready, they stole quietly

out of Solange's boudoir. Turning to the left, they hurried down the hall toward the back stairs that led down to the path through the garden to the servants' quarters.

They did not see the costumed figure of a roguish pirate standing in the shadows of a tall chest to the right of Solange's bedchamber. He saw them, however, watching, with clenched jaw and burning eyes as they disappeared down the back staircase.

Twenty-nine

Streams of silver moonlight danced across the dark waters of the Mississippi, as Philippe's sleepy crew poled the keelboat away from the Nouvelle Orléans wharf. Caresse stood at the rail with Philippe at her side. She stared out across the water at the few dim lights from the grog shops along the quay, rapidly becoming only pinpoints as they moved away from the city into the dark Louisiana night.

"*Merci*, Philippe, for doing this for me," she said softly, watching the receding shore through misty eyes. Everything she had known there was a lie, a masquerade, like the costume she wore, like Solange's party. It had all been built on deception, Lucien's deception and need for revenge.

" 'Tis my pleasure," he replied in a low intimate voice. "I am afraid this has been a terrible night for you. Perhaps you would care to go into the cabin. I have some brandy, and if you will forgive my saying so, although you are always lovely, you look like you could use a drink."

"*Oui*, I could," she agreed with a sigh.

The small cabin was lit by several hanging lanterns, and contained a built-in bunk bed on one side and a rough pine table and chairs near a cupboard fastened to the wall. From the cupboard

419

Philippe took a bottle and two glasses, but standing with his back to Caresse, he also took another smaller bottle from the cupboard and added a few drops of opiate to the glass of brandy he poured for her.

"This should warm you, 'tis cooler here on the river," Philippe said with a thin smile as he handed Caresse her glass. "I fear 'tis not of the best vintage, but I do not like to keep my best stock on board when the boat is docked in Nouvelle Orléans."

" 'Twill be fine I am sure," Caresse reassured him, sipping the golden liquid. It burned going down her throat, and had a strange aftertaste, but he was so solicitous, and had been so kind, she did not want to hurt his feelings. She continued to drink it in small sips.

He sat across from her, watching out of those strange narrow eyes, as he raised his own glass to his lips. "Might I inquire what is wrong, *chérie*? I feel we are friends, and only wish to help in any way I can."

Stifling a yawn behind her raised hand, Caresse began to relate what Solange had told her. Perhaps he could help her to understand why Lucien had done such a thing. While she knew the two men did not like each other, they had been neighbors and Aurore had been Philippe's stepsister. If only she wasn't so sleepy, she thought, finishing the brandy. She could hardly hold up her head.

"I have never understood Lucien St. Amant, *chérie*," Philippe said, with a shrug of distaste. "The man is an enigma, but then his *maman* was insane, and Jacques St. Amant lived out at Sans Regret like a recluse. But I never heard him speak of a Marquis de Villier, although I know Lucien had been several times to France."

Caresse tried to follow his conversation, but Philippe's head seemed to blur, and the room seemed suddenly to spin out of control. What was wrong with her? Was she ill? They were her last conscious thoughts before the blackness came up to meet her, pulling her down, down into their fathomless depths.

Philippe picked up her glass as it fell to the floor, her head slumping across the table. Another thank you to Solange for involving him in her little enterprise of importing drugs from the Caribbean where the ships from the Far East came to port. They had made a nice profit, and tonight he had made such good use of the opiate.

Lifting Caresse up from where she slumped unconscious, he half carried, half dragged her to the bunk. Dropping her on the thin blanket-draped mattress, he murmured, "Soon you will be home, my Aurore." He bent down and brushed her hair from her face, and gently kissed her lips.

The keelboat worked its way up the river as the sun rose over the east bank. Philippe stood at the rail, watching as they passed first Bonne Chance, then Chêne Vert till finally they reached the destination he had sought all night. Sans Regret, the site of so many passionate nights between him and his beloved Aurore. As soon as Lucien left she would send a slave riding one of the plantation mules to invite Philippe for a tryst. The joy they had known in her violet bedchamber, he would soon know again. She had returned to him as she had promised she would. He would never forget how she teased him one night when he was angry with her for insisting he leave. Grabbing her, he had wanted to strangle her for taunting him in one of her swift changes of mood. She had looked up at him and told him if he killed her she would come back and haunt him. She had kept her promise.

As they rounded the bend in the river, the house rose before him. He must go into the cabin and prepare her for her return. The overseer might be a problem, but he had a story ready that Caresse was ill and thought the air at the plantation would be better for her health. Her husband being away on a journey for the crown, he had brought her home. He only hoped she was still under the influence of the opiate.

Caresse felt the dryness in her mouth first, the overwhelming thirst, then the pain throbbing in her head as she tried to open her eyes. She rolled over, pressing her head against the pillows as if she could somehow escape the pain. It didn't work. She had to open her eyes despite the pain, so she could find some water. Slowly, her heavy lids fluttered open as she concentrated, willing them to do her bidding.

A faded purple satin canopy gathered in the middle into a bouquet of oversized blossoms fashioned to look like violets was what greeted her eyes. *"Mon Dieu,"* she whispered. Where was she?

"Bonjour, chérie," Philippe greeted her from somewhere on her right. Turning her head, she saw him standing there, holding a cup of coffee in his hand. "I shall help you to sit up so you can drink this. 'Twill help the headache and the groggy feeling in your head."

"Where . . . where am I?" she stammered as he lifted her up with one arm, placing the pillows up against the headboard with the other.

"At Sans Regret, of course, back in your own chamber. I know you missed it. Violet *is* your color," he said, looking down at her tenderly as he lay her back against the pillows. "Here drink this. 'Twill help. No, it contains nothing but black coffee and sugar, just as you always took your *café*. See, I remembered." He smiled down at her.

Panic like she had never known before welled in her throat as she stared up at him. He thought she was Aurore. Her blood turned to ice as she realized he was mad, but his was a cunning, calculating kind of insanity.

"Drink it, *chérie,* I promise the opiate was only in the brandy. We are here at Sans Regret, quite alone except for the slaves. Zweig is drunk down at the overseer's house. He also has no head for brandy with opiate in it. No one will bother us, and Zoé is preparing one of her special dinners for us, just like in the old days."

Caresse sipped a small amount of the coffee in the cup he held to her lips. That was what was causing the pain in her head, and the terrible thirst. He had drugged the brandy he gave her on the boat. She began to tremble as she realized she was alone in the deserted plantation house with a madman. The slaves would not help her, for they would not raise a finger against a white Frenchman.

"You slept much longer than I thought you would, Aurore, 'tis late afternoon." Philippe teased her, stroking her hair from her face.

She flinched at his touch, a wave of nausea coming over her as he caressed her cheek. Somehow she must keep her wits about her in this living nightmare. It was her only hope at survival.

"Dominique kept all your gowns in the armoire. She aired them regularity, for she, too, believed you would return. I thought the lavender silk, but your earrings are gone. I think that bitch Dominique was wearing them in Nouvelle Orléans when she was pretending to be you. 'Twas why I killed her, it was a sacrilege against your memory. She had to be punished, trying to frighten you by having Pascal put that snake in your armoire. He could deny her nothing. But he is such a fool he used a venomous serpent. He might have killed you. I saw him carrying the snake in a basket into the courtyard when I left my card that morning.

He told me it was only to frighten you into seeking out Dominique's help, but I knew then I had to kill her. She thought she had more power than you, and was determined to prove it. I cut her throat like you used to do the chickens you used as a sacrifice," he said with satisfaction, his eyes gleaming with pride as he told her what he had done for her.

Caresse thought she was going to faint. Philippe was the tall Frenchman coming from Dominique's cottage. Her emotions swung up and down as she realized Lucien was not the murderer, but she was alone on an isolated plantation with a madman.

"Finish the coffee so you will feel like getting dressed. I have planned our dinner to be served on the gallery outside your boudoir like we used to do when Lucien was away," he coaxed, holding the cup to her lips.

Knowing that she had to clear her head if she was to outwit him, she obeyed, even managing a wan smile. Aurore and Philippe had been lovers, trysting when Lucien was away from the plantation. But they had not been blood relations, so why had Aurore not married Philippe instead of Lucien?

"There, I have finished the cup," she said in a whisper, handing it back to Philippe.

"You should have defied your *maman* and married me instead of Lucien," he said as if he had read her mind. "I know you were afraid of her power as a *voodooienne*, the tricks she had learned in Saint-Domingue, but she only wanted Lucien's help with my father's debts so they could return in style to the islands," Philippe told her with a sigh. " 'Tis what made me so jealous that night, to think he was to return, that he would be touching you. It made me lose my head, *chérie*. 'Tis why I did what I did," he explained, his narrow eyes misty with unshed tears. "But you had your revenge, you stayed away from me for seven years, letting me suffer my guilt. I waited so long. You promised even if I killed you, you would return and haunt me. I remember how you laughed because you knew I was so angry I wanted to kill you so he couldn't have you! I really did not mean to do it, but you kept taunting me, standing by the rail laughing at me. I had to stop you," he told her in a reasonable tone as if what he was saying made perfect sense. "You have forgiven me, haven't you, Aurore?" He looked at her with a pleading expression in his narrow amber eyes.

Caresse suddenly realized why they looked so strange, why they had always bothered her somehow. They were the mad eyes of a cold-blooded killer.

"I forgive you," she managed to say through dry lips, her pulse pounding so loud she thought he could hear its beat.

" 'Tis why you came back?" he said with a tight smile.

" 'Tis . . . 'tis why I came back," she repeated, her fear making her stammer, almost overwhelming her control.

"I knew you could not stay away forever, but you are a minx for keeping me waiting so long," he said, lifting her hand to his lips for a moment.

She had to fight to keep from pulling her hand away, the sick feeling in her stomach coming in waves. If he touched her in a more intimate way she knew she would begin to scream and never stop.

"But I must control myself. We have all night. First, our reunion dinner," he said, letting go of her hand with reluctance. "I shall take out what I wish you to wear, all my favorites," he said, rising to his feet and moving toward the armoire.

She watched the waking nightmare, in which she was a feature player, develop in front of her, as Philippe took from the armoire a faded lavender silk dress in a style years out of date. There was a patch of mildew about the bottom of the skirt, but Philippe did not seem to notice. Satin lavender slippers with worn heels followed, along with an orchid chemise threaded with a black ribbon, petticoats, and lavender silk stockings with black scrollwork up the seams, and black satin garters with violets on them.

Caresse shuddered at the thought of donning the dead woman's clothing. But if she was to ever get away from this madman, she must play along with his sick fantasy that Aurore was alive.

"Go see how the servants are doing with our special dinner, while I dress. I want to surprise you," she managed to say with a taut smile. He had to leave. She could not undress in front of him.

"Do not be long. I cannot wait for us to be together," he told her as he paused at the door.

She held her breath, thinking he had changed his mind, but finally he opened the door and left her alone. Moving as quickly as she could with her head still pounding from the drug, she rose from the bed. Searching the room, she looked for anything that could be used as a weapon, but found nothing.

Her mind a crazy mixture of fear, frustration and anger. She knew she would have to don the dead Aurore's clothing if only to buy herself time to figure a way to escape. She recoiled from wearing the undergarments, placing them back in the armoire. She would wear the gown and petticoats as well as the stockings and the shoes, for her own were gone, and he might see them with the movement of her skirt, but she would keep on her own chemise and stays.

Struggling with the gown without the help of a maid, she finally managed to dress. Looking at herself in the mirror she saw that her rouge had worn away, and her hair was a tangled mess. Her fingers recoiled once again from touching Aurore's hair brush, but she had to make the masquerade look as authentic as possible with her wan visage. Taking a deep breath, she picked up the silver-backed brush and quickly pulled it through her tangled tresses.

Noticing that the powdered wig was gone from the stand, she knew that Dominique had taken it, wearing it for her voodoo ceremonies when she tried to convince her followers that Aurore had returned. Pulling her own hair up in a chignon, she had to use the hairpins in a glass-covered dish to hold it up. It made her queasy to use Aurore's hairpins, but turning to stare at the portrait of her above the fireplace, she tried to copy the hairstyle. It was difficult without the aid of a skilled hairdresser. Somehow she managed, and glancing in the looking glass and then up at the portrait, even Caresse was startled by the resemblance. It made the hairs stand up on the back of her neck, so eerie was the similarity between them. She had felt the same cold chill when she had put on Aurore's gown, for it fit her as if it had been made for her. The slippers also were a perfect fit.

As she stood staring at her reflection in the pier glass, she thought she smelled the scent of violets, and the chamber seemed colder. Wrapping her arms around her chest she slowly turned around, expecting to see the specter of Aurore, but there was nothing. There was only the cold, the fragrance of violets, and silence.

"But you are here in the room," Caresse said aloud, staring up at the portrait.

Suddenly the silence was broken by a book falling from the bookcase next to the fireplace. It fell only a few feet away from Caresse, as if someone had pulled it from the shelf and thrown it to the floor. Staring down at the book she suddenly remembered Lucien telling her that there was another hidden staircase at Sans Regret, in Aurore's boudoir.

A knock at the French door startled her as she heard Philippe's voice. "Are you ready, *chérie?* The table has been set, and we are only waiting for you to begin serving."

Freedom lay in front of her, and Philippe stood right outside. He could not come in. She must stall for time.

"I shall be out in a moment, *mon cher.* Do not peek, I want to surprise you, looking just the way you remember," she called out in what she hoped passed for a flirtatious voice.

"I shall wait, but impatiently—although what are a few minutes compared to seven years?" he replied.

Sighing with relief, Caresse began to search the carved woodwork of the bookcase molding, pressing each wooden leaf and flower. Her stomach churning with anxiety and frustration, she moved her trembling flingers up the side of the wall nearest the fireplace. Finally when she was biting back sobs of disappointment, she pressed the center of one of the flowers that she realized were carved like magnolia blossoms, and the bookcase swung open. The smell of damp and mildew drifted out to mingle with the cold violet-scented air of the chamber.

There was a staircase, but she knew with the door shut it would be pitch black. Looking back toward the bedchamber she saw that someone had lit the *veilleuse* on the table next to the four-poster. With a quick step she took one of the tall tapers from the mantel and lit the wick from the flickering flame of the *veilleuse.*

"Merci," she whispered, pausing on the threshold of the hidden staircase, turning for a moment to stare at the empty chamber where she knew an

unseen presence watched and waited. Then she stepped inside the passageway, pulling the bookcase door shut behind her.

Cobwebs, like fine lace, hung from the masonry over brick walls that lined the narrow winding staircase. Holding the taper high, Caresse carefully made her way to the first floor. When she reached the bottom, she stopped for a moment before pressing the knob jutting out from the bricks that she knew would spring open the door. She had no idea where on the first floor the door would open, and if there would be a servant standing on the other side. Where would she go if she was allowed to exit sight unseen?

She stood biting her lower lip, her mind racing through all possibilities. Zweig was unconscious, and would be no help. The slaves could not help her. The path along the river! If she followed it, passing Chêne Vert, she would come to the Sonniers' plantation, Bonne Chance. She had no idea how far it was, and the sun was setting, but there should be a full moon again that night. And, she thought, anything was better than staying here with Philippe.

Placing her hand on the knob, she blew out the candle as the door swung open. She found she was in one of the storerooms, where the foodstuffs brought up from Nouvelle Orléans were stored till needed by the cook. Shutting the door behind her, she moved into the shadowy chamber, the only light coming from a small window high in the wall. Crossing to the door that led out to the first-floor gallery, she paused to hear if anyone was outside. The warming kitchen was on the other side of the house.

Slowly, she opened the door and stepped out onto the brick floor of the gallery. There was no one, but across the garden she could see serving women moving about in the kitchen house, the door open in the warmth of early twilight.

Quickly, she hurried around to the side of the house that faced the river. There, through the branches of the live oaks, she could see the gleam of the river at the top of the levee, the spring rains having raised the river almost to flood stage. On either side of the house, slaves were attending to their various tasks, and beyond lay the swamp, lying in wait like some predatory beast. She had no other choice but to keep to the shadows cast by the large oaks, and make her way down the stretch of lawn that led to the river.

Above her, she heard Philippe's boots on the boards of the second-floor gallery, pacing back and forth like some caged animal. Then she heard him stride to the French door and rap sharply on the glass.

"I am coming in," he said tersely.

As she heard the door open, she moved out from under the shelter of the gallery across the lawn to the shadow of the first large oak, the twining oak. She stopped in front of it, waiting to hear Philippe's voice, but there was nothing.

Cautiously, she ran to the next oak, hiding once more behind its large trunk. Her stays laced so tight made running difficult and she cursed women's fashions. Catching her breath, she waited till she could dash once more to the sanctuary of the next live oak. Moving in her strange fashion, a spurt across to the shadow of the next oak, then catching her breath for the next mad dash, she made her way almost to the shining silver ribbon that was the Mississippi River, shimmering under the full gold sphere of the moon rising slowly over the water.

She rested for a moment, feeling that she was almost free, for the path along the river began a few yards to her left at the top of the levee. Then she heard the sound of a man's boots stepping on a fallen branch. Philippe, he was coming after her.

Fear, stark and vivid, coursed through her as she sensed him coming closer and closer. She could not wait here like an animal in a trap. She had to try.

Picking up the petticoats and skirt of the faded gown, she took a deep breath, and sprinted from the shadow of the tree across the lawn and up to the top of the levee. The keelboat lay tantalizingly close, tied to the dock. Could she untie the rope and jump on, poling it away from the dock before Philippe reached her?

"Aurore! Aurore!" His cries carried up to her on the slight breeze from the river.

She saw him down below, running toward her in long even strides. Turning back toward the dock she saw the boat, but knew there was no way she could make it before he reached her. She was not strong enough to pole the heavy boat away from the dock. But she saw something else, a pirogue gliding over the shimmering water, paddled with a steady even grace by a lone figure. He was heading towards the dock of Sans Regret.

She stood transfixed for a moment. The broad shoulders silhouetted by the light of the moon, the proud head, they looked wonderfully familiar. Was it really Lucien or just a mirage conjured by her tortured, terrified mind?

"You are not leaving me again," the threatening hiss of Philippe came from behind her as she watched Lucien reach the dock. Strong hands reached out for her, around her throat, forcing her to face him.

She stared up into the mad cunning eyes of Philippe as he began to strangle her. She fought him, but her heavy skirt, the satin slippers sinking into the muddy bank of the levee, worked against her.

"You never learn!" Philippe growled. "Always you decide 'tis him you want."

She heard his voice as if from a distance, stars appearing before her eyes as she felt the terrible pressure on her throat. Lucien, oh Lucien, *je t'aime*, she cried silently. She knew she was going to die like Aurore by Philippe's hand.

Suddenly, his hands fell from her throat. She staggered, trying not to lose her balance on the muddy bank. There was the scent of violets all around. Gasping for breath, she watched as Philippe stood transfixed, staring out at the high silver waters of the Mississippi. Then he began to push past her, as if she didn't exist, toward the rushing, swirling water.

"Oui, I understand! She is not you," Philippe called out. "But you have returned to me as you promised. I am coming! Aurore!" He cried out as he ran into the water, his arms outstretched to embrace someone only he could see.

Caresse watched, horrified, as the fast current of the river caught him and he was swept under. Was he gone? She couldn't see anything but the dark water touched by silver moonlight as it rushed on towards Nouvelle Orléans.

"Ma chère," Lucien called to her as he came running in long powerful strides from the dock.

She turned toward him, holding out her arms, too exhausted to move. Reaching her, he swept her slender body, as if it were weightless, up into his arms. Clinging to him, she wept with relief.

Claiming her lips in a long hard kiss, he held her against him in the moonlight. She returned his kiss, rejoicing that fate had been kind. They were alive and in each other's arms. She could ask no more than that she never be parted from this man she loved with all her heart and soul.

"Come away from here, *ma chère*," he said when they both could speak again. "He is gone and will

432

harm you no more." His arm around her waist, he led her down from the levee. The scent of violets had disappeared.

"He was quite mad," Caresse said, wiping away her tears. "He killed both Aurore and Dominique."

"So it was murder and not suicide," Lucien exclaimed, a great weight lifting from his heart. "All these years I thought she killed herself, because she realized I did not love her—that I knew soon after we married, that it was a mistake."

"Do not take the blame, *mon coeur*. She and Philippe were lovers. I think she was tiring of him, and that is why he killed her," Caresse mused. "He thought in some twisted way that I was Aurore returned to him. It was awful," she said with a shudder. As they walked slowly back toward Sans Regret glowing in the moonlight she told him what had happened from the time they left Nouvelle Orléans.

"But I do not understand, *ma chère* why did you ask Philippe to take you to Bonne Chance?" he asked puzzled. "I saw you leave Solange's together and thought that you were leaving for a tryst at Philippe's town house. I went there, and I have to admit there might have been murder in my heart, thinking I would find you together. When I discovered you had never arrived, but that Philippe was planning to leave this morning for Chêne Vert I went to the docks only to find the boat had already departed. Someone told me that Philippe had left with a lady he was taking to Bonne Chance plantation. 'Tis why it took me so long to arrive at Sans Regret—I stopped at the Sonniers', then at Chêne Vert. I only came home because I was exhausted, and planned on resting before I began the search again. When I saw you struggling with Philippe in the moonlight, I knew fate had led me here, but I was almost too late," he said in a raw voice, pulling her closer against him. "Why did you ever go with him?"

Slowly, painfully, she told him everything Solange had said. This was the last remaining secret between them. Why had Lucien sought such revenge against her father and his family? She had to know, for even though she knew she loved him despite what he had done, it was a pain in her heart. She had to know the truth.

"You are entitled to know the story, and how strangely fate has linked our families," he said softly, pressing his arm tighter about her waist.

"Your father, when young, fell in love with my mother. She lived on an estate next to his family's near Lyon. My mother, however, did not return his affection, and was in love with another young man whom the family did not like. When they forced her to announce her betrothal to your father, she ran off with her young lover. They were found weeks later, but when she was returned to her family she was discovered to be pregnant with her lover's child. Beside himself with rage, your father took his revenge and secured a *lettre de cachet* from the Duc d'Orléans arresting her and her family. They were put in the Bastille, the prison for political prisoners, but for my mother the punishment was especially harsh. She was put in with the vagrants, prostitutes, and petty thieves in La Salpêtrière prison, to be branded with the *fleur de lys.*"

Caresse shuddered. "And what happened to her lover?"

"He joined the French army and, with his family's influence, was sent off to where your father could not find him. My mother was not so lucky. Her mind broken by the terrors of the prison, she was sent to the colony of Nouvelle Orléans with a shipment of correction girls, the first brides sent by the crown to the crude settlement. The nuns delivered me on board the ship. Jacques St. Amant saw my poor bewildered mother holding me in her arms when they landed and told me he fell in love with her at first sight."

"Mon coeur," Caresse said, with a sigh for the pitiful woman and her child, victims of the man she knew as her father.

"After both my parents had died of the fever, and Aurore had died, I was afraid I was earning my reputation in Nouvelle Orléans. One day a wealthy titled old man came from France looking for his lost love Gabrielle and their child. He found me and told me I was his only child, and his heir. Heartbroken at finding he was too late and Gabrielle was dead, he succumbed to one of the fevers that sweeps through from time to time. But before he died he made me promise to right the wrong that had been done to both of them by your father. He told me how to go about it, whom to bribe at court, and, of course, I inherited his fortune and had the money to do it."

"If someone had not intervened, *mon cher,* I would be dead like my father," Caresse said, then turned to him with a glint in her eye. " 'Twas you, I often thought so, but it seemed too fantastic. You came to me in prison, 'tis your cloak that I have kept in the bottom of my *cassette,"* she said in wonder. "Why?"

"I did everything as my father wished, but something nagged at me, perhaps 'twas guilt that an innocent woman was suffering because of an accident of birth, because the Marquis de Villier was her father. Although telling him what you had suffered was all part of the plan, something made me go to La Salpêtrière that day and see you before I returned to Nouvelle Orléans."

"How fortunate that you did," Caresse breathed.

"Oui, fate intervened, for when I saw you that day in the cell, I knew that you would be a bride

for La Louisiane, but that I, like Jacques, would be waiting for you there. I tried to tell myself that I was marrying you because of your strange resemblance to Aurore. I felt guilty about how I had treated her. I volunteered to work for the crown to get away from her cloying presence, and when she died I felt a terrible guilt. Seeing you I thought I was getting a second chance to make someone's life happy, to rescue you when I could not save Aurore. But soon after our marriage, I knew you were nothing like Aurore. You were strong, and everything a man could want in a wife. I may have been drawn to you because I wanted to right an old wrong, but also I was drawn to *you*, the person inside the lovely shell that resembled my old failure. And the woman I love is you, no one else but you, *ma belle femme*."

Stopping under the arching branches of the live oaks, the moss swaying in the moonlight, she looked up at him with all the love in her heart shining out from her gray eyes, and said, "I once read that to understand all is to forgive all. I cannot undo the horror or pain my father caused, but the past is over. Let it stay where it belongs." She reached up to touch his handsome visage, staring into the intense black eyes she loved. *"Je t'aime*, Lucien,"* her voice was a whisper on the wind through the live oaks.

"Je t'aime, Caresse," he replied, bending down to kiss those lovely lips that smiled up at him.

Like the jasmine vine around the stalwart live oak, she clung to him, their arms and bodies entwined like their hearts and souls. The ghosts from the past were gone, appeased forever. They had conquered them all. The future stretched ahead of them where they would live the rest of their life together, savoring all of the wonderful experiences yet to be, living each day to its fullest, for they knew what it was to love with every fiber of their being. The past was forgotten in the splendor of the present and the bright promise of tomorrow. And when they were old, they would look back on their life together *sans regret* for what might have been, for they had been given the greatest gift of all, true and everlasting love.

has been done the subject of Philippe's inheritance will guide through the law, see, see, conscience to join than the court." Clamor gave a slight shake to some the loud appressive quiet.

"Do not speak of it, even if had out and all he came before they say to thing say.

and

Epilogue

Let us not burden our remembrance with
A heaviness that's gone.

Shakespeare, *The Tempest*

Sans Regret plantation
August 1750

The sultry heat of deep summer pressed down on the verdant lawn of the plantation. The gray moss hung without moving from the bowed branches of the live oaks, for there was not a breath of air stirring in the somnolence of the afternoon.

Caresse lay on a *chaise longue* in the shadows of the second-floor gallery, lazily moving a fan scented with vetivert. Next to her Yvonne sewed a gown for her son, asleep in his cradle beside her.

" 'Tis so quiet and peaceful here now, no signs of ghosts or things that go bump in the night. Although I must confess when you told me that the chamber Pierre and I were staying in had belonged to Aurore I was a little nervous the first night," Yvonne told her hostess with a smile. "But the new decorations are so lovely, who could not enjoy staying in such a room?"

"I believe Aurore's spirit is now at peace, and

has been since the night of Philippe's drowning. He really thought he saw her beckoning to him from the water." Caresse gave a slight shiver despite the humid oppressive heat.

"Do not speak of it, *chère,* if it upsets you. There is the babe you carry to think about. Only happy thoughts," Yvonne said with a fond glance at her friend.

"My heart is so full of happiness, I can hope that poor tortured Aurore rests in peace. I told you the strange happenings in her chamber that night Philippe brought me here. In some strange way I think perhaps she saved my life. I know I smelled the scent of violets as Philippe let me go, it was so strong and all around me. Lucien thinks I imagined it, but I do not believe that is true. She was there, some essence of her," Caresse mused.

"But you have not felt her presence since that night?" Yvonne asked quietly.

"*Non,* there is only peace and happiness at Sans Regret," Caresse answered with a smile, touching the small mound of her belly where her and Lucien's child was growing. It was due near Christmas, and she had decided to name the child Christiane if a girl, or Christophe if a boy.

"You must be so happy Lucien has ceased his travels for the crown," Yvonne said, a smile curving her lips at her friend's happiness.

"*Oui,* he found the information about the de Vaudreuils' illegal activities, and proof of how badly the governor has handled negotiations with the Choctaw, that the king wanted him to investigate. There is a rumor that the de Vaudreuils may be leaving Nouvelle Orléans," Caresse told Yvonne with a sigh of relief. "Lucien has been allowed to retire from the king's service. He shall be staying home from now on with me and the babe."

"That is good, *chère,*" Yvonne replied, looking up from her sewing as they heard the sound of men's boots coming around the gallery from the back stairs. "You and Lucien deserve happiness after all the turmoil that brought you together. But how romantic it all was, like a story from a novel or a play," she sighed, putting down her sewing as the two men, Lucien and Pierre, came around the side of the house.

"What was so romantic?" Lucien questioned, coming to stand beside Caresse, taking her small hand in his long tapered fingers.

"How you and Caresse came to marry," Yvonne answered, as Pierre leaned down to check on his sleeping son.

"Ah, but the romance is not over," Lucien said, lifting his wife's hand to his lips.

"With you, *mon cher*, as my husband, I think 'twill last all our lives," she murmured. Then a strange look passed over her face, as her hand went to the small round mound of her belly.

"What is it, *chère?*" he asked, his dark heavy brows slanting in a frown.

"Here," she said with a slight smile curving her lips as she placed his hand on her stomach.

He looked at her, shock and wonder in his dark eyes. "He is moving," he murmured in amazement.

"Or she is moving," she reminded him.

Yvonne and Pierre exchanged a smile remembering their own wonder, and awe, when they had first felt the movement of their son. "The next generation of Sans Regret is making her, or his, presence known," Pierre said with a smile.

"The babe seems to have its *maman's* spirit," Lucien commented, staring down at Caresse with all the love he felt in his heart and soul shining out from his expressive eyes.

"And your daring and strong will," she teased, looking up at him, her gray gaze returning his love with such intensity that Yvonne and Pierre looked away, feeling that they had intruded on an intimate moment.

" 'Twill have all the love, all the happiness, we did not have in our childhood, *ma belle femme*. This I vow," he said with solemn tenderness, never taking his eyes from her visage.

"Oui, it shall," she agreed. "But I have no regrets, for the twists of fate brought me to you, and for that I will be eternally grateful."

"No regrets, *ma chère*, only the promise of the future," he said, his voice husky with emotion, as he touched once more the mound of her belly where grew the child conceived from the passion of a rogue and a scarlet lily, the next generation of St. Amants at Sans Regret.

Author's Note

Several of the characters in *The Rogue and the Lily* were real people living in New Orleans at the time of the novel. I have tried to portray their personalities as close as I could to what I had read about them in historical accounts of early Louisiana.

The Ursuline nun Sister Hatchard de St. Stanislas came to the colony in 1726 as a young novice. She gave thirty-five years to her order, dying in New Orleans in 1760. She never returned to France in all those years, although her published letters to her family give a clear picture of what life was like in the small settlement. Sister Xavier tended the convent herb garden, as I tell in my novel. She made medicines from her plants for the hospital, and is considered to be the first woman pharmacist in America.

Pierre-François de Rigaud, Marquis de Vaudreuil, and his wife Solange, governed the colony as I describe in the book. Although he was the governor, she was involved in much of the corruption in New Orleans that reached new heights during her husband's reign. Their years of rule were known for lavish entertainments and elegant ceremonies. They tried to imitate the court of Versailles, and succeeded, as in France, at the expense of the common people. The governor and his wife became known for their elaborate system of kickbacks, profiteering from the supply of army supplies, and illegal traffic in drugs. Leaving in 1753, with his wife Solange, for New France in Canada, he became governor there at the time of the French and Indian War. After surrendering Montreal to the British on September 8, 1760, he was recalled to France and thrown into the Bastille. A few years later his wife Solange died, her husband's name disgraced.

The first women sent to Louisiana by the French king as brides for male settlers were the correction girls from La Salpêtrière prison in Paris. When they proved to not want to become pillars of the community, the French government tried sending out young country girls known as *filles à la cassette*. There is a question whether the casket girls came to New Orleans or were sent instead to the French colony at Mobile. Although they have long been a legend in New Orleans, a kind, well-informed guide at the Herman-Grima House Museum in the French Quarter alerted me to the controversy. Further research revealed that the Ursuline Convent archives show no record of the casket girls in New Orleans. Other history books claim they did come to the colony. I chose to stay with the romantic legend for my character Caresse in the novel.

I wish to thank the staff of the Historic New Orleans Collection for showing me the early map that revealed that the original name of Jackson Square, before it was called the Place d'Armes, was the Place Royale. Thanks also to the friendly staff at the Pharmacy Museum, and Voodoo Museum in the French Quarter.

The free people of color contributed greatly to the history of New Orleans. Much has been written about the quadroon balls, but a more detailed account of their sad, yet very creative past, in the era before the Civil War, can be found in Anne Rice's novel *The Feast of All Saints*.

I wish to thank the knowledgeable guide at Destrehan Plantation on the Great River Road who contributed to my understanding of the running of an early Louisiana colonial style plantation. *Past Masters: The Haunting of Destrehan*, a book written by two Destrehan guides, sparked my interest in haunted plantation houses.

There have been many informative books written about early New Orleans and the French Louisiana Colony. The following books contributed to my knowledge of the time in which Caresse and Lucien lived and loved. *Louisiana's French Heritage*, by Truman Stacy; *Old Louisiana*, by Lyle Saxon; *Gumbo Ya-Ya: Folk Tales of Louisiana; Queen New Orleans: City by the River*, by Harnett T. Kane; *Plantation Parade*, by Harnett T. Kane; *The Voodoo Queen*, by Robert Tallant; *Voodoo, Past and Present*, by Ron Bodin; *Beautiful Crescent: A History of New Orleans*, by Garvey and Widmer.

Last, but by no means least, I want to thank my husband, James Robinson, for understanding my obsession with Louisiana history, and for helping me with my research during those hot summer days in New Orleans. The pictures he took of those special places that had meaning to Caresse and Lucien, helped to jog my memory on those cold, Tennessee winter days when I was writing *The Rogue and the Lily*.

Perhaps some day you will stand on the gallery of a Louisiana plantation house and hear the whisper of long-ago lovers in the wind through the live oaks, or walk the narrow streets of the French Quarter in New Orleans, and sense the shades of Caresse and Lucien, the rogue and the scarlet lily, waiting and watching in the shadows as we did that sultry summer.

DISCOVER DEANA JAMES!